THE BALLAD OF SMALLHOPE & PENNYROYAL

By Jodi Taylor and available from Headline

The Ballad of Smallhope and Pennyroyal

Time Police series
Doing Time   Hard Time   Saving Time
About Time   Killing Time

The Chronicles of St Mary's series
Just One Damned Thing After Another
A Symphony of Echoes
A Second Chance
A Trail Through Time
No Time Like the Past
What Could Possibly Go Wrong?
Lies, Damned Lies, and History
And the Rest is History
An Argumentation of Historians
Hope for the Best
Plan for the Worst
Another Time, Another Place
A Catalogue of Catastrophe
The Good, The Bad and The History

Elizabeth Cage novels
White Silence   Dark Light   Long Shadows

Frogmorton Farm series
The Nothing Girl   The Something Girl

A Bachelor Establishment

THE BALLAD OF SMALLHOPE & PENNYROYAL

JODI TAYLOR

HEADLINE

First published in 2024 by
HEADLINE PUBLISHING GROUP

2

Cataloguing in Publication Data is available from the British Library

Hardback ISBN 978 1 0354 1589 2
Trade paperback ISBN 978 1 0354 1590 8

Typeset in Times New Roman by CC Book Production

Printed and bound in Great Britain by Clays Ltd, Elcograf S.p.A.

Headline's policy is to use papers that are natural, renewable and recyclable
products and made from wood grown in well-managed forests and other
controlled sources. The logging and manufacturing processes are expected
to conform to the environmental regulations of the country of origin.

HEADLINE PUBLISHING GROUP
An Hachette UK Company
Carmelite House
50 Victoria Embankment
London EC4Y 0DZ

www.headline.co.uk
www.hachette.co.uk

This book is for Amelia

Before we start, everyone should be perfectly clear. I am not a nice person. People always think that Pennyroyal's the one to watch and, to be fair, they're usually right. But – occasionally – very occasionally – it's me.

Sorry, but there we go. Definitely not a nice person.

—Smallhope, A.

STARLINGS
The Present

I was with Papa when the news came. He was hanging out of his study window at the time, shooting at the bloody peacock, and I was loading for him when our butler, Cleverly, came in. He stood in silence for a while and then coughed politely.

'I fancy, my lord, you'll find that particular gun shoots a trifle low and to the left.'

Neither Papa nor I even considered asking him how he could possibly know that. Several years ago, Papa had insisted that all our staff learn to shoot. This was in the not unlikely event of us having to fight off an invasion by the massed ranks of evil blood-sucking ghouls – or HMRC as George refers to them. George is my older brother. He walked a different path to the rest of us Smallhopes. As we were about to find out.

Papa emptied both barrels in the general direction of the cedar tree in which the peacock spent each morning, shrieking its eldritch shriek, hangovers for the worsening of. The bird in question lifted its beautiful tail and shat mightily.

Papa swore mightily. 'What is it, Cleverly?'

'A letter from Lord Hardcourt, my lord.'

Lord Hardcourt is brother George. It's confusing, I know, so let's get the details out of the way now. For those less familiar with the peerage of the United Kingdom, Smallhope is our family name. Goodrich is the title. Papa is the Earl of Goodrich – Lord Goodrich. George, as his eldest son – his only son – is entitled to use his second title – Viscount Hardcourt. And I'm Lady Amelia Smallhope. There's no Lady Goodrich – my mother died, along with my older sister Charlotte, when I was about four – a train crash just outside Droitwich – after which Papa spent a while muttering about roping in some elderly and indigent female relative to supervise my upbringing. That did not go well. I suspect we weren't respectable enough even for the most elderly and indigent female relative he could find. Think Henry VIII looking for a seventh wife and every princess in Europe suddenly discovering she was washing her hair that night. Or taking the veil. Keeping her head, anyway.

Faced with his failure to procure someone appropriate, Papa took charge of me himself. The result is that I can ride, shoot, drink, curse and, thanks to Smallhope lungs, make myself heard from one end of the county to the other.

Possibly slightly more importantly, he was raising me to handle the estate. I suspected that at some point he'd taken a long hard look at George, decided he didn't quite have the qualities of guile, deceit and duplicity required to deal with sponging relatives, the local council, our MP, the Lord Lieutenant, HMRC, DEFRA, the parish council, his solicitor, his accountant, his tailor, his wine merchant, and – pretty well

2

everyone, really. Poor George wasn't that good at holding his drink either, so Papa delegated everything to me.

Papa and I got along just fine. He would swear – I would swear back – he would remember his role as a responsible parent and correct my grammar and syntax – and my spelling as well if it was a new word or phrase. Papa and I were very alike.

George was very happy to drift along in his own pretty pink world. In fact, he and I had already sworn a childhood pact. When he became Lord Goodrich, he'd spend his time reading and writing and I would run the estate for him.

I can't remember how old we were at the time. Before George went off to uni, anyway. We were sitting behind the compost heaps – it had been a favourite hiding place of ours. I have no doubt everyone knew we were there but no one ever said anything. We'd made a small fire and were endeavouring to toast marshmallows. It wasn't going well and George had already burned himself quite painfully. I'd had to move pretty quickly to prevent him from setting himself on fire.

I gave him my marshmallow to take his mind off it.

'Thanks.'

He munched for a moment and then said, 'What are you going to do when you grow up, Millie?'

I shrugged. 'Get married, I suppose.'

'Don't you know?'

'Not really.'

'You'll go away, though?'

'Well, yes. You do when you're a girl. You have to go and live with your husband.'

I poked the fire in a manner that indicated my contempt for such stupidity.

3

'Don't you want to be married?'

'Not particularly. A bit of a mug's game. Especially for the wife. What about you? You'll be the earl.'

'I don't think I want to.'

'What – be married or be the earl?'

'Both. Wish you could do it for me.'

We stared at the fire for a while.

'You have to marry, George. Heirs and successors and all that.'

'Yeah.' He sighed. 'It's just . . .'

'What?'

George isn't big on eye contact but for once he looked directly at me. 'It's the weight, Millie. The responsibility. Land, property, people's livelihoods, living at Starlings – I'll get it all wrong, bankrupt the estate, everyone will shout at me . . .'

'George, you know I'll never let that happen.'

'Well, yes, I suppose I do.' He took a breath. 'Um . . . Millie, I've had an idea.'

'Mm?' I was loading more marshmallows. 'What?'

'You do it for me.'

I laughed. 'I can't be the earl. You need a penis for that.'

We'd just done penises in biology and I was rather proud that I'd managed to work one into the conversation.

'No, I mean run things. You run the estate.' He paused. 'Talk to people. Make them do what you want.'

George doesn't do other people very well.

'You can't *make* people do things, George,' I said. Quite wrongly as it turned out, given my career choices. 'You just have to ask them nicely and, most of the time, they will.'

He ignored this. 'If you stayed here then I won't have to.' He peered anxiously through the smoke. 'What do you think?'

4

I considered this. 'What would you do instead?'

'Whatever I like. Get a little flat in London. Read. Paint. It would be quiet.'

George liked quiet.

I shook my head. 'Papa won't . . .'

Again, he looked at me directly. 'Oh, he will, Millie. He already is. It's you he takes with him on estate visits. It's you he buys cider for in the King Teddy. And Jo serves you, which she wouldn't do for me.'

'George, you don't like cider.'

He gazed at me sadly. 'That's not the point. The point is that he takes you everywhere with him. You're his favourite.'

'That's not true,' I said quickly, knowing it was.

'I don't mind. Really. Don't tell me he hasn't already thought of it himself. And probably everyone else has as well. Can't you hear them saying it? *What a pity Amelia wasn't the boy and George the girl.* That sort of thing.'

He was exaggerating, but only slightly. George and Papa didn't always get on. Looking back, neither were to blame. Papa wasn't unkind but he was impatient. And if George had just shouted back – as I did – then everything would probably have been fine. It wasn't that they disliked each other – it was just that each was incomprehensible to the other.

There was the time George crashed the estate Land Rover with me on board. We weren't hurt but there was a staddle stone on the grass verge by the stables that would never be the same again and the Rover hadn't fared that well, either. I pushed him out of the driving seat and pretended it was me who'd done it – which was easy because I'd been driving around the park since I was nine. Papa had roared at me for nearly twenty minutes, something that would probably have killed George.

'There's nothing wrong with you, George,' I said fiercely, handing him another marshmallow.

'Not if I was just George Smallhope, but I'm not, am I? One day . . .' he gestured around, 'all this will be mine.'

'So your plan is to put your feet up and let me do all the work.'

He grinned. 'Something like that. What do you say?'

I grinned back. 'Yeah – OK.'

We shook hands on it. That was our plan. Both of us would get what we wanted and everything would be perfect.

And so it was, right up until the day that Cleverly turned up with the letter. From George. Or Lord Hardcourt, as those of you paying attention will remember.

Cleverly proffered the tray on which reposed the letter. The peacock, realising the day's entertainment was over, pushed off – probably to find the rest of his harem and sire yet another generation of anarchic avians. We usually had a good baker's dozen of the buggers stamping round the grounds, beating up the dogs, terrorising visitors, and continually outwitting poor Papa.

He handed me his gun. 'Put it on my desk, Millie. I'll clean it later.'

Cleverly had brought a letter opener but Papa had already shredded the envelope and was unfolding the single sheet.

'Good God!'

I wasn't paying much attention. The letter didn't have HMRC stamped all over it in blood-red letters so I'd assumed it wasn't anything serious. I was wrong.

'Well, bugger me sideways, Millie. George is engaged to be married.'

'Is he?' I said, astonished. 'Who to?'

Papa frowned at me.

'I mean, to whom?'

'A party calling herself Caroline Dyer.' He looked up. 'Never heard of her. You?'

I shook my head. Faint misgivings began to stir. George didn't write letters. Poetry – yes. Excruciatingly bad poetry, actually. Sometimes he would read us a sonnet or two.

'Dashed good,' Papa would say to these recitations, reaching for the decanter. Like George, he was easily taken in by rhyming words. I did once write to HMRC, explaining this father–son penchant and requesting that they couch all future demands in rhyming couplets because it would make everyone's life so much easier and, believe it or not, I did get a response from their probably optimistically named Customer Care department. In a letter signed by a V. Tepes, they stated they would have been delighted to oblige, but owing to recent government cutbacks, they'd had to let the entire poetry department go.

But back to George. And his letter. The one announcing his engagement to the unknown Caroline Dyer.

'And he's bringing her to dinner on the ninth.'

'What?'

I consulted the calendar on Papa's desk and discovered it to be for the year before last. He'd kept it because the picture of the horse reminded him of one he'd once backed quite heavily at Plumpton and said horse had romped home two days after the race meeting had closed.

Eventually, after Cleverly had done something technical with his mobile, we discovered that the ninth was tomorrow.

This just wasn't how things were done. When meeting members of one's future family, there's a strict procedure to be followed. Beginning with a telephone call giving at least a week's notice. Enough time for us to get the Royal Worcester out. Such a meeting should take the form of a pleasant afternoon tea to introduce everyone and check the prospective candidate's breeding history, bloodlines and financial status. This would then be followed a few months later by a wedding in the local church, St Kyneburgha's, a month's honeymoon in Italy, and then back here sharpish for the start of the shooting season on 12th August. The Glorious Twelfth.

Before anyone becomes inflamed over the Glorious Twelfth's slaughtered birds, here at Starlings – the name of the house, I'll explain later – the odds are very much on their – the slaughtered birds' – side. I suspect game birds actually migrate to our estate knowing they'll be perfectly safe here. The body count rarely exceeds double figures. In fact, about three years ago, the whole event would have been a no-score draw if Higgins, our elderly and incapable gamekeeper, hadn't come across a dead bird – killed by a fox, probably – and actually threw the corpse into the air right in front of Papa and his old friend, General Sir Royston Tindler, both of whom were, at the time, refreshing themselves from their respective hip flasks, presumably to offset the trauma of publicly demonstrating that neither of them was capable of hitting a barn door from a distance of ten feet.

Both gentlemen grabbed for their guns. Both fired. Both missed. The dead bird, obeying the laws of gravity, crashed to the ground. Rosie, Papa's elderly spaniel and mother of

8

Doofus – my dog – woke up, waddled across to the corpse, gave it a good sniff and refused to touch it. Papa stuffed it into his game bag anyway and took the credit. He actually brought it back to the kitchens for Mrs Tiggy to cook.

'No need to hang it,' he said to her, handing over the dilapidated corpse.

I suspect she threw it in the bin and defrosted a chicken. Everyone said it was delicious. Smiles and congratulations all round.

I've forgotten where I was. Oh yes. The day the letter arrived. The day after which nothing was ever the same again.

According to George's non-rhyming missive, a female named Caroline Dyer had inexplicably professed herself willing to become his wife. There followed a paragraph or two where George compared her to several random celestial bodies and a rosy-fingered dawn – to their detriment, obviously – and wound up by announcing he was bringing her for a *meet the family visit*.

I sighed. 'Cleverly, can you apologise to Mrs Tiggy for the short notice and ask her for something special for dinner tomorrow, please. I'll leave it to her.'

'As you wish, my lady.'

He oozed his way out of the door.

I was rummaging through Debrett's – nothing. *Burke's Peerage* – nothing. Google?

'Aha.' I passed Papa my tablet. 'That's her – the one on the left.'

We both peered at the image for quite a while. I remember thinking at the time that it must be a very bad photo. No one could possibly be that vacuous-looking, that skinny, or have that unfortunate a taste in hats. She was wearing spiked heels

9

at some outdoor event and they'd sunk into the soft ground, thus causing her to list to the right a little. Quite a lot, actually.

'Well,' said Papa, handing it back. 'At least we'll know her when we see her.'

I don't think he meant it as a compliment.

I should make it clear that, at this stage – before we'd actually met her, of course – neither Papa nor I had anything against this Caroline person. If she made George happy, etc., etc. And since he spent most of his time in London being a poet . . . or an artist . . . or a writer . . . or a composer . . . whatever that month's chosen profession was – it was unlikely we'd be seeing much of either of them. Life in fashionable London would be far more exciting than life at Starlings. And then, in the course of time, Caroline would be throwing out a couple of sprogs to ensure the succession and that would keep them occupied for a few years, so really this would be quite a minor event in our lives.

I suppose we could have been more wrong, but it's hard to see how.

It would probably be useful, at this point, to include a little information about us, the Smallhopes: where we live, a bit of family history, and so forth.

I know it's fashionable for people to claim their ancestors came over with the Conqueror and, for all I know, ours did – among the mercenaries, murderers escaping justice and general hoi polloi Duke William recruited because he was desperate for manpower. Basically if you could hold a sword, you were in. It didn't even matter if you held the wrong end.

Anyway, our ancestors bimbled their way through the years, emerging in a minor sort of way in the 14th century, which wasn't a century known for its happy times. Not only was there war, rebellion, plague, civil unrest, shit weather and all the rest of it, but the 14th century also produced Black Ralph Smallhope, who was, by all accounts, a bit of a bastard even by that century's low standards. No one's quite sure whether his nickname was due to his ferocious temper, his hair colour, or his armour. Contemporary accounts are scarce and unclear.

The family had settled here at Starlings by then. *Chez nous* at that time was a hastily assembled stone keep with a couple

11

of wooden huts tacked on as required. There were no comforts of any kind – which was how Black Ralph liked it, apparently.

Anyway, even among Smallhope men, he was a bit of a shit. Black Ralph was married to Perfectly Normal Agnes – who, incidentally, is credited with bringing red hair into the family, where it's been ever since – and they had three sons. I don't know about any daughters – they didn't count.

According to the legend, Agnes was pious and kind to the poor and everyone loved her. Except Ralph, one of those men who – due to an unacknowledged but massive inferiority complex and an unwillingness to confront their own inadequacies – are always convinced that their wife is having an affair with every man she meets. Often a self-fulfilling prophecy.

I'm not sure whether chastity belts were a thing then – or ever – but they weren't good enough for Ralph, who went one better and locked Agnes in a cage in 1346, grabbed his sons, and followed Edward III to France. Presumably he forgot all about his wife, because he didn't return for some years.

Fortunately for Agnes, she was able to escape the cage and seduce his younger brother – or possibly she did it the other way around – and the two of them were carrying on very happily at Starlings when Black Ralph finally showed up again. Minus two sons who hadn't made it. The third son brought home a wife and a son but died a year later, supposedly of dysentery, but George and I were always convinced it was the pox.

Anyway, Agnes and her brother-in-law celebrated Ralph's return by hurling him down the castle well. Well, *a* castle well. Buggering up your own water supply is never the best idea and Agnes wasn't a stupid woman by any means. Although it's probably safe to assume that post-cage Agnes wasn't anywhere near as pious and kind as pre-cage Agnes.

Her first priority was to eliminate any and all witnesses to this dastardly deed – namely, the younger brother – by making love to him, there and then, as Ralph splashed impotently some twenty feet below ground level. Their cries of ecstasy intermingled with those of her soon-to-be-dead husband as he roared dark curses and tried to climb out, only to lose his grip on the slippery stones, fall back into the no-longer-fit-to-drink water and injure himself quite badly. He was still struggling to keep his head above water when his brother, literally, landed on top of him – still unlaced and dangling – as Agnes, taking advantage of his post-coital lack of concentration, upended him into the well too, and then leaned over the coping to gloat at the pair of them.

No one knew how long it took them both to die, or even if the story was actually true, until Grandpapa Eustace – whom I vaguely remember as a huge, shouty man – had some work done in the second wine cellar and a quantity of human bones were found at the bottom of an old dry well. Not wanting to be bothered with police investigations and coroner's courts and other irrelevancies, he threw them back and ordered the concrete to be poured immediately.

Black Ralph's wife – Perfectly Normal Agnes – showed no signs of remorse whatsoever, never married again and, possibly because of that, lived well into her eighties. She ruled her descendants with a rod of iron and became a great matriarch.

As children, George and I spent long hours down in the cellar, listening for the piteous cries of long-dead ghosts clamouring for revenge, until Papa very sensibly pointed out that we wouldn't be able to hear them under all that concrete, would we, so we went off to play on my Xbox.

And before I forget, Starlings is named for the sky full of starlings who, for centuries, have flocked around the rooftops during winter sunsets, sweeping, swooping and swirling in complex patterns of magnificent splendour – a murmuration – and, incidentally, crapping over everything in sight. Which just about sums up the Smallhopes, really.

Of Ralph's original castle, only parts of the keep remain, incorporated into one end of the West Wing. The house has since been enlarged, pulled down, rebuilt, burned down, added to, modernised, Gothicised – and the result is a rambling structure which manages to cover an enormous amount of ground but isn't actually that large. It has no particular architectural merit but we do have adequate plumbing and heating, thanks to an Edwardian Smallhope who married an American heiress. He had the sense to marry her before introducing her to her new home. She apparently took one look at the place and very nearly bolted, and only by the installation of mass bathrooms, toilets and central heating could she be lured in through the front door. I always imagine them laying a trail of toilets across the floor to tempt her in.

Obviously the benefits of marrying money were plain for even a Smallhope man to grasp, and from that moment on, all subsequent male Smallhopes would marry well but not necessarily wisely. It's not generally mentioned, but in the early years of their marriage, Grandmama Alexandra actually stabbed Grandpapa Eustace. Sadly, the reason why has been lost to time, but as you can imagine, there was a hell of a row and he always swore he never dared turn his back on her afterwards.

Papa and Mama were at least polite to each other. He lived in

14

the central part of the building and she in the East Wing. Presumably they met on common ground and were polite to each other at least three times to have produced George, Charlotte and me.

Anyway, after that brief guided tour of the Smallhopes . . .

Caroline was appalling.

And that's the kindest thing I'm ever going to say about her. I know that makes me sound arrogant and snobbish but I'm not. Papa insisted I was educated at the local school – Rushford St Winifred's. My best friend was our head groom's daughter, Emily. I did well at school. I was captain of the junior hockey team; I was down to play Katherina in next year's production of *The Taming of the Shrew*, I was year head and a junior prefect with the distinct possibility of becoming head girl one day. And then, if my A levels were good enough, off to uni to study land management.

There were party invitations and sleepovers and all the usual teenage stuff. I went to other girls' houses and they came to mine. We'd have hot dogs and burgers, make popcorn and stream movies. Apart from Papa stamping around in the background shouting about the peacocks, those bastards at HMRC and the imbecilic government, everything was perfectly normal. I did rather worry about what they'd make of Papa but all my friends thought he was lovely. No one was in the slightest bit afraid of him. Rowena said he was sexy and Lindsey thought he was cute. I suppose my house was just like their houses – it's just that mine had twenty-seven bedrooms and four staircases. Although, as I explained to them, we didn't use all of them. I've no idea what they would have made of George but he was wafting around York University at the time so the subject never really came up.

15

Papa, too, knew no barriers when it came to friends and acquaintances. He was almost certainly on nodding terms with every poacher and ne'er-do-well in the district. He was known and welcome in every pub for a radius of twenty miles. And no race meeting was complete without the Earl of Goodrich lamenting his phenomenal bad luck.

And then there was the mysterious Mrs Rugeley who lived in Kew. Papa would take George and me with him to visit her whenever he went up to London, where he decamped regularly to argue with large numbers of people. He would drop us off with her and we'd spend a couple of days there. She had a tall narrow house with a tiny back garden, most of which was occupied by an enormous fuchsia. We would make little cakes and jam tarts and she would read to us from the classics – *Thomas the Tank Engine* and *The Chronicles of Narnia* and Terry Pratchett. George would sit alongside her where he could see the pictures and I'd sit on her lap with my head resting on her comfy bolster bosom. I think she'd been an actress at one time because she could do all the different voices and make the stories sparkle. Sometimes she and George would dress up and sing songs from their favourite musicals and I would laugh and clap and then we'd have fish and chips. I was thirteen or fourteen before I realised what her and Papa's true relationship was. I probably should have resented her and accused her of trying to take Mama's place, but I honestly don't remember my mother, and Mrs Rugeley – Auntie Dee – was so warm and kind and soft and funny. I loved her dearly. I thought George did, too. I miss her even today.

I know you'll think I digress a lot, but I mention Auntie Dee because, with Mama dead, she and Papa were the nearest example I had of a couple in a relationship. The only example, actually. So, I'm not sure what I expected from Caroline and George, but everything started badly and went downhill faster than our local MP's fall from grace when he was discovered with one hand in the till and the other down the front of someone else's shorts.

Back to Caroline. I stood in Papa's study and watched them arrive in a very smart new car. George's engagement gift to Caroline, apparently. It was yellow – which should have told me something, I suppose. Caroline was driving, pulling up outside the side door – we don't use the front. In fact, I wasn't sure the doors even opened any longer. Papa said it was to baffle the revenue when they finally came for us. Apparently the plan was that we'd nip out the back while they wrestled with the front. I had my doubts about that strategy.

Anyway, she pulled up with a flourish of flying gravel, very nearly taking out the pugnacious peacock who just happened to be passing at the time. As was Mrs Tiggy, Milburn the head gardener, and two or three other people who had no business being there but had been unable to resist the temptation. Mrs Tiggy was actually clutching a sprig of mint as if that would offer up some kind of explanation for her out-of-kitchen experience.

First out was George, looking a bit green around the gills. He doesn't travel well. He certainly hadn't travelled well today. Quickly, perhaps, but not well. He leaned against the car door, getting his breath back, and I transferred my attention to the eagerly awaited Caroline.

I've never seen anyone that thin. I honestly couldn't understand why her legs hadn't snapped in half. She wasn't tall – certainly shorter than me. Which might be why she was

17

wearing those massive heels again. Wispy hair blew around her face and she was wearing a short tight yellow dress. She looked like a pencil.

I watched them enter the house and suddenly realised I should be down there to say hello. By the time I came flying down the stairs, Doofus at my heels, Papa was shaking Caroline's hand and welcoming her to Starlings.

They say the onlooker sees most of the game. I was waiting at the foot of the stairs, so it's possible that I was the only one to see the quick appraising look she cast around the hall and its contents. She'd be lucky – the Gainsboroughs were upstairs in the Long Gallery.

'And here,' said Papa, looking around, 'is Amelia.'

Caroline reeled backwards. 'Oh no – I'm sorry – I can't bear dogs.'

It was unclear to which of us she was referring.

'And they don't like you either,' I said cheerfully, as Doofus stood his ground and barked at her.

Even at that stage, if she'd made an effort, we could all have laughed it off. And if she had problems with Doofus, just wait until she met Papa's Rosie, elderly, grumpy and riddled with secondary lifeforms. But George said, 'Millie, do you mind?' So I shut Doofus up in the library. When I came back, they'd taken themselves off to our private sitting room. Cleverly was under instructions to give us twenty minutes and then wheel in the tea trolley.

Caroline was standing in front of the fireplace talking to Papa as I entered, so I was able to take my time observing her. Seeing her now, close up, she had shoulder-length bottle-blonde hair and watery blue eyes. Everything about her seemed pale and washed out. Especially her voice, which was deliberately low-pitched. She had the irritating habit of dropping it still further at the end of every sentence, possibly entering the realms of the subsonic where only elephants could hear her. Not that it mattered – Papa's selectively deaf and George had presumably heard it all before, leaving me, not particularly interested, to perch on the edge of the sofa, trying to look fascinated and absorbed.

I honestly did try to give her the benefit of the doubt, taking advantage of her listing the charities over which she presided to wonder if perhaps she was nervous. Or overwhelmed. Or just trying too hard to make a good impression.

There was no need. Our small family sitting room is just that – small. And very friendly, with slightly shabby furniture, family watercolours – which aren't very good but they were done by the family – and a lovely Empire ormolu mantel clock that hadn't worked in living memory. I had no idea what was wrong with it – for all I know someone had forgotten to wind it up one day in 1947 and it had been like that ever since. The whole room smelled slightly of dog, occasionally of horse, and if it was autumn and we hadn't yet switched on the central heating – damp.

Caroline had obviously made an effort with her appearance. Fortunately she didn't have pillow lips, but they were firmly outlined in brown pencil. Perhaps she couldn't find them, other-wise. They were very thin and, as we were to discover, became even thinner when she was annoyed or displeased. She wasn't silicon-enhanced or in danger of blinding herself with her own fingernails, but to me she seemed a manufactured character. A collection of fashionable features. A persona to show the world. And her laugh was so silvery and tinkling that I feared for the glassware.

19

I underestimated her right from the very beginning.

Cleverly entered with the tea things.

'Ah, excellent,' said Papa, who loved his afternoon tea. 'Millie, would you . . . ?'

Too late. Caroline had already seized the teapot. 'I'm sure you won't mind,' she said, not looking at me. 'After all, as the future Lady Hardcourt . . .'

I don't know whether she stopped talking at that point or her voice dropped into elephant frequency. There's a safari park about twenty miles away. Perhaps they heard. The next minute she was sloshing tea around like a priest swinging one of those incense thingies and telling us about the dear Duchess of Somewhere or other – even the elephants would have had their work cut out for them at that point, big ears or not. Actually, I think I've read somewhere they absorb sound through their feet. Anyway, apparently the dear duchess always asked her to pour because of her special . . . more inaudible words. Ask the elephants.

She got the tea all wrong. You'd think George would have briefed her, wouldn't you. Papa was handed something milk-laden and anaemic. George got something sugared and I didn't get one at all.

Papa and I exchanged a long look. His eyelid flickered so I let her live. Wish I hadn't bothered now.

It was at this point that I made a cardinal error. In later years I would know better than to withdraw from hostilities voluntarily. Never, ever leave your enemy in sole charge of the battleground.

Mindful that I could be ignored much more comfortably in my own rooms, that *Doctor Who* was on later, and that Mrs Tiggy would supply me with a more than adequate care package, I waited until Caroline was in full flow and caught Papa's eye. He grinned at me and nodded his head towards the door. I waited until she was talking about ... something ... and made my escape.

I liberated Doofus, who had made himself a forbidden nest on the library sofa, and went to ask Mrs Tiggy if I could have a sandwich or two. She packed me up a small feast and Cleverly brought me up one of Mrs Tiggy's special chocolate mousses and half a glass of wine. I think they saw the way the wind was blowing much more quickly than I did.

That was my first mistake. And Papa's. We sent the wrong signals. That I was a pushover. That Papa would do anything for a quiet life. That George wouldn't make a fuss. I learned from that. First impressions are important. Start as you mean to go on.

Hindsight is a wonderful thing.

Caroline stayed at Starlings for several days, passing the time by clinging to George's arm as he showed her around, and gushing *darling*s in his general direction whenever he looked at her. I've always been hugely suspicious of people who pepper their conversations with *darling*, and let's not even start on *babe*.

I, Papa and the dogs took refuge in his study.

He was cleaning his second favourite shotgun, I was doing my Spanish homework, and Caroline was being the elephant in the room.

Eventually I said, 'What do you think of her?'

No need to specify who *her* was.

Papa said nothing for a while and then laid down his gun. A sure sign of an important pronouncement.

'Well, she wouldn't do for me, but George seems to like

21

her, which is the important thing. And frankly, Millie, I never thought he'd marry at all. I was convinced he'd hide behind you for most of his life. Let you get on with everything – which would have been fine as far as it went – but the bottom line is that he needs to produce an heir. And a spare, just to be on the safe side. Glad to see he's accepted that.' He picked up his gun again. 'There aren't many of us Smallhopes left, these days.'

'But . . .'

'I know, but she is George's choice.' He stopped again and then said with some difficulty, 'George and I are very different people, Millie. Perhaps if your mother had lived, then she could have . . . well. It was hard for me, losing them both like that. At the time, you were my main concern but, with hindsight, it's George who's been most affected by her death. I didn't mean to be . . . unkind, but I'm afraid I've been unsympathetic to some of his . . . his choices. I think I owe it to him to . . . to be supportive over this one.'

I said nothing. It was true that George and I had had very different childhoods, but Papa's words were making me uneasy in a way I couldn't describe. For the first time I could remember, a shadow lay across my life here at Starlings. And across George. And Papa.

If they'd been on better terms, could Papa, at some point, have taken George aside. Could they have talked about how George saw his future? About leaving his life in London and returning to Starlings to live here? About Caroline and their life together? It never happened. I suspect that, just for once, Papa had bottled it.

Something of my anxiety must have shown in my face because he said, 'Nothing for you to worry about, Millie. I've

22

no intention of kicking off my clogs in the near future – but just in case . . . there's a bit in my will . . . George will take care of you. Probably unnecessary – he relies on you a lot – but it's there anyway.' He stopped and repeated to himself, 'Just in case.'

The wedding took place. I wasn't a bridesmaid. Apparently Caroline was well endowed with sisters – all of whom looked exactly like her. Other than the clones, there were no other Dyer relations at the celebrations. There was a brother, apparently, who was unable to attend because he was abroad or something, and their parents were dead. Probably consumed by their own offspring.

The ceremony was a bit of an ordeal for everyone except Caroline. Beginning with decorating the church. St K's is a small country church and I think everyone had been expecting pretty posies made of summer flowers. Poor Reverend Caldicott could hardly believe his eyes. I don't think he'd ever seen so many purple and orange flowers in all his life.

'Do you think she knows it's not Westminster Abbey?' said Papa, blinking, as we entered together. He was looking very distinguished in morning dress. Apparently Caroline had designated an official colour scheme – purple and orange – with which everyone had to comply. Papa got away with an orange tie but I'd been condemned to wear something stupid in purple, which clashed horribly with my red hair.

There must have been at least twenty-five miles of orange and purple ribbons adorning each pew. Papa caught his foot in the bunting as we sidled into our seats and brought down the whole pew's worth. We stifled our giggles, stuffed it under our seat and didn't dare look at each other.

So busy were we burying the evidence of our depravity that we nearly missed the grand parade of bride and bridesmaids up the aisle. How could one person possibly have so many sisters? All of them virtually identical in their matching dresses.

'Like the *Village of the Damned*,' confided Papa in what he probably thought was a whisper.

The ceremony proceeded. Sadly, no one came up with a good reason why these two should not be joined together in holy deadlock. I didn't actually see the bride's triumphant march back down the aisle – Papa and I were too busy trying not to break anything on the way out.

The reception at Starlings was even worse. George and Caroline – Caroline, anyway – had invited hundreds of guests. Well, probably not hundreds, but that's how it seemed. We had our family and friends too. Some of George's friends from university came. And local people, of course. Most of the family were of Papa's generation – cousins, second cousins, aunts and uncles – who all withdrew to Papa's study afterwards to get some serious drinking done. It was only as I gazed around the troughing masses in the ballroom that I realised how much we Smallhopes had dwindled over the years.

'Are you thinking what I'm thinking?'

I turned. There was Aunt Indira. I'm not sure what our relationship was – she was Papa's now dead uncle's wife's sister's son's wife. I think. There may be another brother or wife in there somewhere.

'What are you thinking?'

'I'm thinking there aren't many of you left. If Caroline doesn't start throwing out some heirs pretty soon, then we could be looking at an extinction event.' She considered me. 'What about you? Any plans to get married?'

'Not likely. The thought of ending up with the male equivalent of Caroline is enough to render anyone celibate. For life.'

She laughed and then frowned. 'Seriously, Millie – I would start looking at alternative living arrangements if I were you.'

'George and I are to run the estate together,' I said.

She sighed. 'Oh, my dear.'

'What?'

'Amelia, you're taller, better looking, younger, more intelligent and more popular. She won't have you around here for long. How old are you?'

'Why?'

'Well, fortunately, your papa's got years of life left in him yet, but I'd definitely put together an exit strategy if I were you.'

I stared at her. Aunt Indira was nobody's fool. She ran her own business, was involved in several more, sat on several committees and was one of the governors of a very posh boys' school up in the Lake District. Any advice from her should be heeded.

'I'll think about it,' I said.

'That would be wise. I strongly suspect the day after Randolph's funeral will begin with you being shown the door.'

'I think I can handle Caroline.'

'Oh my dear, she wouldn't do it – she'd get George to do it.'

She smiled, patted my arm and drifted away. I withdrew to a corner to consider the implications. Indira was absolutely right. Caroline would want rid of me as soon as possible. George wouldn't want to push me out, but he probably would if she told him to. Both of us would be completely isolated from each other. George would remain at Starlings but I'd be out. It wasn't a disaster – I'd never intended to spend all my life here – but I'd always imagined a new life where and when I chose – not being evicted by some . . .

I looked over to where Caroline was laughing with a gaggle of sisters. George stood nearby, staring into space.

As if she felt my thoughts, she looked up and caught my eye. I didn't need to be psychic to know what she was thinking. I was no longer mistress of Starlings. I was the unmarried sister. Too young to be pushed out immediately, but the day would come.

I had two choices. Not whether to go or not – at some point, voluntarily or otherwise, I would be leaving Starlings. No, my choice was whether to go quietly or embrace the inevitable and enjoy myself on the way out.

We regarded each other across the room.

Yes – this really was not going to end well.

3

Papa died. Quite suddenly. In his sleep. Cleverly found him when he took in Papa's morning tea.

There was a funeral. I wanted to invite Mrs Rugeley. They'd been together for years. Left to himself, George would certainly have said yes. They'd been very close once upon a time, but Caroline said no, of course not, George. What were you thinking?

Caroline stood between George and me at the church. The turnout was massive and the place was packed. Standing room only at the back. The day was cool and autumnal. Out among the gravestones, I listened to Reverend Caldicott read the last of the service as I watched the yellow and red leaves slip from the trees and flutter to the ground.

'Earth to earth, ashes to ashes . . .'

The words went round and round my head. Earth to earth, ashes to ashes. Earth to earth, ashes to ashes. I stared at the massed banks of flowers. I stared into the hole in the ground. I stared up at the blue sky. I stared at everything that wasn't Papa's coffin because if I did . . .

Caroline poked me. 'Pay attention.'

And then, from somewhere behind the trees lining the

churchyard – one long, last mournful cry cut through the still afternoon. A lament for an old frenemy. A final farewell. Every Smallhope lifted their head.

That was the day the peacocks disappeared from Starlings. No one knew where they went. There were rumours of feral birds living in the woods for years afterwards. You heard an echo of their cry on the wind, occasionally. Well, I did. With one eye on Caroline, George always denied it and Caroline said thank God those awful dirty birds had taken themselves away before she'd had to bring in pest control. I missed them.

After the funeral, everyone went back to Starlings for the wake. It was just like George's wedding, really. I didn't attend. I sat on my bed, wearing my new black dress, Rosie on one side, Doofus on the other, staring out of the window, trying to make sense of a world that didn't have Papa in it somewhere.

I didn't see George – or anyone – for several days. He was busy being the new Lord Goodrich, I suppose. Eventually, though, he came to see me.

He was wearing a new tweed suit that Caroline must have ordered for him. True, Papa always wore tweeds, but his had dog slobber, mud, spilled beer and horse shit all over them. George had even had his hair cut. This was no longer T-shirt-and-jeans George. This was the Earl of Goodrich.

I thought he wanted to talk about our arrangement. He'd be Lord Goodrich and I'd manage the estate for him, as per our discussion behind the compost heaps. I'd learned a fair bit off Papa and Mr Askwith, our manager, and I wanted to discuss my plans to study land management at uni. But no. He wanted to talk about a new school. A smart all-girls' boarding school

28

in the Cotswolds. He wanted to tell me about how wonderful it would be. How much I would enjoy it once I was there. How much I would benefit from more conventional surroundings. How badly Papa had brought me up. He didn't look at me once. Not once. He looked out of the window or down at the floor. He didn't stroke Doofus or Rosie.

I could hear Caroline behind every word. And it wasn't a discussion. It was all fixed and I would start at the beginning of the next term.

I said, 'George . . .'

He stood up quickly, said, 'Well, that's all settled then,' and left the room.

Seven days later, half the staff at Starlings were handed their months' notice. Mrs Tiggy was in tears. She'd been working in our kitchens since she'd left college. There was no Mr Tiggy, by the way – all cooks and housekeepers are given the honorific of Mrs. It took me ages to calm her down. And I had to make sure everyone had somewhere to go because it was very apparent that Caroline wasn't going to do it.

I only saw my brother once more before I left Starlings too. We met on the stairs. He was coming up; I was going down. I said, 'George, what have you done?' And I didn't mean the boarding school thing.

And then Caroline came along the landing. I think she had some kind of internal radar. Every time George and I were within ten feet of each other, she would materialise out of nowhere and take him away. She started to enquire whether I'd made all the preparations necessary for me to be out of the building by Monday, half past nine, and I just walked off in mid-sentence. Thanks to her, my world was crashing, and I didn't

29

feel I owed her even the most basic of courtesies. I could see, just by looking at her, that she felt the same about me.

I made no effort to prepare for this new school. I made sure I was never around for uniform fitting. Every day I took Pye, my horse, and rode up on the moors or along the coast, slipping in through one of the side doors as it grew dark and blagging some food from the kitchen. Caroline might want me gone but I'd make damn sure that she'd have to do all the heavy lifting herself.

My last morning dawned. Cleverly brought me up a special breakfast and took my overnight case downstairs. I'd refused to don the school uniform and if Caroline wasn't happy about that, then she could come and tell me so herself.

She didn't.

The staff all lined up to see me go. Caroline wasn't there, thank God, so I was able to speak to each of them individually. I knew that I'd never see most of them again and some of them – Mrs Tiggy, for example – had been with me nearly all my life.

My luggage had been sent on ahead. The only thing that would be left of me at Starlings was Doofus.

George was waiting for me at the bottom of the steps. It wouldn't surprise me if Caroline had stationed him there to make sure I actually left the building.

'Well . . . Millie . . . I . . .' He dwindled into silence.

'You promised to look after Doofus for me.'

'I shall,' he said. 'And Rosie, too. Don't worry about them. They'll be fine. And you'll see them when you come home for the holidays.'

'Why are you making me do this?'

His eyes shifted over my shoulder. 'It's a wonderful opportunity, Millie. You should make the most of it.'

30

I leaned towards him and said softly, 'I intend to, George. Trust me – you and Caroline will never be able to show your faces in that part of the country ever again.'

'Now, Millie – don't be . . .'

I turned away from him and bent to say goodbye to Doofus, who couldn't understand why he wasn't coming with me.

The car waited at the door with my hired travelling companion. From some agency, I believe. I don't know – we never spoke. Caroline obviously wasn't risking me cutting loose and coming back home again. I was to be accompanied to the school itself, handed over, and then forgotten.

I could just hear Papa's 'prisoner and escort – quick march' as I walked down the steps of Starlings, and that was it. I never returned to St Winifred's. Never saw most of my friends again. My life turned down a different path.

The new school wasn't awful – don't get me wrong. If it hadn't been Caroline's decision, I'd probably have quite enjoyed it. But her shadow lay over everything.

There was always some reason why it wasn't convenient for me to return to Starlings, so either Aunt Indira or Auntie Dee took me in for the holidays. I missed Starlings horribly. And Doofus. And Pye. But mostly, I missed Papa. They say there are different stages to grief, and anger is one of them. I think I got stuck on anger.

This was when I discovered the really deep satisfaction engendered by never doing as I was told. Or, alternatively, doing *exactly* as I was told. Which, if done properly, can be even worse.

I was asked to paint an angel for the school nativity scene. I created a rather striking Angel of Death, complete with snakes

31

for hair, blood-filled eyes and wings made from the faces of sinners. I thought it looked fantastic hanging menacingly over the stable but apparently I was in a minority of one. There was a bit of a chat with the educational psychologist over that one.

I pointed out that Jesus was born in March. There was another long discussion with the deputy head as to the appropriateness of imparting that piece of information during my reading at the school carol service.

I smoked in the toilets. Well, no, I didn't, because cigarettes taste vile, but I lit one and left it there, which set off the fire alarms, and we were all evacuated and I didn't have to do double maths that afternoon.

They introduced a new system called prefects' detentions – whereby prefects were granted the authority to award detentions for bad behaviour. They announced it at the morning assembly and I'm pleased and proud to say that by lunchtime I'd got two.

I bunked off regularly and was twice brought back by the deputy head herself. She tried so hard with me – opportunities to talk, counselling, the lot – and I just ignored it all. They didn't chuck me out – kudos to them – but I reached minimum school leaving age – and it was made very clear that I wouldn't be welcomed back at the beginning of the new year.

I heaved a sigh of relief and began to entertain thoughts of returning home, and then a letter came. From George. It would seem I was to be packed off to a finishing school. There was a page and a half of how much I would benefit from the experience and how much I'd love it. Oh – and had he mentioned it was in Switzerland?

I crumpled the letter and vowed revenge.

* * *

Mademoiselle Leonie's School for Wayward Daughters of the Aristocracy, or whatever they called themselves, was not what I thought it would be. Well, no – that's not quite right. It was exactly what I thought it would be. Exactly the sort of place Caroline would choose. Dedicated to taking in rich but slightly unconventional young ladies – or misfits, as the rest of the world would describe us – and turning them into something still rich and dim but slightly more marriageable.

It's probably fair to say that didn't quite work out for me.

I was to be there for a term – thirteen weeks – which was twice as long as most students were accepted for, so Caroline was obviously anticipating some difficulties in brainwashing me into becoming something as useless and unpleasant as she was herself. On the other hand, the cost, as George had reminded me several times in his letter, was nearly thirty thousand euros for six weeks. So that was sixty thousand euros straight down the drain, I'm happy to say.

The worst part of all – everything was just *so bloody pretty*.

The school was a lovely old building with pretty fairy-story-style turrets. The windows glinted prettily in the sun. The gardens were bright and colourful – and pretty, obviously – and twice a week, the inmates – or students, as I was constantly instructed to call them – were shunted out to pick blooms for our regular sessions of floral art.

The interior was pretty with impeccably furnished rooms. Real art hung from the walls. No one ever raised their voice. Everything was sweetness and light. Even the toilet rolls were covered in crocheted dolls with pink skirts. I think it was felt that while toilet paper did indeed perform a useful function, there was no need to sit and look at it.

Pretty. Pretty. Pretty.

I wasn't sure I was going to survive this. There was no educational syllabus chez Mademoiselle Leonie so it was just as well I'd had a good foundation at St Winifred's. Although I never got to be head girl. Never got my A levels. Never played Katherina in *The Taming of the Shrew*. Never led the hockey team to victory in the county tournament. And never went to university, obviously. Don't feel sorry for me, though, because Mademoiselle Leonie's was the place where I began my real education. It just wasn't quite the one anyone had envisaged. Because I haven't yet mentioned my roommates.

There were just over thirty girls at the finishing school, most of whom had already completed their education and were near adults. The oldest were in their early twenties. You'd have thought that with all the money Caroline had forced George to fork out that I'd at least have a room to myself, but no – I was in with three others. Not to say it was all bunk beds and threadbare blankets – each bed did have its own curtained alcove, and there were dressing tables and rugs and shelves for personal belongings. I placed my copy of *Anarchy for Fun and Profit* in a prominent position, alongside a mostly empty box of condoms and a poster inviting the reader to *Press This Button to End the Patriarchy*.

I was easily the youngest in our room. Initially I thought they were just silly women whose thoughts revolved solely around men and make-up. I'm not sure what they made of me. I was still in fuck-off-everyone mode. We regarded each other warily and kept our distance.

*   *   *

The breakthrough came one day when we were supposed to be practising floral art in the music studio. I'd grabbed a handful of things with petals and rammed them into what probably wasn't a jam jar – not with those fees – then twisted a piece of rusty barbed wire around the container; my bloodstained thumbprint would be an interesting talking point. If Madame Whatever turned up to complain, then I'd label it *Rage Against the Pretty*.

My roommates were talking about antiques and things – I can't remember why – and I casually mentioned one of the Gainsboroughs at Starlings. I'd had some wild dreams about lifting it from under Caroline's nose, then selling it and living off the proceeds, and I was speculating how much I'd get for it.

'Not a lot,' said Meilin, shoving a random rose into her arrangement which immediately transformed it into something ethereal and wondrous. She looked me up and down. 'Less than twenty pence in the pound. But, if you ever pull it off, come to me and I'll give you mate's rates. Forty pence in the pound.'

I must have looked surprised because Meilin paused and shrugged. 'Family business. Mine one day. Although my stupid brother doesn't know it yet.'

Olga – who had the bed next to me – nodded. She was the daughter of a Russian oligarch. And on her other side, listening carefully, was Lucretzia – niece of someone very important in the world of the not terribly legal. Because this was a school for girls who weren't quite top-notch. Girls with behavioural problems. Girls whose parents were a bit . . . you know. In other words – girls who knew exactly how the world worked, and it wasn't ever going to be in their favour unless they did something about it.

There was a very significant silence. All sorts of doors

35

suddenly opened in my mind. We looked at each other. It was, truly, a universe-changing moment.

I put down my scissors and took off my apron. 'Ladies, I really do feel we might have quite a lot to offer each other.'

So – while the official syllabus was chock-full of floral art, deportment, social situations, style and grooming, social media and how to manipulate it, fine wine and how to persuade someone to buy it for you, how to lay a table for fifty dinner guests, basic diplomacy, etiquette and manners – that wasn't all there was to my time at Mademoiselle Leonie's School for Wayward Women.

It became known as the after-hours curriculum. Olga was her father's heir and already had some standing. She was here to achieve polish and make useful contacts. She initiated us into business management. Sod team-building and mission statements and all that crap. Olga was all about how to plan, strategise and operate while never emerging from the shadows. How to ensure successful outcomes. How to turn failure into success. How to rearrange circumstances to your advantage. The words *risk management* took on a whole new meaning in this context. We discussed how to identify and hire people with very specialised skills. And equally importantly – how not to have them exercise those skills on us.

Lucretzia didn't actually come out and say so, but her father's health was failing and no one was allowed to know. She talked about how her mother worked through him. How she ran her husband's gang of ambitious underlings all of whom were just waiting for the opportunity to slit his throat and take over his organisation. And since this state of affairs had lasted for over seven years and counting, it seemed safe to assume that she and her mother knew what they were doing.

I learned finance from Meilin. How to raise money. How to keep it off the books. How to move it around without attracting attention. And, in a session especially for me, how to fence stolen property without being ripped off.

'The actual theft is the easy part,' she said. 'The real problem is disposal. Art, for instance, unless stolen to order, is very difficult to get rid of. And half the time whatever you've pinched is so hot you have to shift it as quickly as you can. People like my family will take advantage of that. And watch out for the insurance companies as well. They can be bastards.'

'But there must be ways and means,' I said.

'Oh, always. But you'll need to recognise when it's better to move stuff quickly and accept a lower price or when to hold on and reap the long-term benefits. Both are equally risky.' She smiled. 'I plan for my family to offer a complete service all the way through the process. Beginning with actually acquiring the object, its safe disposal, brokering the fees, and ending with laundering said fees. Our clients will pay for it, but it will be a very good service.'

It was all theory, of course, but we drank it in. And then we expanded, moving into successful networking – courtesy of a girl in the next dormitory. Suzanne Somebody was the daughter of a highly placed diplomat. She gave me a list of people in her world I might find useful one day and I did the same for her. The old girls' network at its best. An ever-increasing group would get together every night after lights out, sitting on the ends of our beds, tablets at the ready. There were bottles of illegal wine, some giggling, and then we would educate ourselves. A small group of girls not willing to accept their lives being defined by other people.

We made friendships that lasted most of our lives. In the years that followed, Meilin was always my financial go-to person and our association was mutually profitable. Although to this day I still can't arrange flowers.

Naturally there were a great many rules and regulations at Mademoiselle Leonie's, but since most of them ran along the lines of never wearing blue and green together, never talking across the dinner table, never wearing suede shoes with formal attire – in fact, never wearing suede shoes at all – never bringing lilac into the house, and never lending money to any British politician – ever – I felt under no obligation to comply with any of them.

There was also a ton of stuff about not leaving the chateau grounds except with written permission from a member of staff – and even if you surmounted that obstacle, there was another ton of stuff about being back in the building by 8:30 p.m., in bed by 9:30, with lights out at 10:00.

We weren't held in complete captivity, obviously, so we didn't have to dig a tunnel under the art room or smuggle ourselves out in the laundry van – although I was perfectly willing to give that a go. We were allowed out for Mademoiselle Leonie-approved cultural events. Which did not, we were firmly given to understand, include the upcoming beer festival. A delightful occasion offering big-time beer tasting, live music, street theatre, a food festival and shedloads of young men. Something for everyone, in fact.

Alas – not for the inmates of Mademoiselle Leonie's. We were grounded until these horrors had safely passed.

'I do like a challenge,' I said thoughtfully to Meilin one

afternoon as we regarded the golden perfection of her vol-au-vents and the molten puddles of carbon that were mine.

'You're plotting something,' she said. 'I can tell.'

'I do have a plan,' I said, struggling to unweld a vol-au-vent that had, in Mlle Leonie's favourite phrase, failed to fulfil its true potential. 'Involving an upcoming cultural event and a massive amount of beer.'

Meilin groaned. 'Are you not in enough trouble after sewing Suzanne's skirt to her chair last week?'

'It was a needlework lesson.'

'She was wearing it at the time.'

'Well, you know what they say: when things are bad – make them worse.'

'No – that is what you say. Everyone else just ducks and runs for cover.'

'So I can count on you, then?'

She grinned. 'Of course, but how shall we get there?'

'Bicycles.'

She looked faintly appalled.

'There's a shed full of them by the old stables, for fresh air and exercise. We may be breaking the rules, but we'll be doing so in a healthy, non-polluting and sustainable fashion.'

She groaned and covered her eyes, then uncovered them to say, 'We will need to be out before seven p.m. when they shut the gates.'

'Yes. Olga and Lucretzia will cover for us.'

By which I meant lie like stink as and when the situation demanded. In times of crisis, Lucretzia's superpower was to sob prettily and Olga's was to take refuge in incomprehensible Russian. Between them, they were impregnable.

39

'They'll be on the lookout,' said Meilin, meaning the teachers.

'Not a problem. We'll be conspicuously here. We could be caught playing cards' – which was very much against the rules – 'and they'll send us to our room to think about what we've done. Once there, we shoot down the fire escape and across the lawn to the stables. We liberate a couple of bikes and are straight out of the gates before anyone even suspects a thing.'

She regarded me with admiration. 'Millie, you have a natural talent.'

I nodded modestly. 'And then, after an evening's fun, we cycle back, stash the bikes until later, and climb the wall. Olga and Lucretzia will open the fire escape for us and no one will ever know.'

Well, that was the plan, anyway.

It began well. Our card game in the library was duly discovered by Frau Fiedler, the duty mistress, who was suitably horrified. I think it was the fact we were playing poker that really got her going. If it had been an elegant game of baccarat, she'd probably have joined in and fleeced us.

Getting out of the gates was ridiculously easy. Surprisingly so, in fact. Although we did cut it a bit fine. We were only about a hundred yards away when I heard them clang shut behind us.

Do not expect a detailed description of the beerfest. My memories are a little hazy, although I do remember bands ranging from string quartets to heavy metal, long tables awash with beer, lots of fairy lights, steins, roast pigs, singing and so forth.

I'm certain the first person I saw was Madame Lavalle. And it turns out teachers are like pregnant women – once you've seen one, you see scores of them. They were everywhere. Mrs Newcombe. Frau Fiedler. And Mlle Leonie herself. Fortunately for us, they were all sitting at one of the more respectable tables. We edged our way around the market square to find something a little livelier – and out of their sight – and proceeded to enjoy ourselves. Massively.

Meilin and I were not, however, entirely given over to sin. We'd set ourselves a deadline. Back by midnight. Because midnight is a kind of demarcation line. Get caught *before* midnight, and you're just late back, punishable with extra sessions in floral art and a disappointed look from Mlle Leonie.

After midnight, however, was debauchery, lust, strong drink, STDs, unwanted pregnancies, moral decay and no choice but to become a British politician.

Midnight was our deadline, therefore – and I still maintain we would have made it easily if Meilin had not fallen off her bike. I don't know how she managed it. The road was clear, there was a moon, we had lights on the bikes – one minute everything was fine, and the next minute she and her bike were on the ground.

It took us ages to stop giggling. I got off to help her and then we discovered the wonky wheel. She'd buckled the fork or something.

'Or,' as she said, struggling to get up, 'I forked the buckle,' and we fell about laughing all over again. Then I had to nip behind a nearby bush because . . . beer, laughing, chilly night . . .

Eventually I was able to extricate her from the bicycle and she seemed unhurt, which was a huge relief because she and her bike had been horribly entangled and for one nasty moment I thought I was somehow going to have to cut her free. Of course, by the time we'd sorted ourselves out properly, it was long past midnight and we were well into the debauchery zone.

'I mustn't be caught,' said Meilin, panicking suddenly and

trying to clamber back on her bike. 'I'll be expelled and my family will be furious and I'll be kept out of the business and have to marry my cousin who has very short legs and wears spectacles and whose sweat smells of garlic.'

'Oh yuk,' I said, pot-valiant. 'We can't have that. Come on.'

We wobbled our way past the gates and along the high wall, looking for the place to climb over.

'Leave the bikes,' I said, dropping mine in a ditch. 'We'll collect them tomorrow.'

'Tomorrow I will be on a plane to Hong Kong,' cried Meilin tragically. 'Trying to accustom myself to the smell of garlic.'

'Nil desperandum, baby,' I said, my head swimming.

'But no, Millie – very much desperandum.'

'This is the spot,' I said, pointing. 'There's some missing stones for hands and feet and it's not that high. Over you go. And shush.'

We made a complete mess trying to get over that sodding wall. That sort of thing isn't as easy as people think. Especially when you might have had a few. Eventually, after Herculean efforts, we reached the top, where Meilin overbalanced, grabbed at me and we both fell off. Fortunately, we landed on the right side, because I don't think we could have done that again.

The grounds were perfect for after-hours activities, full of shrubberies and trees. For a reason that might have had something to do with the large number of teachers enjoying cultural enrichment sessions down in the town, the security lights had been switched off. Presumably it's not all right for students to see the faculty staggering back full of beer and good cheer. We took full advantage, however, lurching from shadow to shadow, alternately giggling and falling into a ceanothus and

42

then giggling and falling into the rhododendrons, finally fetching up at the foot of the fire escape that led up to our floor. It was a long way up and, possibly because alcohol had improved our hearing, we discovered the metal staircase had a tendency both to boom and squeak – often at the same time.

Meilin bent over the steps and put her finger to her lips, saying, 'Shh,' which set me off all over again, making me snort, which set her off as well, and much time was wasted while we pulled ourselves together and continued the epic climb to the top.

Which was when we discovered that Olga and Lucretzia had fallen asleep on the job. Literally. The door was closed.

'Arseholes,' I said. But quietly. 'In fact, sodding arseholes.'

Meilin was all set to panic again and I could see I was going to get twenty more minutes of Cousin Whatshisname and his garlicky spectacles.

'I told you,' I said, 'nil desperandum.' I groped in my bag and pulled out the key.

She stared, whispering, 'What is that?'

'The key,' I said, feeling around for the lock and praying the alarm system wasn't activated. If it was and we were caught, then one of us would be sleepwalking and the other making a valiant but doomed attempt to return her to the safety of her bed. That would be the bare bones of my story, anyway. The inconvenient details, such as being fully dressed in inappropriate clothing and reeking of beer, could be addressed later.

Always have a second plan for if – when – the first plan goes tits up.

The system wasn't activated. Another fact I ascribed to the local research currently being carried out in the town by our dedicated educationalists.

43

Meilin attempted sentences. 'Millie, why have you the key? When? Millie? How?'

'The law says if you lock a fire door, then the key must be kept in a case nearby,' I said. 'Which I unscrewed with a carefully procured Allen key. Just in case. Because you always need a Plan B. And – if possible – a Plan C as well.'

I relocked the door behind us and we made our way quietly to our room.

And yes, Olga and Lucretzia were in their beds, snoring their heads off.

And yes, our room did stink of stale beer the next morning. We had to have the windows open for days.

But, most importantly, we got away with it. And I had learned valuable lessons. I'd made the whole scheme much more difficult than it should have been. We could have stayed out all night and returned before breakfast the next day – there were camping sites all over town with public tents for those who hadn't brought their own. But I didn't know that because I hadn't done my research properly.

And I should have realised most of the teachers would attend, that they would be as desperate for entertainment as we were. The gates probably hadn't even been locked. We could have just strolled out. And a taxi would have been a good idea. There were whole fleets of them lined up waiting to ferry people home.

Note to future self – don't be timid. The bigger and bolder the plan – the more chance there is of it succeeding.

4

My thirteen weeks in Switzerland went by much more quickly than I had expected. At the end I was presented with a very pretty certificate from Mlle Leonie herself. I thanked her prettily. She wished me the very best of luck out in the world. I refrained from advising her the world was certainly going to need all the luck it could get, and caught a plane home to Starlings. To find that Caroline had had Rosie and Doofus put to sleep. Because she didn't like dogs.

'You could have given them to Stevens,' I said to George, still rigid with the shock of it. Stevens was the groom. 'Or even Askwith. Rosie was Papa's dog.'

'She was old,' he said feebly. 'It was a kindness.'

Doofus had loved going to the vet because they always made a big fuss of him. I could just picture him bundling into the surgery, tail wagging, eyes shining, tongue lolling. Full of trust because nothing bad had ever happened to him there. Ten minutes later, he'd be dead. Did he die wondering where I was? Did he wonder why I'd left him? I couldn't bear it.

'*Doofus was my dog.*'

'Oh, it's you,' said Caroline, sweeping into the room. 'Obviously.

Back ten minutes and screeching like a fishwife already. There's a considerable sum of money flushed down the drain.'

'Rather like my dog,' I said. 'Let's hope we never have to do it to you. Oh wait . . .'

She shrugged and moved past me. 'George, I want to talk to you about . . .'

She stopped and glared at me. 'Amelia, dear, that is rather your cue to disappear.'

I stayed put.

She sighed. 'As deficient in manners and understanding as ever.'

I stayed put.

'Come along, George.'

As they left the room, I heard her say, 'George, I've told you. I won't have her in this house.'

I noticed the *darling*s and *babe*s had completely disappeared.

I stayed out of everyone's way while I found my feet in a house that had changed beyond belief in the time I had been away. Mrs Tiggy had been replaced by some wannabe TV chef whose idea of a good meal was something the size of a postage stamp served on a black plate. Who the hell eats food that has to be dished up with tweezers? As if a tiny purple flower laid on top of half a lettuce leaf is an actual meal. And served with a dribble of foamy sauce that – as I informed Caroline – looked as if someone had gobbed on the plate.

Cleverly was still here. I suspected George might have put his foot down over that. Cleverly was his only link to pre-Caroline times. The new people were all young, terribly, terribly smart, and didn't have a clue.

Mostly, though, I was shocked at the change in George. He'd always been vague, but now he was remote. He was drifting around the place as if he'd lost all focus. He would shut himself in Papa's study – his study – and I sometimes didn't see him for days on end. No one did. Other than Caroline, of course.

I didn't know if any estate business was being done. Papa had worked from around ten until four in the afternoon – with the occasional half an hour to engage with the peacock, of course – and he'd regularly visited his tenants and properties and generally made himself visible and accessible. As far as I could see, George was neither.

I mostly stayed in my room, but I did go down to lunch one day for the purpose of asking Caroline if she'd had my horse put down as well. She started to tell me not to be ridiculous – Pye had been sold to a very good home and . . .

I walked away and pinched George's car and drove into Rushford where I had a very illuminating chat with Mr Treasure, Papa's solicitor, asking him if he could represent me in the future. He replied that he could, and since George had moved both the estate and family affairs to Caroline's solicitor, there would be no conflict of interests. In fact, it would be his pleasure.

I asked some questions, listened to the answers, issued some instructions, shook his hand, enjoyed a pleasant tea at the Copper Kettle and drove home. Where, it appeared, George had been looking for his car all afternoon and did I know how rude, selfish, inconsiderate, etc., I'd been?

I replied yes, of course I knew how rude, selfish, inconsiderate, etc., I'd been – that was why I'd done it – and left Caroline once again in mid-splutter.

After that, neither of us even bothered to go through the

motions. George was missing in action most of the time. I suspected he was deeply unhappy but, as I pointed out to him, at least, unlike Doofus, he wasn't actually dead. I think that was one of the last times we spoke. We parted bad friends and never had a chance to make up. Perhaps I shouldn't have left him to Caroline's tender mercies. On the other hand, for all I knew, he sincerely loved her.

As much as I could, I lived a separate life from them. Not too difficult. I had my own suite of rooms in the West Wing. Caroline, obviously, had moved George into the rooms traditionally occupied by the Earl of Goodrich. I couldn't even bring myself to walk past. Vivid memories of Papa and the peacock yelling at each other. The peacock shitting mightily and Papa calling for his gun. If I closed my eyes, I could still hear the echoes. So I kept to myself. My Rushford schoolfriends had moved on. Some were taking their A levels and planning for university. Others had apprenticeships or were making plans to travel. It's interesting, isn't it? You can never go back.

I don't know for how long this state of affairs would have continued but along came George and Caroline's Big Party and then the shit really hit the fan.

It was to be a massive affair. Celebrating their acquisition of the title – or Papa's death, as I said to Caroline – together with a wedding anniversary. Can't remember which one. The guest list was massive. All her London friends. All the media people she thought might be useful to her. All the county people. A few local politicians. Even a couple of minor royals. Caroline was nearly fainting with the joy of it all.

Armies of people moved into Starlings to spruce the old place up. A couple of interior designers turned up – I recognised the ones who'd decorated the church at her wedding. They really are from another planet, aren't they? It's very possible they would have displaced HMRC on Papa's list of things to rid the world of. Personally I think he'd have just let rip with both barrels and damn the lawsuits. And I would have loaded for him. Sadly, those days were gone.

The ballroom – and most of the ground-floor rooms – were draped in vast swathes of silver tulle and black wire. Because they made for an interesting dichotomy, darling. Great clumps of black roses sprouted everywhere. Like giant targets. I could feel my trigger finger itch. Except that Papa's guns, like my dog and my horse and most of our lovely staff, had all disappeared.

All the furniture was moved around. The Gainsboroughs – the real treasures – were stored in a remote attic as demanded by the insurance company whenever we had a crowd in the house. I wondered if Caroline – quite inadvertently, of course – had ever had them valued because she thought she could sell them. She'd come unstuck if she tried. They were part of the estate property.

It was during all this upheaval that, walking along the landing one day, I noticed several lighter patches on the walls where paintings had once hung. And when I started to look more closely, there were other items missing as well – a snuff box presented to the fifth earl by the Prince Regent, a glove that might have – but probably hadn't – belonged to Charles II, and a small book of poetry gifted to the probably very ungrateful sixth earl by a young Queen Victoria.

Then the caterers turned up. They took over the kitchen, the pantries, the storerooms. Tents – sorry, marquees – were erected all over the lawns outside. An entire small country's worth of champagne was delivered. Wine by the lakeful. Food by the mountainful. I began to worry for the estate. There was an awful lot of money going in the wrong direction.

At this point I should probably say there was no need for me, personally, to be anxious. Not financially, anyway. Smallhope women look after each other. The way we look at it – it's bad enough that we're lumbered with Smallhope men, without being poor as well. So I had Grandmama Alexandra's money. And Mama's. And Great-aunt Essie had also left me something. So as you can see, I was never going to starve. None of it would be mine until I was twenty-five, but the one thing I did own in my own name were Mama's diamonds. The Skeffington diamonds. Beautiful pieces, bequeathed to me in her will. There was a small tiara, an elegant necklace, and two beautiful bracelets. None of it brash or showy. Good stones, well set.

And mine.

I stood in my window watching the frantic ants milling around below – I suspect our ancestors had gone off to war with less fuss – and drove myself into Rushford to consult with Mr Treasure again, to find he shared my concerns about Starlings. I couldn't do a lot – under eighteen and all that.

'But not for much longer,' said Mr Treasure, which was true. I was seven months off my eighteenth birthday. 'And you have a home at Starlings until then. No one can take that away from you.'

No, but I could still be forced out somehow.

Neither of us gave voice to that thought.

Anyway, I was able to hand him his invitation to the ball. He was delighted. And Mrs Treasure, apparently, would be thrilled.

I left well pleased. Utilising all my recently acquired knowledge, it was time to start gathering friends and allies.

I had no idea the biggest and best friend and ally of all was about to turn up. Uninvited, obviously.

With just over twenty-four hours to go, everyone but me had reached fever pitch. Unlike Caroline, still endlessly indecisive when it came to clothes, I knew what I would be wearing. I had a neat black dress – nothing fancy and it would set off the diamonds nicely.

I asked Cleverly to bring them up and knew immediately that something was wrong.

'I regret, Lady Amelia, that I am unable to comply.'

I asked why, although I already knew the answer.

'Her ladyship asked me to bring them to her yesterday, my lady.'

He stopped there and I wasn't going to embarrass him any further.

Caroline was in George's study, which was no longer full of ancient leather saddleback armchairs, Papa's battered desk, copies of the ancient rent roll bound in leather, and smelling of cigars and port. These days it was draped in limp young people being exquisite and, this close to D-Day, having their own personal meltdowns every ten minutes. The noise was phenomenal. Even the peacock would have given up in disgust.

She saw me at once, knew why I was there and, presumably in an attempt to pre-empt me, said, 'Not now, Amelia. We're all a little busy, you know.'

'Shan't keep you,' I said cheerfully. 'Just come to collect

Mama's diamonds. You know – the ones you've stolen for yourself.'

And that's how to silence a room.

Caroline's lips disappeared completely. I'd done it now.

'What nonsense,' she said. She went to bend back over the table again and paused. Pitching her voice so I could hear – so everyone could hear – she said, 'So after that happens, Tristan, I'll go upstairs, put on the diamonds and make my entrance. Please can you ensure everyone is . . .'

'Mama's diamonds are mine,' I said, equally clearly. 'She left them to me.'

'Don't be ridiculous. She was George's mother too. He's as entitled to the diamonds as you and he's given them to me. Now if you don't mind, we're very busy here and you're just wafting uselessly around the place as usual. Go away, there's a good girl.'

Someone tittered.

That was the moment that changed my life. That was the moment I decided to take the fight to her. And win. The blood of Perfectly Normal Agnes pounded in my veins. From this moment on, my life would go my way or there would be trouble. Lots and lots of trouble. For other people, obviously. I would trample their broken and bleeding bodies. And then I would *still* get my own way.

'Sorry,' I called, 'didn't realise you were busy with such *important* stuff,' and backed out of the door, straight into a man I'd vaguely seen around the place, wearing a smart dark green apron as he carted stuff from A to B and back again according to the whims of various hysterical party planners.

I was unsure whether he was one of ours or one of theirs,

though he didn't look like Caroline's type of person at all. Medium height, stocky build – not one of the skinny exquisites with which she usually surrounded herself. His white-blond hair was cut short – brutally short, actually. His eyes, hard and grey, showed beneath darker brows. Frankly, he looked like a serial killer. Not the ones everyone is astonished to find are serial killers because people thought they were so nice and quiet – but definitely someone who had his very own wanted poster.

I said, 'Sorry,' walked around him and didn't give it another thought.

I sat on my bed, missing Doofus more than ever, and began to think. I mean think properly. Not just thoughts of slow-roasting Caroline over an open fire, not just simple revenge, but actual, full-on, in your face, in-front-of-everyone revenge. Something even she could never come back from. And – it goes without saying – would get me Mama's diamonds back.

I knew where they would be – in the small safe in Caroline's dressing room – and there were several issues to be considered here. Yes, the diamonds were in the safe – but that wasn't the problem. The problem was that of access. Under the terms of the insurance, once they were out of the attic strongroom they had to be stored in the safe in her dressing room. This was the one used for storing smaller, more portable items. Papa had shown me how to open it years ago. Yes, there's a combination, but it's useless if you don't know where to give it a jolly good thwack with the heel of your hand because the door sticks.

My problem was that the door to her dressing room had to be kept locked unless the room was actually occupied. I didn't have a key. And no chance of getting it. I needed to think outside the box. Literally outside the box.

I got up and went to the window and thought some more. Then I threw up the window and stuck out my head.

My rooms are near the corner of the West Wing, adjoining the central block. Starlings is a plain building – thank God the Tudor front had been done away with by some philistine Smallhope in the 18th century – decorated only with tall windows, a handful of slightly wonky pillars around the front door and steps, and a wide-ish ledge running under the first-floor windows to meet the lopsided pediment over the front pillars and porch.

Actually, when I say wide-ish, I mean quite narrow, but certainly wide enough to stand upon. Whether it was strong enough, of course, was completely unknown. The ledge ran all around the older part of the building. Accessing it would be no problem. I could simply climb out of the window and work my way around the building to the front. I'd done it once before when I was about twelve – just to see if I could. On that occasion, I'd only gone a few feet before losing my nerve and climbing back in again, but I didn't remember it being that difficult.

I'd need to inch my way along the side of the building for about forty feet or so, around the corner – which would be tricky but let's not worry about that yet – and along the front. Past the two windows of Caroline's sitting room – rarely used, fortunately. Her dressing room was right next door. Then their bedroom, then their bathroom, then George's dressing room, then Papa's gun room – all locked up now – then around the corner to the East Wing.

I wouldn't have to go that far. It was Caroline's dressing room I was after because that was where the safe was.

The only tiny flaw in it all was the ledge. I hadn't stuck

my head out of the window for years and I definitely didn't remember it being this crumbly. I wondered what I weighed. Very possibly more than the ledge could hold. But it was such a good plan. Tomorrow – the day of the party – I'd wait until she dressed and went downstairs for dinner. Climb out of the window. Along the ledge. In through her window – oh, wait – I'd have to find an opportunity to nip into her dressing room ahead of time and release the catch. She'd never notice, and I could be out in three or four seconds.

OK – so, in through her dressing room window. The safe was behind the little Dutch landscape, a lovely thing. Enter combination. Thump the door. Grab the diamonds – two flat boxes, not large. I'd need both my hands free for the return ledge-creep so I should take a game bag with me to carry them. Out of the window again. Remember to close it behind me. Back along the ledge. Into my room. Change into my dress. Down the stairs. Grand entrance. Wearing Mama's diamonds, of course. After all, Caroline could hardly rip them off me in public, could she?

I do like a good plan.

I kept my head down the rest of the day. If Caroline wanted to picture me weeping helplessly into my pillow that was fine with me. Various members of her ghastly family, plus those guests coming from a distance and staying a couple of nights, would be arriving tomorrow afternoon so everyone was busy anyway.

I let myself out by a side door and walked around the house a couple of times, discreetly sussing things out. Seen from below, the ledge looked narrower, crumblier and much further up. I reckoned if things went wrong then I'd fall about fifteen to twenty feet. It's not the distance, though, it's the landing surface. If I was lucky I'd just end up in a bush. If I wasn't, then I'd fall on to the gravel, which would be much less fun. I'd probably have a broken bone or two to account for. Although I could tell everyone that Caroline had driven me to suicide. Hm – that plan could have merit. I'd consider it as the ambulance whisked me off to hospital. Always supposing, of course, I didn't spend my final hours sprawling undiscovered on the gravel and slowly bleeding to death.

I discarded that idea. Smallhope women don't lie around bleeding to death. In times of crisis, we chuck people down wells.

I walked around the house once more, listening to the sounds of hysteria all about me. Caroline was definitely kicking off about something. I caught a glimpse of George nipping through the kitchen-garden gate. He was pushing off to the pub and I didn't blame him. In fact, I was very tempted to join him even though we hadn't actually spoken for some time. If I had – if we'd enjoyed a quiet drink together in the pub garden as dusk slowly fell, if we'd laughed together over the ridiculousness of the party and everything else, if we'd talked a little of Papa, which we hadn't at all – how much of my future would have been different? And his?

It didn't happen though, so no point in dwelling on it.

No time spent planning is ever wasted. I can't remember who said that, but they were right. That night, I went over everything in my mind. Step by step. I paced it out in my room, trying to anticipate everything that could go wrong and what I would do about it.

The opportunity to fix the window came more quickly than I expected. I heard Caroline's voice moving away towards the other landing where her guests were staying and decided to take a chance. I nipped along to her dressing room and tried the door. I had a book in my hand just in case. Though why Caroline would want to read a book of mine wasn't a question to which I had an answer. Especially as I had strong suspicions she'd never read a book in her entire life.

The handle turned easily. That meant she'd be back at any moment and I needed to be quick. Very quick. No need for lights – the outside lights threw a faint gleam through the window.

Shit – I hadn't thought of that. The exterior of the house would be lit up like a firework display tomorrow night. Think of that later. One thing at a time.

I crossed swiftly to the window. God only knew when it had last been opened so I had a small tin of WD-40 up my sleeve. But it wasn't needed. The catch moved silently. I was surprised. I could have sworn it hadn't been opened in years and here it was, working perfectly. In fact . . . I rubbed my fingers. Was that oil?

I turned away and caught sight of the little landscape on the wall. Should I risk trying to take the diamonds now? I hovered. Yes? No?

No. I had a plan and I should stick to it. If I was caught now, then it would be game over. Caroline could be back at any moment. I nipped back across the room and eased open the door. No one in sight. I slipped through – not without a quick sigh of relief – and closed it behind me.

And opened it to shoot back in again to pick up the book I'd left behind on the table. That was a valuable lesson learned. Always check and check again before leaving the scene of a crime.

She was just coming up the stairs as I crossed the landing. I'd made the right decision by not going for the diamonds tonight. Another lesson learned. Don't swap horses mid-stream. We eyed each other like a couple of tom cats – minus the urine spraying, of course – and carried on our separate ways.

After all that, I found I was hungry so I nipped down to the kitchen for something to eat. An early night, I decided. Big day tomorrow.

The big day dawned clear and sunny. I hadn't actually factored in the weather. Not only would I not have been physically able to ledge-walk in the pouring rain, but appearing at the party with sodden hair and running mascara would have been a massive giveaway and I'd made no contingency plans. Fortunately I didn't need them but that was another lesson learned.

I stayed out of sight for most of the day. A curt instruction through the door conveyed Caroline's command for me to be present and correct at the appointed time. Or else. And for God's sake, try to look a little less like a sulky teenager.

That was fine. She'd go down at six to get in everyone's way and make a lot of inconvenient last-minute changes. Then pre-dinner drinks with family and the guests who were staying with us. A light dinner at seven. She'd then return to her dressing room, adjust her make-up, don the diamonds, and go straight back downstairs to start greeting the hordes of arriving guests. Kick-off at eight thirty. That's the good thing about control freaks – they're easy to predict.

I laid out my dress all ready. And the shoes. I'd do my make-up before I went out on the ledge. After all, there was no point in having been to an expensive finishing school if I never got to display the results.

I made all my preparations – dark sweatshirt and jeans, hair in a ponytail, nonslip shoes – and then sat in the window and watched the sun go down until it was time.

My own window also opened soundlessly. Thank you, WD-40. I sat on the low sill and swung my legs over. Finding the ledge, I cautiously let it take my weight. Nothing crashed into the shrubbery below. Least of all me. I eased the rest of me out of the window, adjusted my swag bag and straightened up. The night was cool with no wind or rain.

I'd debated whether to face inwards or outwards and had gone for inwards, pressing my hands against the bare wall. To this day, I can still feel the rough stone under my fingers. I developed a rhythm. Left foot. Take the weight. Close up with the right foot. Take the weight. Slide the left foot again. About twelve inches at a time. Don't hurry. Don't look down. Thankfully, all the windows on this side were dark. All the action was taking place at the front of the house. Where I would be if I successfully negotiated the corner. Don't think about that. Get there first, then deal with the corner.

Left foot, right foot. I was beginning to feel quite optimistic when something crumbled beneath my left shoe. I threw my weight forwards and dug my fingers into the cracks between the stones, lifted my foot and groped for something solid. My heart was pounding and my fingers slick with sweat. And I needed to get a move on. Caroline would come up just before eight to pick up the diamonds. It was vital she found neither them nor me.

After that little hiccup, things were more or less easy. The ledge was wide enough, comparatively grit-free, and I have quite small feet. I told myself that as long as I didn't actually throw myself backwards I should be fine. I shuffled and shuffled. The West Wing seemed a lot longer outside than inside.

And here was the corner.

OK – I'd practised this at ground level. I extended my left arm and pressed my cheek to the stonework. Weight on the right foot, left leg around the corner. Find the ledge. Test the weight. Seemed OK. Weight on my left foot. Bring up the right foot. Still hanging on with all my fingertips. Ease my face around the corner. Then my right foot. Bring up the right hand. Weight distributed between both feet. And now I was round the corner.

I took a moment, cheek to the cold stone, pulling myself together. The worst was over.

No, it wasn't. Arseholes. In fact, sodding arseholes. There was a lot of activity around the front of the house. Caroline must have had the front door fixed. Waiters, caterers and miscellaneous people were milling around everywhere.

I really couldn't afford to hang around. I shuffled onwards. And now there was another problem. Possibly in an effort to create the impression of welcome, Caroline had commanded every front room to be brightly lit. Light streamed from every window. Well, that wasn't any bloody good, was it?

And there were cars below. I wouldn't be crashing to my death on the gravel but on to someone's cherished motor instead. That wasn't any bloody good, either.

I passed the first lighted window. Caroline's sitting room. At least all the lights made it easy to see inside. The room was empty.

I eased myself past. And then the second window. The third window was the one I wanted. The unsecured window. At least

so I hoped. Because if it had been discovered and relocked . . .
I wasn't certain I had the bottle to go all the way back again –
not empty-handed, anyway. Perhaps I could get into George's
room somehow and access Caroline's dressing room that way.
I'd worry about that if I had to.

And here I was at last. I could see the little landscape on
the wall opposite. I twisted my head to peer further into the
dressing room. Empty. Now to see if anyone had noticed I'd
released the catch. Very carefully – because I didn't want
to push myself backwards off the ledge – I bent and got my
fingers under the wooden frame. I braced myself to lift, and
just at that moment, there were voices at ground level. Right
underneath me. Men's voices. I had no idea who they were.
Staff, guests, caterers, security – it would only take one of
them to glance upwards. I must be a dark silhouette against
the lighted window.

I didn't dare move but I couldn't crouch like this forever.
For God's sake, guys – shift yourselves. Go and get a drink or
something. I'll pay. Just go.

My legs were trembling. I couldn't do this much longer.
Move or fall. Move or fall.

And then – seemingly quite close at hand, piercing the dark
and making my blood run cold – a ghastly shriek. As if all the
souls in hell had cried out in anguish. Or, if you'd lived with
that sound all your life – a Smallhope peacock letting rip in
the woods somewhere. One of them at least was still with us.

The big brave men below gave a kind of mini-shriek of their
own and then laughed in a shamefaced *I didn't really mean to do
that* way and disappeared back up the steps and in through the
front door. I wondered how Caroline had got it open. Looked

at it, probably, which would easily have dissolved the rust and melted the hinges.

I did not hang around. I had that window up in seconds and was over the sill and into her dressing room without even looking. Frankly, I was so traumatised at this point that even being discovered by Caroline couldn't have fazed me. I sucked in some oxygen and then drew the curtains before half the county could see me in here. I yanked at the blue brocade, taking a moment to bury my head in the folds and try to calm down a little because I was going to have to do it all again on the way back. I checked my watch. I needed to get on with it.

Crossing to the little Dutch landscape, I swung the picture aside and opened the safe, hoping against hope that she wasn't already wearing the diamonds. She shouldn't be. I knew her plan was to put them on after dinner and make a grand entrance. If she was already wearing them, then I was stumped.

There were tons of jewellery boxes in there. Mine, however, were dark blue and rather shabby. And there they were. With trembling hands, I pulled one out and opened it.

Empty.

As with the other box.

I really can't describe how I felt at that moment.

It got worse.

The door handle rattled.

I was paralysed with fright. Literally paralysed. I couldn't think. Couldn't move. Couldn't breathe.

A hand clamped across my mouth and a man's hoarse voice in my ear whispered, 'Quiet.'

I didn't really have a choice. An arm reached over my

shoulder, closed the safe, replaced the picture, then circled my waist and I was lifted off my feet and dragged backwards.

It all happened so quickly I had no idea what was going on. Was I being kidnapped? Had someone mistaken me for Caroline? They were bloody dead if they had. The next minute I was in one of the floor-to-ceiling wardrobes. Both of us were in here. Oh God – he was a pervert as well.

'Close the door.'

I did as I was told, easing the door almost closed. We both peered through the crack. My heart was pounding. Whoever was coming in – perhaps I could attract their attention somehow.

The same idea had obviously occurred to my – whoever this was. He said again, 'Quiet.'

I heard Caroline's voice outside, demanding the key from George.

'Just keep quiet,' the man whispered, 'and I'll get us both out of this.' And to my surprise, he took his hand away from my mouth.

I leaned back so he could hear me and whispered, 'Shunt along a bit. If she's come for something in here, then she'll catch us.'

Obligingly he shunted along and I followed him. We stood among more evening dresses than one person could possibly need in an entire lifetime as the door opened and Caroline swept into the dressing room, talking to someone still out on the landing.

She wasn't wearing the Skeffington diamonds. My umpteenth shock of the evening.

No time to think about that. Someone called her name. Obviously yet another crisis was looming. Caroline crossed to the safe, whipped the door open, dragged out my blue boxes, shouted, 'Coming,' and swept out of the dressing room, locking the door behind her.

I felt my fellow wardrobe occupant let out a breath which reminded me to do the same. I couldn't remember when I'd last breathed out. I tumbled out of the wardrobe and made for the window. Caroline would open the boxes, find them empty, jump instantly to the correct conclusion, and head straight for my room. And I wouldn't be there. Because I was locked in here.

The man grabbed my arm. Once again I realised how strong he was. 'Whoa. Where're you going?'

It was the guy in the green apron. The one I'd collided with what seemed like a hundred years ago. Looking at him now, close up, he was younger than I'd thought. Much younger. Around George's age, perhaps. And now that he was uttering sentences of longer than one word, his voice was quiet, hoarse and with a strong east London accent.

'I have to get back,' I gabbled. 'Any moment now, she's going to . . .'

He looked at me. For a long time. Then his eyes dropped to my swag bag. Then over to the safe. Then back to me again. Well, it wasn't rocket science, was it? There was no expression but his gaze wasn't comfortable. I felt my heart thump with apprehension.

And then my brain cut in. Caroline had come for the diamonds. Which meant she didn't have them. I didn't have them. Which only left . . .

I stared at him. He stared back. I stared some more. If I screamed now . . .

I don't know why I didn't.

I held out my hand.

He looked over at the window. Then at me. Then over to the door. Then back to me again. I held out my hand some more. Any moment now Caroline would be bursting back through the door . . . I would be in for a nasty scene but he'd be in for a lengthy prison sentence.

The man obviously came to some sort of decision because he sighed and pulled something sparkly from his pocket.

'Give me that bag of yours. Quick.'

I glared at him. 'No. You give me the diamonds. Now.'

He hissed in what I chose to regard as exasperation rather than homicidal rage. 'Just give me the bag. I'll get it back to you.' He paused. 'I promise.'

Still trying to work out what was going on and very conscious of time flying by, I slowly held the bag out to him. To this day I don't know why I trusted him. Why I didn't just shout for help. I could have saved myself by denouncing him. But I didn't.

He stuffed the diamonds in the bag and slung it over his shoulder, crossed to the window, pulled it down, locked it and drew back the curtains.

'Go somewhere with witnesses who could speak up for you. Kitchen. Stables. Whatever. Move.'

I pointed. 'But the door's locked.'

He did something to the door, eased it open and peered out.

That was the moment I realised he'd been the one who oiled the window lock. Given he seemed able to get himself in and out of the door, the window must have been his emergency exit. Neat planning.

He gave me a small push, interrupting my thoughts. 'Save yourself. Go.'

He shoved me out of the door, followed me out, pulled it to behind him and . . . locked it again, I suppose.

'Why are you still here?' he said impatiently. 'Go.'

He wheeled off to the left, moving silently but at some speed, so I didn't hang around, either. Still utterly bemused, I went right, clattering down the backstairs, along a cold stone corridor and into the kitchen, where, not surprisingly, chaos reigned.

I took a deep breath. I was Lady Amelia Smallhope. This was my home. I had every right to be here. In fact, if Papa had been alive, then I would have been.

I raised my voice. 'Good evening, everyone. I'm just checking everything is all right. Do you have everything you need? Any problems I should be discussing with Lady Goodrich?'

I like to think it was the last phrase that clinched it. There were murmurings I chose to construe as, 'No, my lady, everything's absolutely fine,' rather than, 'The consommé won't set, the souffles haven't risen, the duck's gone dry and half the waiters have been at the champers and are as pissed as newts in the back pantry.' Which would have been far more believable, trust me. In Papa's day, there had been a hugely important but necessarily discreet reception for several foreign ambassadors and a head of state, attended by a princeling, the head of some security organisation, and the Lord Lieutenant and his wife, and part of the ceiling in the dining room had come down during the first course, narrowly missing Cleverly who said afterwards he'd never known he could move that fast, my lord.

Anyway, as I said – only murmurs from the catering people.

'Excellent,' I said, weaving slowly past the laden tables. 'This all looks delicious. My brother and sister-in-law will be delighted. Thank you so much for all your hard work.'

When I thought enough people had seen me, I followed a group of waiters back up the stairs and into the hall, being careful to remain visible at all times. I have no idea with whom I exchanged words, but as long as they remembered me, then it wasn't important.

Instinct made me glance up to see Caroline looking down over the banisters. Looking for me. She made signs indicative of getting my arse up there pronto.

I waved back at her gaily. Perhaps I could infuriate her into some kind of cardiac event before she denounced me. My own heart was thudding like a steam hammer.

Eventually she called out, 'Amelia . . . dear . . . can I have a quick word?'

I climbed halfway up the stairs, staring up at her. 'What is it? I have to go and change.'

'I shan't keep you a moment. Dear.' You have to think gritted teeth for the full effect.

Climbing the remaining stairs as slowly as I dared, I repeated, 'What is it?'

I wanted to stay in full view of witnesses but she grabbed my wrist and whirled me along the landing and around the corner. I'd like to think if she tried that now, I'd have her arm out of its socket and be beating her to death with the soggy end before she realised what was happening. However, this was then.

She slammed me against the wall. For a string bean in yellow tulle, she was amazingly strong. 'Where are they?'

'Where are what?'

'My diamonds.'

'You have diamonds? Good for you. Are they as nice as mine?'

'You know what I mean. Give them to me this instant.'

'If you mean Mama's diamonds, then you already have them. You stole them, remember?'

Spit flew from her mouth. *'George gave them to me.'*

'Sorry, but they're not George's to give. Consult my solicitor. Who is here tonight, I believe. I'll go and find him.'

Her grip tightened, her fingernails digging into my wrist. 'Give me the diamonds.'

I smiled and said softly, 'Caroline, it gives me enormous pleasure to tell you I don't have them.'

'I don't believe you. Give them to me now.'

'Oh my God,' I said cheerfully. 'If I don't have them and you don't have them – have they been stolen? By someone other than you, I mean.'

She was white with rage. I could see two red splodges of blusher on her cheeks. 'I warn you – I will call the police.'

I shrugged. 'If you don't – I will. I leave it to you to decide who will be most embarrassed when I report the theft. Of *my* diamonds.'

Something hard slammed into the side of my face.

We were standing in the little corridor off the south landing, right next to a console table with a tall lamp throwing a soft glow over a series of pretty but valueless ornaments, including an intricately decorated hand mirror that looked Renaissance but wasn't.

Not any more though. It was lying in pieces on the floor and there was blood on it. My blood, actually. And the side of my face was on fire. She'd walloped me with the bloody hand mirror.

I am a descendent of Perfectly Normal Agnes. The Agnes

who upended both her husband and her lover into the well and watched them drown. For one glorious moment, I contemplated doing the same to Caroline. Not the well, obviously – sadly, that was all filled in now – but over the ornate banisters on to the floor below. In my mind I saw her fall. Saw her land. Heard the crack. Watched her blood spread across the tiles . . .

'Excuse me, Lady Amelia, you asked me to remind you.'

I refocused. My friend from Caroline's dressing room stood nearby, now minus the apron and the bag, but with an empty silver tray impressively balanced on the fingers of one hand.

'I believe you said the matter was urgent, my lady.'

Caroline had stepped back, breathing heavily, the snapped-off mirror handle still in her hand. That was how hard she had hit me. I wondered what the damage to my face was. I had an idea I was only seeing out of one eye. However, I'd been granted a lifeline by the person rapidly turning out to be my partner in crime tonight.

'Thank you,' I said, and my voice wasn't steady at all. 'I'll come at once.'

He stood between me and Caroline as I walked past.

She said, 'Amelia,' and her voice wasn't steady, either.

I ignored her. Instinct took me back to my room. I just wanted to get inside and lock the door and possibly never come out again.

He followed me all the way back to my room and opened the door for me. 'Sit on the bed.'

I said, 'No,' but I might as well not have bothered.

He came out of the bathroom with a basin and towel. 'Let me look.' He grasped my chin and turned my face from side to side. 'No – there's no glass. I think the mirror broke when it hit the floor. Your eye will feel like hell though. It's swollen already. Clean yourself up.'

I dipped the towel in warm water and carefully washed the blood and make-up off my throbbing face.

He examined my dress, laid out and ready. 'This what you're wearing?'

I nodded.

He pulled Mama's diamonds – my diamonds, actually – from my swag bag and tossed them on the bed. 'Get dressed, put those on, and get yourself downstairs.'

I blinked. OK – several things wrong with that. Where was the sympathy? My face was killing me. And there was no way I was venturing out tonight. No way at all.

I dipped the towel again. 'But my face. People will ask.'

'Then tell them.'

I stopped dead and stared at him. 'I can't . . . I can't tell people . . .'

'Why not?'

'Well, for a start, I'm a Smallhope.'

'So?'

'You don't understand.'

'You're telling me you're too important to admit you've been subjected to domestic violence?'

Every instinct was telling me to keep quiet. To conceal what had happened. Why, I didn't know. Perhaps it was shame. Or guilt. What could I possibly have done to make Caroline do such a thing? That's what people would say.

'Well . . . perhaps I'm not . . . I mean . . .'

'There are thousands of women out there who think they're *not* important enough to be believed, so tell me – at what

71

point on the social scale *is* it acceptable for a woman to report domestic abuse?'

He had this kind of flat, dead look about him that was far more frightening than Caroline with her mirror. There was a nasty, deadly little pause.

I opened my mouth and then had second thoughts. If I said something along the lines of *what will people think or say*, then I had a feeling I'd disappoint him, and suddenly it was very important that I didn't. Disappoint him, I mean.

'All right,' I said.

'And hurry.'

'My hands are shaking. And I . . . um . . . you . . .'

He sighed and turned his back. 'Tell me if you need help with the fastenings.'

I scrambled out of my clothes and stepped into the dress. 'Zip.'

I was zipped.

I slipped a bracelet over each wrist. He fastened the necklace. 'Tiara?'

I shook my head. 'Wrong hair.'

He put my hair up for me. I know! In all that bizarre night, that's the thing I remember most. He put my hair up for me. And it looked quite nice. I fitted the tiara and squinted in the mirror.

He handed me a lipstick. My hands were still trembling but I did my best, peering into the mirror with fewer working eyes than I should have.

'You look fine,' he said. 'Drink this.'

He handed me a hip flask and I took a swig of brandy. 'Now get yourself downstairs.'

I hesitated.

'She won't do it again and I'll never be far away. Head up. Chin up. Shoulders back. Go and ruin her night.'

'Don't be so unambitious,' I said, the brandy and Perfectly Normal Agnes doing their work in perfect harmony. 'I plan to ruin her life.'

And I did. I took the first steps that night.

6

Heart thumping, I flew along the landing. At the head of the stairs I paused, took a deep breath to steady myself and looked down into the hall. Dinner was obviously finished and the guests had started to arrive. George and an agitated-looking Caroline were approaching the foot of the stairs, all ready to receive them. I could see familiar faces. Old friends.

Some people wear Dior or Westwood or Taylor or Versace. Lady Reeples wears Tigger, her beloved cat. He'd died an age ago – before I was born, I think. A distraught Sylvia Reeples had had him turned into something wearable and Tigger was trotted out – or rather, slung elegantly across her shoulders because apparently it did him good to get out – at every notable social event in the county. I should perhaps say that dear Tigger was looking somewhat the worse for wear these days. Getting out wasn't doing him as much good as it used to. In fact, much more getting out was almost certain to reduce Tigger to a hank of ginger fur, a tail and two glass eyes.

Those meeting Lady Reeples and Tigger for the first time were apt to take a quick step backwards and suddenly spot a dear friend on the other side of the room, but she'd known me since I was born and I was fond of her.

And over by the silver-and-black-draped urns were the Reverend and Mrs Caldicott who had, over the course of their long marriage, grown to look so much like each other as to render themselves liable to speculation of an incestuous nature.

'Nothing to it,' Papa had always said. 'I remember when he was fair and she was dark and they looked nothing like each other.'

However, since the reverend was known to be almost terminally vague, as people said, it was perfectly possible he'd attended a family function back in the mists of time and absent-mindedly returned with his sister instead of his wife, and she'd been too timid to mention it.

I walked slowly downstairs, giving people time to see me.

'George ... Caroline ...' I smiled brightly and stood beside them. A perfect picture of the nice family in their nice home waiting to greet their nice guests.

George, to give him credit, stared at me in horror. 'Millie – what have you done? Your face ...'

'Good evening,' I said cheerfully, shaking someone's hand as our guests moved past us. 'How lovely to see you. Good evening. Thank you for coming. Good evening. How are you? Good evening. Good evening.'

People were staring as they filed past.

Caroline pushed between me and George, her eyes on the diamonds in my hair, at my throat and wrists. What would she do? Actually, what could she do? She certainly couldn't take them off me and wear them herself. Not now people had seen me wearing them.

With an enormous fake smile on her face, she hissed, 'Go to your room.' Which was a huge tactical error on her part.

'OK,' I said and set off for the ballroom, which already had a fair number of people in it.

'Hey, Millie,' said someone. 'What happened to you?'

I took a deep breath. The universe paused. The phrase that changed my life.

'Lady Goodrich hit me.'

What can I say? Papa brought me up to tell the truth.

Within seconds it was all over the ballroom. Within a minute it was all over the house. I heard whispers everywhere. Lady Goodrich . . . Caroline . . . don't believe it . . . look at her face . . .

'Nice one,' said my accomplice, standing before me with a tray laden with glasses. He put one in my hand.

'Now what are you feeding me?'

'Margarita. Get it down you.'

So I did.

The next moment George was at my elbow. 'Millie, can you come upstairs, please.'

'Can't leave our guests, George,' I said, dumping my empty glass on a tray and taking another.

'The police are here.'

'Oh good. I have so much to tell them.'

'Millie . . . how could you do this? You've ruined Caroline's big night.'

Still clasping the margarita, I sucked the salt off my bottom lip, turned to him, and said very quietly, 'George – Caroline is a stupid, vindictive woman. But she can't help it. It's her nature. We just have to work around it. But you're my older brother. Papa trusted you to look out for me. You stood by while

76

your wife killed our dogs. Sold our horses. She stole Mama's diamonds from me and you let her do it. George – I am so disappointed in you.'

I left him standing there, white-faced and shocked.

My shadow was still with me. I asked him where the police were.

'In the library, my lady.'

'You don't have to call me that.'

'I like it.'

Caroline was in the library clutching a very large glass of something. There were two other people with her – a man and a woman. Plain-clothes officers. I suppose if you're the Countess of Goodrich, you don't get ordinary uniformed police.

'Good evening,' I said, leaving the door open so my accomplice could make up his mind whether to accompany me or not. I heard the door close behind me but had no idea which side of it he was on.

They showed me their ID.

'Sorry,' I said, gesturing at my face. 'I'm having a little difficulty focusing this evening. Can you just tell me who you are, please.'

'Detective Inspector Sully and Detective Sergeant Kapoor. We're here . . .'

Caroline intervened. 'As you can see, my sister-in-law has had an accident. She's still a little young for this type of event and the excitement and alcohol have proved too much for her.'

I smiled. This was a professional visit, and I wasn't going to embarrass him, but the inspector knew me. I'd been at school with his daughter. I was friendly but polite.

'Good evening, Inspector Sully. It's very nice to see you again. How is Lindsey? Off to Durham, I believe.'

'She's doing nicely, thank you.' He shifted his weight. 'What happened to your face, Lady Amelia?'

'Lady Goodrich hit me,' I said, for the second time that night.

'I did no such thing,' she said indignantly.

'With a mirror, so technically, I suppose, she's right. She didn't hit me herself.'

He turned to Caroline. 'Do you have any comment to make, Lady Goodrich?'

'It was a complete accident. She walked into it.'

'The mirror you were holding at the time.'

'Exactly.'

'If I handed you, say . . .' he picked up a book from the table, 'this book, could you reproduce the incident. Show us exactly how that occurred.'

'Well, of course not. It all happened so quickly.'

He turned to me. 'Could *you* perhaps . . . ?'

I reached for the book. 'Yes, of course.'

'This is all quite irrelevant,' broke in Caroline.

'Yes, madam. I believe you reported a theft. Diamonds, you said.' He looked at my diamond-bedecked self. 'Would these be they?'

I was impressed. Not many people get that grammatically correct. Especially not me.

Caroline was so agitated that she entirely forgot to pitch her voice attractively low and drop it at the end of each sentence. The elephants would be disappointed not to find out how this ended. Drawing herself up, she said, 'I discovered my diamonds were missing from the safe and telephoned to report a theft.'

He turned to me. 'Did you steal the diamonds?'

'Nope,' I said cheerfully.

'And yet you appear to be wearing them.'

'Yes.'

Caroline stepped forwards. 'As you can see – there has been a mistake. My sister-in-law wanted to wear my diamonds and removed them from the safe without telling me.'

'Is that correct?'

'Yes and yes.'

'You took the diamonds from the safe.'

'That is correct.'

'Why?'

'To wear them tonight.'

'But they aren't your property.'

'Actually, they are.'

'Nonsense. George – my husband – the Earl of Goodrich – gave them to me – his wife.'

There was no expression on the inspector's face or in his voice as he turned back to face me. 'Do you have any comment, madam?'

'My mama left the diamonds to me. In her will. Legally, they are mine.'

'Can you prove ownership?'

'Actually – yes. My solicitor, Mr Treasure – whom I'm certain you will know – is here tonight. I'm sure he'll be delighted to confirm my statement.'

The inspector turned to the sergeant. 'Would you please?' She slipped out of the room.

'Really, this is all quite unnecessary,' said Caroline, attempting a casual air I could have told her was a mistake. 'Obviously no theft has taken place – just a normal family mix-up. We really don't need to detain you any further. No crime has actually occurred.'

'I disagree, madam. This young lady's injury has yet to be explained to my satisfaction.'

That shut her up. We waited in silence. Caroline had another slug of something.

Inspector Sully turned to me. 'Would you like to sit down, Lady Amelia? That eye looks quite painful. Have you sought medical attention?'

'I'm fine, thank you.'

The door opened behind me. I turned. Mr Treasure and Sergeant Kapoor stood in the doorway.

'Ah, Mr Treasure.' Caroline put down her drink and bustled forwards. 'If you could just tell these people . . .'

Sully held up a hand. 'One moment, if you please, madam. A small matter, sir.'

Mr Treasure was peering at me. 'Good heavens, Lady Amelia. What happened?'

'Lady Goodrich walloped me with a hand mirror,' I said, for the third time that night and beginning to get the hang of it.

His eyes narrowed as various solicitor instincts cut in.

'I don't want to minimise your injury, madam,' Sully said to me, 'but if we could just confirm ownership of the diamonds first. Mr Treasure?'

'They are the property of Lady Amelia Smallhope as bequeathed to her by her mother, Fiona Skeffington, in her will. They do not form part of the Starlings estate and are Lady Amelia's own personal property.'

'Amelia is a minor,' began Caroline.

'Immaterial, Lady Goodrich.'

'My husband gave them . . .'

'Again, Lady Goodrich, the diamonds are not part of the estate and are, therefore, not his lordship's to give. They are the personal property of Lady Amelia Smallhope.' He turned to me. 'I do hope you will get that looked at, my dear.'

'I shall,' I said. 'I'm sorry you were dragged out of the festivities. My apologies and best wishes to Mrs Treasure.'

'Would you like me to remain?'

'That's very kind but I think I'm going to take a few painkillers and go to bed.'

'Actually,' said Inspector Sully to me, 'I think we should drive you to hospital and have you checked over.'

'Thank you,' I said, 'but there's no need.'

'Nevertheless, a crime has occurred . . .'

'I thought we'd agreed,' said Caroline hastily. 'The diamonds haven't been stolen after all. Just a silly mistake by my sister-in-law and . . .'

'On the contrary, madam, a crime *has* occurred.' He turned to me again. 'Do you feel up to making a statement?'

'Actually no,' I said truthfully. 'As I said, a few painkillers and bed. If no one has any objections.'

It would seem no one did.

'In that case,' said Inspector Sully, watching Caroline carefully, 'we'll return tomorrow morning for your statement, Lady Amelia. Around eleven o'clock? You can have an undisturbed night. In the meantime, Lady Goodrich . . .'

I made for the door. I had no idea what would happen once I'd left the room and didn't care anyway. I needed a drink and a think.

Mr Treasure followed me out. He assured me of his best service at all times. I wished him an enjoyable evening and headed for the safety of my room.

Where my accomplice was waiting. With another of those margarita things.

'Oh, yes,' I said, necking half of it.

He looked disapproving. 'Have you eaten?'

I shook my head, necked the other half and sat down with a bump.

He sighed. 'How old are you?'

I focused with some difficulty. 'How old are *you*?'

Slightly defiantly, he said, 'Twenty-five.'

I raised my working eyebrow.

'All right – twenty-three. You?'

'Very nearly eighteen,' I said, more or less accurately.

'Oh God. I've corrupted a minor.'

'You did it beautifully,' I said. 'Thanks very much for everything this evening.'

'Where's Medusa?'

'Still with the police.' I looked down at my bracelets. 'I hope you didn't have anything else planned for tonight. Because I'm not handing them over.'

'Actually . . .'

'But if it's the Gainsboroughs you're after,' said the margaritas, 'I can get you forty pence in the pound for them.'

He folded his arms. 'You mean fifteen to twenty.'

'No – I swear. Mate's rates. Someone I know.'

'Someone you know? Yeah – right.'

'Ah,' I said wisely. 'You've obviously never been to a girls' finishing school.'

'I went to butler school. Does that count?'

'Butler school?' I frowned painfully. 'That's not some sort of euphemism, is it?'

'Euphemism?'

'You know – everyone thinks it's a school for the superior manservant but actually it's Assassins 101 or something.'

He drew himself up – courtesy of butler school, I suspected. 'Certainly not, my lady. An exclusive establishment with a two-year waiting list, offering a comprehensive curriculum with a wide variety of subjects and ending with a gruelling series of examinations, all with a minimum pass mark of eighty per cent.'

I was struggling to reconcile accent and vocabulary. And a raging headache. 'I suppose you have a certificate.'

'Diploma, my lady.'

'And you have one?'

'I have twelve, my lady.'

I blinked. With only half my eyes so it was more of a wink. 'Twelve? In what subjects?'

'Among others, cookery, mixology, valet skills, concierge skills, international etiquette, protocols, presentation, all aspects of hospitality management. And floral art.'

'You passed floral art?'

'With flying colours.'

'You have a certificate in floral art?'

'Diploma. Don't you?'

I strove for an answer that wasn't *no*. 'Seriously – twelve diplomas?'

'Seriously – you failed floral art?'

'I don't want to talk about it.'

There was a very long silence. I rather thought I could do with another of those margarita things.

Eventually, I said, 'The police are here. You should get out while you still can.'

'So should you.' There was a somehow significant moment and then he said, 'Come with me.'

I laughed. And then I stopped. 'You're serious.'

'I am. You can't stay here, that's for certain.'

'Well, I know that, but . . .'

'Your family won't bother to come after you.'

'No, but . . .'

'Would you have somewhere else to go?'

I hadn't really considered it. Another lesson. Plan ahead. 'Papa's mistress. Or Aunt Indira, I suppose. But I'm supposed to be giving a statement to the police in the morning.'

He looked at me. 'Imagine if Caroline can't produce you.'

I sat still, imagining just that. Suppose the police turned up for my statement and I wasn't here. What would she do? What would they do? They might even arrest her. That would be fun.

'You could give it a couple of days,' he went on, 'and then let the police know you're OK. Before they start digging up the kitchen garden looking for your body or dragging the lake. We don't want you appearing on the nine o'clock news, but it could make for a very uncomfortable couple of days for Princess Poison.'

I said thoughtfully, 'Yes, it would, wouldn't it? The police . . . the scandal . . . the publicity.'

He grinned.

I grinned back.

As I think I've already said – I'm really not a nice person.

*   *   *

84

I wanted to make a dramatic exit along the ledge again. My accomplice pointed out I could barely see with one eye and we glared at each other. He won that one because he had more glaring eyes than me. I wondered if I should have sipped that third margarita more slowly.

I suppose I should have been sad to leave my home. My only excuses are that I was quite drunk and I honestly thought that one day I would come back. That Caroline would somehow disappear in a puff of ill-natured smoke and George and I would carry on as before. So, I changed my clothes and, just like Nellie the Elephant, I packed my trunk and said goodbye to the circus. Diamonds, money, a photo of Papa and the dogs, toiletries, a change of clothes, and I was ready to go.

Like most seventeen-and-a-half-year-olds, beyond running the estate, I hadn't given a lot of thought to my future, but it would certainly be fair to say I never expected it to turn out the way it did.

Downstairs was chaos. Guests were milling about, wondering whether the ball had been cancelled or not. There was no sign of either George or Caroline. I paused at the head of the stairs. Part of this was my fault. I could go down and make things right. I could speak to people, smile, urge them to drink more champagne, stay for supper, enjoy themselves.

Or I could turn my back on it all. Walk away. Leave it for someone else to sort out.

My accomplice was waiting while I hovered at the top of the stairs. He didn't say a word. No attempt to persuade me one way or the other. It was very obviously to be my decision and mine alone.

I hesitated, my head a whirl of margaritas and conflicting thoughts. If I walked away now, I'd be leaving George to face the aftermath alone. Could I do that? Yes. He'd left me to face Caroline alone. He'd made his choice. But Papa had left him. Our staff had left him. Now, I was leaving him. Did he realise what was happening? That he was completely isolated and surrounded by strangers? Caroline had seen to that.

My poor, sad brother George.

I turned away. 'Let's go.'

My accomplice took me out by the route I would have chosen myself. I suspected he knew the house as well as I did. Through the West Wing, down the west staircase and out of the side door into the small courtyard where we kept the cars. I walked towards them but he said, 'This way.'

He switched on a torch and we walked quickly out under the archway, on to the gravel drive and into the shrubbery. The sounds of revelry died away behind us. From there we crossed into the rose garden, following the crumbling brick wall until we reached the old wooden door leading into the park. Which was unlocked. I was no longer surprised at anything that was happening to me that night.

Actually I was beginning to feel quite unwell. Alcohol, shock, my throbbing face. I had to stop. 'I'm sorry . . . I don't think I can . . .'

He turned back. I couldn't see his face.

'Go on without me,' I said, looking for something to lean against. 'I'll just stay here for a bit . . . You go on.'

It was too far for me to walk across the park to the lane leading to the village, Hardcourt Parva, where he must have left his car.

'It's not much further,' he said.

I shook my head. 'But it is and I don't think I can go that far.'

'It's not much further,' he said again, taking my arm.

It wasn't. There was a small spinney on this side of the parkland – a pretty little wood carefully planted with bluebells. Somewhere quiet to get away from the family, because sometimes living in a house with twenty-seven bedrooms just doesn't cut the mustard when you want a bit of peace and quiet.

Just on the outskirts, deep in shadow, stood a small building I hadn't seen before. Perhaps Caroline had ordered one of those little summerhouse things so she could enjoy nature, although that seemed unlikely – she wasn't that big on the great outdoors and it seemed safe to assume the great outdoors was equally not that big on her.

He opened the door and motioned me inside.

I hung back. Were we to wait here until morning? What would be the point of that? By morning, people would be looking for me and I'd never get away. Why would he bring me here?

And then the penny dropped and I saw how stupid I'd been.

I said, 'No,' and started to back away, wondering how far I'd get if I had to run for it. Should I shout? Although I could barely hear the faint voices and music coming from the house so it seemed unlikely anyone would hear me.

'Oh,' he said, not moving. 'I hadn't thought of that.' He frowned. 'You're not my type.'

I said nothing.

'Look – I'll get you to London. You can get that face looked at. What you do then is up to you. The most important thing is to get you out of this house.'

I said nothing.

'I can't leave you here like this. Come inside.'

I said nothing.

He peered more closely. 'You all right?'

'No.' It came out much more piteously than I intended. And then I threw up.

I don't remember any more.

LONDON
The Present

I opened my eyes. Well, one of them. The other wasn't working so well.

Where was I? I could hear traffic in the distance. And a police siren. I hoped to God they weren't looking for me. Was this London? Must be. I was in London. I'd run away from home. I was a runaway. Oh God, there had been a terrible public scene and I'd run away.

It dawned on me – slowly, because my head wasn't working properly – that Caroline could be telling people anything. That I'd made off with the silver. That I'd stolen the diamonds. That I'd helped myself to the petty cash in George's desk. That I was pregnant and run away in shame. Anything. I had a feeling I'd made a really bad decision when I left Starlings.

I lifted my head. Which, sadly, did not fall off, thus releasing me from the waves of pain and nausea. I'd certainly never drink another margarita again.

I looked at the window. Dark outside. Had I slept all the way through today? Was this tomorrow night?

I was lying on a sofa. Fully clothed. I remembered that I wasn't his type. Someone had tried to make up a kind of bed. The folded-over sheet was clean, crisp and smelled of fabric conditioner. There was an old-style blanket with an eiderdown over the top of that. And a lumpy pillow. A standard lamp in the corner cast a dim glow over an old-fashioned sideboard and knobbly-looking armchair. All the furniture was of dark wood veneer. But clean. There was some sort of wallpaper on the walls. Big blue roses by the look of it. My shoes lay neatly side by side in front of the hideously tiled fireplace.

I was in a house and everything was silent. Not even a ticking clock.

Oh God – where was I?

I sat up and just as I did, a board creaked outside and someone tapped on the door.

Not knowing what else to do, I called, 'Come in,' and in walked my jewel thief cum accomplice cum partner in crime cum getaway driver cum rescuer cum cause of all my problems cum nemesis, whatever. That's a lot of names for just one person.

He was carrying a mug of tea.

'What time is it?'

'About twenty to midnight.'

I must have gaped at him. 'It's the next day?'

'No – same day.'

'Where am I?'

'Twenty-nine Cold Ash Lane, Walthamstow.'

I was bewildered. 'London? How? How can that be? Do you have a helicopter?'

He thrust the mug at me. 'Tea.'

I took it. 'Thank you.'

'Bathroom's at the top of the stairs. Your bag is in there. The blue towels are for you. Come down when you're ready.'

He closed the door behind him. If he was a rapist, he was the most disinterested rapist on the planet.

I drank the tea and looked around the room. Those giant roses were really quite unnerving. When I'd finished, I wobbled my way upstairs to the bathroom. My bag was on the floor next to the bath. The diamonds were still there. I filled the basin and very carefully washed my face. What there was of it. Most of it was black, blue, purple and enormous. There was an eye in there somewhere – I hoped.

I cleaned my teeth, abandoned all attempts to brush my hair, and ten minutes later made my way cautiously downstairs. Drawn by the smell of bacon.

My jewel thief cum accomplice cum partner in crime cum getaway driver cum rescuer cum cause of all my problems cum nemesis – I really couldn't keep calling him all that – was standing at the stove. He indicated the table, which was set for three. 'Sit down.'

I sat. 'Do you have a name?'

He nodded. I'd asked the wrong question.

'What's your name?'

He put a plate of eggs and bacon in front of me. 'Pennyroyal.'

'Pennyroyal what?'

He shrugged.

'Well, thank you for this, Mr Pennyroyal.'

'Just Pennyroyal.'

'Where am I?'

91

'Safe.'

'Did you drive overnight?'

'No.'

'Whose house is this?'

'Belonged to my parents.'

I looked around. 'Are they here?'

'Hope not. They've been dead for some time.'

I peered at the third setting. 'You have a partner?'

'No.'

He crossed to the door and shouted up the stairs, 'Uncle Albert.'

'Here,' said a quiet voice from the back door.

Uncle Albert was tall and rangy with a deeply lined face. I suspected he wasn't as old as he looked but he had an air of ill health about him.

'Breakfast is ready.'

'Do you often breakfast in the middle of the night?'

'Tradition. After a job. Eggs and bacon. And I'm hungry.'

'And we have a guest to welcome,' said Uncle Albert, beaming. 'You must be Amelia. How do you do? I'm Albert. Uncle Albert, if you like.'

'How do you do?' I said cautiously.

'Are you feeling better now?'

'Yes, thank you.'

'That's good.' He turned to Pennyroyal. 'The pod seems fine. How did it perform?'

'Better. Not perfect – I had to bang the coordinates in twice – but adequate.'

'A successful evening, I trust.'

'Yeah . . .' said Pennyroyal, rubbing the back of his neck. 'Well . . .'

Uncle Albert looked at Pennyroyal. 'Did we get the diamonds?'

'The owner declined to part with them, so I brought her back instead.'

Bright eyes looked from him to me and back again. 'This sounds exciting. Do tell.'

The story had not improved while I had been sleeping. Uncle Albert found the whole thing hilarious.

'Not funny,' said Pennyroyal. 'Two weeks I worked my arse off with that catering company and nothing to show for it.'

'Yes,' I said, grinning. 'I do feel bad about that.'

'So where are the diamonds now?' enquired Uncle Albert.

'In her bag,' Pennyroyal said quietly.

They both turned to look at me. My heart thumped so hard it hurt. I was here, alone, with the diamonds and two men. Bad, bad move, Smallhope.

'Well,' I said, over-chirpily because suddenly I was very afraid. 'Thank you for a lovely breakfast. I really mustn't trespass on your time any longer. I'll get my stuff and find a taxi.' I turned to Pennyroyal, saying quietly, 'Thank you for everything. I am grateful.'

No one said anything.

I stood up.

Uncle Albert was buttering his toast. 'Yes, the thing is, my dear, I'm not sure we can let you go.'

'She was unconscious,' said Pennyroyal. 'She doesn't know.'

Know what? What didn't I know?

93

Uncle Albert shook his head. 'Up to you, dear boy. You know I never argue, but do consider our position carefully.'

'I have. I've been thinking about it since I got back.'

'And?'

'Why can't you let me go?' I said.

Pennyroyal poured me another cup of tea. 'Sit down. Finish your breakfast. Then we'll talk.'

I didn't know what to do. I was alone. No one knew I was here. Presumably these two . . . miscreants . . . were concerned about me being able to identify them in the future.

'Look,' I said. 'I'm not going to give you away. Why would I? I'm grateful. But now I'm in London and the time has come for me to go.'

Pennyroyal shook his head.

'Is it the diamonds you want?' I tried to look tough. 'I warn you, I went through a lot for those and I'm not giving them up quietly.'

'What? Oh, the diamonds. No, it's not that.'

'Well, what then?' I said, becoming slightly exasperated at the time it was taking for them to get to the point and completely forgetting I was clearly in the hands of criminals.

'You mentioned Gainsboroughs.'

'Mm,' I said warily. My heart started to thump again. Was I to be forced to steal from my own family? How did I feel about that? Would these men kill me if I wouldn't help them? If that policeman didn't turn up at Starlings tomorrow – today, rather – or if George and Caroline never reported me missing . . . I'd jumped into a car with a complete stranger – well, criminal, actually – and been carted off to an unknown destination . . . How stupid was I? Would helping them be the price I had to pay for my life? After which they'd probably kill me anyway. I put down my fork but retained a grip on my knife, and pushed my chair back from the table.

Pennyroyal reached for the marmalade and by now I was in such a state that I leaped to my feet, put my back to the kitchen sink and waved the knife in what I hoped was a threatening manner.

They watched me in mild astonishment.

'What are you doing?' said Uncle Albert.

I was measuring the distance to the back door. I'd jumped the wrong way when I got up, and the only way I could be further from the exit was if I actually moved to Australia. To say nothing of the two men, the kitchen table and four chairs between it and me. I tightened my grip on the knife and summoned the ancestors. There wasn't a conflict anywhere in the world that hadn't had a Smallhope in it at some point and I wasn't going to let them down. These two . . . miscreants . . . would pay a high price for my life.

'Your eggs are getting cold,' said Uncle Albert.

I swallowed hard. 'I don't think I can help you steal from my family.'

'Fair enough,' said Pennyroyal, whose face, surprisingly, remained uncontorted with frustrated fury and thoughts of revenge.

They carried on eating. I began to feel rather silly. And it wasn't as if I had any great tactical advantage over here by the draining board. And I was very hungry. With great dignity, I sat back down again. Uncle Albert passed me some toast.

'Pity,' he said to Pennyroyal.

'Yeah.'

'Would've solved a few problems.'

'Yeah.'

'Oh well.'

'Yeah.'

Somewhat warily, I picked up my fork and resumed my very excellent breakfast. At some point Pennyroyal enquired if my face still hurt.

'Only a bit.'

We Smallhopes have been bred for fortitude.

Pennyroyal plonked a blister pack on the table. 'Take two when you've finished eating.'

Oh great – I'd been kidnapped and now they were trying to drug me. I prodded the pack with my fork.

'Combined ibuprofen and paracetamol,' he said. 'If it hurts a bit now, it'll hurt like hell later on. You should take things easy for a bit. Go back to the sofa and get some sleep.'

They began to clear the dishes.

I had to know. 'What are you going to do with me? Or to me?'

Pennyroyal, filling up the sink, had just said, 'Well . . .' and then stopped, head cocked. 'Someone's in the yard. One of their midnight visits.'

Uncle Albert shot to his feet – well, climbed creakily to his feet. 'Come along, my dear.'

'What? Why? Where?'

'We'll only be in the way.'

'Great,' I said bitterly. 'Another household where I'm just in the way.'

I was hustled back into the small sitting room with the distressing blue roses. I sat down on the sofa because Pennyroyal had been right about my face. Uncle Albert remained by the door, listening.

96

There was a murmur of voices that went on for some time. And then the clatter of a chair going over. And then the table scraped across the floor. And then the sounds of a scuffle. The back door banged. Running footsteps. Silence.

'Dear me,' said Uncle Albert.

Footsteps approached. I leaped up and seized some sort of hideous vase thing off the mantel and once again prepared to sell my life dearly.

The door opened to reveal Pennyroyal. He stared at me. 'What are you doing with that vase?'

I replaced it in a hurry. 'Nothing.'

Uncle Albert sat down. 'Was that them?'

'Yeah.'

'And?'

'Same as usual. Wouldn't take no for an answer and then I had to thump them.'

'They'll be back. With more friends. This isn't going to go away.'

'Yeah.'

Silence fell.

OK – I'd had enough of this. 'Is there a problem? What exactly is going on?'

Uncle Albert sighed. 'We owe someone some money. Well, no, I owe someone some money. At a somewhat exorbitant rate of interest. They want it back. I haven't got it. They're not happy. Apparently I'm a bad example to others who might take the same casual attitude towards repaying slightly dodgy loans made by people who don't belong to any regulatory bodies.'

'So?' This was nothing unusual in Smallhope circles. 'You just ask for time to pay. Or declare yourself bankrupt.'

Uncle Albert hesitated and looked apologetic. 'Not as straightforward as that. I'm . . . um . . . a criminal.'

Somehow I wasn't surprised. Anyone looking so meek and mild-mannered had to be an axe murderer at the very least. TV news channels are full of people telling the cameras their neighbour was a lovely man, very quiet and polite, always took the right bins out on the right day – this is very important in British society – and they had no idea he had seventeen bodies in the cellar.

Again, before I could stop myself, I said, 'What did you do?'

Uncle Albert looked at Pennyroyal, who said nothing.

'Well . . .'

'Sit down,' said Pennyroyal.

'My face is fine.'

'Nothing to do with your face. Sit down.'

I considered remaining defiantly on my feet, but not for very long. I sat.

'Well,' said Uncle Albert again and stopped and made a helpless sort of gesture at Pennyroyal.

'Uncle Albert's not from round here,' said Pennyroyal.

'Yes,' said Uncle Albert, in great relief. 'That's just it. I'm not from these parts.'

'Oh,' I said. 'You've entered the country illegally. I wouldn't worry too much. It's practically a national sport.'

'Well . . .'

'And you're being blackmailed because of that.'

There was a pause. 'Yes.'

I looked at Pennyroyal. 'You too?'

'No, I'm a home-grown criminal.'

I looked back at Uncle Albert.

'I like to travel,' he said. 'And sometimes that gets me into trouble.'

Pennyroyal rolled his eyes.

'So where have you come from?'

There was another long silence. I looked from one to the other. 'You're really beginning to piss me off now. Ten minutes ago, you were doing the *Oh you can steal from your own family and make us rich* thing, but now it's all *Oh it's much too important to tell you and you wouldn't understand anyway. Go and do your make-up or something.*'

There was another silence. I shivered. This room was cold. I suspected it didn't get a lot of use.

Pennyroyal shrugged. 'You might as well tell her.'

Uncle Albert sighed. 'I'm from the future.'

'The future of what?'

'The future of us all.'

I stopped. 'The future? The future as in a hundred years from now?'

'A little more than that.'

'The *future*.'

'Yes.'

'*You're* from the future?'

'Yes.'

'*The* future.'

'Well – *a* future. There are many.'

There was a lot more from me along the lines of: *You're from the future? The actual future? The future?* They were very patient. It was only after I'd known Pennyroyal for a while that I realised how patient he actually was that day.

Eventually, probably driven insane by my frequent use of

the word *future* and the disbelieving tone in which I said it, Pennyroyal said, 'Come with me.'

'If I want to live.'

I don't think he got the reference.

He led the way back through the kitchen and its disarranged furniture, out through the back door and into a large yard. Exterior lights came on – motion-activated.

Double wooden gates led to the street outside. They were securely fastened with a heavy-duty chain and padlock I suspected Pennyroyal had just fitted. Very new and bright and shiny among all the other drab tat scattered about.

The yard was cobbled, with channels leading down to a central drain. While the drain might be recent, the cobbles had been around for some considerable time.

Between the gates and the house stood a small shed that looked very like the one I'd seen at Starlings. Too big for an outside privy – a workshop, perhaps. There was all sorts of odd stuff stacked around it – old gardening tools, an oil drum, a bicycle without wheels – junk, basically. None of which looked as if it had been touched for ages.

Seen from outside, the house itself was a typical Victorian villa-type dwelling, with dirty bricks and small windows. Again, I could hear the noise of traffic in the distance.

Pennyroyal led the way to the old shed. I could hear Uncle Albert limping along behind us.

I don't know how Pennyroyal opened the door – his body was in the way. Then he stepped aside and motioned with his head.

I stood on the threshold. I wasn't going to add venturing into a strange building to all the stupid things I'd done over the last twenty-four hours, so I stood in the doorway and peered in.

'What am I looking at?'

Uncle Albert gestured. 'This is how I came from the future.'

I stepped back and surveyed the shed. I think I was looking for the wheels.

'In this?'

'Yes.'

'You came from the future in this old shed?'

'Yes.'

I turned to Pennyroyal. 'What about you?'

He shook his head.

'You're *not* from the future?'

'No.'

And off we went again. Me asking the same stupid questions over and over again because . . . well . . . because some things just don't go in the first time round. Or the second. Or even the twelfth. It was all too much. I couldn't cope.

In the end, it was Uncle Albert who called a halt. 'Enough,' he said. 'Come inside, lass. We'll have a nice cup of tea, shall we?'

The kitchen seemed very warm after outside. I sat, shivering. I was here alone with a couple of fantasists, criminals, weirdos, nutters – you name it.

I don't often cry but I was on the verge now.

Pennyroyal came to sit opposite me. 'Listen,' he said, and his voice was, for him, quite gentle. 'Cast your mind back. We were at Starlings. We walked into the pod. The old shed out there. Don't you recognise it? We travelled from there to here. It was night when we set off. It was still night when we landed. The journey took virtually no time at all.'

I looked from him to Uncle Albert. 'I don't want to be rude, but if you're from the future – flying cars and all that – what exactly are you doing here?' I gestured around. 'This house is a little bit . . .' I changed what I had been going to say to, 'a little bit out of the way, don't you think? Why here?'

'Hiding.'

I opened my mouth, but actually – did I want to know?

'You put your finger on it,' he said. 'It's out of the way. It's easily defendable. Lots of warning if anyone comes after me. It's warm and he's a good cook.' He nodded at Pennyroyal. 'Where else would I be?'

I turned to Pennyroyal again. 'Easy for you to say the journey took no time at all – I was asleep.'

'Think about it. How long would it take to drive from Starlings to north-east London?'

I shrugged. 'Two and a half, three hours. If everything went well.'

'Exactly. We left Starlings around half past ten. We arrived here around a quarter to eleven. I woke you at midnight because we were worried you'd choke on your own vomit.'

I ignored that last bit. 'You say it was midnight. It could have been any time.'

'Good point, but it wasn't. You travelled from Starlings to Walthamstow in around twelve minutes. Four of those were me getting you into the pod, laying you in the recovery position on the floor and then setting up the jump. Twice actually, because the pod was being temperamental. Four more minutes were spent this end – shutting down the pod and trying to wake you up. Three minutes to carry you into the house. You sleep like the dead. Lay off the margaritas in future.'

I was doing the maths. Four minutes plus four minutes plus

three minutes is eleven minutes. Leaving one minute to travel a hundred and twenty miles.

It was too much information to take in.

'I believe you,' I said hastily. I thought I'd better be polite in case one or both of them had some sort of psychotic break all over the kitchen table.

I thought his shoulders slumped. 'Yeah. Sure. Of course you do.'

'I'm not ungrateful,' I said, wondering why I was worrying about hurting his feelings. 'I just ... I mean, I can't ...' I stopped. 'I think I should ... you know ... leave now.'

He gave a small smile. 'To your aunt?'

'Yes. No. Oh God, I don't know.'

'Face hurting?'

I nodded and winced a bit.

'Don't make any decisions now. Go and get some rest. Think about it tomorrow.'

'Yes, Scarlett.'

He stared blankly. I sighed. The thought of lying down seemed suddenly very tempting. But ...

'You're quite safe,' he said quietly. 'You have my word on it.'

Strangely, I believed him.

8

The next day wasn't much better. I felt dreadful when I woke up. My face was huge and throbbing and fiery. I didn't even bother thinking about getting off the sofa. I was warm. I was comfortable. I was in bed limbo where I didn't have to think about anything. I kept my eye closed – the other was closed already – put my brain in neutral and left the world to its own devices.

The next day I had to get up. I was starving. I had a bath in the shabby but perfectly clean bathroom and wobbled my way downstairs.

'You look like a rainbow,' said Pennyroyal.

'I wish I felt like a rainbow. Where's Uncle Albert?'

'Made himself scarce for a bit. He'll be back.'

I nodded and wished I hadn't.

'Is he really your uncle? You don't look alike.'

'No.'

'Is his name Albert?'

'No.'

'Is he really . . . ?'

'Yes, he really is from the future.'

'Really?'

'Yes.'

'On the run?'

'Yes.'

'From whom?'

He topped up my mug of tea. 'The thing is, my lady . . .'

'I told you – don't call me that.'

'And I told you – I like it.'

'Well, I don't. Not when you do it.'

'Why not?'

'You're mocking me.'

He looked at his tea. 'I assure you I'm not.'

Well, there was something to be picked over later, but Uncle Albert first.

'You were about to tell me who he's running from. In fact, you were about to tell me everything.'

'I don't think I was.'

'It would be the sensible thing to do.'

'And why would that be?'

'Because I'll just keep asking until you do. I'll go on and on. It will really get on your nerves. I'm a seventeen-year-old girl with everything that entails. You'll be out of your head by this time tomorrow.'

He muttered something which sounded rather like *out of my head now*.

I waited.

Eventually, he sighed. 'Uncle Albert's on the run from an outfit called the Time Police.'

I sat back. 'Seriously?'

'Sadly, yes. They're a bunch of utter bastards but that's because they have to be.'

'Nobody has to . . .'

'Yes, they do. There's a lot of trouble in the future – people doing stupid things with time travel like you wouldn't believe and I don't have time to tell you. The Time Police's job is to sort things out, set the timeline straight.'

'How?'

'Well, usually they just kill everyone in sight and set fire to what's left.'

'Everyone?'

'Yeah – guilt by association. Everyone. And then everything within quite a large radius is destroyed. They're not really interested in the law – the emphasis is on punishment first. Ruthless bastards who do whatever it takes.'

I was horrified. 'And they're after Uncle Albert?'

'They are.'

'And you?'

'No. Although they will be when they find out I've been hiding a fugitive.'

'You're not from the future?'

'No.'

'And he arrived in that shed thing?'

'As did you. And it's a pod.'

I couldn't resist. 'Why isn't it bigger on the inside?'

He stared at me blankly. 'What?'

'Nothing,' I said. 'So it . . . it travels in time.'

'And space. You moved from Starlings to here – remember?'

'A machine that travels in time and space. Are you sure it's not bigger on the inside?'

He stared at me again. 'Should I check you for concussion?'

'No,' I said hastily, because I wasn't sure what that would entail and if I did have concussion, then his cure would probably be to blow my head off. Simple. Cheap. Effective. The solution to so many problems. 'Tell me about this pod thing.'

He said again, 'It can travel in time and space.'

I waited but that seemed to be it. OK – move on.

I narrowed my eyes. 'Are *you* a Time Police thingy?'

'God, no.'

I seemed to have insulted him.

'But these Time Police people were here the other night?'

'No, the people who were here the other night were the people we owe money to. We had to borrow a lot to buy the bits to get this pod fixed but we fell behind with the repayments. I've done my best but the interest is crippling and now they want the whole lot back at once and we haven't got it. And the interest is mounting every day. So yeah – we're in trouble.'

I frowned at the table. Now I knew what my diamonds were for. 'Why don't you just clear off? Get into your shed and . . . go elsewhere.'

He lowered his voice. 'Uncle Albert isn't well. It's difficult for him to . . . travel. And the pod's a bit rough. He's fixing it – when he can. And when we can afford the spare parts.'

'You can actually buy . . . ?'

'No. We buy the closest we can get and adapt them.' He paused, possibly to say, 'You wouldn't understand,' and wisely thought better of it.

I persisted. 'But you used it the other night.'

'We really needed those diamonds.'

'But it's not safe.'

'We thought it would be OK. Probably.'

'You made me get into an unsafe . . . thing.'

'Pod. And you were unconscious. If it had blown up, you'd never have known anything about it.'

'Thank you.'

'You're welcome.'

I returned to the main topic of conversation. 'Why don't you just kill the loan sharks?'

He gave me a long, speculative look. 'Is that what you'd do?'

I thought about it. 'Actually, no. In the long run that probably wouldn't help at all. Others would come after you and the police would get involved. You could end up making things even worse. And if Uncle Albert does succeed in fixing the pod permanently, then all that's unnecessary.'

'You have a good grasp of facts.'

'How did you meet him?'

'He was being beaten up in an alleyway not far from here. I chased them off, went through his pockets in case there was anything valuable . . .'

I looked him straight in the eye. 'No, you didn't.'

He stared right back.

'Not your style,' I said. 'Unconscious old men in an alleyway. You brought him back here.'

'I told you. I'm a criminal.'

'You could have walked off with my diamonds last night. You could have taken them while I was asleep. You could take them now – there wouldn't be a lot I could do about it. You haven't done any of that.'

'Yet.'

I made a derogatory noise.

'Yeah, you're right . . .' he said.

'Told you,' I said triumphantly.

'. . . You *are* beginning to get on my nerves.'

'Give it twenty-four hours,' I said. 'You'll be painting your front room pink, there'll be boy-band posters all over the kitchen, and you won't be able to get into the bathroom for make-up and wet underwear.'

He dug the heels of his hands into his eyes.

I laughed. 'No good deed ever goes unpunished, does it?'

He took his hands away. 'There's something you need to know.'

'What?'

'It's not good.'

'What could be worse than being attacked by my sister-in-law, abandoned by my brother, losing my home, consorting with madmen and having a face like a multi-coloured football?'

He laid a pile of newspapers in front of me.

'There's no point,' I said wearily. 'I can't see the print.'

He peeled off the top one. 'This headline reads, *Where is she?* This one says, *Peer's sister disappears in mysterious circs.* This one says, *Famous Skeffington diamonds – where did they go?* This one says, *Countess questioned.* This one says, *Millie and the Hot Rocks – where are they?* This one says, *MP indicted for serious fraud,* but we needn't concern ourselves with that one.'

'They think I'm dead?'

'They think you're missing. Which you are. They think the diamonds are missing. Which they are. They think your sister-in-law attacked you. Which she did. Pages and pages of excited speculation. You were on the breakfast news this morning.'

'Shit,' I said, in some alarm.

He pulled out a tablet and flicked through the screens. 'The police have announced they're not looking for you in connection with the diamonds although they remain concerned for your safety.' He read a little further and then passed it over. I couldn't see that, either, so I passed it back. He sighed.

I had a nasty foreboding. 'What?'

'She's made a statement.'

My stomach turned over. 'Caroline? What is she saying?'

He read a little longer. 'You've always been unstable. There was a row over the diamonds. You'd been drinking. You attacked her and she was forced to defend herself. Several members of her family witnessed your attack. The police were called. She hadn't wanted to make the matter public but she fears for your safety. Everyone is very sad and very shocked and worried about you. There's an appeal for you to return home and receive treatment for your . . . issues. Bringing the diamonds with you, presumably.'

If Caroline had set out to ruin my reputation – which, let's face it, she probably had – she couldn't have made a better job of it. I was an unstable teenager with a drink problem and prone to violent outbursts. She didn't actually say drug-related but the inference was there for all to see.

Two days ago I would not have reacted well. I would have wasted my time in pointless anger. Futile threats of revenge. But now, forty-eight hours later, I was a very different person. I clasped my hands on the kitchen table and stared at them. For a long time. And then a bit longer. It wasn't impossible. I had the knowledge. He had the skills. It could be done. I grinned at him. Which seemed to make him very uneasy.

'What?'

I said, 'What time is it?'

'It's six in the evening.'

'Excellent. Can I have one of those salty drinks, please.'

'Why?'

'I need a drink and a think.'

And I did. I drank and thank. There would be small difficulties but I had the services of an expert. I had the means. And I certainly had the motivation.

Pennyroyal's face was expressionless but I suspected some disquiet. 'What are you thinking about?'

I grinned. 'Revenge.'

The plan was simple.

'It's simple,' I said. 'The two Gainsboroughs were moved to a secure strongroom – up in the attics – for the duration of the ball. They always are whenever we – they – have a public function and there are other guests in the house. The insurance company insists on it. Caroline's ghastly family are staying on for at least a week so the paintings will still be there. I know their location. I know the best route to get there. I know the codes for the alarms and both the doors. All you have to do is get me to Starlings and then get me away again afterwards. Leave the rest to me.'

'Oh,' Pennyroyal said. 'You know the best and quickest way to get the canvases out of the frames, do you? In the dark?'

I shifted my weight. 'Well . . .'

'Or were you planning to lift the two great heavy frames down all those stairs?'

'Actually . . .'

He folded his arms. 'Yes?'

I sighed. 'All right. Point taken.' I had a sudden idea. 'I know – we could roll them up. You know – tubes.'

He closed his eyes briefly. 'God help me, I'm working with a Philistine.'

'Well how, then?'

'I'll take them out of their frames, leave them on their stretchers, and carry them. They're not large, as Gainsboroughs go.'

'What do I do?'

'You carry the equipment.'

'I'm not just cheap labour, you know,' I said indignantly. 'I'm the one who knows the codes. And how to disarm the motion sensors. I know the route. I know everything.'

'Or we look at it from the police point of view – two valuable paintings disappear only a few days after a major family disagreement. Taken by someone who knows of their existence, knows they're not in their normal location, and knows how to get in and out without activating any of the security alarms.' He assumed an attitude of deep thought. 'Hm. Who could the culprit possibly be, I wonder?'

I slumped. 'I hadn't thought of that.'

'Well, fortunately for you – I have. Cracking on – division of responsibilities. You talk to your mate and make sure she still wants the paintings. Agree a price. I get us there. You get us in. I remove the paintings from the frames. You get us out. I get us away. You take them to your friend. We split the proceeds.'

'I'll need an alibi,' I said, nowhere near as brave as I had been half an hour ago, now that this looked as if it might actually happen. 'A really good alibi.'

'Leave that with me.'

*   *   *

There was a lot more to it, of course. Routes, equipment, details. And the need for speed. Because as soon as things calmed down at Starlings and the last guests left, the paintings would be replaced in the Long Gallery – their usual home – and about fifteen feet off the ground. Stepladders are not quiet. And I'd have to navigate us around the actual house. The secure, but out-of-the-way attic was much the easier option.

Pennyroyal supplied me with a burner phone, and I cautiously contacted Meilin. We talked in a circle for a while because neither of us wanted to commit ourselves, and only when both of us were confident in the other did we get down to business. It took several calls, with a different phone and a different number each time. I always contacted her – never the other way around. No face-to-face contact. Not at this stage. Eventually we reached an agreement.

Pennyroyal and I were up at the crack of dawn the very next day. 'The day of the heist,' I said excitedly.

Pennyroyal rolled his eyes because apparently no one actually says that and sat me down at the kitchen table. 'All right,' he said. 'Rules.'

I nodded, but carefully, because my face still hurt.

'No – I mean it. I'm the one with the expertise which makes me the boss. I want your word you'll do exactly as I say. Think carefully before you give it because if you do, I'll trust you to keep it. Are you a woman of your word?'

I opened my mouth to say of course I was, closed it again, sat back and thought. Was I? If he told me to jump out of an upstairs window – would I do it? Or throw myself into a river? Would I obey him unquestioningly and unthinkingly?

I looked across the table to him. 'Are you worthy of my word?'

I think that was the moment it all began. There was a very long silence.

'Yeah,' he said slowly. 'At least, I hope I am. You can trust me. I promise.'

'Then I give you my word. Freely and without conditions. I promise I will do as you say.'

'And I promise you can trust me.'

He held out his hand. I took it and we shook.

9

Less than a week after leaving Starlings, I was going back again.

'Try to stay awake this time,' Pennyroyal said, as we crossed the yard.

He opened the door and I began to stow our burglar gear inside the shed.

'It's a pod,' he said. 'They're always called pods.'

I began to stow our gear inside the pod while he did something at the table.

'It's a console,' he said. 'They're always called consoles.'

I looked around the pod. The interior was grey, cold and stuffy. A small table – console – covered in dials, switches and levers stood in front of me and a screen had been rigged on to one of those extendable arms. The whole thing looked incredibly steam-punkish. I could just see someone in goggles and flying jacket presiding over this Heath Robinson contraption. There were a couple of metal lockers on the left-hand wall containing God knows what. And that was it. Not even anything to sit on.

'Are you sure this thing is safe?'

'Mostly.'

'Mostly sure or mostly safe?'

'Yes.'

I joined him at the console to watch. 'Can you show me what you're doing?'

'Yes, but not at this precise moment.'

We pulled on paper suits, bootees, face masks and gloves. Nylon gloves because latex can sometimes leave fingerprints. I did not know that. Caroline would be thrilled to see I was getting a proper education at last. I wore the backpack so Pennyroyal could access his tools easily.

'All right,' he said. 'Ready?'

'Yes?'

'Got everything?'

'Yes.'

'Don't just say yes – think it through. Have you got everything?'

I ran through things in my mind, step by step, patting bits of me as appropriate and eventually said, 'Yes, I've got everything.'

'Close your eyes.'

I opened my mouth to ask why, remembered the conversation over the kitchen table and closed my eyes.

The floor seemed to shift slightly and I felt a wave of nausea.

'Oh,' I said, bending forwards and putting my hands on my knees.

'Take off your gloves.'

'Why?'

He passed me a packet of something. 'Have a crisp.'

'Have a what?'

'Crisp. The salt helps.'

'I didn't have a crisp last time.'

'You were full of alcohol. The crisp would have drowned.'

I ripped open the packet and got stuck in. He was right. I did feel better.

'A little disappointing,' I said, crunching away. 'I expected banks of flashing lights and graunching noises and Drama.'

'I'm opening the door. No talking from now on. Gloves.'

I nodded, wiped my hands and pulled on my gloves.

He turned off the lights and opened the door. It was dark outside. I experienced a great wave of disorientation. When we'd left London, the time had been about half past eleven in the morning and now it was dark outside, and I realised I hadn't, until this moment, completely bought in to the whole time-travelling thing.

I followed him out of the pod. The door closed behind us.

It was the dead of night. I could tell. The moon hung low in the sky, throwing long, long shadows across the ground.

As instructed, I listened. Nightly noises. The wind in the trees. A very distant car changing gear. Nothing out of the ordinary. No voices. No sounds of doors opening and closing. No footsteps on the gravel.

And then, again as instructed, I looked. No lights at the windows. No exterior lights on. At one time we used to have motion-activated exterior lights, which isn't always a good idea in the country. Foxes, cats, our resident poacher Amos Cope, even Papa himself lurching home from a convivial evening in the pub – it was like living in a sound-and-light show, and so, finally, Papa put his foot down – especially after the night he and Amos nearly shot each other in the rose garden – no exterior lights after midnight. The house was quiet and still. No signs of life anywhere. Starlings was asleep.

117

Pennyroyal looked at me. I stepped behind him. Those were his instructions – to stay one pace behind. 'I need to know where you are at all times,' he'd said. 'Do as I do. Walk where I walk. Stop when I stop.'

We set off.

I'd given a lot of thought to the best route. Which wasn't necessarily the quickest. I'd walked through it in my head. Over and over. I'd tried to foresee every possible obstacle. All the potential problem areas.

We walked quickly through the shrubbery and across the gravel, which was old and well-trodden and didn't make a lot of noise. George and the dragon slept at the front, guests in the East Wing, and live-in staff at the back. There wasn't a great deal of internal security because in Papa's time we never had less than six or seven dogs. Other than Rosie and Doofus, they'd lived in the stables during the day, but at night they all ran loose around the house. The slightest sound and they would bark their heads off. My own theory was that a couple of drugged chocolate biscuits would render them all unconscious in seconds, but as Papa said, those up to no good had to get close enough to administer the biscuits in the first place. Yes, they could prise open a window and chuck them in, but six or seven spaniels and Labs would be shrieking their heads off with greed and excitement. Now, of course, there were no dogs but probably still no motion sensors, either.

It was easy to nip around to the side door in the East Wing. I'd chosen that one because it had no interior bolts. It was the door Papa used whenever he staggered back from whatever he'd been up to that particular evening.

Getting through the door was easy. Pennyroyal handled that

in about four seconds. He stepped aside and indicated that I lead the way.

I had thirty seconds to disable the alarm. Would they have changed the code? Unlikely. Given recent events, they'd have had other things to think about. And if they had – so be it. If anything went wrong, then Pennyroyal had a plan for getting us out quickly.

Very, very carefully – because it could be temperamental occasionally – I tapped in the code, ignoring my unprofessionally shaking fingers. There was a tiny beep and the red light disappeared. Done. I motioned with my head and we made our way along the corridor to the staff quarters. I had no idea how many staff George had now – or even how many lived in – but I was prepared to bet heavily none of them would have the dedication and commitment of our own people.

We did have motion sensors in this, the mostly unoccupied part of the house. Papa had refused to have them installed in the family living quarters, saying he didn't want bells and whistles going off every time he got up for a slash or went down to the kitchen for a midnight snack. They were activated from a control box sited just outside Cleverly's room. Setting them was the last thing he did before retiring for the night. And he was a light sleeper so we'd have to be careful. I took a breath, recalled the code – who am I kidding? It was my date of birth – and prised open the box. My fingers weren't quite so shaky this time although my heart was thumping so hard I was surprised Pennyroyal couldn't hear it.

Now we could move safely through the building. I led the way. The house used to smell of dogs and damp. Now it was all paint and air freshener. Not an improvement.

119

We took the east staircase to the third floor – the steps were stone and soundless. The walls were thick and the doors heavy, and George, Caroline and the clones couldn't be further away if we'd planned it.

Once on the third floor, it was through the door at the top, turn right, along the corridor, turn right again, along another corridor, right to the very end. There was a tiny door set under a deep arch. Locked, obviously, but we're Smallhopes so you have to keep things simple. The key was on the top of the door-jamb. Through the door. Up another, much smaller, narrower set of wooden stairs. They creaked. I've heard quieter twenty-one-gun salutes. My heart nearly leaped out of my chest with every single one of them. Through the door at the top. Rinse and repeat with the key, jamb, etc.

We were up in the roof now with a maze of dusty corridors and small rooms stretching before us. Left, left, right. Door at the end. Our strongroom. This door was made of metal and there was no key. A code was needed to open the box, to enter another code to open the door. This was the one I was worried about. This was the one that Caroline might have changed. Or she might have had a silent alarm fitted and by now half a dozen police cars could be speeding through the night to arrest us.

Which was nonsense because firstly, this was Rushfordshire and we don't have half a dozen police cars – but mostly because she'd been far too busy spending all her waking hours planning her Big Night and rendering everyone else's lives hideous in the process.

I took a deep breath. Pennyroyal put his hand on my shoulder. Startled, I turned to look. His eyes crinkled behind his mask. My heart was going like a hammer but he seemed quite calm. I

120

could only assume he did stress at the subatomic level. Invisible to the naked eye.

However, somewhat reassured, I did the biz. The door clicked. We were in.

Pennyroyal watched me carefully every inch of the way. Very, very carefully, with one eye on his watch. The reason for which had baffled me when we were planning.

'Why?'

'I need to know the exact time when the crime was committed. The alarm company's records will show that at such and such a time the alarm was shut off and the building entered. That the motion sensors were disabled at such and such a time. The same with the strongroom. And then again that everything was reset and the building exited at such and such a time.'

'Again, why?'

'For your alibi. You're going to be the prime suspect. The only suspect, probably. Therefore you must have a cast-iron alibi for that time.'

'How will I do that?'

'You won't. I will.'

'What do I do?'

'As you're told.'

I said dubiously, 'All right.'

'You're not worried I'll leave you to carry the can, are you? Push off with the paintings and leave you in the shit?'

I looked him straight in the eye. 'No. You promised I could trust you and I do.'

He'd nodded. 'Good decision.'

And now – here we were.

I stepped back because my job was more or less done.

Pennyroyal eased open the door and took a good, long look round. He pointed to the bare floor and I shook my head. No pressure pads.

There were shelves off to one side laden with important Smallhope family documents, old records and leases and so forth, together with a number of jewel cases – I wondered if the empty blue cases were there or whether Caroline would have thrown them out in a temper. Here were the uglier and less used pieces of the family silver, one or two valuable small figurines and ceramics – a ton of stuff that rarely saw the light of day but was too valuable to get rid of – and the family Gainsboroughs. The two paintings hung alongside each other on the wall facing the door.

The one on the left was entitled *Lady Constance Smallhope*, painted in the early 1780s, and very similar in style and composition to *Woman in Blue* except Constance was wearing gold. I'd checked the sizes very carefully. Thirty inches by twenty-four. Manageable.

The second, *Horsebere Brook*, painted in 1756, was roughly the same size and hung on the right. I know they were both quite small as Gainsboroughs go, but they suddenly looked very large to me. I could only hope they'd be a lot smaller out of their frames.

I turned so Pennyroyal could access his backpack and he pulled out a small device, running it around the frames to see if the paintings themselves were alarmed. Nothing. I'd thought not, but it never does any harm to check.

Very, very gently, he eased *Lady Constance* off the wall. I held my breath. Nothing happened.

His job was to remove the canvas from the frame while I

readied the cotton carrying bag. He passed me the canvas and I very gently slid it inside the bag and zipped it up. While I was doing that, he had *Horsebere Brook* off the wall and we repeated the process.

We stacked the empty frames neatly against the wall. I would come to learn that Pennyroyal was a very tidy criminal.

I zipped up the backpack again. He picked up the carrying bags and carefully slung them over his shoulder. We took a swift look around to check we'd left nothing behind – I'd learned from the time I nearly left my book behind in Caroline's dressing room – and ghosted out of the door. Pennyroyal kept watch while I reset the codes. Alibi for the establishing of.

Now, everything was in reverse. Down the stairs. Along the corridors. The house was ghostly and silent. There was still some moonlight through the windows. We didn't need our night visors. I noticed more gaps on the walls as I passed. And one or two items missing from the console tables as well. More than ever I was convinced that Caroline had been selling off our stuff.

Not my problem any longer.

Once downstairs, I reset the motion sensors. The red light began to flash. I held up a finger. One minute to get out. We were at the east door in seconds. I reset the alarm, closed the box and then we were out of the door. He considerately relocked it behind us. Well, you wouldn't want thieves getting in, would you?

We stood in the shadow of the wall, checking for any move-ment on the drive or in the shrubbery. Nothing. The night was still dark and silent. And so were we. Across the gravel. Into the shrubbery. Holding twigs and branches back for each other. Until, finally . . .

123

The pod had gone.

I couldn't believe my eyes. The pod had gone. The bloody pod had gone. What? How? Were we in the wrong place? Had it been stolen? What was going on?

Pennyroyal pushed past me. I went to grab at his arm. 'The pod's gone. Someone's stolen the . . .'

'No, they haven't, and keep your voice down.'

I whispered so hard I hurt my throat. '*The pod's gone.*'

'No, it hasn't. Watch.'

I don't know what he did – the words *blind panic* could accurately have described my emotional state at that moment – but suddenly, through an open doorway, I could see the inside of the pod. I stepped back. I could see the inside but not the outside. Caroline had obviously injured me more seriously than anyone had suspected.

Pennyroyal took my arm – quite gently – and led me inside. Where everything seemed perfectly normal. I stamped my foot on the floor just in case this was another hallucination.

'What is happening?'

'Well . . . I told you it travelled in time and space?'

'You did.'

'Sometimes it's invisible as well.'

I stared at him. 'No, it's not.'

'Yes, it is.'

'But it was in the yard. I saw it there. *Not* invisible.'

'No, but if I engage the camo device, then it is.'

'The . . . ?'

'Camo device.'

'Which makes it invisible?'

'No – nothing is invisible. This is only a complicated system

124

of cameras and projectors controlled by AI. Most pods have something similar.'

'And you were going to tell me when?'

'Just now.'

'You could have told me yesterday.'

'It wasn't working yesterday. I wasn't going to mention it at all until Uncle Albert got it working again. Which he has. And here we are.' He actually smiled. Just a small one but a smile nevertheless. 'Job accomplished.'

It was, wasn't it? We'd done it. We'd actually done it. Suddenly, my legs were all over the place. I carefully propped my backpack against the wall. 'Let's go home.'

'Good idea,' said Pennyroyal.

So, we . . . jumped. Must remember to call it that.

10

We didn't land back at the house.

'Where are we?' I said, staring at the screen. Rather cleverly, there was a camera somewhere pointed outside the pod so you could check what was happening before committing yourself. Cool idea since there were no windows.

'Are we in a petrol station?' I had a sudden thought. 'Do you need to fill her up occasionally? A petrol-powered pod?'

I began to giggle. Reaction setting in. I'd like to think I'm a little more professional these days.

'Sorry,' I said, trying to calm down.

'No, feel free. We're about to get ourselves on CCTV so be as noticeable as you like.'

We pulled off our burglar gear and let ourselves out.

'Turn around,' he said. 'Look back the way we've come.'

'Why? There's nothing to see.'

'Let's assume we need to get back to the pod in a hurry. The camo device is on. How will you find it?'

'You've got some clever electronic doo-da that can . . .'

'Or you can just turn around and look. What do you see?'

'Trees. Broken wire fence.'

'Look for something noticeable.'

'Um . . . old plastic water bottle by the fence post. The pod's somewhere to the left of that.'

'OK. Having made sure we can find our way back . . .'

We approached the brightly lit forecourt.

'Just act normally,' he said. 'We need to buy a few things.'

'Chocolate,' I said. 'And if they've got one of those hot dog machines, then two for me.'

He held open the door to the shop saying, 'I was thinking more along the lines of some fruit and nuts.'

'What? Are you out of your mind?'

'In a way, I'm responsible for you, my lady. And your diet.'

'I absolve you,' I said grandly, as we approached the counter, Pennyroyal laden with two bags of dried apricots and me festooned with steaming hot dogs, chocolate and a Cornish pasty.

We faced the yawning assistant. 'No petrol, mate,' said Pennyroyal. 'Just a ton of midnight snacks. Oh – and I'll have a couple of lottery cards. Time I won something. Cheers.'

He looked at me. 'You got any money?'

'No,' I said, suddenly alarmed. 'Don't you?'

'Fortunately – yes.' He gave the assistant a *women* look. The guy wasn't interested enough to respond. I had strong doubts whether he was awake enough to remember us. Although my still heavily bruised face would help.

'Doesn't matter,' said Pennyroyal, when I mentioned the assistant's lack of interest. 'From the moment we set foot in the forecourt, CCTV cameras recorded our every move. That place gets robbed so often they've installed really good quality cameras, so should anyone ever need it, there will be some excellent and untampered footage of you and an unknown but

127

handsome male companion buying consumables a hundred and twenty miles away from Starlings at almost the exact moment the robbery was committed. You're welcome.'

I stared at him for a moment. 'You are a genius.'

'Yeah,' he said.

The police found us, of course. Which might have been due to excellent policing on their part or – and more likely – me calling Mr Treasure the next day and asking him to reassure the police that I – and the diamonds – were perfectly safe, thank you. I acceded to his almost tearful request that I place the diamonds in a safe deposit box as quickly as possible – which, actually, with Pennyroyal's assistance, I did do.

My unspectacular reappearance and the knowledge that the Skeffington diamonds were safe didn't generate anything like the publicity of my disappearance, because, fortunately, the England football team had crashed to a spectacular defeat against a nation so tiny there were rumours they'd had to field a goat to make up the numbers, and the whole country was in deep mourning.

Obviously we expected the police to pitch up and carry out at least a preliminary interview, even if only to establish whether or not I was involved in what I referred to as the Gainsborough heist.

They never appeared. Nor was there anything on the news, and believe me, I watched every bulletin.

'The insurance company might have told them to keep quiet while they carry out their own investigation,' said Pennyroyal when I mentioned this.

'It seemed to go well, though,' I said, referring to our midnight

128

adventure, of course, not the football thing, although what I had to measure our midnight adventure against was anyone's guess. However, Pennyroyal agreed that yes, the Starlings job had gone well. We'd celebrated with a couple of margaritas, together with, in my case, the hot dogs and chocolate. Pennyroyal had the pasty and a whisky.

Sadly, our celebrations were premature.

'Forgeries,' said Meilin quietly, gesturing at the carrying bag leaning unobtrusively against her chair.

I'd couriered the paintings to her a week ago. An address in Reading, of all places. Since I knew her family firm operated out of Paris, I'd been surprised. Two days later she'd called me. She was in London for a series of business meetings and wanted to meet us at a restaurant in Covent Garden. I thought it was because she wanted to hand over the money in person. Pennyroyal had frowned but said nothing. It would seem his frown was justified.

'Forgeries?' I said. 'You're kidding.'

'*Are* you kidding?' said Pennyroyal, suddenly in her face and looking very menacing indeed. The fact that we were enjoying afternoon tea at a swanky restaurant wasn't going to hold him back. Not for one second.

'Listen to me,' she said sharply.

I glanced around but the place was very discreet.

'My family has built a reputation for trust and probity. Yes, we often work with those for whom trust and probity are things that only ever happen to other people, but that is not how *we* operate. You don't last long in this job if you get a reputation for screwing over your clients. There are some very unpleasant people out there and we deal with most of them. As far as they are able, they trust us and if they can do that, then so can you. I'm sorry, Millie. They're quite good forgeries but forgeries nevertheless.'

I sat stunned. I didn't know what to say. I stared at my plate, trying to take it in.

Pennyroyal, thank heavens, was a little more alert. 'Can you tell when they were done?'

'I can't, no, but my expert thinks recently. Probably within the last twelve months or so.'

Post Papa, then. Caroline. Caroline had done this.

'And they're good forgeries, you think?' I asked.

Meilin drew in a long breath, eventually saying, 'Reasonably. Certainly good enough to fool the general public – especially when viewed from a distance – but my expert didn't even need her magnifying glass. Well, she did, but only to verify what she already knew. Millie, I'm so sorry.' She cast a glance at my still quite colourful face. 'I know things aren't going well for you at the moment.' She paused and then said delicately, 'Is there anything I can do? Money, perhaps . . .'

It would seem she thought I was still the baby of the group who needed taking care of.

'No,' I said, 'but thank you. I appreciate your offer. We both do.'

Pennyroyal did his appreciation silently.

'What will you do now?' she asked.

I shrugged. I had no idea. My brain had stopped working.

She shook her head. 'You must pull yourself together, Millie. Remember what you said that night we couldn't get back in after the beer festival? *Always have a plan. And another plan for if that one doesn't work out. And then another for exactly the same reason.* Millie, this is not like you. You are not a victim. Do not allow yourself to be turned into one.'

I straightened my back. 'No.'

'And what was our motto?'

'When things are bad – make them worse.'

And that was when I had my blinding flash of inspiration.

'You're very quiet,' Pennyroyal said as we racketed home on the Victoria line. He'd obtained two seats by simply staring at two young men until they stood up and moved to the other end of the carriage.

I turned to him. 'I've been thinking. This situation might not be a dead loss after all.'

'We'll talk about it at home,' he said.

I spent the rest of the journey thinking.

I was still thinking as we walked up the hill from the Tube station, past the William Morris place and home to Cold Ash Lane.

It was my turn to make the tea.

'Well?' he said, as I plonked a mug in front of him.

'I'm not sure what you'll say.'

'Tell me and then we'll work out whether it's doable or not.'

'I think it's doable,' I said. 'But it will depend on whether I can keep my nerve.'

I outlined my idea while he sipped his tea, staring at the table. I'd quickly learned that's how you can tell whether Pennyroyal's listening or not. Forget these people who look you straight in the eye while apparently drinking in every word. Your true listener stares at the kitchen table with never a flicker of expression.

When I'd finished there was a long silence.

I opened my mouth to ask what he thought and then shut it again. He'd tell me soon enough, so now I sipped my own tea and stared at the kitchen table.

'It's a good plan,' he said eventually. 'But I think it would be better coming from me.'

I shook my head. 'No – it has to be me.'

'Why?'

'Because I owe her.'

'No. This is where good schemes go wrong. You can't make this personal.'

I shook my head. 'If it's not personal, it won't work.'

'Look,' he said. 'I'm the professional. You're the enthusiastic amateur. You learn from me and . . .'

'This was my idea. I've thought it through. Only I can do this.'

Uncle Albert, who had been out tinkering with the pod and come in to pour himself a mug of tea, was standing safely behind Pennyroyal and grinning his head off at me. I resolutely looked the other way.

'No,' said Pennyroyal again.

'Why not?'

'Because you're too . . .' Pennyroyal stopped.

I gave him a long, level look. 'Because I'm too what? Young? Girlie? Clever? Pretty? Tall? Stupid? Groot? What?'

'On your own, mate,' said Uncle Albert, oozing back out of the door.

'My idea,' I said, banging down my mug with some force. 'My scheme. I don't need your permission. I'm going to go ahead and do it whatever you say.'

132

Pennyroyal finished his tea. 'Found your nerve now, have you, my lady?'

Two days later he and I were sitting around the kitchen table, rehearsing for the umpteenth time. I was me – he was Caroline. We'd rehearsed all sorts of situations, ranging from Caroline slamming down the phone, to threats, hysteria, refusal to play ball, accepting her fate, and everything in between. Theoretically I had a response for every argument she could put forward because, as Pennyroyal said, you couldn't be too prepared for this sort of situation. The slightest hesitation, the slightest lack of credibility, the slightest hint I wasn't prepared to do the worst – and do it all over Caroline – and it wouldn't work. I was the success or failure of this little scheme.

In front of me was yet another burner phone. I really must remember to ask where he was getting them all from.

'Well?' said Pennyroyal. 'This is your decision. You have the lead on this one.'

'I think I'm ready,' I said. 'Well, I'm not completely ready, but I don't think I'll ever be readier.'

'All right,' he said. 'Remember – call the landline – you won't be recorded on that. Don't let her talk you into ringing her back. Only one conversation – this one. She plays ball now or you do your worst. And you'll enjoy doing your worst. She needs to know that.' He sat back.

I'd already programmed in the family's private number.

I could hear it ringing.

She said hello very cautiously – the call was from an unknown number – but this was Caroline and I might be someone important she could use for her own benefit.

133

I needed something to grab her attention before she could put the phone down.

'It's me,' I said. 'Do you want your Gainsboroughs back or do you want to go to prison? You have ten seconds.'

'Amelia?'

'Nine. Eight.'

'It *was* you. I knew it. I told George . . .'

'Seven.'

'This call is being traced. The police . . .'

'Six. Five.'

'Look, George is desperately upset. Return those paintings and we'll say no more ab—'

'Four.'

'I . . . you . . .'

'Three. Two. Prison it is, then.'

'Stop.'

'One. Hanging up now.'

'Let's discuss this.'

'Let's talk money.'

She'd pulled herself together. 'Don't be ridiculous. I don't believe for one moment it's you who has those Gainsboroughs. You've heard something and decided to cash in.'

'Caroline, let's stop calling them Gainsboroughs, shall we? You had our paintings forged and sold the originals on the black market. I know into whose bank account the money went. I even know how much you got for them.'

Silence.

'Have you even reported the theft to the police? You'll have to if you want to claim off the insurance. Although you won't be able to do that once I've made this knowledge public, of course.'

'You . . . I . . .'

'Caroline, you go ahead and claim – I'm not stopping you. But I want the money you got from the original sale. And I want it by close of play tomorrow. I have account details here. You have five seconds to say yes. Or no, possibly. But we both know it's going to be yes.'

'I haven't got . . .'

'Four.'

'Don't start that again. You can't rush this. I didn't actually get a lot for them and . . .'

'Did you miss the bit where I told you I know exactly how much you got for them? And when?'

'I'll need George's permission to . . .'

'George knows nothing about it, Caroline. Did you miss the bit where I said I knew whose bank account the money was paid into?'

Her voice rose. Estuary twang. Here was the real Caroline. 'You little bitch. I told George there was something wrong with you.'

'Two.'

'If you report me, you'll never see the money.'

'No, but I'll see you in court and probably in prison afterwards for fraud. And, in the interests of honesty and transparency, I should tell you that's what I was hoping you would say. Grassing you up has always been my first choice. Which is why I'm hanging up now. Goodb—'

'The money's gone.'

'So?'

'You don't understand. George is hopeless. I'm having to shore up the estate.'

'By stealing from it. A novel approach to finance. You're not a politician by any chance, are you?'

Pennyroyal began to make winding motions and he was right. This was taking too long.

'Caroline, you're boring me. Goodbye.'

'No, wait.'

I disconnected and looked at Pennyroyal. 'Sorry.'

He made an ambiguous noise.

The phone rang.

I looked at it.

'Pick it up,' he said. 'But keep it short.'

I answered. 'Get off the line, Caroline. I need to call the pol—'

'I'll pay. But it will take me some time to . . .'

'Nope. Tomorrow.'

'I can't.'

'Tomorrow.'

'You don't . . .'

'Tomorrow.'

'I can let you have half tomorrow and the rest in a week.'

I hesitated. As soon as she parted with the cash, she was mine. I had her. But this was Caroline.

'Tomorrow.'

There was a long but somehow encouraging silence.

'All right.'

'I'll text you the details. Don't ring this number again. No one will answer.'

I hung up, giddy with exhilaration, success, relief and not having breathed properly for the last ten minutes.

'Not bad,' said Pennyroyal. 'I could have done it in half the time, of course, but not bad.'

Meilin reported the money had turned up. Not all of it. Almost all but not quite. 'As your banker,' she said, 'what would you like me to do with it?'

'Can you take your fee and then deposit the rest of it in my account, please.'

'All right. It will need to move through several other accounts first. Can you wait, say, three weeks?'

'We can. And thank you for your assistance with this.'

Pennyroyal and I discussed whether to go after the full amount. He shook his head. 'I'd say leave it. You got most of what you wanted and you got away with it. In this game that's a success. It was a good scheme – bold and well executed. Learn to walk away while you're ahead.'

I remembered what he'd said about not making it personal.

'I could grass her up anyway.'

'You could – but take a tip from your friend. Establish a reputation for honest dealing and your life will become a lot easier. Meilin is bright and she's successful. Listen to her.'

So I did. We let the rest of the money go.

The Gainsborough heist marked a watershed in my relationship with Pennyroyal. There was another kitchen-table conference on how to divvy up the dosh.

'Fifty-fifty,' I said. 'Less expenses.'

'You did the work. And it was your idea.'

'You supplied the phone.'

'Which makes it the most expensive burner in history.'

'Then think of it as my contribution towards board and lodging.'

He frowned. 'How about this? We split it into three. One-third to you. One-third to me. One-third into the pot.'

'What pot?'

He looked at Uncle Albert, who said, 'Yes. Make the offer.'

Pennyroyal turned back to me. 'This pot. Stay here. With us.'

I blinked. 'And do what, exactly?'

'Whatever you want.'

But I didn't know what I wanted. I'd stepped out of my own world. Did I want to make that permanent? On the other hand, my own world had nothing left in it that I wanted. But did I want this? They were criminals and now, by extension, so was I. Yes, I was all for excitement and adventure, but I was rather less entranced by the thoughts of capture, exposure and prison. And that would only be if I was lucky. Surely it was far more likely that Pennyroyal would annoy the wrong people – and probably already had – and end up in the river with cement overshoes. After a good seeing-to in a dark alleyway some-where, of course. Uncle Albert would flee in his shed thing and I'd be left alone.

Or – a third way – I could strike out on my own. All right, I had no qualifications, no particular skills, but I could learn.

'Think about it,' said Pennyroyal, obviously bored with my cogitations.

'I'll let you know this time tomorrow,' I said.

Always put a time limit on decision-making. Otherwise you can just flounder around in a welter of half-formed arguments for the rest of your life.

Actually, I'd made the decision after about ten

minutes – sometimes you don't have to spend half the night pacing up and down – but I slept on it in case I felt differently in the morning.

I didn't. This was the right thing to do. I'd strike out on my own. I couldn't stay here. I had some money now and in eight years' time, when I was twenty-five, I'd have more. I could travel. Or become a student. Gain a few qualifications. There was a whole world out there – I should go and see it for myself.

'Well?' said Pennyroyal as I sat down. 'Decided?'

I opened my mouth and heard myself say, 'I'd like to stay.'

We lived well during that time. Uncle Albert had been right –
Pennyroyal was an excellent cook.

'Lamb shanks with redcurrant gravy served with dauphinoise
potatoes,' he would announce as I salivated all over the kitchen
table. 'Followed by crème brûlée.'

The kitchen was very obviously Pennyroyal's domain. All
sorts of culinary wonderfulness happened there. Another aspect
of butler school, I guessed.

I asked him once if, in another life, he would have become
a chef.

He shrugged. 'Dunno. Perhaps.' He passed me a tea towel.
'Your turn to dry up.'

They say 'wash up as you go', so I washed up as Pennyroyal
went. He liked things to be neat and tidy. Everything in its place.

'It's a good habit,' he said. 'Especially if you ever have to
work in the dark. Sometimes you need to put your hand on
something without looking, and if it isn't in the right place,
then you're buggered, aren't you?'

I wasn't a particularly tidy seventeen-year-old, but his words
made sense. Doing my share of the housework was boring, but

if I looked at it in terms of ensuring my equipment was always primed and ready for my next dastardly crime, then it became a much more exciting activity. I wasn't hoovering the carpet – I was clearing the route to ensure a quick getaway. I wasn't scrubbing the bath – I was eradicating any incriminating DNA. With this in mind, I reorganised my own few possessions. Later, when Pennyroyal and I were living in a tiny ten-foot-square pod, being neat and orderly stopped us both from killing each other.

For the first time since Regime Caroline, I had money and freedom. The urge to splurge was very nearly overwhelming – but not quite. I opened a savings account and tried to put a little away each month. I believe it was a Persian poet who said, 'This too shall pass,' and wiser words were never spoken. Good times or bad – nothing lasts forever. In other words – plan ahead. I have a friend whose guiding principle is *'Always deal with the now and the future will take care of itself'*. I'm not saying she's wrong – it certainly works for her – but not for me. Recent events had taught me to take the long view.

I bought some clothes and other bits and pieces. Some were cheap, cheerful and throwaway, but every now and then I bought myself a good piece. Trousers that would retain their shape. A winter coat that would look good as it kept me warm and dry.

'Attractive, but practical,' I said to Pennyroyal. 'Just like me.'

He opened his mouth to say something, closed it again, shook his head and walked away.

My toiletries adorned the bathroom. Although Pennyroyal said *engulfed* might be a better word, gesturing at all the sprays, tubes, bottles, sachets, lipsticks and eyeshadow in every colour known to man. I told him we needed another shelf for all my stuff. He muttered something about cuckoos.

I made enquiries about further education at the library because it was free info and often the courses in which I was interested were available locally and considerably cheaper than online or in central London. I signed up for basic accounting and law, both of which were held in the library itself.

I would sit at one end of the kitchen table while Pennyroyal did delicious things at the other. He was never chatty, of course, but I soon learned to frame my questions in such as manner as to elicit a response from him.

Once he learned that ignoring me was a waste of time we actually had some very interesting discussions. Or arguments, if you want the technical term. He wasn't stupid and I often struggled to keep up with the argument he was making. Obviously honour demanded I keep him on his toes as well, and we challenged each other's world view ten times a day. Uncle Albert would come in, pour himself a cup of tea, listen to the discussion, chuck in a provocative phrase or two and then push off again.

It was fun. I suspected their house had never been this lively.

Time passed. I still slept on the couch. There were three bedrooms – Pennyroyal had the big one at the front, Uncle Albert had the small one at the back, and there was a third door which was kept permanently locked. I never asked why and no one ever told me.

And then, right out of the blue, Pennyroyal said, 'We need to talk.'

Filled with sudden misgivings, I sat at the kitchen table. He was the one who wanted to talk so I waited.

He drew a deep breath. 'I've rehearsed this conversation and it goes like this. I tell you I want you to join me permanently. You say in what capacity. I say initially as trainee, then a junior

142

member of the team. You say what team. I say our team – you and me. You ask to what end. I say eventually becoming an equal partner – a nice, clear career path. You enquire as to the team function. I say becoming as rich as possible as quickly as possible. You pause for a moment's internal dialogue, ask a few pertinent questions as to pay, working conditions and life expectancy. I respond with poor, uncomfortable and short. You nod wisely, indicate you're happy to throw in your lot with mine and we drink to our future.'

I stared at him. 'You don't really need me, do you?'

He stared back. 'Yes, I do. Didn't you understand what I just said?'

'You just had several hours' discussion single-handed. What do you want me for?'

'Mutual benefit.'

'Is this a job interview? Because you should know my enthusiasm for cooking and cleaning is still almost zero and I can't see that ever changing.'

He blinked. 'Who's talking about making you cook or clean?'

'You are. Aren't you? Isn't that what you want me for? Junior member of the team doing all the cooking and cleaning?'

'Have I said so?'

'I'd be the girl on the team so it's rather implied, don't you think?'

'No, I don't. And it isn't.'

Conversation lagged for a while as we stared at each other again, lost in the forests of misunderstanding and poor communication.

'Look,' he said eventually. 'At no point while you've been staying here has you doing *all* the cooking or cleaning been

143

discussed or even considered. I'm talking about you joining me in what I do. We continue to split all the housekeeping duties between us. Equal division of labour.' He paused. 'Except cooking, which will always be my responsibility after your abysmal effort this morning.'

I'd like to make it clear there had been nothing wrong with my cooking that morning. It's just that some people can scramble eggs and, apparently, I can't. There had been comments.

I frowned. 'Won't that still leave me with all the cleaning?'

'Pretty much, yes – but now we've taken the decision demo-cratically.'

The line at the side of his mouth deepened which meant he was smiling. He was finding this hilarious.

Well, I'd been worried about my lack of skills and qual-ifications, and here was a chance to do something about it. On-the-job training.

I grinned at him. 'My brains – your looks – we're going to be rich.'

'We need to plan for the future,' said Pennyroyal the next day. 'The first step is for me to teach you what you need to know.'

'No,' I said firmly. 'You'll teach me everything. Whether you think I need to know it or not.'

He considered me for some time. It wasn't comfortable.

'All right,' he said eventually. 'If that's what you want.'

Well, after a couple of days, I wasn't at all sure it was what I wanted. We started with boxing. He asked me if I'd ever been hit before.

I shook my head. 'The occasional hockey ball, but Caroline was my first.'

'It'll be a shock,' he said. 'Remember how you felt when Caroline hit you? Other than the pain, I mean.'

I did.

'Most people are unfamiliar with violence,' he went on. 'Pain isn't the only thing you'll have to cope with. There's shock, outrage, surprise, disorientation, humiliation – all that loses you vital seconds. You need to learn not to dwell on it. Move on. Make decisions. Do you defend yourself or go on the attack? Do you run away? All equally valid options. Circumstances will dictate your decision. Having made your decision – in a split second – you will need to implement it.'

He punched my shoulder. Not hard – more of a push than a punch. I staggered back a few steps.

'Right – now what do you do?'

'Put ground glass in your steak pie tonight.'

'Effective, but that won't save you right at this present moment. How do you know you'll still be alive tonight to do that?'

We started with landing punches. Then hooks, straights, jabs. And where to land them. Avoiding punches. Dodging, slipping. Taking punches. How to recover quickly. From there we moved on to self-defence. Vulnerable points. Base of the neck, kidneys, ribcage. Even the small of the back.

'Do it right and you can cripple your opponent's back and legs,' he said. 'Fingers into an armpit can freeze that arm. And don't forget eyes, ears, nose and groin as well. Aim for just below the ear – just there. And the bladder blow – you know that one's worked if you're both suddenly very wet. Or try to break your opponent's nose. Apart from the pain and the blood, they'll be blinded by tears so you can step in and finish them off.'

I genuinely had no idea the human body was so frail. It's a miracle any of us get through the day.

We went running in the park. This was something at which I was better than him. I'm tall and skinny. I was a long-distance runner at school. Pennyroyal was stocky and muscular – a sprinter. I couldn't match him for initial speed but two hundred yards later I would sail past him, gesturing rudely, and do another two circuits, laughing cruelly every time I lapped him.

I lifted weights. At which I was rubbish – too tall and my arms were too long – but I persevered. Things called muscles turned up.

I could already shoot. Pennyroyal signed me up for his gun club. I had to tick a box saying I had no criminal convictions. I told Pennyroyal I was a criminal who just hadn't been caught yet. He rolled his eyes. He stopped rolling them when I turned out to be a better shot than he was. After weeks of being thrown from A to B in his self-defence classes, I have to admit that felt good. Although in the interests of self-preservation, I kept the gloating to a tasteful minimum.

Most interesting were the first-aid classes from a 'doctor' Pennyroyal knew. I learned to deal with all sorts of physical eventualities, but mostly how to treat bullet or knife wounds. And how to obtain medical treatment without bothering the last sorry shreds of the NHS. What household items could be utilised as medical equipment. I only knew her as Casey but she was good at what she did. Very good. I wondered about her occasionally but didn't ask. No one ever asked me any difficult questions – I returned the favour.

The bits I really enjoyed though – how to plan. Properly plan. Pennyroyal showed me how to start with the desired outcome and work back from there. He would list a set of imaginary circumstances and we'd both have to come up with a plan. Sometimes they were similar and sometimes not.

From there we moved on to the undesired outcomes and how to deal with those. Human failure. Acts of God. Natural catastrophes. Sheer bad luck. How to set up contingency plans and when to implement them. Safety nets and the importance thereof.

Sometimes – and I struggled with this because I'm unwilling to give up – there wouldn't be a successful outcome no matter how much I twisted the circumstances. The trick was to recognise and accept the point at which to walk away. Or, occasionally, run away. How to move on before disaster struck.

'This – all of this,' Pennyroyal gestured at the papers, maps, printouts and scribbled lists scattered across the table, 'everything we're discussing is important, but the one thing – the one essential thing you have to get your head around – *know when to walk away.* Know when to let go and save your own life. It's the most difficult thing you'll ever have to accept – that you can't win them all.'

I folded my hands on the table and looked at him. 'Does that mean that if I were trapped somewhere, couldn't get out, no hope of rescue – you'd leave me?'

He didn't answer for ages. Ages and ages. I waited. Because suddenly this was important. According to everything he'd just said, the answer should be yes. But would he say that?

Eventually he sighed and met my eyes squarely across the table.

'No. I should. But no.'

'You'd die with me?'

147

He sighed again. 'Looks that way. Can you put this stuff away and lay the table, please?'

I loved all of it. I was seventeen. I was exercising my mind and body. Life was exciting. I had a future – quite a lively one, I suspected – stretching out before me. Three months after leaving Starlings, life was better than I ever thought it could be.

Neither Uncle Albert nor I ever got any post. Pennyroyal would receive the occasional piece of snail mail, so when the official letter came through, I took it in to him without a second thought.

Twenty minutes later he'd packed a bag and left the house.

Not a word of explanation – not to me, anyway. No message, no indication of where he was going. Or why. Or how long he'd be away. He was just gone. His room was empty. As if he'd never been here.

I wandered downstairs to the suddenly empty kitchen. 'Will he come back?'

Uncle Albert shook his head. 'I don't know.' He looked terrible – grey and sick – and I was concerned for him.

'What's happened?'

There was a fractional pause. 'I don't know.'

He did know. He just wasn't telling me.

Pennyroyal didn't come back that day. Nor the next. Days turned into weeks. Then into months. There was no word from him.

One horrible dark, rainy day, when I couldn't get my run in the park, I said suddenly, 'Is he dead?'

Uncle Albert was sitting by the fire with a blanket over his knees. He didn't seem the slightest bit surprised by the question. 'I don't know. It's possible.'

I couldn't even begin to imagine such a thing. 'You know why he's gone, don't you?'

'I . . . do.' He sipped his tea. He seemed to need a lot of fluids these days. 'If . . . if you ask me, then I will tell you, because it's important you don't inadvertently say the wrong thing, but think very carefully before you ask.'

I did think carefully. I'd learned enough to know there were things I didn't want to know. I've never been able to decide whether I made a wise decision or not.

'Yes – tell me.'

It was a bald statement of facts. I've never forgotten how Uncle Albert fired the words at me. This is exactly how he told it to me.

'He has a sister. Promising officer in the army. On patrol. Ambushed. Trapped. No hope of escape. Her platoon jumped her. Stripped her naked. Shoved her outside into the crowd. Distraction while they got away. Body never found.'

I swallowed. 'She might not be dead.'

'She's dead. No one could survive . . . that. The best to hope for is that she died very quickly.'

I looked at him. A tear ran down his face.

And mine.

One of the few occasions on which I cried.

We – Uncle Albert and I – began to run out of money. All his – and a lot of Pennyroyal's, I suspected – had gone to pay off his debt, so that was one problem solved. But another appeared to take its place.

Uncle Arthur spent less and less time working on the pod. Some days he didn't go outside at all. I would take him cups of tea, light the fire, and stay to chat – not about anything very much. He slept a lot. I could see he was ill – I just didn't know how ill. And medication is expensive.

I did what I could, dipping into my own reserves. I could do no less. They'd taken me in when I was penniless. They'd saved me – now it was time for me to repay the favour. One should always pay one's debts.

I spoke to Mr Treasure about the possibility of accessing some of my inheritance early. There was no possibility. Gently but firmly, he made that very clear, going on to enquire whether I had any intention of ever returning to Starlings. There was no possibility. Gently but firmly, I made that very clear.

Money disappears very quickly when you have nothing at all coming in.

I thought about getting a job – anything – but Uncle Albert wasn't getting any better and I didn't really feel I could leave him. After a while, he could only spend the day in an armchair by the fire. I had to keep the house warm for him. In the end I gave him my bed on the sofa because he couldn't get up the stairs.

I asked him if he wanted a doctor and he smiled and shook his head, saying he rather fancied his time had come.

I suspected this was him saying that we couldn't afford it. Well – he was wrong there. I emptied my bank account.

That tided us over for a while. Casey came twice a week. I listened carefully to her instructions, and with his medication, Uncle Albert did improve a little. Enough for me to be able to leave him occasionally. I attended self-defence classes at the church hall around the corner. The guy was actually quite a good teacher. I learned a lot from him. And I ran every day just after dawn. I was fairly fit anyway but that was no excuse for not pounding the pavements. I didn't run in the park – I ran round and round the block so I'd be close at hand if Uncle Albert needed me quickly.

I came down one morning and found him on the kitchen floor.

I called for an ambulance. I held his hand. I told him to hang on – help was coming.

He struggled to speak. 'Pennyroyal . . . where . . . ?'

'He's here,' I said, not knowing what to say. I was lying to a dying man, but he wasn't going to live long enough to find out. 'He's coming now. Any moment.'

'Pennyroyal . . .' He closed his eyes.

'Wake up,' I said urgently. 'He's here. Look.'

He opened his eyes and looked straight at me. 'Look after my . . .'

'What? Look after your what?'

He smiled at me – a lovely smile – and then his eyes changed and he died.

I did the ABC thing. Airway – breathing – circulation. It's exhausting but I kept at it, the sweat running down my nose and plopping on to poor Uncle Albert. Compressions – mouth to mouth – more compressions – until my head was swimming. The ambulance took forever to arrive but eventually the para-medics turned up. They tried very hard, working on him for nearly twenty minutes, but we all knew he'd gone.

They rang a duty doctor and hours later one turned up and agreed that yes, Uncle Albert was dead. He looked at Uncle Albert's medication, listened to my description of his symptoms, told me it had probably only been a matter of time, and issued

151

a certificate recording the death of Henry Albert Meiklejohn. He was very kind, actually, and gave me the number for an undertaker. I rang them and they turned up almost immediately.

They were amazing. A very nice lady talked to me in the living room and I never even noticed them taking Uncle Albert out of the front door. Apparently bodies always go out of front doors. She gave me some leaflets and said someone would call to make an appointment for me to visit and make some choices and left.

I had no idea what to do next. As far as I knew, Uncle Albert had no relations. How could he? Only Pennyroyal knew of his existence in this time and he'd vanished. Possibly for good. There was no one to consult, no one to help.

It was an awful time. I made mistakes. I completed the wrong paperwork and it was all rejected. A kindly soul at the register office took pity on me and told me to make a lot of copies of the death certificate because lots of people would need one so I queued for hours to use one of the public machines.

I had to prove who I was and what my relationship to Uncle Albert had been. Mr Treasure helped there. Actually, he was amazing. I'm very happy to think that in later years I found myself in a position to help him with his wife's serious illness. I did it very gently and carefully, telling him he'd helped me so many times and I valued him as a dear friend, and I hoped he'd allow one dear friend to help another and we both got a little teary.

But back to Uncle Albert – the undertaker and I were the only ones at the funeral. I stood in a dreary little chapel. My flowers were the brightest thing there. He was cremated and I took his ashes to the park and, probably against every by-law known to man, discreetly scattered them over a sunny flower bed. I didn't know what else to do.

Somewhere in all that, my eighteenth birthday passed, almost unnoticed and certainly uncelebrated.

And as for Pennyroyal, I'd passed from shock to grief to despair to anger. He'd been gone for months and months and I was lost and had no idea what to do next. Several times I thought about locking the door behind me and just walking away, but where would I go? Nowhere near my family for a start. And what would I do about the house? Surely, sooner or later, there would be rent or mortgage repayments or council tax or something. And if Pennyroyal ever came back, then he'd need somewhere to come back to. Although it would serve him right if he had to live on the pavement.

Really, it was all too much to grapple with so I took the easy way out and did nothing. I worked out. I ran. I paid the library charge and spent all day there, reading, because it was warm. I just lived from day to day.

Sooner or later, I knew my money would run out completely and then I'd have to go somewhere. Do something. What would I do? Get a job, obviously, but I had no work experience, no references – the less said about my brief time at the posh school in the Cotswolds the better – and my pretty certificate from Mademoiselle Leonie's select establishment would be about as much use as a politician's promise made at election time.

And then, one night, just as I was drifting off to sleep, I heard a sound in the kitchen. Nothing identifiable – just a sound.

Six months ago I'd probably have called the police. Or even hidden under the covers and waited for them – whoever they were – to go away. These days I didn't feel that was an option.

I was alone in the house – there was no one nearby on whom to call for help. I would have to deal with this myself. I cracked open the door. By the sound of it they were still in the kitchen. I heard a chair scrape across the floor.

I listened hard, trying to ascertain how many were out there. And what they could possibly want. Uncle Albert's debts had been settled – Pennyroyal had seen to that – and Twenty-nine Cold Ash Lane had poverty written all over it. It was very obvious we had nothing worth stealing.

My heart gave a nasty thump. I was a lone female. Was I what they were after? Had word got out that I lived alone here? Perhaps I should ring for help after all. It would be the sensible thing to do. I heard something clatter and fall to the floor. The bastards were wrecking the place. This was very bad.

And then the thought came from nowhere: when things are bad – make them worse. Yes – I could do that. Time to go on the attack.

I crept down the stairs, grabbed an umbrella, tiptoed to the kitchen door and flung it open. 'Identify yourselves, you bastards, or I'll kick the living shit out of you.'

It was Pennyroyal standing there. Well, leaning there, actually, and even in this dim light I could see he'd been in a terrible fight. I didn't want to think about the sort of person who could possibly have done this amount of damage to Pennyroyal, of all people.

Dropping the umbrella, I ran to catch him just as his legs buckled and he dropped like a dead man.

12

I'd like to say I laid him down gently but he slipped through my arms and crashed to the floor which probably didn't do him any good at all. I tried to ring Casey but there was no response. Reluctantly, and without much hope, I tried for an official doctor. The phone rang for an hour and then went dead. I tried again but a recorded message said there was no appointment free for eleven weeks. I was on my own.

I treated him on the kitchen floor with the ringing phone beside me. There was no way I could move him. In fact, I wasn't sure I should even try. I relocked the back door, pushed the table and chairs out of the way, assembled hot water, a first-aid kit and some torn-up tea towels, cut his blood-soaked clothes off him and began to work. I was pretty sure this was a hospital job but as soon as I said *ambulance*, his hand closed on my wrist.

'No.'

Well, he wouldn't be the first dead man I'd had on the kitchen floor. I allowed myself three deep breaths and tried to remember everything I'd learned from Casey.

I started by checking him for gushing wounds, then moved on to looking for signs of concussion, then broken bones, starting at his head and running my hands over him, comparing one side of his body against the other. I think a couple of his ribs had gone but there was nothing I could do about that and he had no sucking chest wounds – one of those and it would have been an ambulance whether he liked it or not – so I moved on to his other less urgent but still major injuries. Of which there were many.

I started at the top and worked down, sponging away the blood and checking for glass or foreign bodies in the dirt. His face had been badly beaten – boots, I suspected – but his nose and teeth seemed intact. He could breathe. His jaw was unbroken. His neck worked. He could move all his limbs. Not much, but enough. He could flex his fingers and toes. There were what looked like three stab wounds to his right shoulder – two to the front and one to the back – and another long, jagged tear to his upper left arm. His forearms were criss-crossed with deep defensive wounds and heavily bruised and swollen. I cleaned, pressed the edges together and applied butterfly strips.

His chest and abdomen had suffered massive bruising. His testicles were really badly swollen. I'd only ever seen one set of testicles before – thank you, Kevin Aldridge, behind the science block at St Winifred's one rainy Thursday lunchtime – but I knew they shouldn't look like that. I put a cold cloth over the damage. I worried that his right knee and shin were broken but my fingers found no jagged ends. No sinister lumps. Just one massive bruise from knee to ankle.

Mindful of his ribs, I carefully rolled him over to look at his back. Someone had given his kidneys a good thumping. More cold cloths for that. I rummaged in the freezer and found a few packs of frozen peas and sweetcorn, wrapped them in a couple of pillowcases and applied them wherever I thought they could do the most good, especially on his swollen hands. I brought bedding down from upstairs. At least I could keep him warm. I slipped a pillow under his head, rolled him into a sleeping bag and zipped it up.

He lay quietly while I cleared things away. There was clotted blood on his boots – I'd have to clean that off in case the police came looking for him. I shoved the remains of his clothes into a bin bag. I could burn them later.

Then an idea struck me – there are clinics for the very poor, staffed by people with medical experience who had worked for the NHS and had no intention of abandoning its principles. Most of them had been threatened with being struck off for non-compliance and were happily ignoring government commands to do as they were told. I googled the nearest and called for a house visit, told them I couldn't afford a hospital and he was too bad to come to them. I had to leave them my address – not without some misgivings about what Pennyroyal would have to say about that – but it occurred to me that if he died then that would solve the problem, and if he lived he'd be so grateful he'd forgive me anything.

At about eight that evening, I heard a tap at the back door. It was Casey. I should have guessed she worked at the free clinic. That explained why I hadn't been able to contact her on her private number.

'I thought I recognised the address,' she said, dumping her bag on the table. 'What's the stupid bugger done this time?'

She knelt beside him, unzipped the sleeping bag and examined him.

Other than the ribs, there were no broken bones, but

157

Pennyroyal had sustained extensive what Casey called soft-tissue damage. I was to watch for bleeding from ears, blood in urine, blood under the skin. In short – blood.

I was to watch him for signs of a fever or infection. If any of that happened, I was to ignore everything he said and try for an ambulance.

Otherwise I was just to leave him to heal. It was Penny-royal, she said, zipping him back up again and giving me the impression this wasn't the first time he'd bled all over some-one's kitchen. I thanked her. She said she'd never been here. I agreed she'd never been here, gave her as much money as I could afford – because the clinic's need was probably greater than mine – saw her out, and went back into the kitchen.

I slept alongside him that night. I hadn't slept in the same room with someone since I'd left school and it seemed odd hearing him breathe in the dark. In the end I got up and put the hall light on, half closing the door. I felt better in the not quite dark.

I'd like to say he recovered quickly because he was Penny-royal but I can't. He was very ill for a very long time. I had to do everything for him. He lay on the floor, white as a ghost and slightly less chatty. I kept up his fluids, giving him sports drinks because he wouldn't eat. I changed his dressings and did my best to keep him clean and warm.

For a long time he didn't speak a word, and then one day, out of nowhere, he asked the question I'd been dreading. 'Where's Uncle Albert?'

'He died.'

There was a long silence, then he said, 'When?'

I thought. 'Six weeks.'

158

He closed his eyes.

One day I made him soup, holding the spoon for him because of his hands. He took a little then turned his head away so I finished it myself because I couldn't afford to waste it. I made him scrambled eggs and he didn't even complain. I couldn't understand it. His physical wounds were healing but whatever was going on in his head was beyond my tiny skills.

One morning I caught him trying to lift himself off the floor and, rather than argue with him, I helped him up and on to the sofa in the front room. Which made life easier for both of us although I still wouldn't leave him to sleep alone.

One day, right out of the blue, he said, 'You should go.'

'Yes, I should. But I won't. Shut up and drink your soup.'

'People will come looking for me.'

'And find me instead.'

'No.'

'Shut up or I'll take the soup away and do you some more eggs.'

'I'm not joking.'

'Neither am I.'

He took my wrist. 'I've done some bad things.'

'Good for you.' I proffered another spoonful. 'Drink your soup.'

'I've killed people.'

'Stop showing off.'

He was angry. The bowl went flying across the room. Soup sprayed through the air.

'You stupid bint – can't you see I don't want you hanging around any longer. You don't do anything. You can't cook. You don't put out. Not even a fucking hand job occasionally. You're not even pretty. You've been nothing but bad luck since the day you crossed my path. Just fuck off out of it, will you.'

I'd like to say that I realised immediately what he was up to. I didn't though, and my first thought was to undo all the solid medical care I'd put in by laying into him with the poker. It was only after five or six seconds of really quite enjoyable mental images that I saw he was trying to make it easy for me to go. Or possibly I'd been right the first time and he was just an ungrateful bastard who deserved everything that was about to happen to him.

I stood up on shaky legs and crossed to the door. He must have thought I was doing as he'd told me and getting out while I still could, whereas actually I was about to make this a teaching moment. I bent down, picked up the bowl and threw it back at him. It bounced off his head. I told you I was a good shot.

He had vegetable soup in his hair. Yeah – good luck shifting that, mate, because I wasn't going to do it.

I leaned over him. Right over him. In his face.

'You left us. Without a word. Without a penny. I looked up and you were gone. We had to manage on our own. Every day was a struggle and then Uncle Albert died and you weren't here. I didn't know what to do. I spent almost the last of my money on his funeral. And I had to stay on in case you took it into your head to come back again. *Be a team*, you said, and then you pushed off and left us. *Trust me*, you said, and you pushed off and left us. You're the one who was so righteous over whether you could trust me to keep my word and *you pushed off and left us*. You abandoned us, you bastard, and if you weren't already dying on the sofa, I'd do for you myself.'

And just to reinforce the point, I threw the spoon at him as well.

I wasn't sure whether I'd adequately made my views known or not, but I really was feeling quite cross with him.

13

Flying soup aside, the news that people were after Penny-royal wasn't good. He couldn't defend himself and I certainly couldn't. We needed a plan. An escape route. And some money. I sat down at the kitchen table. There was no alcohol in the house, sadly, but I put the kettle on and had a drink and a think nevertheless.

I contacted Meilin. 'Hey, how are you?'

'Busy.'

'Then I'll be brief. I want a lot of money as soon as possible. Can you see to it, please. Lovely to have caught up with you again. Bye.'

She groaned. 'All right, you have my attention. What do you want?'

'To offer you the business opportunity of a lifetime.'

'Oh God, Millie. What have you done now?'

'You'll never guess.'

'I don't want to.'

'I'm offering you the Skeffington diamonds. And get this – at the rock-bottom deal of only fifty pence in the pound because this will be a legitimate transaction.'

I could hear her shaking her head from all the way down the phone.

'Millie – you never, ever, *ever* dispose of a source of revenue unless you absolutely have to. You use it as collateral to raise working capital.'

'You mean pawn them?' I said. I hadn't actually thought of that. I knew from Papa that there had been a bit of a scandal with Cousin Wesley and his informal disposal of several small portable and valuable items after his visit to Starlings when I was about six. The items had been redeemed by his father and returned. Cousin Wesley remained in the outer darkness of family disapproval.

'Yes – I will give you . . .' She considered. 'Thirty pence in the pound for them. It should be forty but you have no choice. On the other hand, there's no time limit. You can redeem the diamonds at any time in the future. I will hold them indefinitely for you. So thirty.'

'Fifty,' I said. 'I need the money.'

She sighed. 'You shouldn't tell me that. It undermines your negotiation.'

'Like you hadn't worked that out. Fifty.'

'Thirty-five.'

'Forty,' I said. 'Because you'll hold them for me and there's no time limit, I won't ask fifty. So forty.'

We agreed forty.

By the time I'd finished organising all that, Pennyroyal had somehow got himself up the stairs and showered. I went in to help and he swore at me. I told him his balls were looking better and went out for an angry run. He was in the kitchen when I came in through the back door. We scowled at each other.

He looked out of the window. 'Actually, you are quite pretty.'

I wiped my sweaty face. 'Yes, I am.'

He looked at the door. 'I didn't mean the rest of it.'

'I know. But say anything like that to me again and I'll come at you with more than a soup bowl.'

'Understood. But you need to know – I've killed a lot of people. Some of them did not go quietly. Their friends and relatives will be looking for revenge. It's dangerous to be with me. I mean it. You shouldn't stay here.'

'If things are that bad, then neither should you.'

'Yeah . . . well . . .'

'I might have a plan,' I announced, thinking it might be a good idea to work up to things slowly. 'No, actually, I do have a plan.'

He said nothing.

'And just to give you fair warning, you're not going to like any of it.'

He said nothing.

I made my voice firm. 'Our time here is done. We have to move on. Somewhere we're not known. I've managed to raise some cash. We'll keep our heads down until you recover. When you're fit again, we'll think about stage two and what to do next. What do you think?'

'You're going to sell your diamonds.'

'Of course not.'

'Well . . . good.'

'You never, ever, *ever* dispose of a potential revenue source,' I informed him with all the authority of someone who'd only recently acquired that knowledge herself. 'You use it to raise working capital. I've pawned them.'

He closed his eyes. 'Oh God . . .'

'The only decision to make is where we go.'

'Amelia . . .'

He must be really shaken. He never used my name. Ever.

'No,' I said. 'It's the only way out. That pod thing belongs to us now and we can't leave it behind. Nor can we stay here. Therefore we go, taking the pod with us. And I've provided us with the financial means to do so.'

I listened to no arguments. In fact, I ignored everything he said. I plonked a very passable fish pie in front of him and told him to eat it. He demanded to know why there were no vegetables. I told him the sweetcorn had given up its life to reduce the swelling on his knee, the mixed veg had nursed his hands, and our entire pea supply had been wrapped around his balls. Strangely, he had nothing more to say after that.

We gave it a week for him to regain most of his faculties and then began our preparations, packing up what little we had. Some of it went into the pod, other stuff to the local charity shops. We ended by sorting out Uncle Albert's few possessions, just in case there was anything important – like money – among them. Pennyroyal was clumsily looking through a chest of drawers and I was rummaging through the wardrobe.

'What's this?'

I'd found a small tin box with a Union Jack on it, wrapped in an old woollen scarf and pushed to the very back of the top shelf.

Injured or not, Pennyroyal made short work of the lock. Inside was an envelope and inside that were two very official-looking ID cards. Citizen's ID cards. In both our names. The one relating to Pennyroyal had a very dubious-looking stain across the back – either his blood or, more likely, someone else's.

He turned them over, puzzled.

'There's more.' I pulled out a sheaf of papers and spread them out. 'All this is in our names as well. Look at the dates. And it seems to relate to those Time Police people you were telling me about.'

He took them off me.

I peered over his shoulder and pointed. 'Authority to act on behalf of the Time Police. Accredited representatives. What does that mean?'

'More to the point – how did Uncle Albert get hold of them?'

There was complete silence in the chilly bedroom as we both looked at the documents. Definitely photos of us – a little older, perhaps, but not much. My hair looked nice. I would do it like that in future. There were our names. Our details. All correct. And our signatures. Everything genuine as far as I could see. Which, admittedly, wasn't very far. Where on earth had they come from and how had Uncle Albert got hold of them?

The phrase *prised from our cold dead hands* was not spoken. Not aloud, anyway, but the truth was horribly obvious. At some point in the future these documents would belong to us. And then, somehow, willingly or not, they would be taken from us. It wasn't a comfortable thought. And that stain on Pennyroyal's card was beginning to look more and more sinister with every passing moment.

I rammed all the documentation back into the envelope. I was wearing a thick hoodie because we had no heating so I tucked it carefully away in the kangaroo pocket.

I could see Pennyroyal was uneasy. I didn't blame him. I was feeling fairly unsettled myself. There was obviously a story here. One that involved us, and whether it was good or bad, or whether there would be a happy ending, neither of us had any idea.

'Strange,' I said.

'You think?'

I scowled at the floor, thinking hard. 'At some point we have these docs; they're worn so they've been well used – by us, presumably – until, somehow, we . . . relinquish them. Uncle Albert acquires them . . . somehow . . . in the future . . . and he leaves them for us here and the whole thing goes round and round. Like a circle. The question is – where and how did they originate? And where and how do they end?'

Pennyroyal rubbed his head. 'I'm too hungry to think. Shall we . . . ?' He stopped.

I'd heard it too. The slight chink of a rattling chain. Someone was at the back gate.

'Bathroom,' he said. 'Quick. We mustn't be trapped up here.'

I followed him along the tiny landing and into the bathroom. And I locked the door behind us because that would delay our intruders for very nearly a whole half-second.

We didn't switch on the light, obviously. When I turned around, Pennyroyal had got the window open. Even colder air gusted in. He whispered, 'You go first. Drop down on to the pod. It's just outside. Wait for me. Quick as you can.'

Pausing only to grab my toothbrush – one has to be practical – I stepped up on to the edge of the bath and on to the windowsill. Somewhat clumsily – you try climbing out of your own bathroom window, it's not the easiest thing in the world, there are badly placed taps and things all over the place – I lowered myself out and hung for a moment, full of doubt. The camo device was on and this was, literally, a leap in the dark.

'Drop down on to the pod,' he'd said but the pod wasn't visible. I couldn't bring myself to let go. I looked up. Pennyroyal was leaning out of the window above me, waiting for me to jump.

'Trust me,' he said quietly. 'Just trust me.'

So I did. I closed my eyes and let go, half expecting a bone-breaking landing on the wet cobbles below.

I dropped about twelve inches. No more. I didn't even fall over. I moved out of the way to give Pennyroyal some room and looked up.

He'd vanished. The window was empty.

What? Where had he gone? Now what did I do?

I crouched – for all the good that would do me – and tried to think. The window above me was Pennyroyal-free. Was he making his escape by a different route? To launch an attack from the rear?

I peered about me. There was a depressing lack of rear attacking happening.

Was he ... I don't know ... building a barricade of some kind to hold them off?

Or – treacherous thought – had he left me behind as a decoy while he himself escaped? He might be half a mile away by now, leaving me to face them alone.

Something moved silently in the night and the next minute he was standing beside me in the dark, whispering, 'Lie flat.'

I lay flat on the roof and whispered, 'Give me a gun.'

Grunting, he eased himself stiffly alongside me. 'No. We're escaping – not starting a war.'

'Who are they?'

'Most likely people looking for me. If we're really unlucky, it's the Time Police.'

'Do you have a favourite option?'

'Neither. We'll be lucky to get out of this in one piece. Here they come.'

There were three of them. Dark shadows drifting in through the now open gate. Tightly bunched, they made their way across the yard.

Amateurs. Even I knew they should have burst through the gate as soon as they rattled the chain – not given us time to get out of the window. They should have split up, each finding their own way to the back door, not moved in a tight clump. And they seriously shouldn't have tripped over the old lawn-mower that had no business being there because we certainly didn't have a lawn, and which Pennyroyal had carelessly left lying around just where anyone might trip over it in the dark. And did.

It and someone went down with a noisy clatter. Someone swore viciously, and the outside light, which should have been the first thing they disabled, came on. Definitely amateurs.

We were still in deep shadow but the bright light exposed three men wearing ski masks. One held a baseball bat, one a sort of cudgel with what looked like nails protruding, and one a vicious-looking baton, thin and whippy. That would hurt.

But no guns.

The light coming on panicked them into hasty movement.

'Come on.'

They charged for the back door. There was the sound of thumping. I craned my neck to see what they were doing. Pennyroyal very gently pushed my head down again.

I heard the tinkle of glass and a splintering crash as our back door gave way, and the next moment they were inside. I could hear voices and the sounds of furniture being overturned as they moved from room to room.

'Now,' said Pennyroyal, but I was already moving. We dropped silently to the ground. Not that it mattered. Stupidly they were making so much noise they'd never have heard us. And they hadn't left a man at the back door to prevent anyone nipping out behind them. I'll say it again – bloody amateurs.

Pennyroyal had the pod open, and a second later we were inside with the door safely closed behind us.

'Aren't we leaving?' I said urgently, because he wasn't doing anything.

He shook his head. 'No need. We're quite safe in here. It takes much more than an old door-breacher to get into a pod. We can sit back and enjoy the show.'

Lights were snapping on all over the house as it dawned on our intruders that they'd missed us. There was shouting and a voice answered faintly from the street. Well, at least they'd remembered to leave a man at the front door.

The voices got louder and angrier as they failed to find us.

'Oh dear,' said Pennyroyal with no signs of regret what-soever. 'We appear to have completely slipped through their fingers.'

'What will they do now?' I said, still not completely re-assured.

'Actually,' he began and then the answer became painfully apparent. There was a sudden orange glow. They'd set fire to the house. I wondered if they thought we were still inside it somewhere, hiding and terrified.

We were a corner house, fortunately, and not part of a terrace, but even so – what about the neighbours?

I had another sickening thought. I'd packed most of my belongings into the pod but some were still in there, and neither they nor the house in which they lived were going to be in this world for very much longer. Once again, I was left with barely the clothes I stood up in. And my toothbrush, of course.

The orange glow intensified. Smoke billowed out of the back door.

'Stupid sods,' said Pennyroyal, obviously determined to make this a teaching moment. 'What did they forget to do?'

His star pupil had the answer ready. 'Leave themselves a way out.'

'Yeah – and good luck to them getting the front door open. It's been raining for days and it always swells with the damp.'

He seemed very put out at the amateurish abilities of our assailants. I suppose it's all a matter of prestige, really. If you're going to be offed, you want it to be by people at the very top of their tree, don't you?

'Who are they?'

'At a guess – relatives.'

I blinked. 'You have relatives?'

'I told you – I killed some people. Their relatives. Looking for revenge.'

'It's a dish best served cold,' I said. 'And things are about to get quite warm for these lunatics.'

The audio system in the shed – pod – wasn't great but I could make out the sounds of smashing glass.

'Kitchen window,' said Pennyroyal unemotionally. I, on the other hand, was quite upset. Twenty-nine Cold Ash Lane had been my home. My second home. I was shedding domiciles like . . . Oh, I don't know. Like something, anyway.

'Don't get attached,' he said, possibly reading my mind. 'Always a mistake.'

The three men were scrambling out of the window now. They'd left it late. Behind them, the kitchen was well ablaze.

'Wow,' I said. 'That fire caught fast.'

'Thank you,' said Pennyroyal modestly.

For a moment I didn't understand him. And then I did. '*You* set fire to the house. *That's* what you were doing just now.'

'Booby traps,' he said briefly. 'Training module three. You haven't got that far yet.'

'I've been living in a house that could have gone up in flames at any moment?'

'Well . . . yeah. I suppose . . . if you want to look at it like that . . .'

I said nothing in that special way.

'You seem cross.'

'Of course I'm bloody cross. You should have told me so I could watch you setting them. See how you did it.'

What he would have said to that I'll never know, because at that moment one of our friends outside ran into the invisible pod and fell backwards.

'Goodness,' I said.

'Happens a lot with these camo devices,' said Pennyroyal. 'Bloody embarrassing sometimes.'

'I can imagine.'

His accomplices stared at their stricken colleague for a moment and then turned and ran. After a moment, the third one heaved himself to his feet and staggered in a circle, arms flailing as he groped his way around the unseen obstacle, and then he too was gone.

172

'As should we be,' Pennyroyal said.

He began to do things at the console. Normally I would have watched closely but I couldn't take my eyes off the screen as the house burned. It was only when he told me to close my eyes that I suddenly realised we were about to jump.

'Where are we going?' I said, suddenly alarmed.

'Somewhere safe.'

'Yes, but where?'

There was no response. Typical Pennyroyal.

NORTHUMBERLAND
The Present

I stared at the screen, now showing a bleak, snowy landscape. A heavy grey sky hung over dark hills. I could see for miles and miles. Sadly there was very little to see except for tiny white flakes drifting aimlessly in the wind.

'Where the . . . ?'

'Northumberland.'

I blinked. I'd heard of the place, obviously, but . . .

'When?'

'Now. Same time. Plus an extra thirty minutes. To be on the safe side.'

'Why?'

'Because you can't be in the same time twice.'

'No, I mean why Northumberland?'

'Not a huge population. A chance to regroup, recover, and decide what to do next.'

'What about food?'

'In the locker.'

'Water?'

'Purification tablets. In the locker.'

'Toilet?'

'Ah.'

'Not in the locker, then.'

He frowned. 'No. Of course not.'

'You're kidding. There's no toilet?'

He grinned. Pennyroyal has a very specialised sense of humour.

I sighed with relief. 'There is a toilet.'

'There's a bucket.'

I folded my arms. 'I demand to be returned to my point of origin – I'll take my chances in the fire.'

'Too late.' He turned from the controls. 'We should talk.'

'About what? You've dropped us in . . .' I gestured at the screen, 'the middle of nowhere.'

'There's a village in the next valley. We need to go there.'

I narrowed my eyes. 'Alibi, I assume.'

'Yes – we might want to go back to Walthamstow one day and we won't want charges of arson hanging over us.'

I decided to deal with that sentence in the order presented.

'Might? Yes, we will want to go back one day. Arson? You deliberately booby-trapped the house. You *are* an arsonist. Alibi? I don't need an alibi. Us? *I* haven't done anything.'

'Just about everyone in Walthamstow knows you were living there too – you need an alibi. Come on.'

'It's snowing out there.'

'Not very heavily. Waterproofs . . .'

'Don't tell me. In the locker.'

We set out for the village. In the next valley it might have been, but it took us a good hour walking single file along some sort of goat track, exposed to a wind that had come straight off the Urals. And Pennyroyal still wasn't up to racing speed. Although I did finally find a use for him as a wind break.

We came down off the moors, followed a lane for about half a mile, and there was, thank God, a village. With a shop. Several shops, actually. A tiny supermarket, a baker, a cheese shop, outdoor wear and hiking gear, and two pubs. Pennyroyal did sensible things regarding a balanced diet. I was carrying the whisky.

The supermarket cashier peered at me. 'How old are you?'

'She's with me,' said Pennyroyal, handing over a credit card. Another good move but I wasn't going to tell him that. 'I only bring her to carry the heavy stuff.'

She stared at him, completely at a loss. Pennyroyal does a really good job of making sure people remember him. Slightly less good at endearing himself to the world in general and the human race in particular, of course.

It was getting dark as we struggled back to the pod. Well, I struggled. The wind was bitter and cut like a knife.

At least I knew to take off my boots and spread my coat and gloves out to dry. Pennyroyal produced a kettle – from the locker, obviously – and we had sandwiches and hot soup in a mug. 'There'll be days when we can't get to the shop,' said Pennyroyal. 'That's what the rations in the locker are for.'

'How long are we going to be here?'

'As long as it takes to get you trained up.'

'In what?'

'Everything. Just as you asked.'

We should all be careful what we wish for.

*   *   *

There was more boxing and self-defence. Every day. Regardless of the weather. There's nothing like dancing around in sub-zero temperatures with a wind-chill factor of minus ten million to ensure lessons are learned really, really quickly. I still can't believe I didn't die of exposure at least three times a day.

Then, when he was up to it, there was Pennyroyal's version of fell running. You pick a remote spot and run towards it in a straight line. You're not allowed to deviate, no matter what you encounter. Bogs, rivers, cliffs – up and down – trees, bulls, waterfalls, people's back gardens, and on one spectacular occasion, an MOD firing range.

That was the daylight programme. Evenings were spent showing me how to operate the pod.

'This is a lot easier than Doctor Who makes it look,' I declared, having successfully identified all the elements on the console and their functions. For the third or fourth time, I might add.

Pennyroyal humphed, which, I'd gathered, was his go-to reaction to people with whom he cohabited. Or *endured* – a word he was using more and more frequently these days.

'Be fair,' I said. 'You actually have things very easy, you know.'

He raised an eyebrow, signifying massive astonishment and disbelief.

I gestured around the pod's tidy interior. 'Is my wet underwear hanging everywhere? No, it is not.

'Is there a constant stream of randy rustics banging at the door, all of them with designs on my virtue? No, there is not.

'Do I continually demand parties and clothes and the latest thing in phones? No, I do not.

'Do I spend the evenings having meltdowns because I hate

177

my hair/face/eyebrows/weight/legs/everything about me? No, I do not.

'Do you have to kick aside discarded female apparel every time you want to get to a locker? No, you do not. You really don't know how lucky you are, do you?'

He said nothing.

I poked him. 'Hey!'

He opened his eyes. 'Sorry, you started talking and I dropped off. Was it important?'

From the basics, he moved on to the slightly more complex pod stuff. Showing me how to calculate spatial and temporal coordinates myself because sometimes the AI could be a little iffy. How to operate the camouflage device, proximity alerts, the various cameras and split the screen. How to check the power levels and use the solar panels to top up.

I asked what happened if the pod broke down.

'We shut the door and walk away,' he said. 'I can fix the easy stuff but the technicalities are best left to the experts. Which we aren't.'

Half an hour a day was devoted to Pennyroyal educating me on what little he knew of the future. Because that was to be our next destination. And, according to Pennyroyal, that was my fault.

I'd been staring at Uncle Albert's paperwork for the umpteenth time when the idea occurred to me.

'We should go to the future.'

Pennyroyal put down his mug. 'What?'

'It's obvious.'

'How so?'

178

I waved the paperwork. 'We've already done it. Will do it. Whatever.'

He took the envelope off me and pulled out the contents again.

I said nothing. You never want to over-egg the pudding.

'We don't know anything about the future.'

'We can learn.'

'What will we live off?'

'Well – our wits, obviously. And we realise every asset we've got, transmute it all into gold, and take it with us.'

'Where would we live?'

I waved around. 'In this. Like we're doing now. Until we make a fortune and can afford somewhere better.'

'It could – it probably will – all go tits up.'

'Then we return to this time. By then the fuss over the burning house will have died down and everyone looking for you will have given up. Really, it's a no-lose scenario.'

He grinned and I realised this had been another teaching moment. Going to the future had probably been in his head all along. Because . . .

The penny dropped. 'You've actually been there, haven't you?'

'Once or twice. With Uncle Albert.'

'Well, you already know what it's like, then. The future, I mean. And we have to go because we've already been. It's meant to be.' I gestured at the envelope. 'And you can brief me. Every evening. An orien . . . orentien . . .'

'Orientation.'

'Orientation. Familiarising me with the future. What it's like. What I need to look out for.' I paused for full dramatic effect. *'Flying cars.'*

I was given to understand there were no flying cars. Not now. Not in the future. Not ever. The world was never gifted with flying cars. Ever.

I was so tempted to ask about jetpacks, just for the pleasure of seeing him go off on one again, but obviously some of the survival stuff had rubbed off on me because I didn't. Personal growth, I told him.

He didn't roll his eyes because, he said, only one of us was a teenage girl. 'But there are things you need to know. And pay attention because they're important.'

I sat up, full of excited anticipation.

'There's something called the Time Wars,' he said, sipping the quarter inch of whisky he allowed himself every night. Apparently he deserved it. I was only ever allowed tea.

'According to Uncle Albert,' he said, 'they discover how to do this time travel thing and, obviously, everyone's at it.'

I nodded vigorously. I would be, too.

'But . . .' he said, and stopped, waiting for my contribution because I had to learn to think for myself. All right – time travel. What could possibly go wrong?

'Well,' I said. 'There's that saying – observing something changes that which is being observed, so I'm guessing people started screwing up the past. Did they mean to?'

'Not always. Often it wasn't deliberate. But when you jump back in time, even something as simple as standing in one place means that the person who should have been standing there has to be somewhere else, which, in turn, affects something else, which affects something else, and so on, and at the end of the day, you had empires rising – and wars happening – that shouldn't have and, worst of all, wars that should've happened didn't.'

'Oh, yes,' I said. 'That's not good.'

He sipped his whisky again. 'Because . . . ?'

'Because people who should be dead – aren't. Which means people form different relationships, and people who should be born aren't and vice versa, which alters the future, which means the people who travelled back in time might never exist to do that, which means that the future never gets altered and therefore . . .'

'Yes,' he said, before I could further entangle myself in temporal dynamics and the English language. 'You get the idea. And that was just the accidental stuff. Then there were the people who thought actually trying to change history would be a good idea.'

'Like killing Hitler.'

'And many others. Uncle Albert said it wasn't a good time.'

'How, exactly?'

'He would never say. History was changed so much – people died, then lived, then died again. Some countries were worse affected than others. America existed. Then didn't. Then it was the Confederation of States. Then it wasn't.' He sipped again. 'The Time Wars are bad. Very bad.'

'So they invented the Time Police?'

'Yes. Ruthless bastards whose remit is to do whatever necessary to stamp out illegal time travel. Unlimited budget. Unlimited resources. And even then, they struggle. At one point, worldwide, they are nearly down to single figures. So they outsource.' He watched me again. Waiting.

I snapped my fingers. 'Bounty hunters.'

He held up the paperwork.

'And we . . . do we become . . . *bounty hunters*?'

181

'Recovery agents,' he said. 'According to this. Although . . .'

'*Oh my God. That is so cool.*'

'No, it isn't, it's . . .'

'*I could have one of those armoured vests with "Bounty Hunter" emblazoned across the . . .*'

'No, you couldn't.'

'*And a really, really big gun.*'

'No, you . . .'

'*I could have two. One on each hip.*' I mimed drawing from the hip and shooting miscreants.

'Over my . . .'

'*And one of those utility belts. Like Batman. With all sorts of technical gadgets and flying things. And a Batmobile.*'

'I don't . . .'

'*And black. I could wear black leather. And my call sign would be Black Widow. You would be my sidekick and . . .*'

'Shut up or I'll throw you out into the snow.'

I laughed a heartless bounty hunter laugh. 'You could try.'

The next moment I was on the other side of the door.

I banged on the door. 'Hey – it's bloody freezing out here.'

Spring turned up. The weather improved and the moment it became a pleasure to step outside the pod and lift my face to the sun, Pennyroyal decided it was time to go.

'We won't have the place to ourselves for much longer,' he said. 'Holiday-makers, hikers, horse riders, dog walkers – we'll be falling over people everywhere.'

'Where are we going?'

'The future. Have you been paying any attention at all?'

We were on one of Pennyroyal's route marches at the time,

following a watercourse upwards. The little valley was lush and green with new leaves and wildflowers. The air was warm and damp. Birds sang everywhere.

I sat on a rock and chugged back some water. 'I have a question.'

'What?'

'Are we a democracy? Do I get a say in anything?'

'When you're older, perhaps. Probably not.'

'Huh,' I said, tucking away my water bottle. 'I'm glad you're not *my* father.'

He actually took a step backwards. 'You think of me as your father?'

'No – *you* pay attention. I just said I was glad you *weren't* my father.'

'How old do you think I am?'

'Well, you told me you were twenty-five. Then you changed it to twenty-three.'

'You're seventeen. How could I possibly be your father?'

'Eighteen,' I said.

'When?'

I became busy with my pack. 'When you were away.'

There was a long silence. 'Did you have a party?'

For one blindingly furious moment, I couldn't speak. Then I said quietly, 'I had a celebration sardine on my evening toast.'

There was another long silence. Pennyroyal's face is not expressive, but at that moment I could follow his thoughts very easily. Uncle Albert dead or dying. No friends. No party. No gifts. No celebrations. The official first step into adulthood and I'd taken it alone.

'Come on,' I said, standing up. 'Another hundred miles to

go before I can hunt down a mammoth for lunch and build you a ziggurat to sleep in.'

That evening, Pennyroyal got the Time Police paperwork out again. Because he was concerned about the dates. 'We've obviously already been in the future so those are dates to be avoided at all costs.'

'Because we're already there?'

'You can't be in the same time twice.'

'But surely, if we've done it then we have to do it.'

He frowned. 'You need to be aware,' he said, 'if we've got this wrong, then we will die and it won't be pleasant. The Time Police are always banging on about the consequences of being in the same time twice, so if you have any doubts then speak up now.'

I leaned back against the side of the pod. Not only would we be jumping into the unknown, which was bad enough, but we had no idea what we'd been up to during our time there. Suppose we were wanted by the Time Police. Or the ordinary police. Or a whole bunch of miscreants were after us for any number of really good reasons. Were we good bounty hunters? Bad bounty hunters? Was there a very bad reason our docs had been taken from us?

On the other hand – at some point we *would* do this. We *were* bounty hunters – the paperwork said so.

I sighed. Uncle Albert leaving us a list of dates, times and places would have been very helpful. And then I looked at the paperwork again. He wasn't stupid. He was from the future – he would have known better than we did what the problem would be.

184

I looked across at Pennyroyal, frowningly going through our documents for the umpteenth time.

My eye fell on the envelope and, for something to do, I picked it up. Everything looked normal. There was no addressee but the actual address was neatly and correctly printed. Twenty-nine Cold Ash Lane, Walthamstow. And the E17 postcode was correct.

The second-class stamp had been cancelled, so at some stage this envelope had been through the postal system.

I turned it over. No return address. I scanned the whole envelope, front and back, turning it over in my hands.

And then I had it. Not on the envelope – *inside* the envelope.

I turned to Pennyroyal. 'Give me your knife.'

'Why?'

Without taking my eyes off the envelope, I simply held out my hand.

He passed it over, but possibly not completely convinced I wasn't going to use it on him, kept his distance.

Very, very carefully, I slit around three sides of the envelope and laid it out flat. Then I picked it up and held it to the light, turning it this way and that.

There was nothing written on the inside. Other than the dark patch in the corner – the stamp – the envelope was completely blank.

Disappointment washed over me like a wave. I thought I'd been so clever. I'd been certain Uncle Albert would have left us a message somehow. I sighed and handed Pennyroyal back his knife.

'Sorry, I thought I had something there.'

He was staring at the envelope. 'You did.'

I blinked. 'Did I?'

He held the envelope up to the light again. 'See that dark rectangle?'

'The stamp?'

'No – it's dark because there's something under the stamp. Can you hold the envelope still while I . . .'

It took a while – and a great deal of gentle manipulation – but eventually he got a corner free and very, very carefully began to peel back the stamp. Fixed underneath was a tiny piece of paper and on the reverse, face down against the envelope to protect the message from the glue – tiny but perfectly readable – one priceless set of coordinates.

'Bingo,' I said.

Pennyroyal looked at me. 'Well done.'

It was just about the first time he'd ever said anything like that to me and I felt ridiculously pleased.

'No,' I said. 'I was on completely the wrong track. It was you who fixed on the stamp.'

'Not without you holding it to the light like that. And that was only because you were the one with the brains to slit open the envelope. Again – good work.'

'Thank you,' I said. 'And well done you, as well.'

'Yeah,' he said, settling back and picking up his whisky again. 'Teamwork.'

My heart was thumping. Because now there was nothing to stop us.

'This is it,' he said.

'Yes.'

'Sure you want to do this?'

'Yes. You?'

He nodded.

I grinned at him. 'We're going to the future. We're going to be bounty hunters. I can wear sunglasses in the dark. This is going to be *awesome*.'

He sighed.

Before we could set off on what I persisted in referring to as our big adventure, however, there were some adjustments to be made to the pod thing.

Pennyroyal wanted me to walk to the village.

'Why?' I said.

'Out of harm's way if this goes wrong.'

'You don't know what you're doing?'

'There are some safety protocols I have to disengage.'

'You're disengaging the safety protocols? Why?'

'There are all sorts of things you shouldn't ask a pod to do.'

'Such as?'

'Carry things out of their own time.'

'How can we become bounty hunters if we can't do that?'

'Exactly. So I'm removing the protocols.'

'How is that a good idea?'

'It's not. That's why I'm sending you away.' He handed me an envelope. 'If there's a big bang then you'll find enough in there to buy yourself a train ticket to wherever you want to go and to survive for a month or so.'

'What you're doing is that dangerous?'

'It's not dangerous at all. If you know what you're doing.'

'And you . . . ?'

'I've seen Uncle Albert do it.'

'But . . .'

'But nothing. I'm completely on top of everything. Now

go. I'll do the practice jump in thirty minutes. You need to be at least a mile and a half away – preferably two. And I'll be watching so don't try just hiding behind a rock or something.'

I gazed around the featureless moorland.

'Go.'

I set off. He let me go a hundred yards before shouting, 'The village is that way.'

Smart arse.

I turned and trudged uphill, over the brow and ten paces down the other side. Where I stopped. This would do.

I lay down in the sun, linked my hands behind my head and closed my eyes. A gentle breeze blew. A bird hovered high overhead, singing its little head off. Fluffy white clouds were scudding about all over the place. It was a lovely afternoon. There were worse ways to go.

I awoke sometime later to find Pennyroyal standing over me, black against the sun.

'Two miles,' he said.

I looked around. 'This isn't two miles?'

'No.'

I held up my hand, he pulled me to my feet and we made our way back to the pod.

The next day, when I came back from emptying the bucket – life as a bounty hunter is not all black leather and witty badinage, you know – Pennyroyal handed me a shop-bought chocolate muffin with a tiny candle in the top. I have no idea where he could have got either.

'I'm sorry I missed your birthday,' he said.

I blew out the candle and made a wish. It came true.

LONDON
The Future
Sorry – no flying cars

The future was hugely unspectacular. I don't know what I expected but I certainly didn't get it.

'Where are we?' I said, staring over his shoulder at the screen.

'East London,' he said. 'I'm trying to make out exactly where we are but I think we'll have to get our bearings on foot.'

'Why?'

'We need to power down. All pods have signatures and the Time Police could track us down. This might be an unlicensed pod. Until we find out, we can't take the risk.'

'But we have papers,' I said.

'And what should we always do first – papers or no papers?'

'Check things out. Know where we are. How to get about. Escape routes. Rendezvous points for if we have to split up. Local conditions and so on.'

'Then let's get started.'

*　　*　　*

189

One scruffy bit of London looks very much like any other scruffy bit of London in any time. Boarded-up buildings, graffiti, weeds growing out of cracks in the pavements and brickwork. Potholes. It was only when we ventured into slightly more prosperous areas that I got a better picture of life in the future. People walked everywhere or cycled. Such vehicles as did exist were electric. There were energy-generating walkways which were fun but demanded a certain level of coordination, and I nearly went arse over tit the first time I saw one of the stately commercial airships trundling slowly overhead, on its way to dock at one of the enormous mooring towers scattered across the city.

Modern apartment blocks towered over the streets with smaller, older buildings sandwiched in between. Something called SmartGlass was very much the thing which, when automatically opaqued, gave the impression most buildings had their eyes shut. The Thames was dotted with flood defences. As were all the buildings along the Embankment. And they weren't there on the off-chance they might be needed. London definitely enjoyed a rainy season.

We spent days walking the streets. I enjoyed it. And the street food was brilliant. Pennyroyal regarded each colourful stall with massive disfavour but I got stuck right in there, trying everything in sight. Particularly the fish stalls – well, we couldn't afford real meat.

I quickly learned that there were massive bans and quotas for the now highly regulated fishing industry because stocks of what I would call *familiar* fish had been depleted to such an extent that now they'd had to move on to the more . . . let's call them *exotic-looking* specimens. And very good value some

190

of them were, as I pointed out to Pennyroyal, showing him the number of tentacles I'd got in just one portion. Actual fish were way out of our price range but, trust me, anal fins fry up quite well, fish-head kebab is nicer than you'd think, and deep-fried caudal peduncle is like savoury crisps. I never got the hang of milt, though. Just didn't fancy it.

We walked as far and as often as we could, getting the lay of the land, making small talk with locals, negotiating the walk-ways – I nearly broke my bloody neck several times – and not fainting at how much everything cost. The weather was pretty shit. In my time, rain had fallen on a fairly haphazard basis – these days it had got itself organised. There was a wet season – a very wet season, actually – when all the flood defences went up and prudent people moved their furniture upstairs. Followed by a corresponding dry season when people nearly killed themselves carting it back down again in the ensuing heatwave. There were about three days a year when the weather was perfect. On the other hand – what else is there to talk about other than the weather?

Having said all that, this was very definitely a conflict zone. There were many no-go areas. I don't mean areas where it was inadvisable to walk – I mean areas where you definitely couldn't go at all. The Time Wars had left – and were still leaving – their mark on London and the whole world. Every day, Pennyroyal and I witnessed scenes disturbingly similar to images I'd seen of the Blitz when I was at school. Burnt-out buildings, craters, torn-up roads – and very ominously – a site where something had gone badly wrong and two versions of St Paul's were struggling to occupy the same space. The flick-ering effect did strange things to people's brains and the Time

191

Police had cordoned off the area, keeping everyone well away until they got things sorted out. 'Sorted out' was Time Police speak for shooting anyone they didn't like the look of – i.e. everyone – and torching everything within a two-mile radius.

Nor was it unusual to walk around a corner and encounter a time slip, often accompanied by a couple of confused Romans or Vikings wandering about. There was a special number for members of the public to contact and the Time Police would appear and 'resolve the situation'. Pennyroyal said they would just shoot the poor bastards – together with anyone stupid enough to be hanging around – and then go home.

Everything Pennyroyal had said about the Time Police was true. They were nasty-looking buggers, almost exclusively men – and big ones at that. They wore black, always kept their visors down and were licensed to do pretty much anything they wanted. Shortly after we arrived in the future, we encountered two of them marching towards us. People got out of their way. I stood and stared until Pennyroyal gently drew me into a shop doorway. We watched as they marched past. Neither of us said a word.

It took us about a month, but eventually we had a working knowledge of our own very downmarket local area and central London itself. And then, finally, the day came.

We stood at the front of TPHQ staring up at the enormous chimneys.

'*That's* the Time Police HQ?' I said.

Pennyroyal nodded.

'That's Battersea Power Station,' I said, amazed.

He nodded again.

'Shit,' I said.

The bloody place was huge.

'Are we going inside?'

'Not until we know what's going on.'

'That's a relief.'

The end of our reconnaissance coincided with the real beginning of the rainy season, so from then on I mostly stayed in the pod. Using my time usefully, I might add. The main languages spoken these days appeared to be English, Spanish and Mandarin. I already had schoolgirl Spanish so I thought I'd get my head around some Mandarin. I worked hard at it and all I can say now is that I understand it better than I speak.

Pennyroyal left me to my studies and went off to investigate the Time Police. 'No point in both of us getting into trouble,' he said. 'And the Time Police don't really do girls.'

I shrugged. 'Their loss.'

He was gone for hours.

I fretted. If anything happened to him, then I was here, in the future, all on my own.

Nearly four hours later, he struggled back in through the door, his waterproof dripping small puddles on to the floor of the pod.

'I have news.'

I closed my Mandarin textbook. '*Shénme?*'

All right – I was showing off. I don't know why I bothered.

'*Wǒmen yǒu gōngzuò,*' he said. 'We have a job.'

'*Cōngmíng dàn,*' I said. 'Smart arse.'

And my accent was better than his.

I handed him a cup of coffee. We didn't have enough money for tea – which was taxed out of existence in this economy. 'Well?'

'Not without misgivings, I presented our paperwork at TPHQ today and believe it or not, it's perfectly genuine. Agents Pennyroyal and Smallhope are authorised to use a pod and act on behalf of the Time Police.'

I hadn't realised how anxious I'd been until I wasn't. 'We have a job?'

'We do.'

'Did they want to know why we hadn't been around?'

'I don't think they could care less. Anyway, we – I – need to call in regularly to collect the job sheets and any bounty owing us. We'll need to invoice them, by the way. That will be your job.'

'And debt collection will be yours?'

He nodded and pulled out a couple of sheets. 'Details of illegals, aka those wanted by the Time Police.'

I rifled through them. 'Are they allocated to us specifically or are we able to choose our own targets?'

'The latter. We're very small fry in the scheme of things.'

'Not for long,' I said, and he grinned.

'The big boys are offered the plum jobs – people like us take what we can get. Fortunately it's a very long list.'

We started small, going after idiots, rather than villains. People whom the Time Police suspected of being naughty but didn't have the time or evidence to proceed against. We'd hang out in pubs and cafés, watching and listening and engaging in occasional small talk as people came and went. It was a surprisingly successful strategy – mostly, as I informed Pennyroyal, because of his villainous countenance. Or, as he informed me, because of my witlessly innocent expression.

A couple of indiscreet conversations later, and after some

very careful sniffing around, we'd have the minimum evidence required and Pennyroyal would be heaving someone through the doors of TPHQ. The bounties weren't huge, but there were always a lot of them to be collected. There was little competition at this level, and we were very enthusiastic.

I stayed well away from TPHQ myself because, Pennyroyal said, if the Time Police thought they were dealing with a girl, they'd reduce the bounty accordingly. I let it go. The day would come when they'd regret that.

'And I don't trust the bloke in charge,' he said. 'Colonel Albay. Bit of a bastard.'

'Be fair,' I said. 'So are you.'

He looked pleased. Well, a line on his face deepened fractionally so he was enjoying a good chuckle. 'True.'

We couldn't have picked a better time. The worst of the Time Wars was over. A lot of people were dead but there were still loads of minor illegals to be picked up. And pick them up we did. We worked hard, often racking up three or four arrests a week.

It wasn't all plain sailing. Once, an illegal got away from Pennyroyal – don't ask me how – and without stopping to think, I set off after him. I love the way men think women can't run as fast as they can. I pounded down the pavement and caught up with him just outside the local chippy, grappling him to the ground. Obviously, he landed on the bottom because I'm not stupid. We rolled around among the vinegar-drenched cartons for a while. I didn't try anything clever – I simply clamped myself around him and yelled for Pennyroyal, who turned up a very long thirty seconds later.

Pennyroyal bundled Chummy off to TPHQ, returning an hour

later to spend a disproportionate amount of time describing my stupidity, my recklessness, because anything could have gone wrong, I could have been badly hurt . . . blah, blah, blah.

I just grinned at him because that always gets his goat.

Finally he paused to draw breath. I grinned a bit more. He drew a couple more breaths and said more calmly, 'He could have injured you badly.'

I suddenly realised he'd been worried.

'That was never going to happen,' I said quietly. 'The bloke who trained me is pretty cool.'

That stopped him in his tracks. 'Well . . .' he said, and huffed a couple of times. 'Good work, anyway. Fancy a celebration pint?'

Because I was so young, my role was usually that of helpless innocent. Or bait, as Pennyroyal referred to it. As soon as I'd lured the illegal into our web, Pennyroyal would step out of the shadows and that was the end of their life as they'd known it. It was fun – I enjoyed it – not least because being bait involved a variety of sub-roles:

Airhead
Aristocrat
Businesswoman
Disgraced academic

And, my favourite – hussy – which initially Pennyroyal wasn't going to let me do because he thought I was too young and he, with the maturity of someone five years my senior, was the guardian of my morals.

When I'd stopped laughing, I told him my morals were my own affair and nothing to do with him, and he said he was responsible for me, and I said he wasn't my father, and he said he was the senior partner, and I said no, he was the equal partner, and he said, 'Go on then, show me how you'll hussy,' and so I pushed him out of the door while I morphed into hussy mode.

I let him back in five minutes later to admire my giant hair, the world's entire supply of mascara, a white top through which could be seen my black bra – always the sign of a hussy, according to Cousin Helen, who hadn't become a nun because she considered their outfits to be too revealing. Presumably she spent her entire life encased in a giant cardboard box with a slit cut for her eyes. I'd topped – or bottomed – off the outfit by chopping six inches off an already too-short skirt – seriously, the belt was wider than the skirt – and completed the look with a pair of silver shoes that Pennyroyal hadn't actually seen yet because I'd planned to introduce them slowly. One at a time, perhaps.

He actually closed his eyes. 'I can see your legs all the way up to your ear lobes.'

'That's rather the point, clever clogs.'

'I can see your bra.'

'Again – that's the point.'

'And your knickers.'

'Only if I bend over.'

'You look ridiculous.'

'Does that matter?'

'Can you even see under all that mascara?'

I tilted my head back and said defiantly, 'Yes.'

He pinched the bridge of his nose. 'Do you have a leotard?'

'I could get one,' I said, surprised. 'Are you taking up ballet?'

'Put that on underneath everything, change those shoes for something you can actually run in, and you can do it.'

'Can you give me some hints on how to hussy?'

'No.'

'Or show me a provocative pose, perhaps?'

'No.'

'I want to look realistic.'

'No.'

'Well, what shall I do then?'

'You don't have to do anything. I won't be far away.'

'Oh – will you be going as my pimp?'

'No.'

'I should have a pimp.'

'No.'

'What sort of a working girl doesn't have a . . . ?'

He got slowly to his feet and that was the moment I decided it would be a good idea to shoot off and buy that leotard.

We began to make a bit of a name for ourselves. Working for the Time Police enabled us to open official bank accounts and access cash, and now that we were ensured a more or less regular income, life became a lot easier. We owed it all to Uncle Albert. These days, everything was heavily documented and without the cards and paperwork he'd left us – the citizen's IDs and the official authorisations – not only would we have failed to thrive, we would probably have died.

Between us, we thrashed out some work rules:

If one of us was detained or injured, then the other would immediately disappear. One of us must always be free to rescue the other.

Both of us had to agree to a job. 'Unanimous,' said Pennyroyal, 'not a majority vote,' although how we'd manage that with just two of us, he didn't say.

Decisions would be made jointly, but if we were actively on a job then he was the one in charge and I did as I was told. He was the one with the experience. I had to accept that or the whole thing was off. I agreed – it made sense. I could argue or discuss afterwards – indeed, I was encouraged to do so – but once we were active then he was the boss.

And, possibly, most importantly – no written records. Ever. We burned as we went. Pennyroyal went one better, somehow getting the AI to carry out an automatic memory wipe at the end of each job. Should the pod be taken, there would never be a record of our activities.

We developed a series of hand signals. Not the official ones used by the military, but our own – unknown and incomprehensible to anyone else.

For the first twelve months we lived in the pod. It wasn't pleasant and that led to the thrashing out of even more rules:

Strict privacy maintained at all times.

Neither walked into the pod unannounced. We always knocked.

The sleeping arrangements were as far apart as we could get them. Each of us was nearly two feet away from the other. We'd have had more space in a king-sized bed.

We each had a half-hour alone in the morning and another half hour at night.

If you got it out – you put it away. The floor space was to be kept clear.

A year of hard work and frantic saving later, together with what we'd brought with us, and we'd amassed enough for the security deposit on some proper accommodation. A second-floor flat in a hideous brick building about forty minutes from the

British Museum as the walkway went. Two bedrooms – well, one and a half bedrooms – a tiny bathroom, a living room with a low-quality basic entertainment wall, and a small kitchen. It wasn't pretty but the neighbourhood was respectable and it was warm and waterproof, which was good enough for us.

Plus – a big bonus – there was a scruffy patch of land at the rear which seemed to belong to our block of flats even though there was no direct access. Perfect for parking the pod.

Having taken every job we could get, we found that we had acquired a certain standing. Smallhope and Pennyroyal weren't showy or high profile. Of necessity we kept ourselves to ourselves, which led to a reputation for quiet competence and reliability. We weren't big shots. We also didn't promise anything we couldn't deliver, and for that reason we had a near hundred per cent success rate.

The Time Police started to call on us instead of the other way around. Once we were invited on a big job. I suspected we were just making up the numbers and we didn't expect to see any action, but there must have been a concealed door somewhere. The first thing we knew about it was when half a dozen or so illegals crashed out of the building, shooting as they came and running directly towards us.

This was the first time I'd actually seen blaster fire. I didn't have a blaster – just a normal handgun – and I made a mental note to raise this issue with Pennyroyal as soon as possible.

I did as those around me were doing – took cover and fired back. Slow and steady. Don't panic. I was surrounded by TPOs and Pennyroyal – I was quite safe.

Two illegals broke away and headed straight for me. Without thinking, I stepped aside, dropped to one knee and fired. Aim for the centre of the body. Nothing fancy. Stay calm. Breathe and fire.

I breathed and fired. I think I put down the one on the left. I don't know who got the other one.

Slowly, silence fell. I climbed stiffly to my feet. A giant TPO stood to my left, powering down his blaster. 'All right?'

I nodded.

'Your first?'

I nodded.

He dipped his chin. 'Good work,' and disappeared.

We did well out of that job, even though the Time Police weren't the greatest payers in the world. True, they always coughed up eventually, but sometimes we had to prod them a little.

We spread our money around. Every now and then I would realise a few assets and jump back to Meilin for her to deposit the results of my labours. I've no idea what arrangements Pennyroyal was making but I knew that we were doing nicely. Jumping to the future had been a good move for us.

Before long, we had the confidence and the reputation to look for additional work outside the Time Police. Pennyroyal came back to the flat one day, scratchpad in hand.

'Have a look at this. It's an invitation to tender,' he said. 'An outfit called Parrish Industries is looking for a firm of security consultants.'

'Parrish Industries? Never heard of them.'

'Well, they're not Portman Weber but they're getting there. Run by Raymond Parrish, who has lots of fingers in lots of pies. Won a couple of big military contracts last year and does the occasional job for the Time Police as well. Hard-nosed bastard. Gets what he wants.'

'And now he wants security consultants?'

'He does. Have a read. Tell me what you think.'

I read. At this stage I wasn't sure whether this was yet another teaching moment or whether he really did value my opinion. He got it anyway.

'First impression – it's a bit ambitious for us, surely. There'll be some big firms after this.'

'We can provide individual attention. Tailor our package to suit.'

I was thoughtful. 'It would have to be a stunning presentation, otherwise it'll just end up in someone's WPB.' I stared into space, ideas forming and reforming.

He made coffee. You couldn't get tea – well, you could – and we would one day – but we couldn't afford it in those days. So the poor man's drink it was.

'You have one hour,' he said, handing me a pad and pen. As I said, we don't do electronics. They leave too obvious a trail. Put a match to your paper and it's gone beyond recall. No clever-clogs IT genius will ever get it back. 'Organise your thoughts,' he continued. 'Let's see what we can come up with.'

I sipped and thought. And thought a bit more. In my own defence, I didn't think a tiny outfit like ours stood even the remotest chance, so I had a fun fifty minutes being outrageous and then handed it over. Pennyroyal gave me his in return, and we read companionably for a while. At the end of which he looked over at me. 'You are quite certifiable.'

'Very probably.'

'This is almost certain to get us killed.'

'I'm sure you'll be able to save us both.'

He flourished my paper. 'Not from this.'

'Don't be so modest. I have every confidence in your abilities. So we're going with my presentation then?'

He closed his eyes, which I took to mean 'yes'.

We downloaded the tender documentation and read it through a couple of times. Many times, actually. Pennyroyal formally registered our interest and we were given a twenty-minute slot at Parrish HQ the following week to present our bid. In front of Raymond Parrish himself. Apparently he was taking a personal interest.

I worked hard on our presentation. And then we rehearsed. Many, many times. Pennyroyal is very big on preparation. I took particular care over my clothes, buying a dark blue business suit. The very best quality I could afford. It wasn't particularly fashionable which meant it wouldn't age. Quiet elegance was what I was aiming for.

I put my hair up because it made me look older, applied a little make-up, and tried not to wish I'd come up with a more conventional scheme.

'All right?' said Pennyroyal.

I nodded.

'Know what you have to do?'

I nodded.

'You can move all right in that suit?'

I nodded.

'You've checked the catch on the briefcase?'

I nodded.

'Got everything you need?'

Remembering his previous instructions, I ran through everything in my head and nodded.

'OK then. Off you go. Good luck.'

Parrish Industries HQ was situated in St James's Square. A very good address. I took the public clipper and strolled through St James's Park, trying not to trip over the pigeons.

I didn't bother checking the lay of the land – the two of us had already spent hours and hours observing the building, the throughput, the staff, the surroundings, routes in, routes out. You name it, we'd observed it and discussed it and then observed it some more.

It was a very warm day. I took my time crossing the park, gazing around me. All the houses were tall and stone-fronted. Papa's club had been a couple of doors down – still was, as far as I could see, although I didn't mind betting its bar profits had plummeted.

A gleaming brass plate announced I'd arrived at Parrish Industries. I made sure to climb the steps slowly. They were wide and shallow but nothing looks more amateurish than arriving at a big meeting looking hot and flustered.

The outer doors were flung open but the inner glass doors stood firmly closed. I held a door open for one of those cycle couriers, which was a useful opportunity to have a quick look around without seeming to. Two receptionists sat behind a smart wooden desk, directing people to the appropriate floors. The entire ground floor was mainly open plan – light and spacious with high ceilings and tall windows. And cool. Very efficient air con. Crowds of people moved around, or conferred on long sofas, twirling data stacks in front of them. All was hustle and bustle.

I gave my name at the reception desk, was awarded a visitor's lanyard and politely asked to take a seat.

No wanding, I noted. It was possible there were more stringent security procedures on the upper floors. Where the important people hung out. Although I doubted it.

For something to do, I watched the courier's interactions at the reception desk. No one asked him for ID. All right, his logo was emblazoned all over his gear, his helmet and his messenger bag, but even so he should have been checked. No one asked him to remove his helmet, either. I shook my head. This place really needed us.

I was distracted by a smartly dressed young man asking me to follow him. I stood up, smoothed my jacket and picked up my briefcase. Slowly, slowly, don't rush. Make him wait for me.

I followed him to the lift. No card access required. I knew that Raymond Parrish lived on the top floor of the building – presumably the P on the control panel stood for Penthouse.

We stopped at the floor beneath P. The young man got out and a woman entered the lift. Taller even than me, dark and very nicely dressed. I'd have worn her cream suit in a heartbeat.

'Miss Smallhope?' she said.

The lift doors closed. Ah – she did have a card. The lift swooped smoothly upwards. She turned towards me. 'I am Lucinda Steel, assistant to Mr Parrish's PA.'

'How do you do,' I said and left it at that. The doors pinged open. I took a moment to adjust the fastening of my briefcase and followed her out.

'This way, please.'

The foyer was unmanned. They really should have some sort of presence here to monitor visitors' comings and goings. Cameras and so forth. And an armed receptionist, perhaps.

Raymond Parrish's office was one of those big corner affairs with pleasant views, very nicely appointed. A little too masculine for my taste – I'm not a big fan of dark brown leather – but it suited him.

He himself was a big man, quite broad across the shoulders, with dark hair only just beginning to turn silver. There was something about him. He had the air of a man accustomed to getting his own way, but there was something not quite right here. He was pale, his mouth compressed, and he looked very tired.

However, he was professional and polite. 'Miss Smallhope, thank you for coming today.'

'My pleasure.'

'Please sit down.'

I sat and slipped off my shoes. His desk was highly polished and wider than I expected but I was confident I could get across it. I was wearing trousers for a reason.

Actually, he was more than professional and polite. He was quite charming. 'I'm sure you won't be surprised to hear we've researched your company, and while your record is impressive, as far as it goes, I must admit to some concerns over the size of your organisation. I'm not sure you have quite the capacity required to . . .'

He stopped speaking as Ms Steel re-entered the office.

'I beg your pardon, sir, but a package has arrived for you, and it's marked "Time sensitive".'

I opened my briefcase.

She stopped as the courier appeared behind her in the doorway, saying over her shoulder, 'I asked you to wait outside.'

I was already moving, sliding over the desk to land with a bit of a thump in Mr Parrish's lap. Indelicate but the shortest route.

I used my left leg to push hard – his chair rolled backwards against the wall, and the next moment I had my forearm across his throat and my gun in his left eye.

At exactly the same moment, the courier's package let out a piercing whistle.

I'm sure Raymond Parrish would have activated his under-desk alarm but unfortunately he had me sitting on his lap and it was beyond his reach. And I'm sure Ms Steel would have initiated some kind of action except Pennyroyal had his arm around her throat and, using her as a shield, was easing himself back against the wall.

She went to kick back at him but he sidestepped her very neatly.

'Yes, that was good, Ms Steel,' he said seriously. 'But next time take a step to the side before initiating that manoeuvre. Your assailant will be expecting you to make exactly that move – as I did just now – but if you can shift to one side and he moves in the same direction then you'll connect with him. Should he move the other way, you'll find yourself with enough free space to hook your leg around his ankle and possibly bring him down. If you both go down, always try to land on top. Would you like to attempt that again?'

I felt Raymond Parrish relax ever so slightly.

I got off him, moved back around the desk, sat down in my chair and put my shoes on again, leaving the gun on his desk in front of me. Raymond Parrish breathed out, smoothed his jacket, and straightened the photo of a small boy that I'd knocked aside. Now for the enjoyable bit.

I made my voice clipped and businesslike. 'Mr Parrish, I regret to inform you you're dead. As is Ms Steel. The whistling package has exploded. Your headquarters have been destroyed. Loss of life and damage to property is extensive. Your business is seriously crippled for the foreseeable future.

'No one searched me or my case when I entered the building. The gun is ceramic and would have escaped your metal detectors, but the most basic manual search would have discovered it. Should have discovered it. No one checked my colleague here, the motorcycle courier. At no point was he asked to remove his helmet for the CCTV I'm sure you must have installed somewhere. My colleague had only to say the magic words *time-sensitive* and *personal delivery* and he was given access all the way up to your office, Mr Parrish. He should never have been allowed to penetrate so far into the building. A set of logo-laden cycle gear and a helmet do not necessarily constitute a legitimate courier. He certainly shouldn't have been left alone outside your office. I'm afraid you will need to bring in a specialist team to locate and neutralise the unknown number of surveillance devices he has been able to deposit in the very short time he has been in this building. Unescorted. You might argue that you have scores, possibly hundreds of deliveries every day, and cannot be expected to escort every single one of them. Page seven of our proposal addresses that very issue.

'You see, Mr Parrish, your security providers have assumed most threats will originate from organisations similar to your own and they've modelled your security accordingly. They have almost completely failed to consider other sources. Small, agile, easily adaptable, creatively thinking organisations, for example.' I paused and then qualified that remark. 'Very talented creatively thinking organisations.'

I put the gun in the briefcase and snapped it shut. 'My honest opinion, Mr Parrish – considering who and what you are, your security is inexcusably poor. I don't know the name of your current provider, but you need to have a serious word with them.'

I stood up and straightened my jacket. 'Now, as you have pointed out, our company is far too small to satisfy your requirements. We are, however, perfectly positioned to advise your security providers and carry out regular audits on your behalf to ensure that the needs of Parrish Industries are being met at all times.

'I have been in this room a little over seven minutes. Please take a moment to consider how these seven minutes have exposed some serious flaws in your security systems and to contemplate how many more might exist, of which you are completely unaware. And now, my colleague and I must be off.'

Pennyroyal had released Ms Steel and politely pulled forward a chair for her. She was so bemused she took it.

Raymond Parrish was on his feet. 'You're leaving?'

'Before you have us arrested.'

'You're right,' he said suddenly. 'Security here is poor. And even worse at my private residence. A while ago there was an incident. I've had to send my boy away . . .'

'I'm sorry to hear that,' I said crisply. 'Our proposal, details of our services and how we think we can best be of future use to you are all in here for your consideration.'

I took our proposal and details of the costings out of my briefcase and laid them on the desk in front of him, together with our rather snazzy business card. 'A pleasure to have met you today, Mr Parrish.'

Pennyroyal bowed, 'Ms Steel,' and we whisked ourselves

out of the room before they could pull themselves together and have us arrested.

The lift was still on this floor and the door was open – another mistake. You can't always prevent people getting in, but you can make it difficult for them to make their escape. And yes, we'd included that on our list of *Issues Mr Parrish Really Needs to Think About.*

Pennyroyal pressed the button and down we went. We moved apart as the lift neared the ground floor because we really had no idea what might be waiting for us there. I was certain Ms Steel would be organising an unpleasant reception.

The doors rolled back. Nothing. Just the usual busy foyer with people in and out, keeping appointments, delivering and picking up packages, all the usual stuff.

'You go first,' said Pennyroyal, so I did. Striding briskly towards the doors. Five yards, four, three . . .

'One moment, please.'

Shit. So near and yet so far.

Pennyroyal swept past me without a glance. Rule One – never be caught together.

I turned slowly, to give Pennyroyal time to get away. 'Yes?'

One of the receptionists was frowning at me. 'Sorry – your lanyard, please.'

'Oh, of course. Sorry.'

I handed it over.

'If you could just sign out, please.'

'Of course.'

According to the book, I'd been in the building less than twenty minutes. It seemed much longer.

They thanked me.

I thanked them.

And then, finally, I was on the right side of the glass doors, out into the hot sunshine, walking slowly down the steps and into the park where Pennyroyal was waiting.

16

Raymond Parrish took us on. Not completely and not full-time, but we were offered a role as part-time consultants. Troubleshooters, Pennyroyal said. Our job was to carry out unscheduled spot checks at all his properties and test their systems. Which we did with great enthusiasm. Pennyroyal was happy because Parrish Industries paid well. I was happy because causing trouble for other people is always enjoyable and now we were being paid for it. The work fitted in nicely around our bounty-hunting activities and the only problem we had now was space. Or rather the lack of it. Weapons, gear, personal possessions – after a while our little flat was bulging at the seams. You would not believe what I had to share my bedroom with. At one point there was a small 16th-century cannon. Don't ask.

After another six months' hard work, we rewarded ourselves with a small holiday and returned to our own time – which seemed unfamiliar after so long away. The weather was better but the smell of traffic fumes was awful.

Pennyroyal disappeared – a couple of promising two-year-olds, he said. Racehorses, I should make clear. He enjoyed a keen interest in the turf and was putting together a very small but very select string of racehorses stabled up at Middleham.

I stayed in London. Meilin came over on the Eurostar and we had dinner together at the St Pancras Renaissance. She shuffled a daunting number of papers in my direction but, according to the summary sheet on the top, things were going well. Very well indeed. I lost on every transaction, of course. Every time she deposited currency in my name, she took her commission, but she was fair, we both knew where we stood, we were useful to each other, and I had complete confidence in her.

She was intrigued by Pennyroyal, asking some very pertinent – and impertinent – questions about him.

I had to confess I had no idea of his marital status. 'I've never actually seen him show affection towards any member of the human race, up to and including me.'

'His sexual orientation?'

I frowned. 'Not sure he has one.'

'His personal habits, his tastes, his background?'

I shook my head.

'Even his real name?'

'Um . . .'

'And yet you entrust your life to this man?' she said. 'You know nothing of him. Is that wise?'

I agreed that it probably wasn't.

'And yet,' she said, looking at me sideways, 'he does have a certain . . .' She stopped.

'Certain what?'

'Attraction.'

I blinked at her, genuinely surprised. 'Does he?'

213

'Perhaps,' she said, much too casually, 'you have an interest there yourself.'

'No, I don't think so,' I said, grinning at her as I speared another chunk of deep-fried Camembert and dunking it in the cranberry sauce. 'The last time I saw his testicles, they were the size of beef tomatoes. Same sort of shape and colour as well.'

She choked on her wine.

'But I don't think it was permanent,' I said hastily, not wanting to spoil his chances. 'He'd been in a pretty bad fight.'

'Hm,' she said, dabbing her mouth on her napkin and changing the subject. 'But what about you, Millie? Surely you have . . . you know . . . someone . . .'

'Occasionally,' I said. I grinned. 'Just to keep my hand in. But not Pennyroyal,' I added quickly, in case she got the wrong idea.

'So there's no one special for you?'

I shook my head. 'Nope. Nor ever likely to be.'

The waiter came with the next course and the subject was dropped. When we'd finished our meal, Meilin pressed a letter into my hand. 'Could you deliver this for me?'

'Of course,' I said, tucking it away, and we said goodbye.

It was addressed to Pennyroyal. I did deliver it and, what's more, I heroically refrained from asking him about it afterwards. I'm pretty sure he contacted her – or vice versa – and several times he disappeared with the pod and came back looking like a cat who'd suddenly found himself living in his very own cream factory.

Despite my brave boast to Meilin, my own social life was somewhat barren. Well, non-existent, mostly. Normally this wasn't a problem, if only because between work and training, I was too

214

knackered to go clubbing until the small hours. I didn't really have the energy for anything more strenuous than the occasional margarita in the Pear Tree on the corner.

And then I met Kester di Maggio.

We'd been assigned a couple of big jobs from the Time Police, one of which turned out to have exciting repercussions. For me, anyway. Pennyroyal – slightly less so. We were involved in bringing down a really quite well-organised professional set-up dealing in black market historical artefacts – no guesses as to how they acquired those. That sort of thing can be very lucrative. There's a massive market for one of Good Queen Bess's fans or a Leonardo sketch and you'd be amazed at the prices they can fetch.

Because this was such a big job, we were working in conjunction with other recovery agents, one of whom I only met when it was all nearly over. Kester di Maggio.

Pennyroyal and I had spent a couple of weeks on this job, keeping our targets under surveillance, identifying the key people and discovering the location of their pods and their warehouse. Then we all moved in simultaneously.

The operation was a success and you wouldn't believe the stuff these people had stashed away. Two warehouses near Regent's Canal – which was how they got the stuff in and out – stuffed to the rafters with what normal people would call treasure and the Time Police would refer to as 'evidence'. If you ever wondered what became of Drake's Drum, I can tell you where it ended up. The whole place was an Aladdin's cave of wonder. And there was the occasional very good fake cleverly mixed in with the real deal. A brilliantly forged Round Table, for instance. Well, six of them, actually, all laid out along one wall. Someone had obviously done their historical research and there was just enough detail for maximum authenticity – ancient wood, the faint traces of different coloured paint denoting each knight's name. Just the occasional dim outline of a few letters. The 'thur' in Arthur. The 'ex' in Rex. The 'vere' in Bedivere and so on. They were really well done. I said to Pennyroyal afterwards – when he was speaking to me again – that we should make an effort to discover who had created them because he or she produced quality work which might come in useful to us in the future.

Anyway, we secured the premises, the pods and most of their key people all in one go. And when everyone had been rounded up and disarmed and things had calmed down a little, I found myself face to face with fellow bounty hunter Kester di Maggio.

The attraction was mutual. He was about the same age as Pennyroyal and big, blond and bumptious. I've always had a weakness for big men and he was very, very big. If you get my drift.

I shut down my blaster – he shut down his – and we smiled at each other for a while. And then for a while longer.

'I'll just secure the prisoners all by myself, shall I?' said Pennyroyal. 'You know – actually complete the job.'

'Mm,' I said.

'Kester,' said Kester, smiling at me some more.

'Amelia.'

Someone behind me sighed very loudly.

'Pleased to meet you,' said Kester.

'Likewise.'

'I didn't know Pennyroyal had an assistant.'

'He doesn't,' I said, scowling, and very keen to correct this erroneous assumption. 'But I do.'

216

'I seem to have used all my zip-ties,' said Pennyroyal, behind me. 'Perhaps that's because I'm doing everything. By myself.'

Without taking my eyes off Kester, I pulled out half a dozen ties and held them out. 'Here.'

There followed the sounds of prisoners being restrained rather more vigorously than was probably absolutely necessary.

'All finished here. Time to go. Now.'

'So,' said Kester, adopting a somewhat overdramatic pose and shaking back his blond tresses. 'You doing anything tonight?' He smiled slowly. 'Amelia.'

Pennyroyal coughed. 'Did I say NOW?'

Even I wasn't desperate enough to say I was free at such short notice. I grinned up at Kester. 'Yes, sorry, I am. Doing something tonight, I mean.'

'Shame,' he said. 'But hardly surprising. What about tomorrow night?'

'No,' said Pennyroyal pointedly.

'Not asking you,' Kester said shortly.

'She's busy,' said Pennyroyal. 'We've got weapons inventory, an hour's self-defence practice, followed by . . .'

'I'm free,' I said. I gave it a heartbeat and then said, 'What exactly did you have in mind?'

Pennyroyal slung someone into our pod. There was a faint cry of pain.

'Oh,' said Kester, still grinning that grin. 'Just a quiet dinner in a little place where they know me.'

One of the prisoners was protesting that his ties were too tight.

'And then perhaps we could look in at that new club down by the river.'

217

I'd never been to a nightclub, though I certainly wouldn't be telling anyone that. 'Sounds great.'

'. . . Hands have gone numb . . .'

Pennyroyal was still droning on. 'Followed by an hour's practice at the shooting range and a weapons familiarisation session followed by . . .'

'. . . Pins and needles . . .'

'And then perhaps a little stroll along the embankment to look at the lights reflected in the river.' Kester looked down at me. 'So pretty.'

I smiled back. 'That sounds absolutely perfect.'

'. . . restocking the pod and doing the laundry,' finished Pennyroyal, who had his own ideas about how to show a girl a good time.

We both ignored him. 'Pick you up at seven,' said Kester. 'We'll eat early, if you like. Beat the rush.'

'Good idea.'

'See you then.'

'Looking forward to it.'

He tossed back his long blond hair yet again.

'. . . Lost all feeling in my hands . . .'

Kester disappeared. I watched him go and then turned to Pennyroyal, noting, to my surprise, that he appeared to have secured our prisoners and loaded them all into the pod without me.

'You're welcome,' he said when I mentioned this. 'No problem at all. Happy to assist you with your love life at any time.'

I was quite surprised. 'Really? You don't *look* that happy.'

'Just get in the pod.'

'. . . Fingers gone blue . . .'

*   *   *

218

'You're not going out looking like that,' said Pennyroyal the next night as I emerged from my room.

'Like what?'

'Like that.'

I looked down at myself. 'What's the problem?'

'If you must go out with that useless pretty boy, why don't you wear the suit you bought for the Raymond Parrish interview?'

'You mean the one where I'm encased from chin to ankle in tailored navy-blue wool?'

He grunted.

For the record, I was wearing a sparkly halter top, velvet jeans and strappy sandals. Nuns have worn less. Ask Cousin Helen.

The intercom buzzed. 'Amelia, it's Kester. You coming down?'

'No, she's not,' said Pennyroyal, shouldering me aside before I could speak. 'You can come up. I want a word.' He turned to me. 'Back before midnight.'

'What?'

I didn't know whether I was horrified or mortified, or just plain pissed off with him. He was treating me like a child. We'd just completed one of our biggest jobs ever and I was in the mood to celebrate.

I grabbed my bag and opened the door to Kester. 'I'll be back when I feel like it. Don't wait up.'

'Eh?' said Kester, puzzled. On the other hand, I hadn't selected him for his brains.

Pennyroyal was determined to ruin my life. 'Take a jacket.'

'It's August. It's a million degrees out there,' I said.

'Nevertheless . . .'

Kester shook his head. 'You might be red-hot on the bounty-hunting front, mate, but you're really crap at dealing with women.'

Pennyroyal folded his arms. 'Don't make me come looking for you tomorrow.'

Kester was openly mocking. 'Yeah – like you could find *me*.'

They were in each other's faces now. I was completely forgotten. It was dawning on me that bounty hunters were really crap boyfriend material.

'I'm off,' I said, slinging my bag over my shoulder. 'When you've both finished your cock-measuring contest, I'll be downstairs and heading for the nearest pub. Where, with luck, I'll be able to pick up a proper man.'

'Saved by your partner,' said Kester to Pennyroyal, grinning as he backed out of the door. 'Luckily for you.'

The only downside to the evening was that Pennyroyal's words had obviously had some effect. Kester was the perfect gentleman throughout. We walked back along the Embankment – and he was right, it was very pretty – sharing crack-of-dawn fish and chips.

Pennyroyal was waiting up. Obviously. Arms folded and with the expression of one impatiently awaiting the opportunity to administer a drugs test.

'You know,' I said, tossing my bag on to the sofa, 'you're not giving me a very good impression of the sort of things you get up to on a date.'

'You don't know what he's like.'

'Kester?' I kicked off my sandals. 'Of course I do. He's an arsehole. Why would you think I didn't know that?'

'And yet you went out with him.'

'Why wouldn't I? I had a great night. We did the chicken dance at the Blue Moon. It was hilarious. You should try a social life sometimes.'

'I go out with friends,' he said huffily.

I couldn't resist. 'Really? Are these friends actually visible to anyone else?'

He scowled massively and, if anything, increased the fold-ingness of his arms.

'Look,' I said, sitting down beside him. 'I know that for you a good night is sitting down with a weapons manual followed by two hours of abdominal crunches and a quarter inch of whisky, and that's fine. Most of the time I'll be bang alongside you. But occasionally it's nice to go out for a meal and a dance and a couple of drinks and stuff yourself on completely unnecessary fish and chips on the way home.'

I toyed with the idea of mentioning a bit of a snog in the doorway downstairs as well and decided that probably wouldn't be helpful at this exact moment.

He huffed his huffing noise. I had no idea what that was supposed to convey. 'I suppose we *could* do something occasionally.'

'That would be great,' I said. 'I'd really like that.'

'I don't dance,' he said hastily, obviously feeling the need to manage expectations.

'I think that's very wise,' I said, patting his arm and wondering how much the world would pay to see Pennyroyal do the chicken dance. 'Anyway, I'm off to bed. Tomorrow is another day.'

*   *   *

221

I couldn't deny that the Pennyroyal and Smallhope combo had developed something of a rep by now. And the need for bigger premises was becoming urgent. I took advantage of one of Pennyroyal's infrequent absences to look for somewhere better to live. Not seriously, just browsing, so to speak, but as often happens when you're just browsing, I stumbled across what we were looking for almost immediately.

Home Farm appealed to me on every level. The property was plenty big enough, with a farmyard and outbuildings and two hundred acres. But there were other, more important, issues. Security, for example. If the worst came to the worst – would it be easily defendable? Nothing protects you from a direct missile attack, of course, but I didn't think we'd made that many enemies. We would later, but not then.

I sat back to have a drink and a think. The price was more than we could currently afford, and I could already hear Pennyroyal asking what the hell I thought we'd do with two hundred acres, but I'd cross that bridge when I came to it.

I took the hyperloop and then hired a private car, using a combination of legitimate and not quite so legitimate paperwork. The Time Police paperwork, obviously, was genuine, but my permit to drive was actually obtained from the man in the corner shop's wife's brother, who produced very good work indeed. Yes, I could have sat the test in this time, but since I hadn't actually sat the test in my own time – Papa had taught me to drive and that was good enough for both of us – I didn't really see the point.

And these days there were all sorts of rules banging on about how many hours people can legally drive each day, and it was expensive to purchase extra mileage – and it's so irritating when your car grinds to a halt because you've exceeded your daily limit. I really couldn't be bothered with all that, so I'd taken the easy way out and obtained an 'unlimited mileage licence' from Hakan's brother-in-law. And I didn't even have to pay for it because Hakan's daughter was having some difficulties with an ex-boyfriend, so I'd popped round to have a quick word, which had solved the problem completely and Hakan had been appropriately grateful.

The property was very remote – which was its main attraction. It was a long journey and the rain was bucketing down for most of it, but everything was worth it when I got there because the place was perfect.

I pulled up at a pair of gates that looked as if they hadn't been closed for a long time, but that could be fixed. A rough hoggin drive led to a redbrick building, very long and low, with eight or nine windows and a front door on the ground floor and eleven windows upstairs. Most of the building was covered in that creeper that turns red in autumn. Late seventeenth or early eighteenth century, I guessed. Almost certainly listed. I wasn't sure whether that was good or bad.

The drive curved up past a very neglected lawn. Pennyroyal would sort that out. He does like things to be neat and tidy. About two-thirds of the way along the building was a deep archway – that would lead through to the farmyard behind. A vulnerability, but a pair of sturdy crash-proof gates and a couple of automatically operated stingers would take care of any attempted unauthorised access.

I looked around. Not another building in sight anywhere. There were hills, fields of crops, trees, grazing livestock and I could hear a small stream tinkling somewhere. This would do us very nicely indeed.

I left the car parked on the verge and walked slowly up the drive. I could faintly hear voices, and some sort of agricultural machinery not too far away, but otherwise just the patter of rain.

I met the agent – a young sapling named Jason – who took me into the house. Through the back door, obviously. I stood looking about me. A long, fairly narrow passageway stretched in both directions – half-open doors on one side, windows on the other.

To me, the place was perfect. Old-fashioned, of course, in need of some modernisation, and there was a slight smell of damp, but the windows were too small to climb through and the walls nearly twelve inches thick in places. A single wooden staircase twisted up through the middle of the house – the only access to the floor above – and upstairs the layout mirrored that of downstairs. Extensive attics, I was told.

The Faraday family still occupied the building, but being farmers, presumably were all out doing something agricultural. Jason and I went out into the farmyard. Jason had thought to bring a spare umbrella – he deserved the sale.

I'm no stranger to farms and farmers – we had a good half-dozen on the estate rent roll and I'd often accompanied Papa when he went to visit. The yard was tidy but the signs were all there. Lack of cash. Make do and mend. Old-fashioned equipment. I declined the invitation to inspect sties and stables but I did want a look at the big barn which didn't stand that far from the back door. We could extend the farmhouse outwards, which would give us access from the house into the barn without ever having to go outside. Very useful to someone looking for a safe place for their pod. There was plenty of room inside the barn, power was already laid on – although we'd need more – the roof looked sound and the floor in good condition. Yes, it was stuffed full of fodder and equipment but that needn't be a problem. I walked back out into the yard again and stood for a while in the soft rain, looking around and thinking. It was more than just liking the place. It called to me.

Jason had the sense to shut up.

I shook my head at his invitation to inspect a few fields – I wasn't interested in the land – and asked if it would be possible to meet Mr Faraday, or some member of the family, at least.

Jason disappeared into a building and I waited, listening to the rain patter down on my umbrella. I'd had an idea, but if the Faradays wouldn't play ball then there was no point taking it to Pennyroyal.

I liked Mr Faraday immediately. Farming was in his blood. I reckoned if he stood still for long enough – not that there was any chance of that – somehow he would be absorbed back into the land. His brick-red face was almost exactly the same colour as the soil. He offered a paw with no apologies for its grubbiness and we shook hands.

At his invitation, we went inside, sat in the kitchen and I put my proposal to him.

I started by enquiring why he was selling. A reasonable enough question from a prospective purchaser. This simple enquiry unleashed a torrent of information. The bloody government, the idiots at DEFRA, supermarket buyers, rules and regulations, the increasing costs of everything and the impossibility of making farming pay – let alone turn a profit – were all paraded for my inspection. I said nothing, letting him get it all off his chest and waiting until he ran down. It was sad, he said, because he'd wanted to leave the farm to his children – the farm had been in his family for generations, etc.

'Mr Faraday,' I said, 'I might have a proposition for you. In fact, I have an idea which could benefit both of us.'

I outlined my idea, and after I'd finished speaking, the kitchen was very quiet. I noticed again the smell of damp.

'Obviously I must talk to my partner,' I said, 'who will need to come and view the property for himself before we make any decisions, and I expect you'd like to discuss it among yourselves as well. Can you anticipate any problems with the proposed arrangement?'

Mr Faraday, looking somewhat shellshocked, shook his head. He walked with me to my car. We shook hands again. Now all I had to do was talk to Pennyroyal.

On his return, I poured him a beer, warned him it was a bribe, spread the details of the property in front of him and took myself off to my room with a book. I certainly wasn't going to queer my pitch by rushing him.

Thirty minutes later there was a tap at the door.

I called him to come in and he sat on the end of the bed. He'd brought the details with him which I considered to be a good sign.

'The building's OK,' he said. 'Ideal, in fact, but what the hell would we do with two hundred acres?'

'Nothing,' I said, and told him of my plan.

He listened in silence then said, 'If they don't agree . . .'

'If they don't agree then we look elsewhere, but I think they will. It's the perfect answer to their difficulties and Home Farm is perfect for us. Extending the barn to cover the back door leaves us with only one defendable front door. Park the pod in the barn and we can easily get to it in an emergency without ever going outside. There's electricity in the barn, I checked. And water. We can install gates in the archway. There's no clear access through the farmyard. There's a good kitchen in the farmhouse with plenty of storage. And cellars for gun cabinets and things. One or two are secure enough should we need to stash anyone there overnight. It's long enough for us to have our own private quarters at each end. I'll take the archway end and you can have the other, and even then there's still more than enough space for offices, equipment storage, spare bedrooms and the like.'

'You've given this a lot of thought,' he said, flipping through the details again.

I had.

'How did you leave it?'

'I told Mr Faraday I had a partner to consult. He's talking to his family about their end of the deal.'

'So nothing definite?'

'Not without you seeing it first.'

'And if I don't like it?'

'Then there's no more to be said.'

'Really,' he said suspiciously. 'You'd let it go? Without any arguments?'

'Of course. It's no good if you're not happy, and living with a grumpy Pennyroyal is no fun, trust me. I had enough of that with my father. Stamping about, massive sighing, hard looks, grunting, slamming doors . . .'

He heaved a massive sigh, gave me a hard look, stamped to the door, paused, and shut the door very quietly.

We went two days later. By hyperloop again, enjoying a sumptuous lunch on the way. Although Pennyroyal was heavily critical of the sauce – lumpy, apparently. He did, however, refrain from sending the whole meal back and executing the catering crew.

The hired car was waiting for us at the station. I drove. Beside me, Pennyroyal twitched. He doesn't like being driven.

We cruised through the rather pleasant countryside. At one point I had to brake hard to avoid chickens. Pennyroyal drew a sharp breath. 'You're driving far too fast. How did you ever pass your test?'

'There's a test?'

There was a short silence during which, presumably, he checked for the location of the emergency exits.

'You never took your driving test?'

'Papa said I didn't have to.'

'Well, that I can believe, but his reasoning was . . . ?'

'Because I only ever drove through the park – private land – or to the village – most of which we owned.'

'I think I already know the answer to this, but did he have one?'

'One what?'

'Driving licence.'

'There's a driving licence?'

He sighed.

I let another mile roll by and then said, 'Do *you* have a licence?'

The silence was much longer this time.

He folded his arms. 'You took that last bend much too fast.'

Ned Faraday was waiting for us in the yard. I appreciated he hadn't made any attempt to smarten himself up. Although he had washed his hands and the kettle was singing on the range. A good sign, I thought.

I introduced him to Pennyroyal and he showed us round personally this time. Then we sat at the kitchen table and I ran over my plan again.

'I know we talked of this before, and I've discussed this with my partner as well, but I just want to make sure we're all on the same page.'

I sipped my coffee and then put down the cup. 'My proposal, Mr Faraday, is that we buy the farmhouse to live in, together with the barn for storage. We're not farmers and we have no interest in the land. You say you're selling up because the farm isn't viable any longer. My partner and I are willing to pay top whack for the building and renovate it to our requirements, but leave you the farm itself – land, outbuildings, stock, the lot. I'm hoping the injection of cash from the sale of the building will enable you to finance the modernisation you need to carry out. We're both from landowning families, Mr Faraday. I know you don't want to part with your farm. It's been in your family for generations. It's more than your income – it's your heart – so we take the house and you keep the farm. And if or when the time comes for us to move on – you'd be guaranteed first refusal at a fair price. Can you confirm that is your understanding of the deal?'

'Aye. It is.'

'And what are your thoughts?'

'I've discussed it with the family – all of them. The missus and the two kids.'

'How did they feel about it?'

'Missus were a bit down. I reckon she thought she were

leaving the life behind.' He sighed. 'The last few years haven't been easy. She were looking forward to something with less mud and hard work.'

'You have other properties on your land,' I said. 'Convert one of those into a nice place with a modern kitchen and bathroom and she might come round.'

He grinned. 'That were my thought and all.'

We'd finished our coffee. There was no point in hanging around. I stood up. 'Well, you've had our offer, Mr Faraday. Please take some time to think about it. You can contact us through the agent.'

He nodded and we shook hands.

'What do you think?' I said to Pennyroyal as we made our way back to London.

'He'll do it,' he said. 'It's a good deal for him. You were right about him not wanting to sell. He can use our money to begin to pull the farm together. It won't be enough for a complete modernisation but it will start to bring him in more cash, which he can then use to raise a proper loan. He's unlikely to get a better offer. Yeah – I reckon he'll do it.'

'It's a good deal for us, too. Our flat is much too small and we're established now. We don't need to be in London any longer. And it's secure. In fact, Home Farm could be a little fortress.'

'We should keep the flat.'

'Good thought. We can use it for storage or even a bolthole if necessary.'

'Mm,' he said, and I shut up because I knew I'd got my own way.

17

HOME FARM
The Future

The sale went through without a hitch. The Time Police had been very happy with us over the Drake's Drum thing and Pennyroyal had taken advantage of their rare approval to up our rate a little – well, quite a lot, actually – and we were able to follow up that success by breaking up one of those English National Liberation Army cells who were plotting something ridiculous to do with Richard the Lionheart.

ENLA are a bunch of shaven-headed numpties whose stated mission is *England for the English*. When pressed to define *English*, they're slightly less assertive and tend to lose themselves in a tangle of incoherent maunderings and dribbling, accompanied by gestures they fondly imagine give them a quasi-military background.

They tend to be male because most of them hold strong views on the position of women in the world. Obviously, a few of them do have girlfriends who are actually real – or don't have to be inflated every night – but most of them enjoy a loving

231

relationship with their right hand. Frankly, if you wired the whole bunch together – and Pennyroyal and I might just do that one day when we're bored – they couldn't power a light bulb.

Anyway, we were definitely moving up the league and our rates reflected that fact. Which was just as well. The purchase of Home Farm took the bulk of the company money we'd been putting aside, and even then we had to top it up with contributions from our own private accounts. It left us a trifle short on the financial side, but six months' hard work would take care of that.

Our connection with Parrish Industries had enabled Penny-royal to assemble a bunch of men he referred to as 'builders', who put together one or two little security bits and pieces for us at Home Farm and then replastered over everything and slapped up a couple of coats of paint. Oh – and they modernised the kitchen because both of us agreed that was the most important room in the house.

I'd lived with Pennyroyal for some years now – at the house in Walthamstow, the pod in Northumberland, our poky flat in Bloomsbury, and now at Home Farm – and during all that time I'd never ceased to wonder at his need to impose order on himself and his surroundings. And, to some extent – me. For someone who brought chaos and catastrophe to anyone who crossed him, everything in his own world was always neat and tidy. I don't mean he rushed around washing plates as soon as they were used, or cleaned the kitchen floor three times a day – I mean that somehow, quite unobtrusively, without fuss or bother, everything was always in its place and ready for use.

I watched him personally supervise the kitchen alterations,

stating his requirements clearly and concisely. The implication that noncompliance was not an option was never spoken but somehow clearly understood.

After the work was completed, he placed his cooking implements in the spaces allocated. He arranged the contents of his cupboards logically. He paced out the triangle between sink, cooker and fridge – because apparently that's important. He folded napkins and tea towels neatly and precisely, stored candles, batteries and torches where they could be easily accessed, arranged his storage jars and spices alphabetically, and generally brought order and beauty to his kitchen kingdom.

From there, he turned his attention to the outside. The yard was not his to command, but he had the hayfield that was our front lawn brought under control and he himself attended to cutting out the dead and diseased wood from the willows bordering the stream. It was a huge improvement. You could almost hear the landscape sigh with relief.

I suppose it's what he does – wherever or whenever we are, Pennyroyal imposes himself on his surroundings. Yes – it's a control thing.

As well as the ones down in the cellars, he installed two additional gun cabinets in his own quarters, because, he said, he liked to have a few weapons to hand.

'Really?' I said. 'I thought you just liked to cuddle them in your sleep.'

He really does have a very nice line in expressionless stares that somehow say a lot.

The rest of it – our quarters, the office, spare bedrooms and so forth – was done bit by bit, so the whole renovation took some time to complete. Especially as we were working throughout.

We had to. Like every property renovation on the planet, we ran well over budget.

And there were arguments, of course. Apparently men don't allocate the same importance to cushions as do women. I told Pennyroyal that his lack of cushion appreciation might be an explanation for the many social issues with which he was burdened, and he threatened to shoot me on the spot and burn them all. We compromised with me remaining unshot and him ignoring the cushions.

Once the builders had left, he prowled around the barn, armed with power tools and a determined expression, while I set up the pod. One of the advantages of working for the Time Police was that we were entitled to free pod maintenance, which saved us a packet. I suspect their thinking was to ensure any semi-official pods weren't going to blow up at any moment, taking a sizeable area and a large number of officers with them. It was easier and cheaper in the long run for them to fund regular servicing for their agents' pods. And it was something we didn't have to worry about.

Unasked, the Time Police mechs had installed seats, which made jumping a great deal more comfortable. And they'd upgraded the camo device and fitted a new fascia to the console. In fact, the whole pod looked a great deal less Heath Robinson than it used to. Fewer exposed wires hung from the ceiling. It was no longer necessary to thump the console in a certain place in order to activate the proximity alert. And the rattle had been dealt with, which sounds quite minor but apparently pods should be soundless. Any rattle anywhere is bad news. The mech said we'd dodged a bullet there, but since we dodged at least one bullet every time we got up in the morning, we didn't take a lot of notice. And they'd hung a pine air-freshener from the ceiling. I thought it was a big improvement but Pennyroyal said they were just taking the piss and threw it away.

He installed a row of metal lockers in the barn (we had rat issues) and I packed away rations, clothing and equipment – all on hand and ready to be grabbed in the event of an emergency.

I have no idea what Pennyroyal did to his own rooms at the other end of the building, but I ended up with a very pleasant sitting room, bedroom and bathroom.

Because I'd lived most of my life among the faded elegance of Starlings, I thought I'd have something a little more modern now. And comfortable. I wanted somewhere to relax. Some of the days I had at work required massive winding-down afterwards.

Creamy white walls set off some nice art I'd acquired along the way. The plain wooden floors showed off one or two Turkish rugs. I'd selected similar but not identical fabrics for the curtains and sofa because I really don't like matchy-matchy. It was only after the 'decorators' had departed that I realised that although I'd called it jade, the main colour scheme was actually peacock blue. Obviously you can take the girl out of Starlings but not Starlings out of the girl.

Two shallow steps led to the bedroom, which I kept simple and quiet, but the bathroom was the last word in opulent luxury. Especially the wallpaper. Pink and gold flamingos strutted their stuff around jade foliage and turquoise pools. Gold taps – not real gold, sadly – and huge, fluffy pink towels completed the look. I fully intended to spend every non-working moment in there.

Pennyroyal, I suspected, slept in a coffin.

*   *   *

Six hard-working months later, we were just about done. Our HQ, as I said to Pennyroyal, who simply shook his head and went off to fetch a bottle of wine and two glasses.

We arranged ourselves outside on the now neatly trimmed lawn. I'd found a rickety wooden table and three chairs. Spring had well and truly sprung and we were practically into summer, which was the best time of the year. In the future, the end of July, all of August, and the beginning of September tend to be tests of endurance if you're not fond of the heat. Out here, though, in the country, with the benefit of cooling breezes sighing through the willows and the sound of running water, everything was very pleasant, and two bad-ass bounty hunters sat in scruffy T-shirts and shorts with their feet up and a very well-deserved bottle of wine between them.

Well, obviously, one bottle turned into two. Which might have been a bit of a mistake. Afternoon turned to evening. The Faradays called goodnight as they left, locking the archway gates behind them, racing down the drive on their quadbikes, and then it was just us, a couple of persistent insects, the warm, velvety dusk and the slowly emerging stars.

'This is nice,' I said, stretching out my legs.

'Mm.'

'Back to work on Monday.'

'A couple of days yet.'

'Any plans for your time off?'

He shook his head. 'Nothing involving power tools, anyway.'

'We've done it, though.'

He turned his head to survey our new home. 'We have, haven't we?'

'And it's legitimately ours.'

He nodded.

'Did you ever think . . . ?'

'What?'

'When you tried to steal my diamonds . . .'

'I didn't try,' he said, quite offended. 'I *did* steal your diamonds.'

'And then gave them back.'

'Yeah. Don't tell people that. Bad for my image.'

'OK. Did you ever think though . . . ? I mean, I remember that time at Starlings when I bumped into you outside Papa's study, and if this was a romantic novel, I'd have had some sort of premonition and spent the next couple of chapters thinking about you non-stop.'

'You mean you didn't?'

'Never gave you a thought.'

'Typical.'

'Not until you turned up in Caroline's dressing room. Had you noticed *me*? At all?'

'Course not,' he said, staring off into the darkness. 'Those endless legs and that great mane of red hair – why on earth would I ever have noticed you?'

'You make me sound like a horse.'

'I like horses,' he said, apparently genuinely surprised I might take issue with his comment.

I snorted, which, now I come to think of it, didn't help my case. 'Do you compare all the women you know to horses? Asking for a friend.'

'Only the ones I like,' he said, suddenly serious.

I couldn't think of anything to say. All at once the night was very warm. Very dark. Very quiet. A cool breeze sprang up and every square inch of my skin was goosebumps.

I looked at him over the table. He was looking at me. I could see the gleam of his eyes.

My bare feet were resting on the chair between us, only inches away from his hand. He had only to lift his hand to touch my ankle. We'd been living and working together for some time now. He'd seen me in my underwear. I'd seen him naked. Handled his body when he was hurt . . . But we'd always been very careful of each other's privacy. Not in all our time together had I ever thought about . . . well, anything . . . because . . .

The breeze blew again, bringing with it the scent of fresh-cut grass. The Faradays had been bringing in the hay. Behind the willows, out of sight, the stream gurgled in the night.

Pennyroyal was still looking at me. He hadn't moved an inch. I suddenly realised this was my call. Why, I don't know. He wasn't chivalrous. Or sensitive. Or kind – well, there had been the birthday muffin, but he certainly wasn't kind to other people. And that was OK, because neither was I. It was why our partnership worked.

We were on the very brink of . . . something.

And then – almost a whisper on the wind. Faint but unmistakeable. The harsh call of a peacock far away. The hair rose on the back of my neck.

I finished my wine and stood up. 'I think I'll turn in.'

'Good idea,' he said, topping up his own glass. 'Goodnight, my lady.'

I was cursing myself all the way back to my brand-new bedroom, but as events turned out, I'd done exactly the right thing.

* * *

After that moment – about which neither of us ever spoke – there was nothing to hold us.

The Time Wars had made us both a very great deal of money. One-third of our profits still went back into the business and we split what was left. Pennyroyal had his horses while I gave most of my remaining share to Meilin to launder into my accounts. I don't know why I was squirrelling it all away – I certainly didn't have any premonitions that I might need it one day. It was just what I did.

We weren't the only ones in the game, of course. There were other teams out there. The Hussain sisters – with whom we had very little to do. Their reputation was not the best. They'd turn on anyone for money. Friend, foe, absolutely anyone at all. Then there was the Key Group, who ran international teams of well-trained, efficient bounty hunters with whom it was a pleasure to work occasionally. And Femke de Vries, who always worked alone. Kester di Maggio danced in and out of my life just enough for us to engage in a little highly enjoyable but completely meaningless sex. Pennyroyal disliked him intensely – I think on the principle that no one should be that good-looking or that irritating. I could practically hear his trigger finger twitch every time he clapped eyes on him.

But we were solid. We were established. We were quick, quiet and discreet and we had a reputation for delivering.

And then, one day, something very strange happened. It was one of the very few occasions when we didn't have any other choice than to do as we were told.

Pennyroyal, glass of whisky at his elbow, was doing the accounts. He was sitting at the kitchen table, the ledger open in front of him. We always try to avoid leaving an electronic trail. A ledger, however hefty, can easily be incinerated with a blaster should the occasion ever warrant it.

It was a rare, peaceful evening at Home Farm. The kitchen was warm and comfortable. I'd drawn the curtains against a rainy night and was curled up by the range reading, with a glass of wine nearby.

Pennyroyal sighed heavily, closed the ledger and drained his glass.

I glanced over. 'Problem?'

'Buggers haven't paid it again. Invoice 34/B/4007.'

'Still?' Invoice 34/B/4007 was a regular thorn in his side. 'What's the problem? We've got the signatures, there's no queries, no irregularities – they've paid everything since then. What's going on with them?'

He shrugged. 'I fired off a stern reminder yesterday. In fact . . .' He checked his scratchpad. 'A response. An appointment has been set up. Tomorrow 1100 hours.' He read further. 'With you.'

'With me? Do they think I'll make it easier for them to wriggle out of paying?' I frowned. 'Big mistake, if so.'

'Agreed,' he said, and spent a few moments in deep thought. 'I might hang around outside. Just in case.'

I nodded. Always keep your big-hitter in reserve.

I made sure I was through TPHQ doors at 1100 hours sharp. Punctuality is important. The atrium was chaos, as usual. Half the people here had been grassed up and the other half were doing the grassing. There were struggles, protests, shouting and general mayhem.

I reported to one of the Time Police officers at the front

240

desk and as I did so, an officer I didn't know peeled away from another group and approached me.

'I've told you before,' he said before I'd even had a chance to say good morning. God knows the Time Police have no social skills, but this was just plain rude. 'You know as well as I do that there's no chance of payment without the appropriate documentation.'

About to refute this with well-justified indignation, I paused. The documentation was complete. Neither Pennyroyal nor I made mistakes with our paperwork and the docket had been signed off – by the Time Police themselves – some time ago. They simply hadn't followed through with payment. Where was this going?

'I beg to differ,' I said, which he could take any way he pleased.

There was a short pause. I could see other officers watching us from a distance.

'Look,' he said. 'I'm not denying you've done good work in the past – and I look forward to more of the same from you in the future . . .'

'Not if you're going to renege on your legitimate debts,' I said evenly, watching his face, because something was going on here and I didn't know what.

He raised his voice over a couple of men nearby who seemed quite determined not to be taken into custody. 'This is ridiculous. I can't hear myself think here. Come up to my office.'

Well, that was something new and different. The atrium and the series of rooms behind it at TPHQ were specifically set aside for gentle conversation with members of the public. Less gentle conversations were carried out below ground level in their cells.

241

In all the time we'd been dealing with the Time Police, not once had Pennyroyal ever got beyond the public area. The time and place of our meeting – here in the atrium – had, presumably, been this officer's choice. Why was he moving me out of public view? He was up to something. And by allowing myself to be removed, I could be doing something foolish, even by my standards. However, life is for taking chances. I smiled at him and indicated happy compliance.

We took the lift. Neither of us spoke. From there it was a short walk down a corridor. Don't ask me which one. Rumour has it that every single corridor at TPHQ is almost identical to the others. Presumably the Time Police hive mind can't handle variety.

Once we were in his office with the door closed behind us, he passed me the stamped docket. I hadn't even had time to sit down.

'All completed and paid in full. The money should be in your account before you even return home.'

I took the docket and perused it carefully. If nothing else, at least invoice 34/B/4007 was paid. Pennyroyal would be pleased. 'Then why am I here?'

'I have a job for you. Please sit down.'

I sat. 'This has been a somewhat elaborate scenario for just a job.'

'I consider it to be necessary. Listen carefully. I shall say this only once. Please make a note of these coordinates.'

He rattled them off.

I made a careful note. 'And?'

'You will find a house there. Two adults. One child. An infant. You will collect the infant and transport it to this location.'

He rattled off another set of coordinates.

I made another careful note.

'And what of the two adults?'

'They will not present a problem.'

Well, that was interesting. Did he mean they would happily hand over the infant? Or was there some other reason they wouldn't be a problem? Already dead, perhaps?

'And the reason for transporting this infant?'

'None of your business. Nor will this be a job for which you can invoice the Time Police. This is a private matter involving me alone. On successful completion, I will pay you three times your going rate.'

'What will happen to the infant?'

'Again – not your business.'

Oh no. No, no, no, no, no. I stood up. 'I regret to inform you this style of operation falls outside our remit. May I recommend the Hussain sisters?'

He sighed. 'The point of the operation is to remove the child from a hazardous environment and convey it to a place of greater safety.'

I maintained a polite but disbelieving silence.

'If it puts your mind at rest, had you not raised your objection, then I wouldn't have continued with this conversation.'

I increased the ratio of disbelief. 'Is there some reason you can't do this yourself?'

'Yes.'

I waited, but that appeared to be it.

Eventually, he said, 'You may be assured no harm will come to the child. You have my word on that.'

Oddly enough, I was inclined to believe him. Don't know why.

I sat back down again. 'So – to make sure I have understood you correctly: we jump to the first set of coordinates and retrieve an infant who will be handed to us.'

'That is correct.'

'We then jump to the second set of coordinates and hand over the infant?'

'Yes.'

'To whom?'

'To me. And only me.'

I have to say at this point every alarm bell I possessed was going into overdrive but I kept my voice businesslike.

'You are very specific on this point. Is anyone else likely to be there?'

'Where?'

'At either or both destinations.'

'Unknown, but it would do no harm to be prepared for the worst. Circumstances will dictate your actions – I leave everything to you – but there is to be no evidence of any kind. No trace of your presence and absolutely no record of your final destination. You will eliminate whatever is necessary to ensure that.'

I wondered if Pennyroyal and I fell under that heading. No witnesses.

I shifted in my seat. 'At this point, I should advise you that any attempt by anyone – anyone at all – to eliminate Pennyroyal and me at the same time will set in train a series of events that will ultimately lead to their undoing. Which is just a fancy way of saying if you screw us then we will screw you.'

He inclined his head. 'That is expected and understood. However – if anything goes wrong – not that I expect it to because your reputation is second to none – please be aware I will be unable to protect you. This operation is not only off the books – it never happened.'

'Understood.'

'Will you accept the job?'

At three times our already astronomically high hourly rate? Of course I would. 'Plus expenses.'

He didn't even blink. 'Agreed.'

I thought I'd probe a little. 'To whom shall I address any queries?'

'There will be no queries.'

He wasn't going to give his name, was he? No name badge on his uniform – although he wore Hunter flashes on his shoulders – and nothing on his office walls – if indeed this was his office, which I doubted.

I should perhaps say here that although I'd never met this man before that day, I did become aware of his identity later. Several of his identities, actually. As a Hunter, he had more than one. Never by word, look or deed did he intimate we'd already met. Pennyroyal and I always took our cue from him and did likewise.

Taking the plunge, I nodded. 'Then the job is accepted.'

'Do you have any questions?'

I tilted my head to one side. 'Why us?'

'You get the job done. You don't talk about it afterwards. You have nothing to prove.' He stopped and smiled mockingly. 'And, most importantly – you're not from this time, are you?'

My heart might have stopped but I knew my face wouldn't give anything away.

I said politely, 'I'm sorry?'

'Don't be. It's what makes you – both of you – perfect.'

'Because . . . ?'

He stared at me for a moment and then leaned over his desk. 'You asked why I couldn't do this job myself . . .'

He stopped.

I'd got it. He couldn't do this job himself because he couldn't jump to at least one set of those coordinates – the first set, I guessed. Because he was alive at the time. Pennyroyal and I could. Because we weren't. We hadn't yet arrived from the past. And he knew it. I was conscious of standing at the top of a very slippery slope.

'I see you've worked it out,' he said.

'Are you threatening us?'

He smiled coldly. 'I'm not so stupid. I wouldn't care to cross you and I certainly wouldn't cross your partner. Although I will if I have to.' The room was very quiet. 'You have only to carry out this job and I'll forget this conversation completely.'

'Will you?'

'You have my word. And you will remember you had already accepted the job before I made my threat known.'

'A job which we now have no choice other than to accept.'

He smiled again. 'True. However, let me reassure you – I have no interest in your origins. None at all. Other than your suitability for this job, I don't care whence you came. Let me down, however, and I'll revoke your licences, put you at the top of the red list and probably kill you myself. Do we understand each other?'

246

I stood up. 'I believe so. Good morning.'
'Good morning.'
I found my own way out.

18

We spent a long time preparing for this one. The first thing –
obviously – was to check out the coordinates. Even an idiot
doesn't jump blind. I'd been right about the first set. The second
set were several millennia ago. Pennyroyal shook his head but
said nothing.

We acquired maps and images where possible. We discussed
weapons and equipment. We ran through every possible scenario.
We rehearsed as far as we were able. And then we armoured up
and climbed into the pod.

I settled myself while Pennyroyal handled the jump. We
landed safely and took our time before venturing outside.

'Right time, right place,' I said, checking the read-outs.

'No other pods here that I can see,' reported Pennyroyal,
consulting a very sophisticated signature reader he had acquired
after it fell off the back of someone else's pod. 'What's the
weather doing?'

'Cold. Clear. Dry.' I picked up my gun. 'Well, given we won't
be paid until we hand over the sprog – shall we get a wiggle on?'

'The time is 0350 hours,' he said, setting his watch. 'Dawn
in just under three hours.'

'Should be long enough for us to bag a baby. Let's go.'

We opened the pod door to a cold night. The sky sparkled with stars. I knew we were in the depths of the countryside, and I knew where and when. And I knew there was an infant somewhere in the vicinity. Other than that . . .

Somewhere far away a fox barked. The sound carried clearly in the crisp night air. Pennyroyal signalled to our left. I nodded and followed. Another rule: he always led the way – I always watched our rear.

We were in a country lane with tall hedges running along both sides. The impression was of being in a deep dark tunnel. All I could see was starry sky overhead. There was a gate on our right. Gates tend to squeak when opening and this was a very silent night so we climbed over. Ahead of us a wide path led to a dark shape with chimneys. A cottage. There were no lights, no dogs, just a light breeze and total silence. So far so good. Contrary to expectations, this could be a piece of doddle.

The explosion took off almost all the front of the house. A brilliant white and yellow flash lit up our surroundings with painful clarity. I ripped off my night visor, rolled as far under the hedge as I could, and pressed the heels of my hands to my eyes. It didn't help in the slightest. I was blind. Only temporarily, I hoped, but until our vision cleared neither of us was going anywhere.

I could feel Pennyroyal beside me. We were helpless. I could only pray nothing crept up on us. If anyone out there had heat detectors then we were sitting ducks. On the other hand, there were lumps of burning thatch dropping out of the sky all around us and part of the hedge was alight, so finding us among that lot could be tricky.

My eyes and nose were streaming. I let the tears roll down my cheeks. You can't rush something like this. The only thing to do is sit tight and wait for your eyesight to drift back when it feels like it.

Beyond the roaring flames, the night remained silent. No screams or shouting. No gunfire. Someone had blown most of the front off this cottage. For access? Hardly. There are quicker and easier ways of getting inside a house than taking out an entire wall. Had someone overestimated the amount of explosive?

Or, possibly, had someone planned to destroy the whole building and everyone in it and *underestimated* the amount of explosive required? What exactly was going on here?

Or – and here was a third option. Could the front door have been booby-trapped by the two adults inside? Which told us they had been expecting trouble. More importantly, they wouldn't bother sorting out the good guys from the bad – they'd just shoot everyone who wasn't them. Which meant just about anyone here tonight would have it in for us one way or another.

Using my sleeve, I carefully wiped my eyes dry. I was beginning to see green and purple shapes against a darker background but I certainly didn't have enough vision to leave the shelter of the hedge yet. Orange flames were leaping skywards – I could see the glow easily enough – showering the area with sparks. Could anyone possibly have survived that explosion?

I blinked a couple of times, snorted snot, and risked a look. Not as bad as I had thought. A good part of the cottage was still intact.

I dragged my arm across my eyes one final time and refitted my night visor, just in time to see four blurred figures emerge from the shadows and very cautiously approach the cottage. They weren't that far away from where we lay; if we hadn't been motionless and under the hedge, they would have seen us.

Pennyroyal nudged me and indicated we should move. He went first – I hung back a little. Given the way the evening was going, there might well be other people on site we had yet to meet.

The four figures advanced towards the cottage, silhouetted against the flames, which told me they were either inexperienced, too stupid to know any better, or very confident. We moved in the other direction, looking for a way around the back. Not a door. Doors didn't seem to be that good an idea at the moment. That said, we couldn't hang around. Hostiles were already on site and we had a baby to secure.

Pennyroyal picked up a large stone and smashed a window. The sound of shattered glass was barely audible over the noise of roaring flames. Smoke billowed out. He put his arm in to unfasten the catch while I watched our backs. We were very vulnerable. There was nothing on my proximity meter but that could change at any moment.

Pennyroyal climbed in first, checking out what looked like an ordinary sitting room. At his signal, I followed and took up a position where I could see what was happening but still cover the window. The temperature was very much higher than outside and rising every moment. I could see flickering flames through an open door in the far wall. We needed to get a move on.

We had one advantage. We were aware of the hostiles – hopefully they had no idea about us.

Given the recent explosion though, it seemed reasonable to assume the occupants – if they were still able to – would be barricading themselves in somewhere. We stood either side of the doorway and peered cautiously out into the flame-lit hall, looking for the stairs, which we found just off to our right.

Smoke was curling around the doorjamb and the temperature was climbing every moment. I looked at Pennyroyal. He indicated we'd search downstairs first, then head up.

Suddenly, two people appeared at the end of the hall. A man and a woman. They were under a wet blanket to protect them from the smoke. Both were coughing. The man held a baby-shaped bundle tightly to his chest.

OK – this could be easier than we had thought.

They turned in our direction, but before we could move or make our presence known, before we could do anything at all, two figures stepped out of the smoke. They'd been waiting. There was a brief burst of gunfire and the couple with the baby crumpled to the ground.

Arseholes. Sodding, sodding arseholes. We hadn't been quick enough. Pennyroyal would not be happy. He really doesn't like failure. I'm not fond of it myself. And who knew how our lovely client would react?

Before our opponents even finished shooting, Pennyroyal stepped out of the doorway, knelt, and opened fire. They both dropped to the ground. I turned the other way to cover his back just as the other two hostiles appeared at the other end of the hall. We all saw each other at the same time and the long narrow hall blazed with gunfire as well as flames. Somewhere in the distance I could hear crashing timbers. A ceiling was coming down. And when one falls, the others won't be far behind.

Pennyroyal signalled to me to grab the baby, rolled into the room on the other side of the hall and unleashed a continuous hail of gunfire, covering me as I ran, gun raised, towards the two still figures lying face down, entangled in their blanket. The flames were roaring more loudly down this end of the hall. Stinging sweat ran down into my eyes and my clothes were sticking to me.

I bent, twitched the bloodstained blanket aside and reached for the baby, which was half shielded by the body of the man who clutched it.

It was a pillow.

The adults – parents, possibly, or guardians, or even bodyguards – were both dead. They had given their lives to head off their attackers. Did this mean the baby was still in the house somewhere?

I chinned my mike. 'Adults dead. No baby. Checking upstairs.'

The stairs were over to my right, made of wood and beginning to char. I took them two at a time, expecting the whole lot to collapse at any moment. There were four doors on the landing. One was obviously a bathroom. I was about to ignore it and search the bedrooms first when I had a sudden thought.

And I was right. A mattress had been heaved across the bath. I pulled it aside and there, lying in the bath, tightly swaddled in a soaking wet blanket, lay a baby. I'm not an expert but it looked about six months old to me. It was awake but just lying quietly.

I grabbed it. First baby I'd ever held. They're a lot heavier than you'd think.

'Target acquired,' I said to Pennyroyal.

'Bottom of the stairs are burning. Hostiles still alive in the hall. Can you go out of a window?'

Well, I'd have to, wouldn't I?

I ran down the first flight of stairs because there was a

window on the half-landing. Closed but not locked. I opened it up and stuck out my head. Behind me and to my right, the flames roared louder. Bloody hell, it was hot. I could hear gunfire again. Pennyroyal had obviously found more little friends to play with. That was nice for him.

Escape was no problem for me. For the baby – slightly more difficult.

In the end I laid it down on the floor and ran back into the bathroom. There was a dressing gown behind the door. I struggled into it and tied the cord tightly. Then I stuck the baby down the front and pulled the two sides around it. It didn't feel particularly safe and I was forced to use my left hand to keep it in place. Plus, the baby didn't seem to appreciate the efforts I was making to save its life and had begun, very unhelpfully, to yell its head off.

Returning to the window, I sat on the sill and swung my legs over. It wasn't the largest window in the world and I now have a new appreciation of the difficulties faced by pregnant women every time they try to climb out of a burning building through an inadequate window, in the dark, with a major gunfight happening close by. Especially when you discover that at some point you've cut yourself quite badly and not noticed and then, much later, your partner complains bitterly about the bloody handprints all over the pod and tries to make you clean them up. But I digress.

I didn't want to jump – especially with a baby on board – but I was very conscious I was silhouetted against an orange glow and a shot could come out of the dark at any moment. I should not hang around.

I wrapped my left arm around my passenger, tossed my gun down ahead of me . . . and jumped.

I had it all planned. Land gracefully on hopefully soft, squidgy ground. Extend right arm for balance. Utilise left arm to keep baby safe. Bend ankles and knees to absorb the shock. Half a second to regain composure, locate gun, rendezvous with partner and make quick getaway.

A number of stifled curses beneath me indicated I might have landed on top of said partner. The ground heaved and I toppled sideways – baby-side up.

I sat up. 'What the hell?'

'We need to move.'

'Why? Surely they're all dead.'

'Yes – and they all have friends. Time Police friends.'

I was trying to get up, floundering around and struggling to extricate my legs from Pennyroyal. All while not letting go of the baby, which was indicating its displeasure in the traditional manner. Piercing cries rent the night air.

'You mean . . . ?'

He heaved me to my feet. 'Yes – our late friends here are working for the Time Police.'

'Bounty hunters? Like us? Shit. Did that bastard at TPHQ double-cross us or his esteemed colleagues?'

'Unknown. And no time to talk about it now. We need to leave. Very, very quickly.'

'It can't have been him – why despatch people to take out a baby and then us to save it? What would be the point?'

'Well, obviously he wasn't the one who despatched them.'

'Then who?'

'No idea. Can we go?'

'But that means . . .'

'You have the listening skills of a teenage girl. Move.'

'I'm twenty-three,' I said indignantly. 'You know that. You came to my party.'

'I did no such thing. Will you move?'

'Well, at half past nine you stuck your head round the door and told everyone to go home, which is more or less the same thing.'

'Can we go? Before others turn up with revenge in mind. Or the rest of the cottage falls on us.'

'You realise what this means, don't you? Two factions within the Time Police. Which begs the question – which one is employing us? The goodies or the baddies?'

'Let's forget leaving, shall we? Let's sit down and have a picnic instead. Out here in the dark and danger. Who could possibly want to discuss this in the comparative safety of the pod?'

'We might even be interfering with a legitimate mission. In which case . . .' I turned to him. 'Why are we hanging around? We should go.'

He really shouldn't use language like that in front of a baby.

Back in the pod, I left Pennyroyal holding the baby – literally – while I shoved on a quick Flexi-glove and got us out of there. We seriously did not want to linger. If our client had used us to interfere with a legitimate mission, then we could be in some serious trouble.

Actually, there was no reason Pennyroyal couldn't have handled the jump but I just wanted to see him holding a baby. He stood quite still, holding it slightly away from him as if it might explode at any moment. Which I've heard they can do. From either end. Sometimes both. Simultaneously.

I had the new coordinates already programmed in and we didn't waste any time. Seconds later we were somewhere else.

Stonehenge – three and a half thousand years ago.

We both drew a long breath.

I struggled out of the dressing gown and Pennyroyal told me to burn it when we got back.

'Of course.'

He was unwrapping the baby from the wet blanket. It didn't seem that grateful. 'We'll ditch everything we used tonight. Bonfire, I think. I'll handle that. You make sure the automatic memory wipe functions properly. We were never there.'

'Or here,' I said, doing a very careful sweep, just in case there was a welcoming committee here, as well. Nothing.

'The bodies will be found in the burnt-out ruins,' he said, peering dubiously at the baby. 'Hopefully, they'll assume the baby's remains were so tiny they were missed.'

'They'll know something went wrong when those they hired don't report back.'

'They might assume both sides wiped each other out. After all, someone booby-trapped that cottage. Whatever they believe, with luck they'll never know it was us.'

I frowned. 'Why would the Time Police want to kill a baby?'

'Perhaps they were just after the parents.'

'Then why does our client want the kid?'

'Perhaps he couldn't stomach killing a baby.'

There was a short pause as we both thought that one over and simultaneously came to the unlikeliness of that conclusion.

'We're involved in something shitty here,' I said, picking up

257

my gun and checking the charge. 'Let's just get tonight over with, shall we?'

Pennyroyal carried the baby because, as I pointed out with a perfectly straight face, I was the better shot.

'Foggy,' he said as I opened the door.

A thick mist swirled around vast dark shapes that came and went. Silence was all around us. Moisture hung in the air and beaded on my sleeve. I wasn't happy with this, and Pennyroyal even less so. An atmospheric Stonehenge is all very well for the tourists but not when you're transporting a stolen baby to an illicit rendezvous that might be – probably was – crawling with a bunch of legalised killers. Because while the Time Police might not have been able to jump to the cottage, there was absolutely nothing to prevent any of them being here. Concealed behind the massive stones. Waiting for us.

We'd been instructed to rendezvous at the eleventh stone. Yeah – bounty hunters are that stupid. We took up a very careful position behind a convenient trilithon with a good view of the eleventh stone. Wouldn't do us any good if whoever was here had heat sensors, of course, but we crouched anyway. The baby, thank goodness, had either gone back to sleep or fainted when it caught sight of Pennyroyal.

He faced one way and I the other and we waited. Everything seemed refreshingly cold after the burning cottage.

I whispered to Pennyroyal, 'Anyone out there?'

'No.'

'Did you engage the camo device?'

'Never took it off.'

We waited some more.

'How long have we been here?'

258

'Five minutes.'

'Seems longer.'

'You have no patience.'

I sighed very ostentatiously.

Silence happened for a while longer.

'So,' he said. 'You and di Maggio . . . ?'

'Seriously? We're doing this now? What about me and Kester?'

'Is that still on?'

'Off and on. Off at the moment. Why?'

'Just wondered. Do I need to beat the crap out of him?'

'I can do that for myself, but thank you for the offer.'

'It would be a pleasure.'

'I'll let you know.'

'Movement. He's here.'

No, he wasn't. This was another someone I didn't know.

'Shit,' breathed Pennyroyal, and drew back further behind the stone. And if Pennyroyal was concerned then I definitely was.

I whispered, 'What?'

'That's Albay. Time Police boss.'

Sodding arseholes. I'd been expecting our client and instead we'd got . . . What the hell had we got ourselves into?

Without another word, Pennyroyal handed me the baby and disappeared into the fog. Damp silence resumed.

I laid the baby at my feet and felt its face. I think you're supposed to keep them warm and dry but this one was cold and wet and inhaling fog. However, my job was to keep it alive long enough for it to catch pneumonia. I stood up and pressed my back against the stone, offered up a quick prayer to the spirits of the place for our survival and tried, very unsuccessfully, to make out shapes in the shifting murk.

Faintly, but unmistakeably, I heard the sound of a body hitting the ground. At the same time, the fog swirled. Someone was over there. At the eleventh stone. I tried to squint through the mist. Who had just been sonicked? Pennyroyal? Should I move? Leave the baby as bait and wait to see what happened? No – anyone could fire at a bundle on the ground. They wouldn't even need to get close. A brief burst of blaster fire – no more baby.

I pulled out my second blaster, stood over the baby, and waited, Janus-like, trying to face in two directions at the same time.

The baby began to cry. Not helpful. I contemplated picking it up and moving, but Pennyroyal was out there somewhere and I didn't want him mistaking me for someone else. I tried to jiggle it with my foot. For some reason it didn't like that at all. Stones came and went in the mist. At least, I hoped it was just the mist causing the impression of moving monoliths. I had enough on my plate without a bunch of giant rocks cantering around the landscape.

Who had hit the ground just now? Pennyroyal? Or our client? Or Albay? None of those would be good. We especially didn't want a reputation for gunning down the commander of the Time Police.

The baby was making enough noise for ten. I couldn't see a sodding thing. What was going on? Had they disabled our pod and jumped back home, leaving me here with a dead Penny-royal, a crying baby and a bunch of moody monoliths? It would be many millennia before English Heritage turned up to save me.

And what would happen when the sun came up properly and the mist burned off? I'd be completely exposed.

Pennyroyal's voice sounded in my ear. 'I'm still here.'

'Never doubted it for a moment.'

'Liar. Behind you. Don't shoot me.'

He emerged from the other side of the trilithon.

I stowed one gun and picked up the baby. Whose yells redoubled. I handed it to Pennyroyal, who tucked it firmly under one arm. It shut up immediately.

'Albay's taking a little nap,' he said. 'Did he see you?'

'No. You?'

'I sonicked him from behind.'

'Not very sporting.'

'Says the daughter of someone who shot birds out of the sky for fun. And rabbits.'

'Papa couldn't shoot a peacock out of a tree twenty feet away,' I said, still trying to develop fog-penetrating eyesight. 'And very few rabbits can fly. Besides, bunnies are the epitome of evil.'

'Speaking of which . . .'

The mist swirled and suddenly our client was with us. No warning. Just fog and then – client. If I'd still been holding the baby, I would probably have dropped it. And he was lucky Pennyroyal didn't take his head off.

If we'd expected thanks, we were to be disappointed. He handed me an envelope.

'Fill in the amount you are owed and present it to the bank of your choice. It will be honoured. This never happened. Don't make me come after you.'

Our normal response would be to scoff, but of all of the Time Police officers we ever knew – actually, of anyone we ever knew – he was one of the few whose threats should be taken seriously.

261

Taking the baby off Pennyroyal without another word, he disappeared back into the mist. We remained quite still for a very long time afterwards.

'Well . . .' said Pennyroyal eventually.

I turned to look at him. 'Do you know who that was?'

'I've seen him around.'

He said no more and I didn't ask.

'Why was that kid so important? It was only a baby.'

'It was important to him. Did you see his face?'

I nodded. 'Do we even know if it was a boy or a girl?'

'Didn't think to look.'

'Nor me. Let's go home. That other bloke will be awake in a minute. And I'm hungry.'

'You're also still bleeding.'

'Stitches, margarita and a bacon sarnie, I think. And not in that order. I wonder if we'll ever know what that was all about.'

'Hope not.'

I could only agree. 'And we've been paid rather handsomely to forget.'

'Forget what?'

19

After the events at Stonehenge, Pennyroyal and I decided to keep our distance from the Time Police for a while. Colonel Albay hadn't seen our faces, but a fairly low profile seemed advisable. The days passed and there was no dawn knock at the door, but Pennyroyal installed yet another layer of security around Home Farm and I sometimes heard him patrolling the house at night.

It was the perfect moment to busy ourselves in other areas. Our single attempt at corporate security had gone well so it made sense to move in that direction. Raymond Parrish would give us good references. Pennyroyal was putting out feelers when, without any warning at all, the Time Police issued an official notification. Colonel Albay had stepped down from his position as head of the Time Police. His successor would be announced in due course.

'Oh my God,' I said, panicking. 'We didn't kill him, did we?'

'No,' said Pennyroyal, still studying his scratchpad. 'Although *stepped down* is Time Police-speak for dead.'

'How?'

'They'll never say.'

'But nothing to do with us.'

'I think we would have heard if so. Our recent client would have tipped us off.'

'Or just killed us to save trouble in the long run.'

'Or that.'

'In fact, might still do so.'

'Could do, yes.'

'Should we be worrying?'

He shrugged. 'No point. It's not as if we'd ever see him coming.'

'True. Are we dead men walking?'

'I don't think so.'

'When will we know who's replacing Albay?'

'Whenever it suits them to make that known.'

'A blood-soaked arena,' I said dramatically. 'All the contenders stripped to the waist, armed only with their nails and teeth and a determination to succeed.'

I expected Pennyroyal to scoff but he didn't.

'I wouldn't be surprised,' he said slowly. 'Not the arena thing but certainly the corporate, political and military equivalent.'

'Suppose,' I said slowly, 'our client is a serious contender. He's obviously high-ranking, ruthless, enigmatic and a Hunter. He'd be perfect.' I frowned. 'I'm not sure whether that would be good or bad for us. Where are you going?'

He was putting on his coat. 'Off to see what I can discover.'

Bounty hunters love to gossip, and tongues would be wagging faster than the tails of a pack of Labradors eyeing up a plate of sausages. Similar amounts of dribble, as well.

'Back before midnight,' I said, tapping my watch, because I still hadn't forgiven him over his comments on my date with Kester.

He threw me a look and disappeared to embark on a giddy whirl of social interaction and alcohol to see what he could discover, returning several days later looking very much the worse for wear. I told him this sort of thing took it out of a bloke his age and reminded him he wasn't as young as he used to be and perhaps I should consider taking up with Kester di Maggio who probably partied seven days a week. I plonked a glass of fizzing relief in front of him, together with a pot of strong black coffee and a foil packet of paracetamol, sat down and awaited revelations.

'It wasn't easy,' he said.

I agreed. I could see he'd had to put in some solid work.

He sipped his coffee. 'I don't think whatever's going on is anything to do with us. Albay's death didn't even happen in this time.'

'What happened?'

'They – the Time Police – moved against some sort of historical organisation. They must have thought it would be easy, but it turned out to be a really bad move on their part. The history people fought back. In a perfect world they should have gone up in a ball of greasy flames ten minutes into the engagement, but they didn't. Not only did they survive – they triumphed.'

'Against the Time Police. How?'

Pennyroyal shook his head, but very carefully. 'There were . . . exploding condoms.'

I sat back, not quite able to believe my ears. 'I didn't know that could happen. Does it occur often? Were people actually wearing them at the time? Was friction a factor?'

'I don't know,' he said wearily. 'Does it matter?'

I waved my arms in frustration. 'Of course it does. It's the most important part of . . . How could you not find out? Suppose one day you're . . . you know . . . doing it for England . . . and suddenly – BOOM – your todger's over the other side of the room.'

'A merciful release,' he said, covering his eyes.

'You're such a lightweight,' I said, seriously annoyed he'd come back without this vital information. 'If this situation ever arises again, I'll go and you can stay behind and catalogue your cutlery drawer.'

He got slowly to his feet, alternately wincing and swaying.

I didn't offer to help. He could have bought my sympathy with exploding condom details but inexplicably hadn't. He was on his own.

Some facts did slowly emerge. It was too good a story not to be repeated. The operation had taken place at the Institute of Historical Research at St Mary's Priory, just outside Rushford. Not that far from Starlings, ironically.

I knew of them by reputation. The whole county knew of them by reputation. The Institute of Historical Research at St Mary's comprised a bunch of lunatics who – far from being academically minded historians spending their days peacefully perusing ancient documents and arguing over the fate of the Princes in the Tower – were, in reality, a bunch of complete disaster magnets who could set fire to water. And had done so on several occasions. They'd obviously been a thorn in tender Time Police flesh for some time. The whys and wherefores never emerged and having established it wasn't anything to do with us, Pennyroyal and I left the matter alone. Everyone is entitled to their secrets, after all.

We would get to know St Mary's better in the future, but at that point in our lives, we regarded them as just a bunch of unstable but not too dangerous eccentrics who could be safely ignored.

As I said to Pennyroyal later, the august firm of Smallhope and Pennyroyal didn't get much wrong, but when we did, it turned out to be a doozy.

Albay's death led to an internal power struggle within the Time Police, and that's putting it politely. The reality was a bit of a bloodbath. The winner – astonishingly – was a woman. No idea how that happened. I suspect balls of steel were involved somewhere along the line. She had a face to frighten children but a reputation for straight dealing. Initially she had her hands full consolidating her power base, and gently easing out all the thugs who had served the Time Police so well, but were now very surplus to requirements. I should imagine that was hard work. People don't surrender power easily and working for an organisation licensed to do pretty much as it pleased will always attract the wrong sort of person.

Nor did those only loosely connected with the Time Police escape the cull. Certain of our bounty-hunting brethren were given to understand their services were no longer required. The Hussain sisters jumped before they were pushed. Femke de Vries quietly disappeared. The Key Group scaled back quite drastically. Kester survived the cut, however, as did the firm of Smallhope and Pennyroyal.

Relieved of our anxieties over Albay, Pennyroyal and I relaxed somewhat. Life for us was really rather good. With Meilin's help, I had invested very carefully in recent years and,

267

together with the inheritance that came to me on my twenty-fifth birthday, I was doing very nicely, thank you.

Which turned out to be just as well.

Twice a year I would jump back to my own time, and it was during one of my six-monthly meetings with Meilin, when we would go over the figures, drink prosecco and settle who owed who what, that she said, 'Are you in contact with anyone at Starlings?'

I shrugged. 'Not really. My solicitor occasionally, but that's about it.'

'Talk to him,' she said suddenly.

I was a little puzzled, but she'd never led me wrong in all the time I'd known her. 'All right – I will.'

I rang Mr Treasure.

'Lady Amelia, I'm so pleased to hear from you.'

'And I you,' I said, and we spent some time talking about his family, mutual acquaintances and local doings in general. All perfectly normal stuff and I was just beginning to wonder why Meilin had even bothered to mention Starlings, when he suddenly said, 'She's put two farms up on the market.'

My mind was still running on Meilin and it took a moment to register what Mr Treasure had said.

'Caroline? Can she do that?'

'With the earl's knowledge and consent – yes.'

'What about Young George?'

Yes – by some process unfamiliar to man – or mitosis, perhaps? – Caroline had managed to throw out a sprog. Young George. I'd never met him, but he must have been around five or six years old.

Mr Treasure's silence answered that question.

'Which two farms?'

'Hill Top and the Langleys' – can't remember the name.'

'Ashburton,' I said.

'That's the one.'

'Together? Or separate lots?'

'Separate.'

'Auction?'

'Yes.'

'Who?'

'Laxton Knowles. From London.'

'When?'

'The third of March.'

Shit. Less than two weeks. 'I'll call you back.'

I had a drink and a bit of a think – because quick decisions aren't always good decisions – and left a message for Meilin.

The answer came through about thirty minutes later. 'Yes. But don't make a habit of it.'

I went back to Mr Treasure who agreed to act for me. Well, not him personally because he was too well known locally, but he would appoint an agent. We set a limit. And then a ten per cent overrun in case it was needed. His agent, said Mr Treasure, was an expert at reading an auction and would know whether exceeding the set price might be justified. I concurred. Too infuriating to reach the limit and have the farm go for only a couple of thousand over.

And then I crossed my fingers. Because I knew these farms. They were well managed and profitable. Which would be why Caroline was selling them off, of course. Well, officially it should be George, but it would be Caroline handling the sale.

What sort of financial hole had she mismanaged the estate into if she was being forced to sell off our land? Mr Treasure

269

would almost certainly have strongly advised against such a course of action, but Caroline – via George – had given him the old heave-ho years ago and transferred everything to her own man – the second Flint from Flint, Chert, Chalk and Flint, who, no doubt, was much more amenable.

It was an effort, but I stayed well away from Starlings in the run-up to and for the duration of the auction. In fact, I stayed out of the whole county. I found a quiet hotel in Sidmouth and kept my head down. The last thing I needed was for Caroline to get wind of what I was doing. Either she'd withdraw the properties or – more likely – try to push up the price. Farms with good land attached aren't cheap. This would be making a very sizeable dent in my holdings. But I knew these farms – and the families who ran them. Long term, I reckoned it would be a good investment. Fingers crossed, anyway.

Mr Treasure's agent was successful. She bided her time and swooped in at the last moment and secured both properties. One for much less than we had expected. So, in addition to saving the farms, I'd pissed Caroline off as well.

I put Mr Treasure on a watching brief for any subsequent sales – in case Caroline decided to make up the shortfall by selling off a third farm – and requested that he inform the current tenants the new owner would be obliged if they stayed on. Without divulging who the new owner was, of course.

I returned to the future and Home Farm, considerably poorer than when I'd left. When I told Pennyroyal about it, rather to my surprise, he agreed, saying that he couldn't see what else I could have done. Another one who reckoned you should sell your kids before your land.

*   *   *

It was not long after that we became properly involved with the aforementioned people at St Mary's. I think both Pennyroyal and I were surprised to find that time travel had actually existed in our own time – neither of us had known a thing about it until we met Uncle Albert. And he was from the future anyway. Someone was keeping a very tight lid on that particular piece of information.

Our paths hadn't yet crossed – not until Bannockburn – but one of the Key Group operatives said something interesting one boozy evening at the Flying Duck pub, up by Barricade Bridge.

'Troy,' slurred Dave, fumbling for his pint and obviously well away. 'Something happened. They did something.'

'Who? The Trojans?'

'No. Other lot.'

'The Greeks?'

'No – the idiots. St Mary's. Big fuss about it. Still don't know how the buggers got away with it.'

'With what?' I asked, closing his fingers around his glass for him.

'Dunno. That's just it. No one knows. Not even . . .' He jerked his head in the general direction of TPHQ and slowly fell off his chair.

His colleagues thought this was hilarious and somehow the subject was dropped.

Anyway, historical researchers, my arse – you never saw such a bunch of mischief-making catastrophe merchants in all your life. The charmingly informal nature of their adventures struck no chord within Pennyroyal's soul. Of course, at the time, we had no idea how important St Mary's would be to our future. The future of everyone, actually.

271

We first encountered them at the Battle of Bannockburn. An episode which doesn't really reflect well on anyone. Except Robert the Bruce, of course. The story is told elsewhere so I shan't recount it here, but they saved our lives. And then, being St Mary's, invited us to Christmas lunch afterwards. Pennyroyal and I don't get asked out a lot – well, I do; Pennyroyal slightly less so – and we were happy to accept.

I was especially keen to do so as it meant I was able to renew my acquaintance with Mr Evans. We'd met briefly during the battle. He'd been unconscious for most of the time, but we'd still managed to make an impression on each other. And when Pennyroyal and I arrived at St Mary's for Christmas, Mr Evans was my designated security escort. They had secrets – more went on behind some of those closed doors than they were letting on – and they weren't too sure about us in those days. None of that mattered, however, because Mr Evans took his escort duties very, very seriously. An excessively conscientious young man is our Mr Evans and, believe me, he conscientioused all over the place. Obviously I was moved to reciprocate – the honour of the firm was at stake – and neither of us could stand upright afterwards.

It was easily the most enjoyable Christmas lunch I'd ever had. At least it would have been if he and I had actually made it downstairs to eat.

Pennyroyal and I celebrated our return to Home Farm with a drink and congratulated ourselves – as not many others have been able to do – on surviving a St Mary's Christmas.

I asked him how everything had gone after lunch.

He grinned. 'Food coma.'

'Really?'

272

'But not for long.'

'How so?'

He poured me a margarita and himself a glass of whisky.

'Dr Bairstow, Max, Markham and I sat down for a highly enjoyable but cutthroat game of whist. No quarter asked.'

I made myself comfortable. 'And none given, I should imagine.'

'Indeed. Anyway, for about twenty minutes there was that rare thing at St Mary's – almost perfect silence.'

I grinned at him. 'Until . . .'

'I don't know how – someone must have left a door open somewhere.'

'Accidentally?'

He frowned. 'I don't think so. Not given subsequent events.'

'Do you have a prime suspect?'

'My first choice is that little bugger, Matthew Farrell.'

'Ah. Like mother, like son.'

'It would appear so.'

'So a door was left open . . . ?'

'Swans.'

'*Swans?*'

'Swans.'

'You say swans plural. How many?'

He sipped his whisky. 'Difficult to say. More than two – probably less than a hundred.'

'Good God.'

'Nasty buggers, they were – well, all birds are.'

'You don't have to tell me,' I said. 'The Smallhope peacocks are a perfect example of biologically and chemically weaponised winged ex-dinosaurs. Do you know one once threw a snake at Papa?'

'Dead?'

'No – he got away by climbing in through the estate office window.'

'I *meant* the snake.'

'Oh. No.'

'Why?'

'Well, obviously because he was able to climb . . .'

'No, I meant why did it throw a snake at your father?'

'Probably in revenge for being shot at every morning. That's what they do, you know.'

'Throw things at your father?'

'No – peacocks catch snakes. That's why people kept them.'

'Do you have many snakes at Starlings?'

'Not any more. Can we get back to the swans? Were they throwing snakes?'

'Not that I saw.'

'So a stupefied St Mary's is engulfed in a tsunami of *Cygnus olor* . . . what happened?'

'Well, obviously it was senior staff to the rescue.'

'You and your whist partners defended St Mary's to the last man?'

'We picked up the table and chairs, retreated to the half-landing and continued the game. Although I believe Dr Bairstow did poke someone awake with his stick as he passed and requested the situation be rectified with all speed.'

'What happened?'

'A great number of unfortunate events in a very small space in a very short period of time.'

'Goodness.'

'Unfortunately for all concerned, the pokee turned out to

be a Mr Bashford, who leaped to his feet shouting, "What?", subsequently fell over a small chicken and banged his head on an occasional table.'

'You're kidding.'

'I am not. As you would know had you actually been present instead of . . .' He paused.

'Debauching and being debauched,' I said helpfully.

He huffed.

'Go on.'

'Well, the chicken leaped to her owner's defence, standing on his body, squawking defiance at everything feathered. And unfeathered. Several people were quite badly beaked. The swans, possibly feeling theirs should be the starring role, took exception to her intransigence. The confusion was considerable. And very loud.'

'What time was this?' I asked, wondering why I hadn't heard any of it.

'About half past four.'

I cast my mind back to what I'd been doing at half past four. 'Oh. Yes. Well, carry on.'

'While the chicken engaged friend and foe alike, I trumped Markham's ace and . . .'

'Never mind your stupid card game.'

'Well, there were feathers, confused people, hissing swans, overturned furniture, and swan shit, and all of St Mary's – other than the chicken – was losing badly.'

I shook my head. 'Typical of them, don't you think. Triumph over the Time Police then lose to a herd of swans.' I frowned at my margarita. 'Herd? Pack?'

'Whiteness,' he said.

'Really? Are you sure?'

'Or the other and far more appropriate term – a lamentation.'

I was pretty sure he was making this up. 'A lamentation of swans?'

'Or whiteness.'

'You're making that up.'

'If only.'

'So how did it end?'

'Believe it or not – Dr Maxwell . . .' He sipped his whisky again.

'Dr Maxwell what? Set fire to the building? Was crushed under a . . . a . . . ?'

'Whiteness.'

'A lamentation of swans?'

He shook his head. 'The phrase you are looking for is *saved the day*.'

'No, I really don't think I was.'

'As you wish.' He lapsed into silence, staring into his whisky.

'You can't leave it there,' I said indignantly. 'How exactly was the day saved?'

'Dr Maxwell battled her way through the . . . battle . . . threw open the front doors, grabbed Mr Markham by the . . .'

I narrowed my eyes. 'By the . . . ?'

'By the scruff of his neck, shouted, "Here he is – come and get him," and pushed him out through the open doors.'

I blinked. 'Ruthless.'

'Indeed, my lady.'

'And that worked?'

'It did. To a man – well, to a swan – the entire . . .'

'Whiteness.'

'. . . Lamentation followed the hapless Mr Markham out of the door.'

'Harsh,' I said, topping up my glass. 'But effective, it would seem. When's the funeral?'

'While seemingly brutal, this is, apparently, standard procedure in the event of avian incursion. By the time the swans had sorted themselves out, Mr Markham was already galloping around the building to hurl himself, rather in the manner of your papa, I imagine, through one of the library windows which Dr Maxwell had previously opened for him. The defeated swans continued with their own plans for Christmas Day, St Mary's went back to sleep, we continued with our game and I won seven and sixpence.'

I stared thoughtfully at my glass. 'They work well together, don't they? Max and Markham.'

'They do.'

'I think that's worth bearing in mind.'

'As do I, my lady.'

 20

Pennyroyal and I ran across St Mary's fairly frequently after that. One thing led to another – as it so frequently does. We helped them, they helped us. And then one day we found ourselves working together in the face of a common enemy. Max and Markham joined us at Home Farm and we took on a bunch named Insight – ultra respectable and ultra nasty. The two frequently go together.

To begin with, we didn't realise quite how nasty until Max infiltrated their ranks and exposed the full extent of their nefarious activities. Plundering the past, relocating criminals, even manipulating events in contemporary times. Trust me, Insight's plans for America would have blown your socks off. And I wouldn't be surprised if they hadn't been secretly funding those ENLA nutters as well. Nasty, nasty people and the world was a much better place without them.

This too is a tale told elsewhere. None of it was as straightforward as we had anticipated, and being St Mary's, also involved detours to Runnymede, 13th-century Lincoln and Victorian London. It was all go for Max and Markham.

Pennyroyal and I took a different path and found ourselves

up to our necks in the anarchy and civil unrest in Europe 1848 – the Year of Revolutions. I should probably make it clear – these were not *our* revolutions. Yes, Pennyroyal and I have started a few over the years, but this time our job was – not to prevent them, exactly, but to make sure each one proceeded down the correct path.

Max had briefed us well. This period was sometimes known as the Springtime of Nations. Across Europe, countries were unifying, overthrowing monarchies, instituting social reform – you name it, they were at it – and it was our job to keep things on track.

Our plan was to let Insight do all the hard work. Fund the uprisings. Take all the risks. Then, at the right moment, Pennyroyal and I would move in, remove a few inconvenient people, change a few minds, and encourage key players down a slightly different path. I would bribe – Pennyroyal would threaten. A winning combination.

We began in France. I like France – it's so easy to start a revolution there. In almost less time than it takes to recount the story, the citizenry were out on the streets expressing their dissatisfaction in the traditional manner and we could safely leave them to get on with it.

Once things were ticking over nicely, we jumped to Germany. The Peasants' Revolt looked a little dodgy for a while until I hit on the idea of winding up the middle and upper classes by publicly calling for reformation of the monarchy. Demands for constitutional monarchies always keep people arguing among themselves for months.

Hungary took us a while. By now, I think Insight were becoming aware – not of us, specifically, but that there was definitely someone out there shoving spokes in their wheels at every opportunity. They tracked us down eventually and things got a little hairy for a while. We hung on for as long as we could, because at the very least Insight were having to throw more and more resources at us – which, to some extent, distracted them from what Max was up to – but in the end we had to go. Well – we had to run, actually.

They'd cornered us in a small room over a bakery. I was covering our rear when Pennyroyal kicked open the back door and realised that they'd cut us off. There was an almighty hail of gunfire. Pennyroyal absorbed most of it.

A game-changing moment, obviously. I readjusted my priorities and concentrated on getting him somewhere safe for emergency treatment.

Fortunately, we'd made some good friends among the local people. It's amazing how much bonding can be done over a few glasses of pálinka. A couple of locals picked up Pennyroyal, and we fought our way to a small street off Váci utca. We split up – I think our friends were intending to provide a distraction. The pod was against a wall under a bridge. I had to drag Pennyroyal there myself, all the time expecting to feel a bullet between my shoulder blades.

I was nearly there when I tripped over my skirt and fell heavily to the ground, dragging Pennyroyal down on top of me. I broke my wrist, though I didn't realise it at the time. Pennyroyal said afterwards that it was me dropping him face down on to the cobbles that convinced him he was going to have to save his own life and he heaved himself to his feet. I did what I could to keep him upright and seconds later we were back in the pod.

I saw our Hungarian friends safely away and then had us out

of there and back to St Mary's before Insight could do anything imaginative with EMPs. One of our closer shaves. And given that Pennyroyal had what Max described as a record-breaking number of bullets removed, I still can't believe he survived.

Once we'd recovered from that, then it was off to the Boxer Rebellion. Minus Pennyroyal this time, although by that point he was looking a little less like that Swiss cheese with the holes in it. We took Mr Evans along with us instead, despite Pennyroyal's dire predictions that the whole enterprise would go tits up if he wasn't there to supervise.

'I'm fine,' he rasped, ashen-faced as he attempted to rise, Lazarus-like from his Bed of Pain.

'Yes,' I said. 'Being unable to stand up straight is always a sign of peak physical fitness.'

'There's a bloody revolution going on – bullets, flames, explosions, riots, murder, wholesale destruction – and you're taking St Mary's.'

'Don't you prefer to have them inside the tent pissing out rather than the other way around.'

'Evans is from St Mary's. They're *all* from sodding St Mary's. They'll be pissing in all directions.' Once again, he struggled to stand up.

I went to sit beside him, saying quietly, 'Seriously, my friend – no. Not this time.'

He folded his arms. Pennyroyal has very eloquent arms.

I pressed on. 'I am the first to say there is no substitute for the real Pennyroyal but I think, in this case, Evans is a very nearly adequate replacement, don't you?'

And he was. It was Evans's strength that helped us free that woman from the burning hut. I've no doubt he would have dealt

281

equally efficiently with her very unpleasant father or husband, too, but I got in first and broke the little shit's arm. Evans and I had rather a lot to drink on our return and discussed arm-breaking techniques deep into the night.

And Max flirted briefly with Ancient Egypt. Nothing was straightforward – it never is if St Mary's are involved – and for heaven's sake, don't mention the donkey to Pennyroyal. Theirs was not a happy relationship and I suspect it was only the fact that he – the donkey, not Pennyroyal – brought his own gold that saved him from becoming premature donkey burgers.

The whole job came to a head in 1895 at an elegant residence situated in Swan Court, London. Pennyroyal and I were guarding two fugitives, Svetlana and Anastasia Koslova – a mother and daughter, both on the run from Svetlana's husband. A dangerous and unpleasant man. In exchange for a colossal sum of money, Insight had undertaken to jump Svetlana and young Anastasia back in time and give them a whole new life there. The part of the deal they never mentioned to their victims was that after only a few weeks, Insight would kill them, strip their bank accounts, throw the bodies in the Thames and do it all over again with fresh customers. A lucrative business. There never seemed to be any lack of those who, for various reasons, were eager to escape their own time.

Pennyroyal and I were to act as butler and housekeeper, which would give him a chance to exercise his fabled butler skills – about whose existence I was still not completely convinced. A diploma in floral art? I don't think so.

Whether he did actually possess twelve diplomas or not – he was perfect for the job. The household staff – all female – thought he was wonderful and hung on his every word. He was coddled and cossetted, always given the largest slice of cake, and I don't think he poured his own tea the whole time he was at Swan Court. Every one of his utterances was met with a bobbed curtsey, a breathless 'Yes, Mr Jeeves,' followed by another bobbed curtsey. I began to feel quite nauseated.

The job itself was quite easy, the house was comfortable, Mrs Proudie was an excellent cook, our charges gave us no trouble and by then, Pennyroyal and I had been working together for years and knew each other backwards. Even if Insight did turn up, nothing we had learned about them in our encounters so far had given us any real cause for concern. We were slick and professional and competent.

It would be fair to say things did not go according to plan.

We'd had word from Markham that it was time to pull the plug on Swan Court as a safe house and to get out of there asap. I sent the servants away immediately – we didn't even allow them time to pack up their belongings. We were actually on our way out of the door ourselves, all set to whisk Svetlana and Anastasia away in our pod, when Insight turned up unexpectedly early. One team came through the front, the other through the back, and we were caught between them, trapped between the main part of the house and the servants' areas.

If it had been just the two of us, there wouldn't have been a problem, but we had civilians to protect and that always changes the game.

'Go,' I said to Pennyroyal. 'Hold them off. I'll stash these two somewhere safe and join you.'

He nodded and disappeared.

We had advantages and disadvantages. The house was pitch-dark but we knew every inch of it, and Pennyroyal had emergency weapons stashed all over the place. Insight, on the other hand, had night visors and were well armed. But not as well as us.

The Koslovas and I were in the front hall, just outside the servants' door leading downstairs. I whirled my charges around, meaning to head down to the servants' region. There's always a strongroom in this type of house – the place the family keep their valuables, the silver, all sorts of things. The one at Swan Court was located in the butler's pantry and was easily big enough for both of them to hide in. With mother and daughter safely stashed away, I could get back to Pennyroyal.

There was a sudden hail of gunfire and Svetlana, standing right next to me, gave a kind of sigh and slipped to the floor.

I had choices. At best she was seriously wounded, but most likely she was dead, and I had a child to save. I didn't hesitate. Through the door. Down the stairs, pulling the little girl along with me.

The strongroom was just off the butler's pantry. I knew that we had more weapons stored in there. I unlocked the door.

'Inside,' I whispered.

'Where's . . . ?'

I'm not tremendously child-oriented. And I was here to save her life; I didn't have time for an emotional crisis.

'With Jeeves,' I said. Pennyroyal had taken to calling himself Jeeves while at Swan Court, so I'd retaliated with Mrs Danvers. 'Inside now.'

In she went. She was a very obedient child – I quite liked her. I seized as many weapons as I could carry – we definitely had one or two things stashed away that would give these shits from Insight something serious to think about – locked her in and slid the key under the door. This old wooden door wouldn't hold for a moment – not against Insight's weapons – but it would make her feel more safe and secure.

'Stay here,' I said. 'Don't come out for anyone except me or Jeeves. And stay quiet.'

There was no sound from inside the strongroom so I assumed Anastasia was already obeying instructions. I'd done what I could. Time to get back to Pennyroyal, still upstairs somewhere, holding off any number of hostiles.

I'd only been away a minute or two but it was already too late. Insight had broken through the back door and were advancing down the servants' passage. And I could hear gunfire on the floors above, as well. We were well and truly trapped. I needed to deal with this lot, which would protect Pennyroyal's rear and clear the way to the pod. Once there I could deposit the kid, arm myself with something a little more substantial and really do some damage.

The passageway dog-legged slightly so I stepped into the kitchen. They wouldn't be able to get too close without exposing themselves. I set both blasters to charge.

They came pouring around the dog-leg, chucking out a couple of light sticks and firing short sharp laser blasts. Professionals. I took aim and both sides got stuck in.

The passageway rang with gunfire. Lumps of plaster were exploding from the walls. A small fire started somewhere – whether deliberately or not I don't know but I could definitely smell burning.

I saw one of them go down but there were many more. It was a bit of a stalemate down here. They couldn't get past me, but I couldn't get past them to the pod. In the meantime,

285

a major war was being fought overhead. Which was encouraging. Pennyroyal was obviously open for business and being enthusiastic about it.

My hands grew hot and slick with sweat. Plus I was wearing any number of starched petticoats for that authentic housekeeper rustle and bustle, and they don't lend themselves to freedom of movement.

My blasters were both charged by now. I laid down the handgun in case I should need it again, set the first blaster to maximum and fired at the wall just a little ahead of the dog-leg, hoping for a lucky ricochet. Obviously I couldn't see the results but there was a lot of frantic shouting which I thought was encouraging.

This was some quality opposition though. They did exactly the same to me. I was enveloped in a blast of heat and a large lump of wall fell on me. That hurt. And there was a lot of dust. I couldn't see very well and hanging around here was no longer an option. I grabbed my remaining weapons before they could capitalise on their advantage and wriggled backwards. One of the storerooms would give me the same sightline but was nearer the stairs up to the ground floor. Not my first choice but better than nothing.

They took advantage of me changing position to work their way further along the passage. Nothing I could do about that. From now on, all I could do was hold my position and trust to luck. Still no sign of Pennyroyal. Things were not looking good.

I wiped my hands on my skirts, picked up another blaster and tried to keep up a slow steady discharge that would encourage Insight to stay exactly where they were – or, if I wanted to be wildly optimistic – call it a day and go home.

Except I couldn't allow that to happen. If even one of these buggers made it back to Insight knowing who we were and what we'd done, Max would be a sitting target. She'd die and Markham with her, probably, so I gritted my teeth, ignored everything slowly disintegrating around me and just kept at it because more lives than ours hung on this.

What changed the game was the sudden and very worrying silence from upstairs.

Shit. What was going on up there? I told myself it was Pennyroyal changing position – as I had done – preparatory to unleashing something lethal.

I was wrong. There was a sudden silence down here too. The opposition had stopped shooting. There could be only one reason for that. They were gearing up to mount an offensive.

Another group burst through the servants' door and came racing down the stairs and along the corridor, firing as they came. I was caught between the two teams but at least that meant the buggers to my left had to pack it in if they didn't want to end up shooting each other. I wriggled about, switched to wide beam and swept the passageway left to right, right to left, left to right, holding them back and hoping Pennyroyal would miraculously appear from somewhere and back me up.

He didn't. There was no sign of him anywhere.

I emptied one blaster and reached for the other. This one had rather a neat little rocket attachment. I knelt up, heaved it up on to my shoulder and fired up the passage. The heat blast knocked them all off their feet and hit the wall with a great ball of flame. It also sent me arse over tit but this was my chance.

I staggered to my feet, grabbed the little handgun as well and made for the servants' door, trampling the fallen as I went. I heard shouts behind me and ignored them. My plan was to lead them away from Anastasia. With luck, Pennyroyal was around somewhere doing something murderous to someone.

I was also able to grab one or two Insight weapons as I passed.

I emerged into the hall. I knew exactly where I wanted to be. Behind the red armchair in the corner, which would give me a neat view of the front door, the servants' door and the stairway. A nice commanding position.

Or would have been if someone else hadn't got there first. And not Pennyroyal, either. As my friend Max would say, 'Bloody bollocking hell.'

Fortunately, he was as surprised as me, which should have given me a vital second to deal with him, but it just wasn't to be my night.

The man kicked my legs out from underneath me and the next minute we were both rolling about on the floor. I nutted him and made a poor job of it in the dark. I couldn't get a grip on him and sadly he used his brains – and his voice – to shout for help.

Yes, I know, but there were a lot of them and only one of me. On the other hand, there were more than one or two downstairs who wouldn't be getting back up again, plus another group of stunned and scorched miscreants at the bottom of the stairs. Plus Sunny Jim here was going to have a splitting headache, so I reckoned I wasn't doing too badly. And little Anastasia was still safe downstairs. It would take them ages to secure the house and make sure there weren't any more like me waiting for them in the dark, so I was pretty certain that she'd be on the back boiler for a bit. And, of course, my partner was still out there somewhere. Yeah – short term this might not be good for me, but the situation could be worse.

Not by much, though. Half a dozen hands hauled me away from Sunny Jim and to my feet and I really don't know why they bothered because the first thing they did was knock me straight back down again, with a couple of swift kicks, as well. Not tremendously pleasant, but it was all distracting them from anything happening elsewhere.

Someone said, 'Where's Eddie?'

'Upstairs.'

Well, obviously, I couldn't have that, so I kicked out. Not terribly effectively – stupid petticoats – but I did connect with something.

And paid for it. I vaguely remember being dragged along to somewhere – the kitchen, as I discovered when I'd recovered a little. There was some conversation to which I didn't bother listening, though I do have a memory of a voice saying, 'Remember, lads, he needs to hear her scream.'

I only remember the pain. Big red spirals of pain. There was some damage happening and there wasn't anything I could do about it. Except not scream, of course.

I did hear the door slam back. I managed to lift my head as Pennyroyal appeared in a sudden eruption of flame and smoke – like something spat out of hell. He raked the kitchen with gunfire. On and on and on – demolishing the room in front of my eyes. China dishes, pots, pans, plates – everything exploded in a hail of destruction. And still it went on. Lumps of plaster, wood and earthenware ricocheted around the room and were as dangerous in their own way as the bullets. A part of the ceiling came down. And then he started with his big blaster.

I just had time to think, *well, about bloody time, mate*, before painfully rolling away behind a chair that would afford me all the safety and protection of a sheet of newspaper.

There was a gun. I reached out for it. Even that small movement was almost too painful to bear. A solid jag of pain ripped straight through me. I'd been done some serious damage. Very serious, actually. I tried to sit up and felt something tear and had to content myself with balancing on one elbow. I fired until the gun was empty.

Pennyroyal was behind the overturned kitchen table, laying down a very useful wall of blaster fire. Men lay everywhere. We were going to get out of this.

No – we weren't. The door was smashed off its hinges and a man entered. There might have been others – I saw only him.

Everything happened in very slow motion. Even the sound dragged.

I heard him say, 'You.'

I heard Pennyroyal say, 'Yeah – me,' and all of a sudden – in that instant – the game changed completely. We – everyone – Insight – Anastasia – me – we were all forgotten. The two of them dropped their weapons and closed with each other, crashing back through the remains of the door and out of sight.

Pennyroyal never came back.

He left me.

Because – after everything he'd ever said – after all the training – after all the years we'd been together – Pennyroyal made it personal.

I don't think anyone knew quite what to do next. The kitchen was in pieces. I could barely move, let alone take the opportunity to escape. I lay very still among the wreckage of the kitchen and hoped that Insight would think I was dead.

Unfortunately – no. With one accord, they all turned and looked at me. They raised their weapons. I tried to grope around but there was nothing. Well, there was a broken kitchen chair. I stared at it. I really should have been thinking about utilising it as a weapon, or how to turn this situation around or some-thing – anything – but all my mind seemed able to do was run through the same phrase over and over again.

He left me. He left me. He left me. The bastard had done it again. He left me.

Pennyroyal had left me to die. Not a backward glance. Not a second thought. He left me. I closed my eyes and laid my cheek against the cold tiled floor. I'd been a fool and nothing mattered any longer.

The room rang with gunshots. I opened my eyes and braced myself for death. Which was turning out to be a lot more pro-tracted and painful than I could have wished.

The three men dropped. A weapon skidded over to me. I stared for a moment and then instinct kicked in and I reached out and grabbed it. Pain. Great pain.

'It's me,' said Markham, somewhere overhead. 'Can you walk?'

'No. Leave me. No good to you. Little girl.'

'Max has all that in hand. She's taken her and gone for help. Where's Pennyroyal?'

He might well ask.

I couldn't have told him anyway. My mind was still refusing to move on. This is how amateurs die. The personal overwhelms what's really important – survival, for instance – leaving the

291

body paralysed and unable to defend itself. It occurred to me that it would be very pleasant just to close my eyes and die. The central pillar on which I'd built my life had been kicked away. I wasn't sure I wanted to survive this.

Fortunately – although I didn't think so at the time – I wasn't given the choice.

Markham seized my arm and a handful of skirt and dragged me backwards into one of the pantries off the kitchen. Full of shelves and bins and sacks. Smelling of coffee and spices. I tried not to cry out with pain.

Remember, lads, he needs to hear her scream.

Well, I'd really have to raise my voice for Pennyroyal to hear me now, wouldn't I? He could be anywhere.

With that thought – Insight were back, shouting to each other in the passage.

'The kid's gone. Can't find her anywhere.'

'The fucking pod's gone, too. With Eddie. And that bloke.'

That bloke. Pennyroyal. He'd really gone. He hadn't just left the kitchen. Or the house. He'd left London. This time period. Everyone and everything. And he'd left me to die. *Trust me,* he'd said. And I had.

Wouldn't be making that mistake again.

There was more gunfire. Markham holding the door. Me trying to load for him. Shaking hands. Blurry. Pain. Voices. Shouting. Time Police. About bloody time. Good old Max. Close my eyes. Sleep now. Perchance to dream. With luck to die.

Sadly, my luck appeared to have run out. Kindly death did not appear. I opened my eyes to a large room divided into cubicles. I could tell from the smell it was a medical facility. The Time

Police's MedCen was my best guess, although really, I was too sick to care.

Medical personnel came and went. I was very good. I swallowed this. I swallowed that. I had my dressings changed. I agreed that yes, I felt much better today, thank you. I didn't, but after a while, lying to everyone, including yourself, becomes second nature.

I sat up when told. I ate what was put in front of me. The posh school in the Cotswolds, Mlle Leonie, Meilin – even Caroline – would have been astonished at my docility. My only thought was to recover, leave this place, return to Home Farm and kill Pennyroyal slowly and at leisure. And then dig him up and do it all over again. I hadn't hated even Caroline as much as I hated him.

I spent hours brooding, reviewing my grievances – and there were many – but it all came back to that one thing. He'd abandoned me. Left me to die. He hadn't even looked back.

All these years and I'd been completely wrong about him. How stupid was I? And it wasn't as if the evidence hadn't been there. Leaving whenever it suited him was what he did. He took off. He did it when we were living in London. Vanished without a word. I'd glossed over it. I'd accepted it and we'd moved on. And now he'd done it again. And he couldn't have picked a worse moment.

He'd left me there to die alone.

How long had I been here at TPHQ? Some weeks, I thought. In all that time there hadn't been any word from him. We had our rule – never the two of us injured in the same place – especially with these Time Police bastards. You never knew what they might take it into their heads to do – but he could have got

293

word to me somehow. Via Max or Markham. Perhaps he was dead. Well, if he wasn't now, he very soon would be once I got hold of him. The pendulum always swings back the other way. The coin always flips to the other side. Loyalty and friendship on one side. Betrayal and treachery on the other.

After a while, I stopped wondering where he was and how he could have done this, and moved smoothly into hoping I never saw him again. Ever. Because that was the easiest way. Lock it all down and move on. Consider my future. Count myself lucky I had one. No thanks to him. And off I'd go again. Staring at the wall and plotting my revenge.

Because he'd left me. Left me to die alone.

21

The Time Police had picked up our pod. My pod now, I suppose. It was waiting for me in their Pod Bay on the day of my discharge some weeks later. I was certain they'd have availed themselves of the opportunity to probe our secrets. Yeah – good luck with that, boys. There's an automatic memory wipe after every jump. We're not stupid. *I'm* not stupid. No more we – remember?

There was no reason to stay any longer. I'd given hundreds of statements – keeping my wits about me all the time because overburdening the Time Police with information never does anyone any good. Commander Hay had thanked me personally. I quite liked her. Shame about her face. Anyway, she came down to MedCen to say thanks for everything and to wish me a speedy recovery.

I smiled and said we'd be invoicing her – *I'd* be invoicing her – in the near future. She took it well, I have to say.

And then, finally, I was free to go. They wanted me to stay another few days but bedrest in one bed is much the same as bedrest in another. And I wanted to go home. There was nothing for me here. Max and Markham had already returned to St Mary's. They'd come to see me before they left, and we'd caught up on our individual adventures.

Inevitably, they wanted to talk about Pennyroyal, and I needed to shut that down. Quickly. I could barely even think about him, let alone discuss his desertion with anyone else. I asked Markham if he could find me a coffee and as soon as he'd gone, I turned to Max and said, 'This is not for discussion. Ever.'

She gave me a long, level look, finally saying, 'OK,' and then the doors crashed open with Markham bearing coffee for three and the conversation moved on to individual bounties.

Commander Hay was kind enough to escort me to my pod. Although I think she just wanted to be sure I was out of their building without causing any mischief on the way. It's nice to have a reputation.

I shook hands, thanked her politely for their care of me, and told her she'd be hearing from me – she did flinch a little at that point; I'd love to have seen her face when they eventually got the final invoice – and entered the pod. The door closed behind me. I took a moment to check they hadn't inadvertently downloaded any tracking software or anything of that nature – I would have if I'd been them – decided I'd do a complete reset when I felt more like it – and headed back to Home Farm.

I touched down, sat for a moment, then began to shut everything down. In fact, I powered down completely. I'd run a systems check when I felt a little more enthusiastic about life. Until then, a warm bath and a margarita. But first I needed to set about the complete annihilation of my partnership with Pennyroyal. With extreme prejudice.

I opened the door and stepped out. As always, the barn smelled of hay, manure, dust and creosote. I was home. At last.

I had to squeeze past another pod parked alongside ours. Presumably the one Pennyroyal had arrived in.

The back door opened as I approached and Pennyroyal stood silhouetted against the light.

He said, 'Welcome home, my lady,' and it was as if a guillotine came crashing down, severing my life into two parts. Pre-Pennyroyal betrayal and post-Pennyroyal betrayal.

I stared him in the face. One of the many advantages of being tall.

'Never say that again. You've lost the right to call me that.'

I pushed past him into the passageway and from there into the kitchen. I was blind with rage but somehow I found my way. My hands were actually shaking. Even Caroline hadn't reduced me to this – but then I'd known what Caroline was almost from the moment I clapped eyes on her. I'd never trusted her with my life. I'd never made the mistake with her that I'd made with Pennyroyal.

I turned to face him. I didn't recognise my own voice.

'You left me. We were in the middle of a job and you ran away. You had more important things to do. You left me. In a house full of hostiles. With a little girl to protect. You left us both. If Max and Markham hadn't turned up, I'd be dead. That little girl would be dead. The whole job would have gone down the pan. They'd have taken out Max when she got back to Insight and Markham would have died protecting her. Because she's luckier than me in her choice of partners. *Trust me*, you said – you always say – and yet, when he needed you, you weren't there for Uncle Albert. He called for you but you had more important things to do, didn't you? *Trust me*, you said, and then, when I needed you, you left me to die alone at Swan Court. That I'm here, now, is no thanks to you, but to Markham who held Insight off long enough for Max to fetch help. Your share of the bounty is on its way. God knows why – you did precious little to earn it. I'll send it on. Now get out of my sight.'

Again, I pushed past him and down the passage to my own quarters where I locked the door for the first time ever. I had to sit down and just breathe for a long while. I'd never known such fury. If I thought I could physically manage it, I would have killed him with my bare hands.

After about thirty minutes, I made myself a cup of tea, took some of the medication the Time Police had sent me home with and fell on to my bed. I don't know why – there was no chance of sleep. My adrenalin levels must have been off the charts.

I tried reading – that didn't work at all. There was some paperwork on my table – bank statements and such – but I couldn't concentrate. I tried rearranging the furniture – please don't ask me why. All I did was hurt myself trying to shift the heavy stuff. In the end I curled up on the sofa and waited for the sun to come up. Then I unlocked the door and went looking for him.

The door to his rooms was half-open. I'd never known that before.

I knocked on the door because I didn't want to be shot. And not a gentle *I'm sorry, can we be friends again?* tap, but a bloody great *I'm coming for you, you duplicitous bastard* thump.

He was gone. His bed was stripped, his wardrobe empty. His personal gun cabinet – his emergency weapons, I always called them – had been emptied. No books on the shelves. Other than a few marks on the walls where things had been hanging, it was as if he'd never been there. I went down into the cellars and punched in the code for the gun cabinets. He'd taken a few guns and left me the rest.

Wearily, I climbed the steps back upstairs and went out into the barn. The second pod had gone.

I hadn't slept a wink last night, but I hadn't heard a thing. It must have taken him hours to achieve all this. Especially in his condition. He was as badly injured as I was. I had only vaguely registered it at the time, but there had been a long red angry wound through his eyebrow and a huge stitched-up gash across the back of his head. He'd looked to be missing half an ear and he was wearing Flexi-gloves on both hands.

And he hadn't made a sound. Pennyroyal doing what Pennyroyal did best. When the going gets tough, the tough creep away into the night.

Bastard.

I slammed the back door. The sound echoed through the quiet house.

There was a note on the kitchen table.

Accept my share in lieu of notice.

'So,' I said, aloud. 'Gone for good this time, have you?'

Outside, the sun came up on a lovely day and the birds sang.

I did not get over any of this in a couple of days. It was quite a while before my urine stopped looking like rosé. Before I could bend and twist again. It was even longer before I could contemplate my future. And I refused to think of Pennyroyal at all.

I tried to make a plan. One day I sat down with pen and paper to make a list of pros and cons and then had to scrunch up the paper and throw it away, because Pros and Cons had been the team name Markham had suggested. Before I knew it, I was lost in bitter memories again.

I had choices. I could continue alone. I could take on another partner – Kester di Maggio would join me like a shot. I could retire and live here at Home Farm. I could sell up and continue in this time, but in London, working for Raymond Parrish, perhaps. Or I could return to my own time and . . . do something. Really, I was spoiled for choice, and perhaps because of that, I found myself unable to make one. I would wake in the morning with the decision made, change my mind by lunchtime, change it again by the evening, and go to bed as undecided as ever.

There was no message from Pennyroyal. I never really thought there would be and I certainly didn't log on every morning expecting one. In a way I was rather glad – I wouldn't have known how to feel or what to do if he had messaged me.

Yes, I did – who am I kidding? I'd have shot the bastard in ten different places and then stamped on his face. And then *I'd* have left *him*. Left him slowly dying in his own blood. On the kitchen floor. That was a very agreeable image. I spent a lot of time dwelling on that one.

In the meantime, I had to get myself fit again. I started walking. Not far to begin with, but a little further each week. I walked across country to various beauty spots. I extended my range, taking lunch with me so I was out most of the day. I began to run, gently at first and on the flat, and when nothing fell off and my wee didn't turn purple, I ran up hill and down dale as I'd done in Northumberland. That had been a few years ago now, but I was glad to see I could still do it.

Finally, one rainy afternoon, I made myself a margarita, sat down in the warm kitchen, pulled together all the Insight paperwork, and started work on invoicing the Time Police. Three days I spent on that. I charged them for everything I could think of. Max and Markham's time – that would be a nice surprise for them both – my time, the bastard's time, and damage incurred – especially to Home Farm. I was chancing my arm a bit with that, but nothing ventured, nothing gained. I added in everything I could think of, and even I was faintly horrified at the total. They'd never pay all that. And so, because I was in the mood, I added in a mark-up of ten per cent, called it hazard pay, and fired off the invoice.

I retired to my own room, enjoyed a few reward margaritas and went to bed.

As I said, I never thought the Time Police would pay up. I thought they'd query a few items – all of them, actually – challenge the mark-up, and generally prevaricate. Imagine my surprise when they paid – in full – and well within the twenty-eight-day period. A bit of a first.

On the other hand, Insight had been a tremendous coup for them. And they hadn't actually had to lift a finger until the final takedown. Yeah – they hadn't done too badly out of us.

I deducted expenses and fees, shoved the usual one-third into the business account – one day I'd have to think about what to do with that – and divided everything else into four. Me, Markham, Max and the bastard. I set aside a sum for Evans, as well. He was a latecomer to the Insight job but he'd still been a member of the team.

We hadn't been poor before but now we were about as far from poor as you could get. I gloated over the figure in my bank account for a while – and what a pleasant experience that was – and poured myself another reward margarita.

I jumped back to Paris to see Meilin, firstly for a financial update and secondly to unload my share of Ramses' gold, a Fabergé egg and a couple of Chinese books we'd acquired along the way.

Her jaw dropped when she saw me.

'I don't look that bad,' I said, dropping into a chair.

'Yes, you do,' she said. So much for self-delusion. 'You look terrible.'

'A job went bad,' I said, not wanting to give any details.

'And your partner?'

'Gone,' I said and she could construe that any way she pleased.

She picked up the books and examined each of them very closely. 'Millie, do you know what these are?'

'I do.'

'How did you . . . ? No, don't tell me.'

'Perfectly legitimately,' I said. 'They're not stolen and no one's looking for them. Can you dispose of them?'

'Certainly not.'

Oh well, it wasn't as if I needed the money. I'd donate them to a museum.

I'd been too hasty. She was in love.

'These are so beautiful.' She ran a gentle finger over the fine yellow silk. 'I would like to keep these for myself. My own private collection.' She looked over at me. 'How much? And for the egg?'

'Market value less mate's discount,' I said wearily.

'To go into your usual account?'

'Yes. Will there be a problem?'

'No. I'll sell the egg – and I know to whom – but the books

302

will belong to me and I shall never sell them. They will be treasured heirlooms for my family.'

We haggled a little but not much and I left everything with her.

I spent a day walking around Paris, reminding myself that, if I wished, I could do this sort of thing for the rest of my life. Travel the world. See the sights. Stay in pretty boutique hotels. Eat good food and drink fine wine. Never be shot at again. For some reason, it didn't hold any great appeal. No, I needed a proper job. Something that exercised mind and body. I couldn't think of anything just at that moment but something would occur. What was it I'd always said? Have a plan. And then a plan for if the first one failed. And another one after that. I needed to stop drifting, pull myself together and sort out the rest of my life.

I checked out of the hotel, returned to the pod and went back to Home Farm. To decide what to do with the rest of my life.

Not as easy as you might think. A successful plan rather depends on identifying the desired outcome and then working backwards from that. I didn't have a desired outcome. I didn't know what I wanted. I didn't even know what I didn't want. I walked for miles, hoping the exercise would jar something loose in my brain. Which, sadly, remained very unjarred.

I went to bed early that night, read for a while, turned out the light and settled down to sleep. Which didn't happen. My mind wouldn't stop ticking over. I couldn't rid myself of the fear that if I didn't find something soon, I'd drift aimlessly for the rest of my life. Amelia Smallhope – showed promise but failed to follow through. I was actually quite cross with myself – I had

303

brains, I had money, I had opportunities other people would die for, and I was wasting all of them.

Someone knocked at the front door.

I was so surprised that initially I couldn't think what the noise was. I can honestly say that was the first time anyone had ever knocked at our front door. Other than those from St Mary's, no one else had ever been here. It couldn't be one of the Faradays – they always came round the back. Intruders tended to come through the roof. Perhaps someone's car had broken down and they'd seen my light on and come for help.

That had never happened before, either. I really couldn't think of a reason why anyone would be out here at this hour. Not a good one, anyway.

I threw on a dressing gown, slipped a small pistol in my pocket, shoved a stun gun up my sleeve and went downstairs, carefully not switching on the lights as I went. The camera controls were in the office, next to the wardrobe room. There was a fuzzy green image. I jiggled the controls. The image turned its face towards the camera.

Pennyroyal.

I drew in my breath with a hiss. He'd come to kill me. Yes, by banging on the front door and standing still for the camera. Pull yourself together, woman.

I went to the front door and opened it, leaving the chain up. We looked at each other. Actually, the image hadn't been that fuzzy. It was chucking it down with rain.

Neither of us said anything for quite a long time. Eventually, I said, 'Yes?'

'News,' he said. 'Bad news.'

I unhooked the chain, pressed the hidden control to disable

one or two devices deliberately designed to discourage visitors, and pulled open the door. He stepped over the threshold. He was wet but not *trudging through the night in the rain* wet. He'd only walked from his pod.

'Where's your pod?'

'Two fields away.'

In that case, he probably hadn't come to kill me. If he had, the pod would be outside on the lawn, prepped for a quick getaway.

I led the way into my personal sitting room. What now? Did the normal rules of hospitality apply? Did I offer tea? Something stronger? I suddenly wished I'd paid more attention at Mlle Leonie's establishment. A large part of the syllabus had been devoted to awkward social situations and how to resolve them and I hadn't bothered to listen because I'd planned to be the one causing the awkward social situations.

I stopped in the middle of the room and turned to face him. 'What is it?'

He stood in the doorway, dripping water. He'd never been in here in the same way I'd never been in his quarters.

If I still didn't look well, he looked even worse. The wound over his eye had not healed gently and his hands were badly scarred. The last two fingers on his left hand hadn't set properly. And he'd lost weight. He'd always had a stocky build but not any longer. Now he looked diminished. And there was a shadow across his eyes.

I waited. And waited some more. I was determined not to speak. The only sound was water dripping off his coat on to the floor. Small pools began to form.

'George is dead.'

I stared at him, unable to take it in. This was silly. How

could George be dead? He was only six years older than me. He couldn't possibly be dead. How could George be dead?

Pennyroyal had remained standing just inside the doorway, making no effort to come further into the room. He still wasn't looking at me, just staring at the water collecting on the floor.

'How?'

'They said he was cleaning his gun.'

'Cleaning his gun? George has never fired a gun in his life. He hates them. Besides I'm pretty sure Caroline got rid of them all and—'

I stopped dead, taking in the implications. George being dead was unbelievable. George picking up a gun, let alone cleaning one, was utterly inconceivable. It just couldn't happen.

I tried to get my brain to work. Had Caroline killed him? Personally? Had she actually picked up a gun and fired it at him? Or had George killed himself? Which was worse? Having your life end in a crescendo of violence and terror at the hands of someone else? Or suffering such agony of mind – such despair – that the only way out was to end that life? What were George's last thoughts as he stared down the gun barrel? And who held the gun? I couldn't believe he'd killed himself. Caroline had killed him. She must have done. But how? Surely her fingernails wouldn't be up for the job. No, how much more likely was it that she had created the conditions for George to take his own life? And I hadn't been there. I'd left him completely at her mercy. We hadn't even been speaking when I left all those years ago. I'd never made any effort to contact him. George had been entirely alone and now I knew how that felt.

Caroline would pay for this.

Pennyroyal was still blocking the doorway.

'Get out of the way.'

He didn't move. 'Where are you going?'

'I'm jumping back. To Starlings.'

'Why?'

'Revenge.'

He still didn't move and I could still hear water dripping to the floor.

At long last, he lifted his head and looked at me with those dead, dull grey eyes.

'Let me tell you how you feel. You're consumed with the desire to kill. It fills your heart and your head. You want to avenge George and quiet your own conscience. Because you weren't there to save him when he needed you and no power in the universe can ever change that. Your heart burns for revenge. Nothing will stop you. And once you've taken your revenge – once you've killed all those responsible – you think everything will be all right again. Well, it won't. It certainly wasn't for me. It lost me you – the only person who means something to me – and I can tell you from experience that if you go down that route, you'll find nothing but loneliness, desolation and, if you're very lucky, a quick death.'

There was a huge, long silence as his words reverberated inside my head. I'm not gifted with enormous self-knowledge – no Smallhope is – but at that moment, the blinding flash of revelation made me catch my breath. I actually staggered.

Because my instincts had been exactly the same as his. Revenge. To abandon everything in my life and embark on a journey from which there might be no coming back. To make others suffer as I was suffering. To hurt others as I was hurting. And now, here was someone who had stood where I was standing now and he was warning me . . . trying to prevent me from making exactly the same mistake.

'Sit down.' He caught hold of me and pulled up a chair, but I was rigid. My body refused to bend. I couldn't move at all.

For a moment nothing happened and then he made a small sound and held me tightly. He was cold and wet and I didn't care. I almost couldn't breathe and I still didn't care. My mind had stopped working. There was nothing for me beyond that moment. My world had stopped. George was gone. Forever. Why had I never found the time to jump back and talk to him? Somewhere away from Caroline's influence, just the two of us? But I hadn't. In all the excitement of my successful new life, I'd barely given him a thought and now it was too late. The chance for us to talk together behind the compost heaps like we used to – gone forever. There was nothing I could do to change anything. It was all too late. Because I'd left him.

'Breathe,' Pennyroyal said hoarsely.

I wasn't sure I could handle the pain of breathing.

'Breathe,' he said, again. 'Please.'

I squeezed my eyes tight and tried. What came out was a kind of gasping sob that hurt my chest, hurt my throat, hurt everything. But the next one was easier, and the next.

And then the tears came.

A second later, so did mine. For quite a long time. I could feel his tears soaking into my hair.

'I'm sorry,' I whispered.

'Are you talking to me or George?'

'Both of you.'

He wiped away my tears with his thumbs. 'I'm sorry, too.

Sorrier than I can ever say. It haunts me. If, because of what I did that night, you had died . . .'

He couldn't go on and neither could I and so we stood together, holding on to each other as if our lives depended on it. And at that moment, I think they very probably did.

He slept on the sofa in my sitting room.

He was still there the next morning. I'd slept like the dead – he'd obviously slept like the more than dead.

I suddenly realised I was hungry. Slipping on my dressing gown, I went into the kitchen to make some breakfast. I'd like to think it was the smell of bacon that woke him but more likely it was the sound of banging pans and cursing.

He stood in the doorway. I waited for the traditional exasperated comment about my scrambled eggs. It never came. Both of us looked pretty awful. We stared at each other. What now? Where did we go from here?

I moved the frying pan off the heat, turned to face him and said, 'Why?'

There was no need to say any more. He knew what I was asking.

He was silent for a long time, then said, 'I had a sister. She . . .'

I held up my hand. His pain was too painful to watch. 'I know. Uncle Albert told me.'

He swallowed several times, and then said, 'It was him. That bloke in the kitchen. It was Derek. Eddie. The last one left. The one whose idea it was to . . . push her out into the mob. I couldn't . . . I wasn't thinking properly. Or thinking at all. I had to kill him. Whatever it took. As soon as I was able to think clearly I came after you but you were safe at TPHQ by then so I just . . . waited for you to come home.'

I didn't know what to say. I'd been so wrapped up in what he'd done, I'd never asked myself *why*. This was Pennyroyal. He wouldn't have done what he did without a very good reason. And Eddie was dead. It was over. Finished. And was I so very different? Hadn't I too experienced that overwhelming desire for revenge?

For something to do, I put the frying pan back on the heat and poked the bacon. Decision time. There was George's death to deal with. And what of Pennyroyal? He'd exposed his soul to me last night and in those moments he'd spoken the truth. Revenge was not the magic cure for guilt. He'd killed to avenge his sister – many times – and it hadn't helped. His guilt had not been assuaged. Probably mine wouldn't be either. I should sit down calmly and try to reason things out.

I indicated the table and he sat down in his old seat. I put a plate of food in front of him and sat opposite. He looked down at it, saying, 'I've been where you are. Don't make my mistakes.'

'You always say don't make it personal.'

He was still staring at his plate. 'Personal blinds you to everything else. You need to stop and think. Revenge is a dish best served cold.'

I pushed a knife and fork across the table.

'What would you do if you weren't here?' He gestured around at Home Farm. 'If you were living a normal life in your own time?'

I considered this. 'Short-term – attend the funeral.'

'There you are, then. A starting point.'

He was right. I'd attend the funeral and then . . .

310

'I have a suggestion,' he said.

'Yes?'

There was a long pause. This wasn't easy for him. This wasn't easy for either of us. I'm sure there are people who can talk about their own personal feelings from morning to night. Clarify the issues. Discuss successful outcomes and the means of achieving them. And then there's me and Pennyroyal.

Eventually, still not looking at me, he said, 'I want to come back. I want to resume our partnership. I don't know how you feel about that, and I suspect you don't either. So, a suggestion. I'll escort you to the funeral because you shouldn't go alone. Then we'll come back and spend a month here. Perhaps take on a small job or two. Perhaps not. At the end of twenty-eight days, we decide whether to continue or whether to make a clean break. Part, but as friends. That . . .' he paused and then continued heavily, 'that would be important to me.'

I needed a moment to think about this.

'Take your time,' he said, watching my face carefully. 'I'll be waiting in the other pod if you need me. Two fields over.'

My professional instincts weren't entirely dead. 'Anything useful in the memory?'

'Yeah,' he said, getting up and, like me, not having eaten a thing. 'One or two things you or I might find useful.'

'Good.'

On his way to the door, he paused. 'One more thing.'

'What?'

'If you want to engage with Caroline, then you can't afford to go back looking anything less than perfect. At the moment you look exhausted. Ill. Like a victim. You need to be sleek, glossy, prosperous – a successful businesswoman. The way you look right now she's more likely to give you a fiver and the address of the nearest Salvation Army hostel. When she's stopped laughing at you. And if you are going to kill her, you need to make sure you do the job properly. I thought he was dead. Derek.'

'Eddie,' I said.

'I thought I'd done for him and he was the last of them. Only it turned out I hadn't. Don't leave the job half done the way I did. That blows up in your face when you least expect it.'

I considered my own plate. Good advice.

He turned away again. 'Get well. Plan your strategy. Execute without mercy. Succeed.'

More good advice.

I ate my breakfast alone, took a shower, looked myself squarely in the mirror for the first time in ages and made a decision.

By mutual consent, we discussed nothing before the funeral. I put my energies into improving my appearance. Pennyroyal, somewhat embarrassed, presented me with a voucher for a spa weekend. I thanked him politely and took myself away.

Away from Home Farm and its dark memories, I lay, wrapped in a waffle robe, in the Japanese gardens, listening to the humming bees, the tock of the deer scarer and the tinkling fountains. The koi pools were spectacular. There's something very soothing about watching brightly coloured fish swim around in crystal-clear water. And these were friendly – very unlike those finger-chomping bastards in TPHQ, which rumour reckons are not koi at all but some kind of multi-coloured attack piranha the Time Police breed specially.

Everything was peaceful and harmonious. The food was

good. I've never been to Japan but I made a mental note to get myself there one day. I booked myself into just about every treatment going – excluding colonic irrigation because who does that? – and returned to Home Farm a little over forty-eight hours later looking and feeling very much restored.

I gave it another week, lying around reading, eating, drinking and running a little further every day and there was a definite improvement. Make-up would do the rest.

HARDCOURT PARVA
The Present

George had a beautiful day for his funeral. Early May can be lovely. The horse chestnuts around the churchyard were in full flower. The beech leaves were green and glossy. All the colours, all the scents were bright and sharp and clean. I was hit with a wave of unexpected nostalgia. I had forgotten . . .

There were surprisingly few people in the church and even fewer of them were local. The bulk of the congregation consisted of Caroline's family. I assumed everyone else was what passed as friends, useful social contacts or those she considered good enough for her to be seen with in public.

I'd meant to sit quietly at the back, but this lack of George's family, George's friends, George's tenants, and local people who had known him all his life and would probably have liked to pay their last respects made me angry. Very angry indeed.

Pennyroyal slipped quietly behind a pillar at the back and sat down.

Tradition has it that you tiptoe around in a church. Especially on solemn occasions such as a funeral. That didn't suit me at all, so I walked very slowly and very deliberately down the aisle, my heels sounding loud over the murmuring organ. Still played by Mrs Harris, the butcher, I saw.

Heads turned as I made my way to the front. Caroline and Young George had the front pew all to themselves. Selecting the row behind – deliberately kept empty so everyone could have a good view of the grieving but brave widow and her young son, I suspected – I bowed to George's coffin, ignored the panicking usher trying to funnel me somewhere inconspicuous, slipped into the pew and sat behind her. Directly behind her. She half turned her head, trying to see who I was from the corner of her eye. I shifted my weight away from her gaze. If she wanted to know who it was, then she'd have to turn around and face me. I waited but it didn't happen. Although the back of her neck began to turn a fiery red. I found I had no pity.

Reverend Caldicott stepped up, the organ dwindled into silence and the service began.

It was all surprisingly traditional. Definitely un-Caroline. I wondered if George had discussed details with Reverend Caldicott at some point. Which led to more internal speculation as to the mystery of his death. I made myself concentrate. We sang the 'Old Hundredth'. And 'Crimond', of course. Reverend Caldicott spoke very movingly of George as a young boy. George in the church choir – until his voice broke so disastrously in the middle of 'O for the Wings of a Dove'. George coming second in the school poetry competition. George's unfailing modesty and consideration for others. Caroline flapped a lacey hankie. I did not slap her. Not in church. That would not be seemly.

From what I could see of him, Young George must have been

around eight or nine. He didn't look terribly robust – his shoulders showed sharp and thin beneath his jacket. But, plenty of time for a growth spurt or two. He looked very like the photo of his father at the same age. It had sat on Papa's desk – along with one of me – until Papa's death, when they'd both disappeared. Along with the desk itself. And Papa. I caught my breath.

Young George had our family colouring. His hair was the same colour as his father's. And mine. And Papa's before us. There was no blond in Young George's hair. In fact, I couldn't see much of Caroline in him at all.

He stood quietly, singing from his hymn book. He didn't fidget while Reverend Caldicott delivered his address. I wondered if he was naturally quiet. Or shy. Or terrorised. Or, given it was Caroline – drugged. No – not even Caroline would do that.

The service concluded, the pallbearers stepped forwards and my brother George was carried out to see the sun for the last time. There was quite a crowd of villagers in the churchyard, all at what Caroline would fondly imagine was a respectful distance, but was actually because they didn't like her.

I kept my own distance. Let her wonder if she'd been imagining things. I stood in the shadow of a yew tree and watched George laid to rest. I wondered how much rest he'd been allowed these last few years. I said my own prayer and wished him well. Rest in peace, George.

Caroline took Young George's hand and whisked him away. Apart from a very cursory word with the Caldicotts, she spoke to no one. Even after all this time, she didn't have much of a clue, did she? Her family trailed behind her as they climbed into the waiting cars and were driven the hundred yards back to Starlings.

I watched them go. I could just imagine the 'Well, thank God that's over'. Said in front of Young George, as well.

Smallhopes had been buried in this churchyard for centuries, except for those who have fallen in various actions around the world – which is quite a sizeable number, actually. There were enough here, however, to have filled up the ancient family vault, no matter how carefully they'd been packed in, so from the late 19th century onwards, we'd been buried in the family plot alongside, shaded by three ancient yews. I've always thought it appropriate for the descendants of those who fought at Agincourt to lie under the descendants of the trees that supplied the famous bows and arrows. Papa was buried here. With Mama and Charlotte beside him. Now, George was here as well. I'd be there one day. Alongside Papa. My plot was already reserved so even if Caroline outlived me there wouldn't be a thing she could do about it. Although I was buggered if Caroline would be outliving me. I took a moment to enjoy a few thoughts inappropriate for consecrated ground.

Standing between George's grave and Papa's, I whispered one final goodbye to George, wishing him the peace I suspected he hadn't had much of in his married life, and then – and I don't know what made me say it – I turned to Papa. 'I'm sorry – I was supposed to look after George, and I failed. But I will look after his son. I promise.'

I stayed among the trees until most people had left before speaking to Reverend Caldicott and his wife. They greeted me warmly and we talked a little of George. They asked me if I was going back to Starlings.

'Not invited,' I said.

'No one is,' said Mrs Caldicott. 'Not from the village, anyway.'

I said nothing because I had Young George to think of – or just George now, I supposed. It's medieval and old-fashioned, I know, but one day these people would be as important to George as he was to them. Responsibility and duty work both ways. He would be many people's landlord or employer. Village families and ours had marched together down through the centuries. Fighting, poaching, arguing, dying together on some foreign field . . .

'I think Jo's putting on a bit of a do at the Teddy,' said Mrs Caldicott, referring to the local pub – the King Edward.

'Good idea,' I said.

Jo was talking to someone I didn't know so I waved to attract her wife's attention.

'Now then,' said Ellie, coming over and shaking hands. 'Who's been a stranger?'

'As if I'd ever forget the place I had my first illegal drink.'

'I nearly had a heart attack when they told me you were only fourteen.'

'It's legal if you have a meal.'

'A packet of crisps is not a meal. Are you coming back to the Teddy? We've put on a bit of a spread.'

'Good,' I said, pulling out my credit card and handing it to her. 'I'd like to put something behind the bar.'

She handed it back. 'No need. I reckon you're good for it. We'll settle up at the end.' She signalled to Jo and disappeared in the direction of the King Teddy.

I lingered in the churchyard. Pennyroyal approached. 'All right?'

I explained there was a bit of a do at the King Teddy if he was interested.

He thought for a moment. 'I might see if I can lend them a hand.'

'I think that would be greatly appreciated.'

He disappeared among the tombstones.

That is such a Pennyroyal sentence.

I made my way out under the lychgate – where George's coffin would have paused for a few traditional moments – and out into the main street.

The King Teddy was on the left, about halfway down. The third part of the traditional village triangle – manor house, church, pub. The place was packed and noisy. I made my way to the bar, acknowledging smiles and nods. Pennyroyal was already there. I raised my eyebrows – he shook his head. The bar was fully staffed and they didn't need him. Using my eyes, I asked him if he wanted a drink and he shook his head and pointed to his pint so I left him to drink it in peace.

I took half a pint of cider for myself – this was not a margarita moment – and began to circulate. There was no lack of people to talk to. I simply said I was working in London these days and left it at that. It was broadly true. I circled the room, renewing old acquaintances and making new ones. Nothing stays the same. Not even in little backwaters like this one. Some people had died – others had been born. No one said a word about Caroline – which, in itself, spoke volumes.

Jo came out from behind the bar and made a formal toast to the memory of George. Then we raised our glasses to the new Earl of Goodrich. I blinked at the floor. Someone put their hand on my shoulder for a moment and I blinked some more and turned around.

Pennyroyal was behind me. 'Look outside.'

Young George was standing on the grass verge. Not doing anything. Just gazing up and down the road and looking very lost and alone.

My mind flew back over the years. The day of Papa's funeral. Sitting on my bed. Doofus on one side, Rosie on the other. Both long dead themselves, now. I'd sat in my room and watched the darkness fall. Alone. In every sense of the word. Because my papa was dead.

I gave Pennyroyal my drink to hold and slipped outside.

'Hey. Do you know who I am?'

He turned and shook his head.

'I'm your wicked Aunt Amelia. Don't bother with the aunt bit if you don't want to. Just Millie is fine. That's what your papa called me. How are you, George?'

He drew a breath and then said formally, 'Very well, thank you.'

'Should you be here?'

He shook his head.

'Well,' I said, 'I'm not sure if you know this, but it is the sworn duty of every aunt to lead their nephew into temptation at every opportunity. You coming in?'

He looked uncertain. 'Mummy says . . .'

'I expect she does, but you're an important person now, George, and there are people here who wish you well and would like to meet you. You won't be on your own. I'll be with you. If you want, of course.'

He squinted up at me. 'Mummy says one day you'll be sorry.'

I grinned. 'Mummy's not wrong. But not today. So are you coming in?'

He stumped across the verge. I followed him in through the door.

Pennyroyal approached him with a glass of orange juice. 'Can you play dominoes?'

George shook his head.

'Want to learn?'

We sat him down at a corner table and were joined by old Amos Cope, poacher extraordinaire whom Papa had publicly threatened to shoot on at least three separate occasions.

'Mr Cope,' I said, shaking hands. 'How are you?'

'Not bad,' he said. 'Not bad at all.' He looked at George. 'Now then, young squire.'

Completely at sea, George stared at him. Then at me. Then at Pennyroyal. At that moment, my feelings for Caroline were even less friendly than usual. I strongly suspected she was isolating Young George in the same way she had his father. Something unpleasant was definitely going to happen to her one day.

'He's asking how you are,' said Pennyroyal, lining up his dominoes.

Again, George said formally, 'I'm very well, thank you, Mr . . .'

'Cope,' I said.

'Mr Cope. I hope you are as well.'

'Not so bad,' he said again. 'We playing for money here?'

'We are not,' I said. 'Your skill precedes you, Mr Cope, to say nothing of your sleight of hand. George – beware Mr Cope and whatever he has up his sleeve. To say nothing of his poacher's pocket.'

George wrinkled his forehead. 'What's a poacher's pocket?'

Mr Cope winked and tapped his nose. 'Tell you later. When your auntie's gone.'

We played a quick game – you'll never guess who won – and then I took the hint and moved away. Pennyroyal followed me, leaving Young George to play another game and broaden his horizons in a way that would horrify his mother.

I was angry. Everyone here should be a big part of Young George's world. He should know them. The regular duels between Amos Cope and Papa – which had usually taken place in this very pub – had been a part of village life. Each seeking to outwit the other and thoroughly enjoying themselves in the process. I know for a fact Papa had tried to have Amos transported to Australia on several occasions and had been bitterly disappointed to discover the practice had been discontinued. He'd attempted to raise the matter in the House of Lords with a view to reinstating the appropriate legislation. I'd had to point out that transporting Amos Cope to a blameless and unsuspecting nation probably came under the heading of 'Act of War'. Although, as Papa had said, it would have been fun watching Amos trying to stuff a kangaroo into his famous pocket.

The afternoon wore on. I beat Pennyroyal at darts. Twice. And reminded him I'd always been the better shot, just to rub it in a little. I leaned on the bar and listened to the story of someone's ploughing drama. There were ham rolls – apparently there are always ham rolls at funerals – and these were very good. I had another drink and listened to the voices around me. I hadn't realised how much I'd missed all this.

'That's your problem,' said Pennyroyal, materialising beside me.

'What is?'

'This. All this. It's bred into you. You can't escape it.'

'I can and I have.'

He shrugged. 'We'll see.'

It came out before I knew it. 'I have no plans to change my life.' And suddenly realised I didn't.

He shrugged again. 'We can't do what we do forever. People age. Even us. We'll get older and slower and one day – poof.'

'Poof?' I said, suspecting he'd been at the scrumpy.

'Someone younger and faster comes along. They have a reputation to make and taking us on is their way of establishing themselves. The secret is to recognise the moment and get out at the right time.'

'Hm,' I said. Because that had started a train of thought I would return to later.

Rescuing George from Amos, I took him around the room, introducing him to various people, many of whom were his tenants or worked for the estate in some capacity. He really should be getting to know them. Papa had taken me everywhere when I was younger. We'd careered around the country lanes in one of his rickety old vehicles, him shouting greetings out of the window and me waving. I'd joined in the discussions and arguments. I'd sat in on estate meetings. Papa knew everyone and had made sure I did too. Caroline should be doing the same for Young George. Was she making sure his only access to the world was through her?

It was easy to see that, for most people, this was the first time they'd met him. People were wary but polite. George had beautiful manners. If he was overwhelmed, it didn't show. He seemed completely at home with adults. I wondered if he knew anyone his own age. Other than at school, I mean. He shook hands with everyone to whom I introduced him and remembered their names.

More drinks were served. More ham rolls consumed. Time flew past and the sun had gone down. The windows outside were darkening.

George tugged at my sleeve. 'I have to go, Auntie Millie. They'll miss me at dinner.' He looked over his shoulder. 'Although I'd rather stay here.'

Again, I spared a thought for those who'd left Young George alone on the day we buried his father. And again, it wasn't friendly.

'Don't blame you,' I said. 'But duty before pleasure – always.'

Pennyroyal drained his pint. 'I'll walk you back, mate.'

'I do know the way,' he said, a little stiffly.

'Good,' said Pennyroyal. 'You can show me. Now – it's polite to thank your host and say goodnight to the room. I'll wait here for you.'

We watched George approach the bar, stand on tiptoe and speak to Jo. She smiled so he'd done that right. And then he walked to the door, cleared his throat, closed his eyes, and piped, 'I have to go now. It was nice to meet you all. Goodnight.'

There was a massive chorus of goodnights, which seemed to reassure him greatly. He opened his eyes, anyway, and he and Pennyroyal disappeared out of the door.

Ellie and I settled up. She warned me to be sitting down when I got my next credit card statement and I began to say my own goodnights, suspecting – correctly – that it would be a long business. It was completely dark when I eventually left the King Teddy.

I breathed in the cool air – it was still a little chilly at night – and set off back up the road towards the pod, parked carefully behind the churchyard, strolling past cottages that had been here for centuries. There were lights at all the windows. Someone's dog barked. I was just thinking that other than the modern street lights and the chippy, Hardcourt Parva must have looked this way for hundreds of years, when a shadow stepped out from the shadows and tried to drag me behind a laurel bush.

If I hadn't been me, it would probably have worked. On the other hand, if I hadn't been me, I probably wouldn't have been attacked. But it was me. And I'd had a bit to drink. And I was still pretty pissed at Caroline. Who, granted, wasn't here at this particular moment, but whoever this little shit was would do just as well.

Seriously, the whole thing was massive bad planning on someone's part. I'm five foot nine. I box. I run. I lift weights. Not enthusiastically, but I do it because Pennyroyal says it's good for upper body strength. *And I'm a fucking bounty hunter, for heaven's sake.*

This little twat didn't cause me any problems at all. So much so I felt honour-bound to pick him up a couple of times to show him where he'd gone wrong, following through with a demonstration highlighting his weak areas and then having to pick him up all over again.

Eventually, my arms got tired so I left him down there. I leaned against Mrs Peggotty's garden wall and took a moment to straighten my clothes and hair. As I continually tell Pennyroyal – we're representing the public face of the firm and it's in our own interests to look smart at all times. Actually I can count on the fingers of one hand the number of times Pennyroyal hasn't looked neat and tidy. There's no middle ground with him – he either looks immaculate or as if he's only one step away from death itself.

I was just putting the finishing touches to my appearance when Pennyroyal emerged from a random bush, sporting his familiar disapproving look. 'That took you far too long.'

'I was enjoying myself. I wanted to savour the experience.'

'Even so . . .'

'And combine it with a teaching moment.'

'For whom?'

'Him.'

He bent over Chummy and rolled him over. 'Know him?'

'Oh God,' I said. 'I think it's the male of the species. Caroline's brother. Rodney or Gilbert or Rupert or something.'

'Why haven't we seen him before?'

'Rumour has it he's spent some time serving at His Majesty's pleasure.'

Pennyroyal leaned closer. 'Pretty boy. Either he'll have done very well in prison or very badly.'

'Do you care?'

'Not even a little bit. George has been safely delivered. Slipped in through the west door in a manner very reminiscent of his aunt. Nice boy. Anyway – feeling better now?'

'Very much so. Now I see why there are so many fights at funerals.'

He blinked. 'What sort of funerals do you attend?'

'Well, so far, only family ones.'

He shook his head.

'And Uncle Albert's, of course. At which there wasn't any

sort of civil disturbance of any kind, so I suppose you're right –
it's a Smallhope thing.'

Pennyroyal stirred the groaning Gilbert – or Rupert – or
Rodney – with his foot. 'What do you think he was up to?'

I shrugged. 'Looking for George, perhaps, saw me instead
and thought he'd have a bit of fun.'

Pennyroyal prodded him again. 'Wonder how that worked
out for him.'

BACK AT HOME FARM
The Future

The twenty-eight days were up. Decision time.

We seated ourselves at the kitchen table. There was an awkward silence.

I cleared my throat. 'Shall I begin?'

Pennyroyal nodded.

'I've thought about this a great deal. You want the partnership to continue and I do, too. However, neither of us is match-fit at the moment – for various reasons – and I think we need a period during which we can both readjust ourselves to working together again.'

I stopped in case he had a comment to make. Which he did.

'You have the expression of one planning something.'

'I have and I am. Several somethings, actually. I was thinking about what you said about the inadvisability of going on too long in this profession and I think you're right – we should move into other possibly slightly less strenuous areas. Although how less strenuous they'll be once we turn up, I don't know.'

'We?'

'I'm sorry,' I said. 'I didn't mean to take anything for granted. You go ahead and tell me what you want to do. How you see *your* future.'

I clasped my hands on the table and waited.

Eventually he said, 'I'm sorry.'

'No, it's OK. Take your time to get your thoughts in order.'

'No. I'm sorry.' He stared down at his lap. 'Desperately sorry.' He made to say something else, appeared lost for words and fell back into silence. I waited and eventually he said, 'What I did . . .'

'Was exactly what I would have done to Caroline if you hadn't stopped me. I'd have killed her – probably not very cleverly because I was too angry to think clearly. I'd have traumatised Young George, got myself arrested – and perpetrated who knows how many other disasters. I . . . I can understand now . . . I think . . . a little of how you felt when you saw him again. So suddenly. Derek, I mean. Or was he Eddie?'

'He was Derek when I was beating the living shit out of him the first time. Can't believe he survived that.'

'Nor me. Were you having an off-day?'

'Must have been.'

I said softly, 'I wonder how he got from this time to the future. To Insight. To become Eddie.'

'Not our problem,' Pennyroyal said curtly. 'He was the last of them and now he's dead.'

I should stop talking about this. Derek and what he and the others had done to Pennyroyal's sister was still an unbearable wound for him. Always would be, I suspected.

The silence went on and on and on, as it does when you get

two people who don't find it easy to talk about important things. Finally, he stirred and said, 'I swear to you, on the memory of my sister, that I will never leave you again. I will stand with you to the end. Always. Without fail.'

I felt my eyes fill with tears. I couldn't look at him. Which didn't matter because he couldn't look at me. We sat for some time, each of us not looking at the other, and then I took the easy way out – for both of us – and steered the focus of the conversation to safer waters. 'Our future.'

'You've had an idea,' he said. 'I can tell.'

I made a decision. 'It's a personal matter and nothing to do with the firm, but it's something on which I'd appreciate your thoughts.'

'Hang on.'

He got up and mixed a margarita and poured himself a small whisky. 'Go ahead.'

I sipped. 'Caroline's selling off the estate. Some of it is tied up legally but most of it isn't. At the rate she's going, I worry there won't be anything left for Young George. Nothing of value, anyway.' I took another swig. 'I want to buy up as much as I possibly can.'

He said nothing so I carried on.

'It would be from my own share of the profits. I wouldn't touch the firm's money. But it might leave me short. Very short, actually. How would you feel about having a partner who might not be able to support herself?'

He leaned back in his chair. 'It wouldn't be the first time we've looked after each other.'

'That's true.'

'And anything you did acquire would, if I know you, be

properly managed and rented out. Sooner or later you'd be getting an income from it?'

'Yes.'

'We can always take on extra work.'

'It's not fair to make you take on a larger workload to pay for my extravagance.'

'Let me ask you a question. Why are you doing this? You don't owe your family anything. You don't owe Starlings anything.'

I took a deep breath but my voice still wasn't steady.

'I left him there. My brother George. I left him.'

'You had no choice. I was there at the time, remember? Staying would not have helped anyone. Least of all you.'

'He was all alone. She cut him off from everyone and everything. I wonder if he knew she was robbing him blind. Or whether he only realised it at the end.'

He frowned. 'She can't dispose of the entire estate, surely?'

'No – but I'm not sure she isn't fatally crippling it. Financially, I mean. The only thing that will be left for Young George will be the title. There's nothing she can do about that.'

'Are you sure?'

I stopped. No, I wasn't sure. Suppose – just suppose . . . Caroline was well endowed with female relations. She wouldn't find it hard to dredge up a cousin from somewhere. Not too closely related, of course – you don't want the kids having six fingers and the Habsburg chin – but there was a possibility George might one day find himself married to a mini-Caroline and then he would be lost indeed.

Pennyroyal had more questions. 'What about the house itself?'

I paused. 'Actually, I don't know. I don't think anyone's ever tried to sell it before. I'll speak to Mr Treasure. If it can be done, then I'm sure she'll give it a go and if she does, then he'll let me know. If it's not all too late by now, of course.'

'Too late for your brother – but not too late for his son.'

'No.' I picked up my glass. 'You do see why I have to do something, don't you?'

'Could the family help?'

'There are so few of us now. Really, there's only me.'

'If you think you're responsible for keeping a watchful eye on George's son, then do it.'

'It's hard to explain. Even to myself. I think it's what you said – it's bred into me.'

'An ancestor thing.'

'Not necessarily. Everyone has ancestors. The only difference is that mine have been in one spot for a long time. Lots of people say we didn't earn the lands or title – although don't try telling that to the Elizabeth Smallhope who laboured under Charles II for night after night. Yes, her compliant husband was awarded the earldom but she was the one who earned it. And yes, I know I'm descended from cattle rustlers, court prostitutes and thieving warlords, but all that's bloody hard work, you know. To say nothing of hundreds – possibly thousands – of dead Smallhopes and parts thereof littering foreign fields.'

I stopped. I wasn't explaining this at all well but I didn't really understand it myself. 'It's just . . . I suppose it's a sense of duty. Papa had it – I have it. To preserve . . . no, to protect the estate and hand it on to the next generation.'

He nodded.

'And . . .'

'Yes?'

'What you said at the funeral – about the firm not going on forever.'

'Yes?'

'We might need a bolthole one day. Somewhere to hide. Somewhere to recover from illness, injury, whatever. Somewhere to retire to, even. Why shouldn't that be at Starlings?'

'Always plan ahead.'

I smiled. 'Another teaching moment. Haven't had one of those for a long while.'

There was a short silence.

'Well,' he said, topping up his glass. 'Land rarely depreciates. Long term – a good investment. Short term – as I said, not the first time we've looked after each other. If you still want my advice – go for it.'

I did go for it. Mr Treasure agreed to advise me of anything he thought I should know about. Especially if it related to Starlings itself. On his advice I formed a housing company – the Battersea Corporation, of which I was sole owner and director. I put him on a retainer and quietly, through his agent, began to pick up parcels of land here or there.

There were other jobs to attend to, as well. Loose ends to tie up from our Insight adventure. We delivered Max and Markham's share personally, combining it with another job. Can't say too much about that because the warrants are still active – a politician and an arsehole – although we haven't had to execute either of them yet. The warrants, I mean, not the subjects of said warrants.

*   *   *

333

The worst of the Time Wars was over and our Time Police work had declined accordingly.

'We need to respond to changing circumstances,' I said to Pennyroyal.

He agreed. 'But without burning any bridges behind us. I wouldn't want to sever all ties but we should start moving into other areas. I'll put the word out – see what that brings forth.'

It brought forth very quickly, actually. Raymond Parrish put one or two well-paying assignments our way and then, one day, he called us in to his office. Well, no, he sent us a politely worded request to which we equally politely responded.

This visit was very different to our first. Their reception area was as bustling as before, but now there were scanning booths for anyone entering the premises. Everyone's bags were searched – manually – whether their owners liked it or not. There was a visitors' list off which we had to be checked. And – most importantly – we had to surrender our ID cards, to be kept for the duration of our visit and collected on the way out.

Pennyroyal became very twitchy about this, which was a little unfair because it had been one of his suggestions. However, we complied like good little recovery agents and were handed a randomly generated number which would get us our docs back when our visit was finished.

Pennyroyal peered suspiciously at his number. I think he suspected they were either auctioning off our IDs at this very moment or, worse, probing our personal info as it related to our employment history, blood groups, medical history, police records and bank details.

I tucked away my number very carefully because if I lost

that then Pennyroyal would have to take the building apart to retrieve our stuff and that, I guessed, would not endear us to Raymond Parrish even a little bit.

He'd had his office redecorated since we saw him last, in shades of brown, cream and pale green. A little less masculine – perhaps he didn't feel he had so much to prove. Parrish Industries was worldwide by now. We sat down on one of his very comfortable sofas and waited to see what he had in mind.

He got straight to it. 'I find myself experiencing some unease about the actions of one of my main competitors. Well – my one main competitor.'

By mutual consent, I did the talking. 'Is that the cause of your unease? That it is your main competitor?'

'No. I hear things. Often I hear things I'm not supposed to. May I get you some refreshments, by the way?'

'Coffee, please,' I said.

'Nothing stronger?'

'We don't drink while working.'

He nodded.

Ms Steel brought in refreshments.

He had his naughty side, did Raymond Parrish. Quite straight-faced, he said, 'I think you will remember Ms Steel.'

She cast Pennyroyal an unloving look. She certainly remembered him.

'Ms Steel has recently become my PA. If, for some reason, I am not available and your matter is urgent, then you may safely leave a message with her.'

I frowned. 'What sort of urgent matter might we want to contact you about?'

He stirred his coffee. 'It has, once or twice, crossed my mind that this major competitor is, shall we say, pursuing certain commercial opportunities that some might find . . . disturbing.'

I put down my coffee. Pennyroyal hadn't even picked his up. He was pursuing his usual silent-menace routine. At which he was extremely good. He usually left all the talking to me. Each of us playing to our own strengths.

'If I understand you correctly,' I said, 'might these commercial opportunities involve a temporal dimension?'

'They might.'

'Surely then, it would be more appropriate to take your concerns to the Time Police.'

'While they would certainly be more suitable – they might be less effective.'

'That does not seem likely.'

He paused. 'Let me just say that a Time Police element is already involved.'

'We don't trespass on their territory. While perfectly happy to accept commissions from them – we are not in competition.'

'I understand. This Time Police element is, however, not official.'

Well, bugger me sideways – as Papa once said to a princess – Raymond Parrish had a TPO in his pocket. I did not look at Pennyroyal. Who was almost certainly very carefully not looking at me.

'We would not care to find ourselves in conflict with this element,' I said. 'That could prove unfortunate for all parties.'

'That is clearly understood. It is unlikely that your paths will cross.'

'Would this element be aware of us?'

'Yes.'

'Is there likely to be a conflict of interest?'

'No. My instructions will be that this Time Police element would, wherever possible, smooth your path. With luck – and some careful planning – direct contact can be avoided.'

'I hope,' I said carefully, 'that this element is of a rank sufficient to be able to perform that function effectively.'

'You need have no fears on that score,' he said.

Pennyroyal was almost certainly reviewing what he knew of certain TPOs. I needed to concentrate on Raymond Parrish.

'Might we have some details before coming to a decision?'

'Of course. I shan't insult you by swearing you to secrecy before you actually accept the commission. Your discretion is well known.'

That's the sort of comment that leaves a happy glow in the heart of a hard-working recovery agent. Pennyroyal and I are proud of our reputation. Reliable. Effective. Discreet. And bloody expensive, of course. Which doesn't matter because some of our clients have the resources of a small country behind them. One or two have the resources of quite large countries. For anyone considering following us into the business – we've generally found that the larger the country, the less keen they are on paying. They seem to think the normal rules of invoicing don't apply to them. We've had to be quite firm on several occasions. There was one case where even stern invoicing proved ineffective, forcing Pennyroyal to spend a happy Sunday afternoon calling up old acquaintances and setting in hand various events that boded badly for that country's political stability. Two major coups and an army mutiny later, their government paid in full. Plus our punitive late settlement fee. All calculated at compound interest, obviously. $P = C (1 + r/n)nt$

337

No one invoices quite like Pennyroyal.

But back to Raymond Parrish. We accepted the commission. Portman Weber was the organisation involved – which we'd guessed anyway. They were a multi-national conglomerate with tentacles in every pie and, based on what he *didn't* say, a particular thorn in the Parrish Industries' pie. I do love a good mixed metaphor.

We settled the finer details – the budget, for instance – fixing our fee and negotiating our expenses. Pennyroyal happily accepted a substantial down payment and we returned to Home Farm to get stuck in.

We began by spending a very enjoyable day inventing criminal pasts for ourselves. Actually, not that much invention was required. We simply rifled through our memories and listed the appropriate skills. Breaking and entering, industrial espionage, illegal time travel activity, tax evasion – that would be Pennyroyal – blackmail and extortion – the two are not the same – theft, GBH, ABH, arson, fraud, political agitation – I have to say, even I was impressed.

Without any prompting from us, the Time Police added us to their amber list. Thanks to Raymond Parrish's unofficial Time Police element, no doubt. On the strength of that and together with our newly colourful CVs, we waited. Not for long. Pennyroyal was approached by an oleaginous little twat named Geoffrey who was so discreet and oblique that he – Pennyroyal – confessed afterwards he hadn't known what he was on about half the time. He rather thought, at the end of the interview, that we might have been offered a job, but he couldn't be one hundred per cent certain.

There was a follow-up interview which both of us attended. I wore my favourite smart business suit and Pennyroyal wore his favourite expression of glowering hostility. There were four of them – three women and one man and no formal introductions.

It was an interrogation. Oh, it was all very nice and friendly – and the refreshments were superb – but it was an interrogation nevertheless.

They started with me. I smiled and trotted out my cover story. I'd been a hard-working and vastly under-appreciated admin officer in local government until a series of unfortunate coincidences, accidents and downright bad luck had left me with no alternative but to seek employment elsewhere. Quite quickly. In other words, I'd had my fingers in the till. From there I'd moved smoothly into a life of crime, where I'd been surprised and delighted to find my talents had been greatly appreciated and – much more importantly – appropriately rewarded.

'And you?' they said to Pennyroyal.

'I've always been a criminal.' He said no more.

Looking at him in his leather jacket and heavy boots, it was very obvious in which areas he had specialised and wisely, they'd left it at that.

I had questions of my own, obviously, since, despite their fond imaginings, we were interviewing them, wrapping mine up in the usual queries concerning pay, holidays, working conditions, pension scheme, etc.

Sadly, I didn't glean as much info as I would have wished – most of my questions were met with brain-numbing amounts of corporate gobbledegook, evasion and downright lies. I was very impressed with their performance. Politicians couldn't have done it better. It would probably be accurate to say Pennyroyal and I were the most truthful people in the room and it's not often we can make that claim. I hadn't enjoyed myself so much for ages.

They'd be in touch, they said, and eventually, after a tediously long and drawn-out period, we were offered undefined positions in an unnamed organisation with unspecified duties and responsibilities.

'Exciting,' I said to Pennyroyal, who sighed deeply and assumed the expression of one who could see that this was going to end in tears. Although not for him.

The job took longer than we thought – nearly six months, in fact. We spent some time supposedly hopping around the timeline in our very enjoyable role as tour reps for a firm purporting to offer really stupid rich people the opportunity to see the sights of history. Temporal tourism, no less. Although actually, it wasn't – the whole thing was a massive and very lucrative scam. Basically we wore very smart uniforms and showed bunches of rich plebs sights they couldn't have begun to appreciate even if they'd actually been looking at what they thought they were looking at at the time. Yes, sorry – that sentence got away from me towards the end. Even I found being pleasant to so many idiots day in and day out to be quite wearing, and I assume it was only their extremely generous tips that prevented Pennyroyal just shooting everyone in sight and going home early.

We were just beginning to think this was a normal, bog-standard scam – nothing major – when, presumably having passed some sort of probation period, we were inducted into the whole point of the operation – which was to earn vast sums of money to fund the mysterious and sinister Site X.

Site X was a filthy business. Not many people emerged

unscathed, let alone alive, and Pennyroyal and I had no sympathy for any of them. They deserved everything they got. I can't say too much because the Time Police investigation is still open. They have a very good idea of who was behind everything but bringing charges is proving difficult.

What I will say is that there are a great number of rules and regulations pertaining to the testing of new pharmaceuticals on humans. Clearly, you can't just feed people new products willy-nilly and hope they don't grow a third head or start to glow in the dark. Legal testing procedures, however, are expensive and time-consuming, and obviously manufacturers want their product on the market as quickly as possible.

So, to that end, some genius came up with the idea of jumping back into the past – a long way back into the past – and building a research centre there. Away from any awkward oversight issues. Suddenly there was a free, never-ending supply of test subjects with no rights and no protection because, technically, Neanderthals weren't human at all. Site X was the answer to all of Big Pharma's prayers. No unions, no regulatory bodies, no oversight, no limits – just a bunch of free, easily available subjects with whom they could do as they pleased.

We saw some dreadful things. The laboratories and operating theatres were nothing less than torture chambers. Anaesthetics, apparently, are too expensive to waste on a species so completely outside the scope of the law. Pennyroyal reined himself in – all credit to him – because we were supposed to be professionals on a job, but I know he took advantage of the chaos and destruction at the end to settle a few scores on behalf of those who couldn't. I suppose a nicer person would have stepped in at some point and made an effort to restrain him. I am not a nice person. I kept watch at the door so that he could give his full attention to the job in hand.

We were just getting ready to jump back to London to report our findings to Raymond Parrish when the Time Police arrived and went through Site X faster than a banker collecting his farewell bonus before the Fraud Squad turn up.

I've always thought it quite ironic, given that Pennyroyal and I were working for him, that it was Raymond Parrish's son, Luke, who led the undercover operation. A clever boy, Luke Parrish. God knows what he was doing in the Time Police. Though not so clever that he didn't bite off a little more than he could chew when everything kicked off. It took some quick thinking on our part to ensure he and his colleague didn't freeze to death in the snow.

The Time Police rounded up those Site X staff still capable of being rounded up and then released the Neanderthals. We watched from a distance as the sad straggle of survivors made their painful way through the snow to safety.

Anyway, Pennyroyal and I completed the job we'd been well paid to do, and emerged with all sorts of useful info for Raymond Parrish, so happy endings all round. Although not for the Site X employees, of course. Those that survived the Time Police incursion – and Pennyroyal – fell down any number of stairs on their way to the cells.

We passed names, dates and info on to Raymond Parrish. What he did with it I don't know.

'Biding his time,' said Pennyroyal and I think he was right.

There was a huge scandal when all the facts came out, and for a while it looked as if Parrish Industries would be in the firing line as well, but everyone knows how that ended, even though most of the murkier details were suppressed. And given that Luke Parrish came out of the whole Site X thing minus a couple of fingers, we were rather apprehensive as to Parrish senior's reaction, but not only did he not hold it against us, he went on to offer us a rather special family job. And that one I definitely can't talk about.

As part of the fun, Pennyroyal and I had had a side bet on the identity of Raymond Parrish's tame TPO. We each wrote a name on a piece of paper, sealed them both in an envelope and tucked it away until the right moment. Although we'd written two different names, we were both right. I have no idea what game that particular officer was playing. Deep, dark and dirty seemed a fair guess. We encountered him on several more occasions, although it's always the memory of him appearing so suddenly out of the mist at Stonehenge that stays with me. A truly dangerous man who kept his hand well-hidden right up until the end. He's gone now, of course. Too clever for his own good, that one.

24

We took a couple of weeks off after the Site X affair. The years were racking up – and the injuries, too. Pennyroyal was playing host to larger and larger areas of scar tissue.

And then something rather unsettling happened.

I was leaning against the embankment wall outside TPHQ, watching the river go by and waiting for Pennyroyal, who was handing in some dockets. Something he could do electronically, but he liked to network, maintaining he always picked up a surprising amount of useful information when bounty hunters got together and gossiped. I was in no hurry. It was a lovely day, the river sparkled, and TPHQ loomed massively over everything. Pennyroyal and I had planned to head off for a nice lunch when he eventually emerged. We weren't after anyone, no one was after us, and everything was right with the world.

And then a voice said, 'Millie?'

I nearly fell over. No one here in this time called me Millie. I was Smallhope, my lady, or you fucking bitch, depending on who was addressing me and under what circumstances. Various possibilities flickered through my mind, but to my certain knowledge, absolutely no one knew me as Millie.

I put one hand in my pocket – the one with the gun – and turned slowly around to a face from the past. The very last person I expected to see.

Uncle Albert. It was Uncle Albert. Young and fit, and with a little more flesh on his bones – but definitely Uncle Albert. And alive.

I know this can happen but it's still disconcerting to find yourself suddenly face to face with someone who died in your arms some years ago and for whom you grieved. And then, without warning, they're back. Standing right in front of you.

I tried to pull myself together.

He was watching me anxiously. 'I have got it right, haven't I? You are Millie?'

How did he know? He hadn't met me yet. And yet he knew I was Millie.

'Yes. And you're Uncle Albert.'

His shoulders sagged with relief. 'Yes. Well, if you say so, then I expect I will be. We haven't met yet, have we?'

I shook my head. 'How did you know to call me Millie?'

He smiled. 'Oh dear – am I not supposed to know that yet? Sorry. Anyway, I've come to ask you a favour.'

Sudden relief surged through me. So this was how it happened. Our papers were not prised from our cold dead hands as I had always feared, but just quietly handed over on request.

'Let me guess. You want our papers.'

'I do. Does this calm acceptance mean you've already surrendered them?'

'You leave them for us in an old tin with a Union Jack on the lid, hidden on the top shelf of the wardrobe in your bedroom.'

He smiled. 'Well, that was much easier than I thought it would be. And informative, too. Thank you.'

'Just make sure we get them back, otherwise there'll be loose bits of time flapping about all over the place.'

'All right.'

Speaking of loose bits of time, I had a sudden thought. 'I have to ask – what did you mean when you said, "Look after my . . ."'

He frowned. 'I've no idea. When did I say that?'

Carefully omitting the phrase *dying words*, I said, 'You will say, "Look after my . . ." – and then we were interrupted and never got back to it.'

He looked puzzled. 'Was it important?'

I thought back to that moment on the kitchen floor. 'I don't know.'

At some point Pennyroyal had arrived. I could see him standing very still, watching us.

'Turn slowly,' I said. 'He's just off to your right.'

Uncle Albert turned away from me. I couldn't see his face. I couldn't see Pennyroyal's either. I saw them shake hands. They talked for a while; their heads close. I'd walked away to give them a moment but I heard Pennyroyal say, 'Walthamstow.'

He was giving the future Uncle Albert his address. As Max would say – the circle was closing. It's a strange feeling.

When they turned back, I had my papers ready.

'Here you are. Citizen's ID and Time Police authority.'

Uncle Albert was already holding Pennyroyal's documents. For anyone who remembers, the bloodstain on the back wasn't his. Someone at Site X didn't get out of his way quickly enough.

He tucked everything away. 'Thank you.'

'Should we ask?'

Uncle Albert shook his head. 'No. Will you have to report the loss of your papers?'

'We'll say they were taken from us at Site X. There will be hard looks and sarcasm.'

'I'm sorry.'

Pennyroyal grinned. 'We didn't say who would be doing the hard looking and sarcasm.'

Uncle Albert smiled suddenly. His lovely smile which brought back so many memories. I couldn't speak.

'Well,' he said. 'Will I be wasting my time if I tell you to take care?'

'Yeah.'

'Well, take it anyway.'

We were both very quiet afterwards.

Finally, I said, 'That brought back memories,' and he nodded.

There was more silence and then he said, 'Does he remind you of someone?'

'Yes, but I don't know who.'

'Me neither.'

There was more silence and then I asked him how he'd got on at TPHQ.

He showed me the total on his scratchpad.

'Good heavens,' I said.

'Yeah – not too shabby, is it? You going back to deposit your share?'

'Yes, I think so. Catch up on what's happening at Starlings. Take a week off to recharge the batteries. You?'

'Not sure. Time off, anyway. Are you ready for lunch?'

*　　*　　*

Meilin had bad news for me. Well, no, not me personally – the bad news concerned the estate.

'Caroline has put a large part of the estate up for sale.'

'How large?'

'Dangerously large. It's the tipping point. It is likely the estate will be unable to support itself on what remains, thus justifying the decision to sell off the rest of it.'

'The place is being asset stripped.'

'As much as she is able, yes.'

'You said "tipping point".'

'For the estate.' She eyed me. 'And possibly for you, as well.'

I sat back and thought. I had a very nice property portfolio. A good, solid, regular income. You can go too big. Acquire too much and the profitable part can be subsumed by the unprofitable and everything crashes to the ground. Like the EU. Was this the point where I stopped acting in my own interests and took on those of Young George? To my detriment? After all, as Pennyroyal had said, what did I owe Starlings? In the normal course of events – if I hadn't met Pennyroyal and gone off gallivanting around the timeline – I'd probably have married some poor sod – anything to get away from Caroline – and gone to live somewhere else and my interest in what happened to Starlings, the estate, everything would be zero because, technically, I wouldn't be a Smallhope any longer.

It doesn't work like that, though. At least, not for me, anyway.

'I can hear what you're thinking,' she said.

'Going to talk me out of it?'

'Not necessarily – the decision is yours. Just make sure it is an informed one.'

'That's very good advice.'

'Well, naturally. It is coming from me.'

I contacted Mr Treasure and he came up to London. We had a long talk. A very long talk.

'What about the trustees?' I said, over lunch. 'Surely they have something to say about this.'

'Your brother named the countess, her brother, and her solicitor as trustees of the estate.'

'Well, they're hardly likely to argue with her, are they?'

'No, but it is unlikely any of them will have acted outside the law. I'm sure if I check there will be the appropriate Land Registry Transfer Forms, TR1s, TP1s and so forth. Nothing that could render her liable to prosecution. And her solicitor would have to ensure everything is legal and above board or he himself could be struck off. It's just that their actions might not necessarily be in Young George's best interests.'

'Yes,' I said bitterly. 'Not morally scrupulous but nothing illegal. Difficult to deal with.'

'Indeed. I think it most likely this state of affairs has been brought about by . . . shall we say . . . poor decision-making.' He looked at me. 'You, however . . .'

'Don't get carried away. I'm just as capable of bad decision-making as everyone else.'

He finished his meal and laid down his napkin. 'I shall await your instructions, Lady Amelia.'

I thought I'd better go and have a look at the place first. I didn't want to start any rumours so I donned a pair of walking boots, acquired a rucksack, tied a scarf around my head, wore sunglasses – and went quietly.

The village looked unkempt. There were empty houses, trees

349

that were badly in need of attention, and chimneys that needed repointing. The outlying fields had been left fallow. Standing at Starlings' main gate, I could see the front garden had at least received some attention – that was the bit that showed, after all – but other parts of the garden, the shrubbery and the rose garden, were completely overgrown. The water garden was halfway to becoming a swamp.

Under the terms of George's will – and Papa's – funds would have been set aside specifically for the maintenance of the house and grounds. It didn't look as if this had been happening, which might very possibly be a useful negotiating tool in the future.

Three or four bright, shiny and very new motors were parked outside. Mr Treasure had said several members of Caroline's family had moved in. 'Like bloody locusts,' I said to Pennyroyal afterwards.

Young George, now around thirteen or fourteen, was, apparently, benefitting from a small, unfashionable, but probably very cheap boarding school in the East Midlands.

I met with Mr Treasure to discuss his findings.

'The late earl – your father . . .'

'Call him Randolph,' I said. 'That's how he was known.'

'Very well. Randolph was no fool.'

That was true. Papa might not have been able to hit a peacock in a tree twenty feet away but he wasn't an idiot. 'What did he do?'

'The estate comprises various parcels of land – all with their own title number at the Land Registry – and, well, he landlocked some of the more valuable parcels, meaning there's no access except through other parcels of land, thus rendering them – the landlocked parcels – very difficult to sell.'

350

'And that's what she's selling off now? The access land?'

'Yes. Possession of that will considerably increase the value of the landlocked parcels. No doubt she hopes to make a killing.'

I considered his words. 'Can you acquire the access parcels on behalf of the housing company?'

'I'm not sure. It's possible she might have buyers already lined up.'

This was it. This was the moment when I had to commit myself – acquiring these parcels of land would not be cheap – or stick with what I'd got and let the estate go. How much did I value Starlings? How much of a Smallhope was I? Either I stepped in – to my own detriment, perhaps – or I let it go and walked away. Meilin was right. This was my tipping point.

All right – look at things the other way around. What if I did let it go? How much would I regret that in the future? Max always says it's better to regret an action than a non-action. She doesn't actually put it like that – especially after a couple of margaritas – but I know what she means.

And what of Pennyroyal? And the firm? Should I let it go? Live out my life in peace and prosperity?

For the first time in my life, I dithered.

And then, quite casually, Mr Treasure said, 'There is a rumour that the house itself might be up for sale.'

I lifted my head. 'House and land? Or just the house?'

'Either. Any offer considered.'

'Is she that desperate for money? How? Her living expenses must be tiny – the estate pays for everything.'

'Her ladyship enjoys a lifestyle appropriate to her station in life.'

I said nothing.

351

'Along with all the rest of her family, of course.'

I still said nothing.

'Except for his young lordship, perhaps. She does appear to have done a good job of isolating him from . . . well, the world, really. If I may be permitted to comment.'

I looked at him.

He looked back at me. Nothing to read in his expression. Nothing at all. 'In a possibly connected matter . . .'

He paused and coughed. Mr Treasure has a whole repertoire of coughs, much in the same way Pennyroyal has a whole repertoire of nasty looks. Some were significant and others less so. This was a significant cough. 'You may not be aware, Lady Amelia, but the dowager countess has a large number of . . . personal debts.'

'Again – what on earth is she spending her money on?'

He coughed again. 'Lady Goodrich's brother is reported to have expensive tastes.'

I wracked my brains for his stupid name. 'Gilbert?'

'Hugo.'

'Oh. Are you sure?'

'Certain.'

'OK then. Drugs, do you think?'

'And horses. Cars. Travel.' He blushed. 'A wide variety of . . . sexual partners. And he has expensive friends.'

'I don't know him at all. What's he like?'

'Mr Dyer is the centre of a group of lively young people with no discernible means of support.'

'You're saying he supports them. He buys their friendship. I'm sure in return they tell him he's wonderful.'

'Popularity has a price.'

'And Caroline supports him. And the estate supports her. It's just like the bloody Woodvilles, isn't it?'

He blinked. 'Is it?'

'Edward IV married an impoverished widow – Elizabeth Woodville – thereby causing all sorts of grief. Not least the sudden appearance of an enormous number of rapacious relatives who battened on Edward and the court and stirred up all sorts of trouble. For everyone, in the long run.'

He stared thoughtfully out of the window.

I stared thoughtfully at my teacup. If there's one thing Pennyroyal and I look for in any assignment, it's weakness. Everyone has a vulnerable point. Was it possible I had just found Caroline's?

'Would it be possible for me to acquire these debts?'

'Debts are frequently bought and sold, I believe. However, there are certain restrictions. Anyone buying those of the dowager countess would, for instance, be unable to impose new conditions – increase the rate of interest, perhaps. They must abide by the original terms.'

I must have slumped.

'But,' Mr Treasure continued, 'should the repayments fall into arrears, the creditor does possess the right to call in the debt. Which, of course, the debtor is almost certainly unable to pay off or they wouldn't have gone into arrears in the first place.'

He began to fold his napkin. 'I believe the term is leverage.'

I preferred the term *revenge*.

Very discreetly, Mr Treasure began to snap up strategic parcels of land. Meilin acquired Caroline's personal debts on my behalf. And she hardly charged me for it at all. I remarked on this and she laughed and said she was enjoying herself.

353

I was back and forth. Working from Home Farm and then jumping back to sign endless documents and part with horrifyingly large sums of cash.

Throughout all this, Pennyroyal said nothing, other than the occasional enquiry as to my progress. And then, one day, at his request, he and I sat down at the kitchen table for a discussion. He came straight out with it and asked if I was considering retirement.

I shook my head. 'No – I don't think I can afford to.'

'You think you can do both? Run the estate and carry on with the firm?'

'Yes. Although initially I might have to spend some time setting everything up. Become George's legal guardian, perhaps. Because otherwise Caroline will reappear as soon as my back's turned and who knows what sort of influence she could exert. I can appoint Mr Treasure as one of the trustees – with Aunt Indira as the other – and then you and I can carry on as before. Why would we not?'

'I suspect that once you return to Starlings . . .'

I shook my head. 'My primary responsibility is to you and the firm. That will never change. Do you have concerns about that?'

'I have concerns, yes, but not about the firm.'

I blinked. 'What then?'

'Have you considered that for Caroline, the quickest and easiest way out of her difficulties will be to sweep you aside? Your will leaves everything to your nephew, which, effectively, means it's all up for his mother to grab all over again.'

'I'm not so easily swept.'

'Car bomb. Road traffic accident. Accidental shooting. Fatal food poisoning. Ordinary poisoning. Falling down the stairs.

354

Riding accident. Drowning in the river. Mugging gone wrong. Falling under a bus. Hit and run . . .'

'Yes, all right,' I said, before his litany of doom could gather pace. 'I get the picture. But I can look after myself.'

'Not as well as I can.'

I started. 'Sorry – not with you. What are you saying?'

'I'll do this with you. As your bodyguard. She – or that lightweight brother of hers – will think twice if I'm standing at your shoulder.'

'They'll take you out first. That's what I'd do.'

'I'm not so easily taken out.'

'Hit and run. Falling in the river. Shooting. Stabbed in an alley one dark night. Bitten to death by a horse. Direct nuclear strike . . .'

'Yes, all right,' he said. 'The point I'm trying to make is that we're in this together. We both take a year out. It's not as if we don't deserve a break. You exterminate the entire Dyer clan – I'll watch your back. And I'll be able to keep an eye on my horses. One of them is looking quite promising. At the end of twelve months, we'll sit down and discuss what to do next. What do you say?'

I suddenly realised how much better I felt knowing Pennyroyal would be around. 'I say it's a good idea.'

'Deal, then.'

We shook hands over the kitchen table.

We didn't shut down Home Farm but I told the Faradays we were going away for a while. Ned just nodded. 'I'll keep an eye on the place if you like,' he said.

'That would be kind.' I paused. Thanks to Pennyroyal and

355

his 'builders', our security could best be described as ferocious. Anyone attempting unauthorised access wouldn't be attempting it for very long. 'Just from the outside, you understand.'

'I do,' he said, grinning.

He did. Home Farm has seen some action in its time.

'In that case, thank you. I expect one or both of us will check in occasionally.'

'How long will you be gone?'

'I'm unsure,' I said. 'About a month, I think.'

That's the beauty of time travel. Twelve months at Starlings, but we'd only be gone a month in this time.

I packed a few things – Pennyroyal packed even fewer – and then we were ready.

'OK,' I said. 'Let's do this thing.'

25

STARLINGS
The Present
Revenge at last

'You're very quiet,' said Pennyroyal from the front of the car. He'd insisted on driving, styling himself as my chauffeur. He produced a peaked cap and sunglasses to prove it.

I told him it would take more than a fancy hat and a pair of Ray-Ban Aviators to make him look respectable and he'd told me to get in the car. No, not in the front – in the back, because now I was the new owner and important.

We travelled in silence. I stared out of the window and reflected on my life so far. I don't know what Pennyroyal thought about. Speed limits, road safety and the best route to Starlings, I hoped.

'Five minutes,' he said. 'Hair OK? Lipstick? Been to the toilet?'

'I'm so glad you're not my mother.'

'Don't start that again.'

We turned in through the gates. I reached out and touched

my briefcase, stuffed full of the results of the last six months. We pulled smoothly up to the front steps and he turned off the engine.

Nothing seemed to have changed. The pillars supporting the pediment were still slightly wonky. The paint was still peeling away. I found it hard to believe I'd been away for so long, but I had.

Pennyroyal reported that we were being watched from an upstairs window. The Regency sitting room. I'd forgotten he knew the place as well as I did.

'By whom?'

'The dowager countess, her snake of a brother whose name we can never remember, and someone I presume is their legal representative, which makes him a Mr Jacob Flint.'

'They still don't know it's me, do they?'

'They're not hurling boiling oil from the battlements and they can't see you through the tinted windows in the back, so I'm going with no. And remember, they're only expecting Mr Treasure and some minor official from the housing company who's turned up to deal with a few loose ends. We'll have the element of surprise on our side. Just remember – if it all goes tits up, I'll never be far away.'

My stomach was in chaos. Because this was personal. And personal rarely ends well. 'Thank you.'

'Don't get out just yet. Make everyone wait.'

'OK.' I opened the briefcase for the umpteenth time and surveyed the contents.

'Have you got everything?'

'I hope so. If I don't, Mr Treasure will.'

'Here he comes now.'

Mr Treasure's car pulled up alongside ours.

'Wait,' said Pennyroyal. He got out and held open my door.

I remembered long sessions with Mlle Leonie and emerged gracefully. And without showing my knickers. 'Thank you, Pennyroyal.'

'My lady.'

'We're back to that again, are we? Good morning, Mr Treasure.'

'Good morning, Lady Amelia.' He nodded politely at Pennyroyal. 'Good morning. Shall we go in?'

I handed Pennyroyal my briefcase. 'If you'd be so good . . .'

'Of course, my lady.' He reached in through the window and deposited his cap on his seat. Now he was just a man wearing a black suit, sunglasses and the sort of expression that bodes badly for everyone.

Mr Treasure climbed the shallow steps and rang the bell. I could hear a faint and very unmelodic clonking. That hadn't changed, either.

I turned to Pennyroyal. 'How do I look?'

'Like an avenging angel.'

Since that was exactly the effect I'd gone for, I was quite pleased. I was wearing a tight-fitting black suit with a high-necked white blouse and I'd put my hair up. That and the heels meant I was now well over six feet tall. I'd probably be the tallest person present. That's always fun.

It was Cleverly who opened the door. He hadn't changed at all.

His eyes drifted across Mr Treasure – whom he was expecting.

Then Pennyroyal – whom he wasn't, but then, people rarely are.

And then me, standing at the back.

His eyes widened.

I put my finger to my lips.

He stepped aside and held the door open. 'Good morning, Mr Treasure.'

'Good morning, Cleverly. How are you?'

'Very well, thank you, sir. You are expected. Her ladyship is in the Regency sitting room.' He glanced at us and said uncertainly, 'How shall I announce you, please?'

'Donald Treasure, of Treasure, More, Treasure, and Treasure . . .'

'And Lady Amelia Smallhope,' said Pennyroyal.

Cleverly twitched a small smile. 'If you would follow me, please.'

I grinned back and winked.

He strode slowly and majestically across the hall – seriously, Black Rod himself couldn't have done it any better – up the stairs and around the east landing. Flinging open the double doors, he announced – surely far more loudly than was absolutely necessary – 'Mr Donald Treasure and Lady Amelia Smallhope.'

Strictly speaking, I should have gone first, but then Cleverly wouldn't have had the pleasure of ensuring my name echoed quite so resoundingly around this part of the building.

Someone somewhere dropped something. I didn't get a chance to find out who because the next minute we were across the threshold and I needed to concentrate.

Caroline was still favouring tight yellow dresses. Her previously wispy hair was now improbably long and thick. Hair extensions, I suspected. Good ones, though. Her nails were fashionably rectangular. If she went to pick her own nose, her entire brain pan might cave in. Although these days she probably had someone to pick it for her.

Her brother – thingummy – was sprawled in an armchair by the fire. He didn't get up. Actually, I wasn't sure he could. Good. One less to deal with. Not that he represented any sort of threat.

I was aware that the two solicitors were maintaining civilised standards of behaviour, exchanging polite greetings and enquiries as to the health of their respective families. Not Caroline and me, though. We were staring at each other exactly as we'd done all those years ago. Again, it was as if I'd never been away.

Except that I had. If I hadn't, I certainly wouldn't have allowed her to desecrate this room so shockingly. Its classic Georgian lines had been almost completely obliterated by some interior design guru. Gone was the elegantly striped wallpaper, the splendid portrait of Gervase Augustus George Smallhope, the Earl of Goodrich who'd survived Waterloo and then died, two years later, when his horse put his foot in a rabbit hole in the South Hangar. They'd been at full gallop and the fall had killed them both. The artist had portrayed Gervase leading the charge. *A* charge, anyway. Sadly, everyone was a bit vague about which particular one. Not that it mattered now because the painting had vanished. An attic or a saleroom was my guess. I tried to suppress the familiar burn of anger.

Something resembling a diseased spleen hung in its place. Really, if she had to smother the place in contemporary art, she could have gone for something decent. Sarah Lucas's *Chicken Knickers* – one of my favourites – would certainly have given people something to talk about.

The room's colour scheme was no longer the familiar faded

blue and gold, but green, orange and mustard. Not the sort of colours you want to encounter after a good night on the tiles. I could just hear Papa calling for a bucket of whitewash and his shotgun. And not in that order, either.

The two solicitors, still professionally polite, were each laying documents across the table and talking earnestly as they did so.

Pennyroyal was eyeballing Caroline's brother – what *was* his bloody name? – and Cleverly, bless him, had left the double doors open – so any staff inadvertently finding themselves up on the landing at this opportune moment – during the normal course of their duties, obviously – would be able to hear every word spoken. Not only that, but he'd cleverly – sorry, but I've been dying to do that – stationed himself against the wall where he could enjoy a first-class view of hostilities as they unfolded.

I was encouraged. No one knows what's going on better than the staff and obviously Cleverly had already picked his side. And if Caroline dragged her eyes away from me and demanded to know what he thought he was playing at – and she was insensitive enough to do that in front of everyone – he could simply reply that he was waiting to ascertain whether refreshments would be required. There would be a fractional pause before he added, *my lady*, and then he would depart with more grace and dignity than his employer could muster in a million years.

It dawned on me suddenly that I was going to enjoy this. Perfectly Normal Agnes stood at my shoulder. At my other shoulder, obviously. Pennyroyal had the first one. I rather thought each would approve of the other.

Caroline was still staring as if she couldn't believe her eyes. She'd expected a low-level minion from the housing company and instead she'd got me.

In this sort of situation – any sort of situation – one should always move swiftly to take advantage of one's opponent's befuddlement. Keep them off balance for as long as possible.

I gestured around the room with its ever so slightly too large furniture jarringly at odds with the room's gracious proportions.

'Congratulations, Caroline. Not everyone can take high-end furniture and make it look as if it's just come from a flat-pack bargain basement.'

Her gaze encompassed Pennyroyal before turning back to me. 'You really have no class, do you?'

'Apparently not,' I said cheerfully. 'Although my interior design genes are recoiling in horror at this monstrosity. How much did they have to pay you to put it in?'

I promise I don't usually pass comments on people's homes but it was truly heartbreaking to see this lovely old room looking so uncomfortable in its present ugly and incongruous setting.

I hadn't been asked to sit down. I contemplated the sofa in front of me – just fractionally too low, with its seat fractionally too short and its back fractionally too upright. I could easily envisage the struggle to extricate myself from its clinging embrace – although I am Mademoiselle Leonie-trained so I expected to be equal to the challenge.

Across the room I could see Mr Treasure and Mr Flint were still immersed in all things legal. I was very aware of Pennyroyal standing at my shoulder and a little to one side. Perfectly positioned to deal with the brother – what was his bloody name? – Rodney? Rupert? – should the occasion arise.

That left me and Caroline.

'Do I need to call the police and have you removed?'

I smiled my special Caroline-annoying smile. The one I'd

363

perfected when I was seventeen, and could still do, even after all these years.

'You called the police once before, remember. How did that work out for you?'

'It got you out of this house and my life, so as far as I'm concerned – very well. I'm happy to do it again.'

'I'd be even happier if you did. Use that phone there. I can wait.' I smiled again. Strangely, this failed to conciliate her in any way.

'Get out,' she hissed. 'You're not welcome here.'

'I was born here. Just on the other side of the landing, in fact. This is my home.'

'No, it is not. Not any longer. Starlings does not belong to you. It never did. You have no right to be here. Starlings – all of it – belongs to me.'

It didn't, actually. Starlings belonged to Young George, but she'd given me the perfect opening.

I grinned. 'Funny you should say that.'

Across the room the conversation stopped, and legal heads turned our way.

This was it. This was the moment. Don't make it personal. This was just business. I was Smallhope, facing down a couple of minor villains. Getting the job done so we could collect our fee at the end of it. Yeah – I'd got this. I was me and she was mine.

She was talking. I can't remember what she was saying, but I deliberately cut across her.

'I don't have all day, so let's get started, shall we?'

Her solicitor whispered in her ear.

'She's lying,' Caroline said, and turned back to me. 'What's this nonsense he tells me about you representing the housing company?'

I couldn't resist. 'Caroline, I *am* the housing company. As Mr Treasure will be happy to confirm.'

Mr Treasure laid down a set of papers – for general perusal should anyone care to peruse generally.

I continued. 'Ashburton Farm . . .' Pennyroyal flipped open my briefcase and pulled out a document. 'Hill Top Farm . . .' and again with the document. 'The properties in Streetley, the parcels of land known as Five Hangar Farm, Cranham Woods, Redmire Moor, Low Moor . . .' Documents were coming thick and fast. 'In fact, nearly everything you've quietly disposed of over the years – it's all mine. Rights of herbage, turbary, estovers, marl, pannage and so forth – everything belongs to me. As does all the income derived from these properties. You have made me a very rich woman, Caroline. I suppose I should thank you.' I paused. 'No – I just can't bring myself to do it. However, we digress. Allow me to broach the real reason for this afternoon's little chat. I understand you are considering putting Starlings up for sale.'

'If you think for one moment that I would ever even *contemplate* selling Starlings to you . . . over my dead body.'

There was a very long pause.

'I'm sorry,' I said. 'Were you waiting for someone to talk you out of that?'

'Cleverly – show these people out. And if they won't go, then call the police.'

Cleverly appeared to have been stricken with sudden deafness.

She turned back to me, contempt written all over her face. 'I wouldn't sell you Starlings if you were the last person on earth.'

I gestured to Mr Treasure to lay the relevant papers across the low table in front of her.

'Allow me to put your mind at rest, Caroline. I'm not buying Starlings from you. I'm *taking* it and you're going to surrender it to me. To save you asking why – you'll do it because I tell you to. In fact, from now on, you're going to do exactly as I tell you to.'

'I can assure you I have no intention of—'

I cut across her again.

'You do appear to have got yourself into a bit of a financial tangle, don't you? Bad management, perhaps? Or simple extravagance?' I looked around the room. 'Abysmal taste, definitely. The estate isn't the bottomless pit you had hoped, is it? Or should we be laying your perpetual cash shortage at . . .' I gestured. 'Whatshisname's door.'

'Hugo, my lady,' murmured Pennyroyal.

I turned to him. 'Hugo? Are you sure?'

'Yes, my lady.'

'Not Rodney?'

'I believe not, my lady.'

'Or Rupert?'

'No, my lady.'

'Oh. Well, never mind. To continue. Should we be laying all this at . . . whatshisname's door? He does have some interesting but expensive habits, doesn't he? Nor is he tremendously scrupulous about establishing a young person's age before embarking on . . . well, the things on which he likes to embark.'

Pennyroyal picked up the conversational oar and shoved it in. 'I have frequently heard it stated, my lady, that those who have served a spell at His Majesty's pleasure often emerge with more bad habits than when they entered. Although it would appear that in this case, Mr Dyer had a good many unsavoury practices even before his incarceration.'

'Good heavens, Pennyroyal – say it's not so.'

'Alas, my lady . . .'

'Oh dear me. How embarrassing for the Dyers. Never mind. Every family has its black sheep. I think we can all remember Second Cousin Selwyn and the unfortunate affair with the professional young lady from Bermondsey, the jar of Vaseline and the two chilli peppers. He required urgent medical treatment, you know. The press had a field day. *And* he was a member of the House of Lords, too. Not any more, obviously. Even with their notoriously low standards, they couldn't allow him to sit there any longer. Sit anywhere, now I come to think of it. Not without medical assistance, anyway. Still, at least both the professional young lady and the chillies gave their consent – unlike Hugo's little friends, of course.'

Pennyroyal looked solemn. 'It would appear, my lady, that the dowager countess's attempts to conceal her brother's bad habits have very nearly drained the estate dry. Mr Dyer's personal credit being utterly shot and hers not much better, she has been forced to obtain money by a series of disastrous personal loans. Lacking any sort of business acumen, she was unable to secure these at anything other than punitive rates of interest, which has resulted in her failure to maintain the repayments. In short, my lady – the dowager countess is on the verge of bankruptcy.'

'Goodness gracious,' I said. 'How is such a thing even possible? Why, not even Vincent Smallhope – the fifth earl, you know – the one who was best friends with Charles James Fox

367

himself and who had more gaming debts than brain cells – not even he managed to get himself and the estate into such a pickle.'

No one seemed willing to comment on the fifth earl and his unfortunate habits.

I readjusted all the paperwork slightly, lining it all up with the edge of the table. Waiting for the silence to become thicker and thicker.

Caroline drew a breath to speak. Suddenly very wary indeed, her solicitor cleared his throat and shot her a warning look. She swallowed hard and said nothing. Which was very encouraging.

'Nothing to say, Caroline? I'll just carry on then, shall I? The thing is – and you'll be so thrilled to hear this – I'm actually in a position to assist you. And . . . um . . .'

'Hugo, my lady.'

'Dammit, why can't I remember his name?'

'Few do, my lady. Sadly, Hugo Dyer does not possess the happy knack of making an impression.'

'Thank you, Pennyroyal. Where was I?'

'Explaining how you intended to assist the Dyers with their present financial predicament, my lady.'

By this stage, both Caroline and her brother were giving the impression they were on the verge of some sort of collective family aneurism. Mr Treasure's compassionate instincts took over. I know he was a member of the legal profession with everything that entailed but, with the exception of Cleverly, he was easily the nicest person in the room today.

'Perhaps this next part should be broken quite gently, Lady Amelia. To soften the blow a little.'

I nodded solemnly. 'Of course, Mr Treasure. Caroline, I

personally have purchased all your debts. They now belong to me. As do you. Unless you play ball, I'll call them in and ruin you.' I looked at Team Smallhope. 'How was that?'

'Magnificent, my lady,' said Pennyroyal.

I said nothing because modesty is a virtue to which we should all aspire.

Everyone stared at everyone else. Caroline looked completely bewildered.

'Perhaps, my lady,' said Mr Treasure, 'you might like to explain the situation to the countess in slightly more detail?'

'Of course. Let me lay things out as they stand at the moment. Income from the estate has been vastly reduced. Foolishly, you've sold off the best bits. To me – just to rub it in. You've let the house and grounds run down, which leads me to believe that the monies set aside for their maintenance under the terms of the late earl's will have been diverted elsewhere, which really is just a little bit naughty, you know. To make good the ever-increasing deficit, you've increased rents to such an extent that you've forced people out and now there's property standing empty and bringing in no income at all. Fatally, you've failed to reinvest and modernise. Have I left anything out?'

Caroline had regrouped by now. 'None of this is anything to do with you. You're not one of the trustees. You have no say in what happens here. You're just some cheap, troublemaking trollop who's turned up to try and make herself look important.'

I sighed. 'I wonder if this is the moment to remind the countess that I own the housing company that owns a significant amount of the estate and that I personally own her. What do you think, Pennyroyal?'

'Normally I would say this is the ideal moment to remind

369

everyone that you own the housing company, my lady. And to keep reminding them at every opportunity. At this precise moment, however, I feel our attention should be concentrated on the fact that you also own Caroline Dyer. And, within a very few minutes – everything she owns.'

Caroline was doing her best pillar-of-salt impersonation. 'I see you've brought your own personal thug.'

'Well, fair's fair,' I said. 'You've brought yours.' I jerked my chin at Hugo. 'Given the ease with which I put him on the ground after George's funeral – my money's on mine.'

We all looked at Hugo who, at a guess, had been a little too enthusiastic with the mid-morning recreational substances and was struggling to keep up.

Caroline was still wrestling with current events. 'This is . . . this is utter nonsense. I don't believe it. I don't believe any of it.'

'It's all very true, I'm afraid, Lady Goodrich,' said Mr Treasure gravely. 'Lady Amelia owns your debts.'

She tossed her head. 'That's illegal. I'll see you in court.'

'I regret to be obliged to correct you, but – no.'

'I've heard of this,' said Hugo suddenly, only a few minutes behind everyone else. 'You might say you own the debts but you can't change the terms.'

I gave him a bright smile. 'Well done, Gilbert. If only Caroline had kept up the repayments. Alas, falling into arrears means that I can call in the whole debt. And I am. So pay up, Caroline – now – in full – including the outstanding interest – or take the consequences.'

Her solicitor whispered something in her ear.

She shrugged him away and narrowed her eyes in a way

that made her look like a stroppy whippet. 'Rubbish. That can't possibly be legal.' She turned back to me. 'This is my home.'

'It's George's home.'

'George is a minor. And I am his parent. You can't force me out.'

'Wrong. I can and I am.'

I looked at Mr Flint who obviously had a better grasp of facts than *la famille* Dyer.

He said quietly, 'What exactly are your intentions, Lady Amelia?'

'Very simple. I want Caroline out of this house and out of George's life. Give the poor lad a chance to grow into who he is. She's bought a villa in Tuscany – let's not go into how and from where she obtained the means to do so – but if she goes there – and stays there – then I won't enquire too closely as to where the money came from. Go now, Caroline, and I won't call in your debts. Otherwise . . .'

'You'll cancel all my debts?'

'I'm not that stupid. I'll still hold them and I'll call them in the moment you do something to annoy me. Get it through your head, Caroline – you belong to me. You'll do as I say or I'll ruin you. And enjoy every moment.' I paused. 'Go on – annoy me. *I dare you.*'

The silence practically reverberated off the walls.

'You can't deny me access to my child,' she cried, suddenly remembering she was a mother.

'You mean the child you shoved into boarding school last year and haven't seen since? That child?' I shook my head. 'Go abroad, Caroline. Find some doddery foreign aristocrat with loads of dosh and leech off him for the rest of his life.'

Mr Flint was straight in there. 'And her ladyship's allowance? What will she live off?'

I shook my head. 'Alas, the money she's siphoned out of the estate over the years has left it unable to support her in the future. The only thing I'm offering her is this one chance to leave with dignity. No one will ever know what she's done. She's simply gone abroad to live. I'll move in – I am George's aunt, after all. Caroline has been bravely holding the fort, but I'm back now and she's taking the opportunity to start a new life.'

Mr Flint nodded. He'd already worked out that, under my influence, George would be transferring all estate business back to Mr Treasure. He wasn't stupid. He could accept that the good times were over. If he didn't make a fuss, he'd probably be able to keep what he'd managed to acquire over the years. Smart man.

Not so Caroline. 'And if I don't comply with your demands?'

'Then I'll ruin you. You can bankrupt yourself trying to pay off what you owe me and stay out of the courts, but you won't succeed and my legal team will take you apart. There will be allegations of fraud. Embezzlement. Financial misconduct. And all your brother's dirty linen will be on full public view. The publicity will be horrendous. Although not for me, of course. Or you can go now. You can keep what you've got, but you'll never again be able to use the estate to raise money. Mr Treasure here will see to that. Whatever you choose to do – I'm in and you're out. The only detail to settle now is which flight you catch tomorrow.'

I could almost see Caroline's mind working. I had no idea what her brother's mind was doing. Nothing very much, I suspected. Would she dig in her heels? Was I going to have to fight her every inch of the way? For Young George's sake, I'd hoped this would be quick and clean.

And then Mr Treasure saved the day. 'I believe our first move, Lady Amelia, should be to demand a thorough audit of the estate accounts. Give the three trustees – all of whom are in this room – a chance to account for themselves and their actions.'

Mr Flint stepped back. 'I've only ever carried out my instructions. I was never included in the decision-making process.'

Great – the rats were beginning to desert the sinking ship. I had no doubt he was right – he would never have been involved to that extent. And it was possible that his part *had* all been completely above board. But no one likes an audit.

The two solicitors were holding a hurried consultation. Pennyroyal pulled out the appropriate paperwork and handed it to Mr Treasure. He and Mr Flint sat down. Mr Flint pored over the contents, reading each document slowly from beginning to end.

This would take a while but I waited quietly. Meilin had handled the purchase of Caroline's debts and I knew that everything would be perfectly in order.

Caroline, on the other hand, was hampering her man by continually interrupting him with demands that he do something – which he was trying to do – that he couldn't allow this to happen – which he had no choice about – that he should call the police – we all stared at her over that one. She was such an idiot. It was a good deal for her but her hatred of me was getting in the way of her recognising that. She was allowing the personal to affect her judgement. She was going to fight me all the way and it was going to be ugly.

Pennyroyal caught my eye. 'With your permission, my lady.'

'Of course,' I said, not having a clue what he wanted, but this was Pennyroyal and I trusted him to the ends of the earth.

Facing Hugo head-on, he said, 'Lady Amelia would like to discuss the late earl's death.'

From over by the table, Caroline lifted her head. A moment later, she scoffed.

'Silly little cow. If that's your game, then you're wasting your time. It was an accident. There were witnesses. Independent witnesses. Take your thug and his malicious accusations elsewhere or I'll have you in a court of law for slander.'

But there was fear. Sudden, overwhelming, bone-deep fear. I'd seen it too often to be mistaken. What could make her so afraid? What was I missing?

Pennyroyal smiled. She really didn't know how much danger she was in. 'Not George – Randolph.'

It was as if someone had suddenly sucked all the air out of the room. I felt my lungs empty.

Caroline's face drained of blood. I saw it. She stared at Pennyroyal, her mouth open. No sound came out. She was frozen to the spot. Paralysed. If it had been anyone else, I'd have been truly concerned. I'd have sat them down. Shoved a brandy inside them.

Something flashed across Hugo's face.

And with a sudden crash of realisation – I knew. I knew what they'd done. My stomach plummeted like a lift. I'd had my suspicions over how George had died but Papa's death had never entered my mind. I'd just accepted it. I couldn't . . . A red-hot fury was burning a hole in my heart. Not George – Randolph. Papa. My darling, darling papa.

Thank God for Pennyroyal.

He crossed the room, gently took Mr Treasure to one side and suggested he might like to see to Lady Amelia. Having thus moved a possible witness out of earshot, he spoke very softly to both Hugo and Mr Flint. Not for very long but for long enough. No one spoke to Caroline. She still hadn't moved.

Neither had I.

Faintly I heard Mr Treasure say, 'Lady Amelia . . .'

I was still waiting for Caroline to come out with some sort of denial. Waiting to hear what she would say. Threats of prosecution for slander and so forth. But she didn't. Perhaps she knew it would be useless. Perhaps she knew she'd already waited too long to make that denial. Perhaps she knew her guilt was written all over her face. Not just guilt – fear. And, for once, not fear for herself. Because now she was looking at Hugo. It was Hugo, the beloved brother, for whom she feared. Yes, of course it would have been Hugo. With or without her knowledge, he'd just hurried the succession on a little. They'd never met but Papa wouldn't have tolerated Hugo for one single second and both Hugo and Caroline knew that. Papa would have done everything he could to ensure no Dyer had any say at all in our family affairs. Ever. Yes, it all made perfect sense. Now that it was too late.

Still she said nothing. No threats to have us thrown out. No attempt to call the police and have us arrested for something. Not a word. Actually, I didn't think she was capable even of thinking, let alone saying anything. She'd turned a very dirty white – I could actually see her foundation sitting on top of her skin – and then she gave a fluttering gasp and sat down suddenly.

At the same moment, Hugo took two steps forwards to stand between us, his fist raised and his eyes glittering. I'd thought there was something not quite right about him and now I was certain of it. Whether he was threatening Caroline or me was unclear. Not that it mattered. Pennyroyal was suddenly there. I don't think his feet even moved. He was just there. And making a bloody sight better job of projecting looming menace than Hugo ever could.

I caught a glimpse of Cleverly who had also moved towards me. He'd enjoyed some exciting times when Papa had been around – ceilings crashing down, compulsory target practice against the day HMRC invaded, lying through his teeth for us when George and I set fire to the dining room curtains – but this morning must have easily made his top ten.

He'd brought me a brandy.

'Thank you.'

I tossed it back. Without taking my eyes off Caroline. Whom no one had brought a brandy. Her eyes and mouth were slack with shock. I wondered if I looked as bad as she did. There was a fresh series of documents on the table. It would seem there were some signatures required.

Somewhat blindly, I signed.

Caroline signed. Well, she moved a pen across a series of papers, but Mr Treasure seemed satisfied.

Cleverly and Pennyroyal witnessed the signatures.

Hugo – who had armed himself with a brandy because it was obvious no one was going to get one for him either – assumed a sneer. 'Surprised your ape can even write.'

I wasn't even conscious of making the decision. My body acted all by itself. There was a brief flurry – from me, obviously. Hugo's only part in the proceedings was to fall heavily to the floor. Face down. Like toast. A couple of ornaments bounced on impact but they were quite hideous so no one was particularly bothered. He lay very still. Cleverly actually stepped over him as he brought me another brandy.

Caroline blinked and came back to life. 'You've killed him.'

I sighed. 'Sadly, no. But by all means, call the police if you wish.'

She pointed to Pennyroyal. 'You're as big a thug as he is.'

'You're very kind,' I said, 'but no one is as big a thug as Pennyroyal. He is unique.'

Pennyroyal bowed. 'Thank you, my lady.'

'You're welcome. Are we done here?'

'I believe so,' said Mr Treasure, gathering up the documents. He turned to Caroline. 'Starlings still belongs to the earl, of course, but Lady Amelia will take over his upbringing.' He held up the documents. 'New trustees will be appointed. You, Lady Goodrich, have agreed to live abroad and relinquish all claim to the estate. You may return for family occasions only at the express invitation of the earl himself. Mr Dyer . . .' we all looked down at the slowly returning-to-the-world Hugo, 'may never return here at all. Under any circumstances. Should either of you break these conditions, then appropriate action will be taken.'

Caroline made one last attempt. 'Go ahead and try. There's nothing that will stand up in a court of law.'

Pennyroyal grinned. 'Appropriate action will have nothing to do with a court of law.'

We gave it a minute for the words to sink in.

Caroline made one last effort, dragging words from somewhere. 'I – we – can't just go.'

377

'Of course not,' said Mr Treasure. 'Obviously you will want to collect your own personal belongings. With the assistance of Mr Pennyroyal, of course. To do the heavy lifting,' he added tactfully.

'And to make sure nothing small and valuable inadvertently falls into your suitcases,' I said, not bothering to be tactful at all.

'You're not staying here,' snarled Caroline. 'I won't have you under this roof.'

I turned to Cleverly. 'Pennyroyal will remain here to render assistance where needed. In the event of you needing me suddenly, Cleverly, I'll be at the King Teddy. Lady Goodrich and Mr Dyer will certainly be finished packing by this time tomorrow. Please ask the staff to render them every assistance.'

'I shall be delighted to do so, my lady. And welcome home.'

I had a quick word with Pennyroyal before I left.

'Well, that went better and more smoothly than I thought it would. Although I'm sorry you never got the chance to shoot either of them.'

He sighed sadly for missed opportunities.

I paused and then said, 'How did you know?'

'About Randolph? I didn't. I wanted to hurry them away. I thought it was just an empty threat. Until I saw her face.'

'I didn't have a clue,' I said, staring out of the window. 'Why didn't I work it out?'

'Not your fault. No one sees clearly when it's personal.' He bent his head, saying softly, 'I am concerned for you. Are you all right?'

I made an effort to smile. 'I am coping, my friend. And who knows, an opportunity to slap Caroline may yet arise.'

He nodded. 'Leave everything here to me. You go and put some ice on that hand. And watch your technique next time. You're lucky you didn't break a bone.'

26

Caroline left the next morning. I watched her car pass the King Teddy. Off to Tuscany to gnash her expensive dental implants. Hugo went with her. Pennyroyal had someone at the airport to ensure they actually made their flight.

Later that day I left the pub and walked the short distance back to Starlings. I turned in through the gates and stopped, taking it all in. Even after everything that had happened yesterday, I was still finding it hard to believe. I was back. I was actually back home. A Smallhope returning to Starlings.

I took a deep breath and was just about to set off for the front door when something blue moved in the tree above me. I jumped a mile and as I did so, a peacock screamed from over my head and shat mightily.

'Missed me, you bastard,' I shouted.

'What *are* you doing?' said Pennyroyal, emerging from the shrubbery.

I grinned at the peacock. 'We're celebrating my return.'

All my stuff was gone, obviously. My room had been locked after I left. Apparently Caroline had wanted it gutted the second

I was out of the door, but my brother George – thank you, George – had put his foot down for once. Perhaps he thought I would come back one day. And I had. Just too late for him. Anyway, he'd ordered the door locked and the room left alone. Obviously all that had changed once he was dead. In some distress, Cleverly told me he'd done his best, pretending the key was lost, but all to no avail. Everything I'd once owned had been taken away and utterly destroyed. School prizes, sports cups, books, photos of me and the dogs, photos of Papa, one or two of Mama and Charlotte, rosettes won with my pony, scrapbooks, clothes – everything was gone. Absolutely nothing left. The room had been completely stripped. My entire life up until the night I met Pennyroyal had been ruthlessly exterminated.

I patted Cleverly's arm and told him it didn't matter.

The only good news was that Caroline hadn't bothered converting my rooms into another taste-free zone. They'd been locked and left. Now they smelled musty, but other than their emptiness and a ton of dust, they were exactly as they had been.

I left Cleverly supervising a quick spring clean and the acquisition of some furniture and drove off to see George at his grim little school just outside Leicester.

I told him that his mother had gone to live abroad – he took the news warily but without any distress, I'm glad to say – and I offered him a choice. Continue at this school or come back with me and I'd get him into Rushford St Winifred's. He'd be plain George Smallhope with all the advantages and disadvantages that entailed. What did he think?

He raced me to the car. I told the school to send his stuff on and we were out of there.

He was a quiet boy – very like his father – although physically, he took after Papa and me. Here was another one who would be tall. There was very little of Caroline in him. I casually mentioned her brother and he confided he'd always been a little frightened of Uncle Hugo. He said no more, and I didn't ask, but I did mark Hugo down as something that might need future attention.

I turned over some ideas on the way back. We needed to expand George's world a little. I hoped he'd make friends at his new school. I would encourage him to invite schoolmates for sleepovers. Or they could camp overnight in the gardens. They could have BBQs. Build a treehouse, perhaps.

He needed proper male role models. I'd start with Pennyroyal. Yes, I know, but I've seen him with kids and – mostly because he couldn't give a rat's arse whether they liked him or not – they loved him. George needed someone to take him fishing, tinker with oily things, teach him to ride, get him wet and dirty and just generally enjoy life. Actually – none of that would do Pennyroyal any harm, either.

It did worry me that George was so quiet. Almost as if he'd learned not to draw attention to himself. In general, we Smallhopes are not shrinking violets and if that was his nature and not learned behaviour, then that was fine – as long as it was rooted in confidence and not fear, he could be anything he liked.

Cleverly and I picked up the household reins. I gave him permission to hire and fire staff as he saw fit. Most of Caroline's people left of their own accord. Everyone was thanked for their service and paid off. We were shorthanded for a while. Pennyroyal took George downstairs to learn how to do the washing-up. He loved it. Mrs Tiggy came back to us. There were nearly as many tears as the day she left. And a couple of others, including Milburn, who cast one look at the gardens and tutted in the manner of one who had always known the place would go to rack and ruin without him.

I wanted to un-isolate us from the outside world. Wherever possible, Cleverly ordered locally. The butcher, the local shop and the pub. I planned to resume the annual summer fête. There would be a Christmas party for the children. And a carol concert in our hall. We'd donate the giant Christmas tree that had always stood on the green. We'd open up part of the gardens for everyone to use. George made a substantial donation towards the new roof on the village hall – which put them within spitting distance of their target. Now the crèche could reopen. And the keep-fit classes. And the art group. I thought Reverend Caldicott would faint with joy.

And dogs – I chose a spaniel for myself, a relation of Doofus, and George picked out a pair of Labradors. There were unexpected damp patches all over Starlings for a while.

George liked his new school. His teachers reported a growing confidence. He made one or two friends. He joined the chess club like his father. He was good with computers. And, like me, he was a long-distance runner.

As Papa had done with me, I took him along when I went out. He met his tenants. He asked questions. We were at Ashburton Farm one day and John Langley got him to assist at a calving. There was no need – everything was perfectly straightforward, I think it was her second or third calf and mum knew what she was doing – but George was right in there. I was quite proud of him. And of the way he washed his hands in a bucket of dirty water afterwards, talking over his shoulder as he did so. And then sat down on an old feed bin in the yard with a mug of tea and piece of Mrs Langley's chocolate cake. When he bent to stroke one of the cats, I caught John Langley's eye and he nodded. Yeah – well done, George. It took a little while but I could see him growing into his role. And he was a nice lad. Quiet, yes, but with a sense of humour. He'd do.

Throughout all this time, Pennyroyal lived at Starlings with me. He had a room in the East Wing in which he got up to heaven knows what. Initially he hung around in case there was any fallout from Hugo or Caroline. There wasn't. Not a peep. I wasn't sure whether that was good or bad.

With everything on an even keel, he disappeared up to Middleham to check on his three horses, returning in a state of huge excitement. *Two* of his facial lines deepened fractionally. It seemed that one of his colts was turning out to be quite exceptional. And I know he went up to London to sort out the Walthamstow house. I didn't go with him. Other than that, he seemed quite happy to settle into life at Starlings.

Initially, I was relieved and then, after a couple of months, I don't know, something wasn't right. I had no idea what. Outwardly he was just Pennyroyal being Pennyroyal, but there was something. When you've been together as long as we had . . . A sudden thought stopped me in my tracks. Was that it? Had we been together too long? We were coming up to fifteen years. He was thirty-eight. In his prime, as he would no doubt inform me if I asked. Was he bored here at Starlings? True, no one had tried to kill us for ages, neither of us were wounded, we were rich, we could even retire if we wanted to. I knew we'd agreed to twelve months away from the business but was he missing the old days?

I said nothing but I began to worry. He might want to leave but be afraid to broach the subject. No, that was too ridiculous for words. This was Pennyroyal. If he wanted to go, he'd get up from the breakfast table one morning, say, 'I'm off now. Thanks for everything,' and just go. I began to consider ways and means of broaching the subject but as it turned out – I didn't need to.

We were returning from a quiet evening drink at the King Teddy, walking slowly up the drive towards the house, and right out of the blue, he stopped and said, 'It's her birthday next month. She would have been forty.'

Sometimes it's better to say nothing at all.

He stood in the dusk, staring out over the park, not looking at me. The wound still hadn't healed. It probably never would. I kept very still and very quiet. I was here if he wanted me. In case he needed to talk.

Who was I kidding? This was Pennyroyal. Of course he didn't need to talk. I myself am not a big fan of talking about *issues*. Waste of bloody effort if you ask me. Your time would be much better spent getting up off your arse and kicking the living shit out of your issues. Issues should always be clear about which of you has the upper hand. However, I suspect I'm a babbling brook of spilled secrets compared with Pennyroyal, whose issues were so firmly and deeply embedded that it would require heavy-duty excavation equipment to get to them.

And yet he'd actually mentioned it . . . for the first time ever. And after all these years. His sister's death had overshadowed his entire life. Well, obviously it had. How did anyone even begin to survive something like that, far less get over it? He hadn't, obviously – keeping it buried safely inside himself. Year after year. Pennyroyal's heart – that mythical organ – was the only place in which she still lived. There was no body, no grave and, as far as I knew, no memorial. Although she must be remembered somewhere, surely. The army doesn't forget its people.

I remembered Papa's grave with its by now well-worn headstone. And George's alongside. Less well-worn but getting there. The Smallhope family plot. Forever ours. A sunny spot in which to sleep the centuries away. I'd never thought about it very much. It was just there. Our ultimate destination. Where did his sister lie? Had she even been granted the dignity of a grave? Or had her remains been left for the weather and wild animals, as exposed in death as she had been in life?

I was roused from my thoughts by the sound of the door closing. He'd gone into the house ahead of me. I followed him in and went to my room for a drink and a think. Standing in the window, I looked down. It was almost dark and I couldn't see much. The formal gardens were at the front of the house. The kitchen garden was on the east side. The rose garden, the sunken garden and the shrubbery lay to the west. And the pretty little wood beyond, where Pennyroyal had parked his pod that first night. The night we met.

She'd still been alive then.

There was a space, between the garden wall and the rose garden – just a wide path with grass verges, really – running between two brick walls. Nothing special. It was just a way to get from one place to another. But put a gate at each end . . .

I stood for a long time, turning over all sorts of ideas. The next morning I went down to see our head gardener, Milburn. We sat in his immaculate cabin behind the compost heaps. I inhaled the familiar smell of earth and wood and creosote. Shelves of neatly labelled jars held seeds. Fearsome garden implements hung around the walls. I wondered if Pennyroyal had ever been in here. You could invade a medium-sized country with this lot.

Milburn made some tea and pulled out a tin of surprisingly good biscuits. I explained what I wanted, handing over one or two quick sketches I'd made.

'Water,' I said. 'And somewhere to sit. Quiet and calm. Lots of scent. Private. A door or a gate at each end which can be locked.'

He laid my sketches in a row along his potting bench.

'Just give me a few days, my lady, and I can do you a proper drawing. And a planting plan.' He looked at me. 'Cost?'

'Not important. And get in whatever help you need.'

'In that case – Baileys. For the hard landscaping and the pool. Work'll go quicker that way.'

Baileys were a local company. A good choice.

'Agreed. I'd like it completed by mid-summer.'

'I'm not one of them TV garden shows,' he said with some contempt. 'But yeah. By mid-summer.'

'You'll oversee the work,' I said and he nodded.

'Leave it with me.'

Just under one month later – well before mid-summer – it was done. Except for the plaque.

I contacted Mr Treasure. 'Can you track down a name for me?'

'Possibly,' he said cautiously.

I explained.

'Is that his real name?'

'Probably not. But I have a London address you might find helpful and . . .'

I stopped.

'Lady Amelia – are you still there?'

'I've had second thoughts, Mr Treasure. Can I get back to you?'

'Of course.'

Discretion is the better part of valour. Or so they tell me. But if Pennyroyal wanted me to know his sister's name, he would have told me. And, more importantly, there might still be people out there looking for him. I didn't want my search to wake any sleeping dogs.

No – I should leave all that alone.

The finished garden was beautiful. Now for the tricky bit. I needed to proceed with extreme caution. Or, possibly, I could kick caution to the kerb and jump straight in.

Guess which option I went with.

'I've done something you might not like,' I said.

We were in the estate office. He was at my desk, leaning forwards, peering at something on his screen. 'Not narrowing it down.'

'No, I mean you really might not like it. I meant well but you could end up shooting me.'

He sat back and looked at me. 'What have you done?'

'Come and see.'

I led the way outside and paused before a white-painted wooden door, handing him two keys.

'This one is for this door and the other is for the door at the end. This part of the garden is now private to you and no one – including Milburn – will ever come in here without your permission.'

He was suddenly wary. 'Why?'

I drew a deep breath. 'Because you don't have any sort of memorial to your sister. Not your fault – you've never had a proper home. Now you have this. It's all yours. A place you can come to think about her. Or just think in general. If you want to.'

I waited.

He looked down at the keys.

I held my breath.

Slowly, he inserted the first key. The door swung open.

I'd seen it before, of course. Milburn had overseen the work and I'd overseen Milburn, but now I was seeing it through Pennyroyal's eyes.

A white garden.

A herringbone brick path led from this garden door to another, some sixty feet away, widening out in the centre to accommodate a circular pool. Two curved wooden seats were placed on either side. One in the shade and one in the sun.

Two wide borders ran either side of the path. Since the layout was formal, the planting was symmetrical. Each side reflected the other.

At the back of each border, along the walls, they'd planted white climbing roses, white clematis and honeysuckle. One day they'd smother the walls in flowers and scent.

Everything had been chosen for its white flowers or silver-coloured foliage. Roses, magnolias, peonies, daisies, lilac, tulips, snowdrops, hellebores, lily of the valley, artemisia, lamb's ears and hydrangeas. Whatever the time of year, there would always be something for him to look at.

The pool had white water lilies and in the very centre sat a small statue of a young girl. One hand trailed in the water; the

389

other held a jug, pouring a never-ending trickle of water. Her head was lowered as she peered down into the clear depths and her hair hid her face. The lines were lovely.

Some of the plants were still very small but the bones of the garden were strong. It was easy to see how it would look in six months, a year, two years. Cloud after cloud of white flowers smothering the walls and spilling across the path.

Around the pond stood pots stuffed with white nicotiana and night-scented stocks. When he sat here in the evening, the air would be filled with their perfume.

If he wanted to sit here in the evening.

If he wanted to sit here at all.

Pennyroyal still hadn't said anything. He hadn't even entered the garden. He was still standing in the doorway. I resisted the urge to gabble at him. To make things worse as I tried to make them better. Every instinct said to run. I stood my ground as he looked around.

'What's this?'

I said again, 'Your garden. To sit and think about your sister. To remember her. Somewhere for you alone. No one will ever come in here – not even me – unless you allow them to.'

He took a single step through the door. Just one.

Despite the bright sunshine, I'd gone very cold. I'd made a big mistake. I'd stepped over our undrawn line. All the years we'd been together, we'd survived by never stepping over any number of undrawn lines and now I'd made a cardinal error. I'd invaded his most private area. In a moment he'd turn around, thank me politely and meaninglessly, return to his room, pack, and thirty minutes later he'd be gone. I'd never see him again. Because we'd had a perfect balance, carefully built up over the years, and I'd wrecked it. If I listened carefully, I would be able to hear the sound of my world crashing down around my ears.

He turned back to face me.

I stepped aside. I wasn't going to get in his way. I'd let him go and then return to my room to reflect on my own stupidity.

He stood stock-still. Obviously working up to saying something. I recognised the signs and braced myself.

'Her name was Amelia.'

I sometimes think the universe removes the power of speech for very good reasons.

He wouldn't look at me. I couldn't look at him.

I laid my hand on his forearm – just for a second – and then walked away, leaving him to the peace and silence of his garden. I did briefly look back. Just once.

His back was to me but he was reaching out to a flower.

Months passed. We settled down into our own daily routines. The dogs learned what the small sandy patch in the shrubbery was for. George was doing quite well at school. Not a mental giant – none of us Smallhopes are particularly bright – but he was doing much better. Not so pale. A little more robust. Making some noise. I suspected he'd deliberately stayed as quiet and as far away from other people as possible. It seemed unlikely Caroline had been a nurturing parent.

He gained the confidence to venture out by himself. He would go down to the local shop to buy things. I sent him down to the chippy every Friday night. He didn't push himself forwards and probably because of that, he was quietly and matter-of-factly accepted.

And watched over. Jo shot out of the King Teddy when he

came a real cropper off his bike one day. Half a dozen people crowded round to help. Including Amos Cope, who offered him a swig of something from a dirty flask on the grounds that it would kill or cure. Ellie drove him to hospital while Jo rang me to tell us what she'd done.

He was fine – discharged the next day. No concussion but with a fine set of cuts and bruises which, I suspect, he wore with pride.

He learned to ride – he enjoyed it. He showed no signs of wanting to learn to shoot and I didn't force it. I didn't take it up again myself, either. I'd done enough of that over the years. The peacocks shouted derisively and undisturbed.

He settled down to work for his GCSEs and then, of course, it would be his A levels. His father had his, of course, but I'd missed mine and I doubt Papa had even been aware of their existence.

All this time, I was managing the estate, with George at my elbow a lot of the time. I sold off the unproductive land and property, each time explaining what I was doing and why. That it wasn't his purpose to preserve but to improve. His duty was to move with the times and hand a prosperous estate over to the next generation for them to improve in their turn. Because nothing stands still.

One thing I was very careful to consult him over – and to include Mr Treasure as well – was Pennyroyal's surprise offer to rent an old cottage, its outbuildings and three small fields. A little over four acres in all. The property was a couple of miles away – certainly within easy walking distance. A place of his own, he said. Although if it was a problem he could look further afield.

'Oh yes,' I said in excitement. 'A bit of TLC and it could be

392

lovely. New kitchen and bathroom, new wooden floor, colourful throws, lots of light, bright, warm and comfy.'

He folded his arms. 'I was thinking more along the lines of a place for the pod, full CCTV coverage, no sightlines to the windows, remote alarm system, underfloor gun cabinets, bulletproof glass and security shutters.'

'Still no cushions, then?'

He sighed.

I asked George's permission, making it very clear that if he said no then that was the end of the matter. He didn't say no – I think, in his own quiet way, he quite liked Pennyroyal.

I had the property's rentable value assessed, obtaining three estimates from three separate estate agents, and we took an average. Less ten per cent mate's rates. I couldn't knock off any more because it belonged to the estate and it was my job to get the best price.

Pennyroyal's plan was to divide his time between doing up the cottage and his horses in Middleham. Because – and you'll be as gobsmacked as I was – one of his horses was running in the Derby.

I'd been to Epsom several times with Papa, who had never missed a Derby. A chance to exercise his legendary bad luck in elegant surroundings, he'd said. He'd even been in the Royal Box once or twice. Whether legitimately or not I've no idea, so let's not go there.

Apparently, Pennyroyal's horse was called Bounty Hunter. 'Seriously,' I'd said, and another line had deepened fractionally so he was obviously thoroughly enjoying the joke.

'Out of Coconut Shy by Predator,' he said. 'What else would he be named?'

Bounty Hunter had shown promise right from the beginning and so had been entered as a yearling. Pennyroyal had reckoned he was worth a punt and paid the entry fee – just under £600. He'd had to reconfirm when Bounty Hunter reached three years old. And again in May. More money each time. I was beginning to get his point about racing not being cheap. But now his horse was one of the final field of fifteen and he invited me to go with him to Epsom.

I thought for a moment and then said, 'Why just me? Why not hire a bus and take everyone?'

'Why would I do that?'

'Because this is the most exciting thing that's ever happened here. Apart from Perfectly Normal Agnes chucking her husband and brother-in-law down the well, of course.'

He stared. 'Why?'

'He locked her in a cage and went off to France for a few years. She was very peeved.'

'Oh, yeah, I could see that.'

'Anyway, stop changing the subject. Let's put on a coach and anyone who wants to can watch your horse run.'

'Will anyone actually want to?'

We had to hire four coaches in the end. And a lot of people made their own way. The village just about emptied. The King Teddy shut for the first time in its long chequered history. Even a stray bomb in 1941 hadn't managed that.

Hats were bought, luggage compartments stuffed with booze, children shoehorned unwillingly into clean clothes, and off we set. Pennyroyal had gone on ahead some days ago so George and I went by coach with everyone else.

We left them all on the Hill – somewhat reluctantly because

they were going to have a great time there, whereas George and I were wearing our best clothes and, in my case, a silly hat.

I won't bang on about the race – you can watch the holo any time you like – but the field was tightly bunched all the way until, as they rounded Tattenham Corner, the favourite Loopy Loo was just in front by a nose. It was looking as if the Aga Khan had it in the bag yet again when Bounty Hunter made his late run, stormed up on the outside, swept past Loopy Loo as if he was standing still and won by half a head.

The crowd, as they say, went wild. George and I shrieked ourselves hoarse. Pennyroyal twitched with emotion and then made his way into the Winner's Enclosure to be presented with the trophy.

George and I disgraced ourselves utterly.

We left Pennyroyal to do whatever victorious owners do afterwards, boarded the coach and sang all the way home. Well, I did. George fell asleep just outside Swindon.

Pennyroyal returned to a rapturous welcome and was swept into the King Teddy where he didn't buy a drink all night. I guided his steps home afterwards, rather hoping he might burst into song, wear a traffic cone, or somehow morph spontaneously into a fluffy ball of frivolity – but no.

His triumph coincided with George's fifteenth birthday, so obviously, as I said, major celebrations were called for. George, Cleverly and I put our heads together. There were to be two events. One outside in the gardens in the afternoon for those attending with children. There would be a massive tea tent, pony rides, skittles, a small funfair, a bouncy castle, races and competitions. The other would be an evening do – inside, with lots of good food and alcohol. And, I suspected, a lot of adults would want to giggle and fall over on the bouncy castle after nightfall.

An expressionless Cleverly made a note to extend the hire period accordingly.

27

I dressed carefully for the party. My usual outfit – a simple black dress. And I'd finally redeemed Mama's jewels from Meilin. The ones that had once been so important to me and I'd almost forgotten about. Meilin laughed, couriered them to me and said she was glad to see the back of them. I was only wearing the necklace and one of the bracelets – any more would have been a bit over the top.

I met Pennyroyal at the top of the stairs. 'Well,' he said, with one of his rare smiles. 'Haven't seen those in a long time.'

'Hands off,' I said.

He made a rude noise, indicating he could take them any time he wanted.

I made an equally rude noise indicating I was more than equal to anything he could do. We grinned at each other.

'Did I ever thank you for taking me in?'

'You did not. Did I ever thank you for picking me up off the kitchen floor?'

'You did not. We have terrible manners,' I said.

'So I've heard on many occasions.'

So that was both of us in a happy mood and looking forward

to the party. Well – I was, anyway. It was a long time since Starlings had enjoyed a good old-fashioned knees-up.

The only fly in the ointment was that Caroline would be attending. She'd contacted us through Mr Treasure and demanded to attend her only child's birthday bash. Mr Treasure had advised us to agree.

'You have no reason to keep her out,' he said. 'It wouldn't look good in court should the issue ever arise. She has faithfully kept to her side of the bargain. And she won't be bringing Hugo.'

'Where is that particular ray of sunshine at the moment?'

'I don't know. Not with his sister, it would seem. I could find out, if you particularly . . .'

'No, it's OK – let's just forget about him.'

Pennyroyal and I went downstairs together. George was already waiting. Pennyroyal disappeared in the direction of the drinks while George and I greeted the guests as they arrived.

They were a pretty mixed bunch, including a dozen or so of George's school friends and another half-dozen from the village, all of them looking shy and awkward in formal clothes.

'Dancing through there,' I said, gesturing. 'Food through there. And drink. Take a tip from one who has stood where you are now – pace yourselves. The night is young – you don't want to spend two-thirds of it puking in a flower border wishing you'd never been born. The catering staff are under instructions not to serve you cocktails or anything too lethal so don't even try. For obvious reasons don't do drinking and the bouncy castle simultaneously.'

They giggled and disappeared. Well, I'd done what I could. It was out of my hands now.

And Caroline. She and two of her sisters had arrived

mid-afternoon. George had greeted them politely and shown them their rooms. I stayed well out of the way and since then we'd all avoided each other, though now, sadly, no one could put it off any longer and here they were. Praying mantises in posh frocks and bling.

No one even bothered with the false smiles. Caroline stared at the diamonds. Well, like Pennyroyal, it was a long time since she'd seen them. I'm sure she would have said something, but at that moment Pennyroyal materialised at my shoulder.

'Your drink, my lady.'

'Thank you,' I said. 'Do you remember George's mother – the dowager countess?'

'Vaguely,' he said, obviously in a carnival mood that evening.

She flounced off, trailed by her two sisters.

I turned to the hovering Cleverly. 'Everything OK downstairs?'

'Not in the slightest, my lady. I suspect the sack of Troy caused less chaos and confusion than current activities in the kitchen.'

'All quite normal then?'

'Absolutely, my lady.'

'Well, I think everyone's here now. Let me know if anyone turns up you think I should know about. I'm off to enjoy myself before the next crisis engulfs us all.'

He left.

'Don't believe a word of it,' I said to Pennyroyal, as we strolled across the hall. 'Things will be running like clockwork down there. It's his employers who usually manage to balls things up.'

'Speaking of which,' he said, 'would you like to dance?'

I like to think I didn't hesitate. No surprise that he should ask. No surprise that he could actually dance.

'I'd love to.'

I put down my drink and we moved into the ballroom. Which was packed, but the noise levels certainly dipped as we made our way on to the dance floor. The band was playing a slow number and we slowly circled the room. Of course – this was just his unobtrusive way of keeping tabs on what was happening around us.

We circled again.

'See anything?' I said.

'What?'

'Anything suspicious?'

'Why should there be anything suspicious? What normally happens at these sorts of events?'

'I thought this was a bit of unobtrusive surveillance.'

'No – I just wanted to dance with you.'

'Oh. OK then.'

The music stopped.

'Well, that was very pleasant,' I said.

The music started.

'Shall we go round again?'

'If you like.'

'You look very beautiful this evening.'

'Thank you. You dance very well. Let me guess – butler school.'

'I have a diploma,' he said gravely.

'I'm beginning to doubt the very existence of this butler school of yours.'

'Can't think why.'

We twirled a little bit more and then the music stopped.

He bowed slightly. 'Thank you.'

'My pleasure,' I said, and meant it.

He moved away, and I re-embarked on my hostessing duties.

As well as George's friends, loads of local people and the plague of George's maternal relations, there were Smallhopes here, too. Some of them had been invited out of affection – Aunt Indira, for instance. A few, out of duty, had come to pay their respects to the head of the family, but most had come out of curiosity. I was keeping an eye on them. I'd already had to rescue George from Second Cousin Selwyn's scheme to sell sand to Dubai – apparently they were running out and here was George's chance to get in on the ground floor. I'd flagged down a passing waiter, handed Second Cousin Selwyn another glass of champagne and taken George away to meet someone. Anyone. Selwyn's mother and sister glared at me as I passed. And they weren't the only ones.

I found myself near the bar. How strange. And also near Aunt Indira who, like me, was taking refuge from the family.

'They hate me,' I said cheerfully.

'Not all of us, Millie. Some of us think you're the best thing that ever happened to this family. I think Randolph would be very proud.'

I swallowed down the familiar red-hot ball of pain experienced whenever I thought of Papa, who could have been – should have been – here with us today.

She nodded at Pennyroyal. 'What's the position with him?'

'Why do you ask?'

'The rumour is that he's your lover. That you're completely under his thumb. Don't shoot me – I'm just repeating the gossip.

That perhaps – horror of horrors – you'll even marry him. Which would embarrass the Smallhopes, expose us all to Dyer ridicule, and cripple the estate forever. And worst-case scenario – he forces you to make a will leaving everything to him. Just before he kills you.'

'Really?' I said, trying to remember the last time anyone had forced me to do something I didn't want to.

'Mm. They've talked about nothing else. I'm supposed to be discreetly interrogating you as to your intentions.'

'Really?' I said, again.

'Yes.' She looked at me. 'How do you want to play this?'

I grinned at her and waggled my eyebrows.

She laughed. 'You're really never going to heaven, are you?'

'I sincerely hope not.'

'Well, I don't see why you should have all the fun. Brace yourself.'

'Why?'

She drew back – a look of horror on her face.

'What?' she exclaimed. Her voice rang around the room. People stopped and stared. She made a dramatic gesture, dragging the back of her hand across her forehead like the helpless heroine in a silent movie. 'Are you out of your mind? How could you even contemplate such depravity?' Her voice vibrated with passion. 'Are there no depths to which you will not sink?'

All conversation stopped. I saw Caroline turn to look at her. And then at me.

Indira hadn't finished. 'Does the honour of the Smallhopes mean nothing to you?' She clasped her hands together at her bosom and uttered throbbingly, 'Are the shades of Starlings to be thus polluted?'

'Aren't you getting rather carried away?'

She unclasped her hands and drained her glass. 'This is me, Millie – never knowingly understated.'

I grinned at her. 'You're just going to push off now and leave me to deal with the embarrassing aftermath, aren't you?'

'My glass is empty – can't have that. Enjoy your embarrassing aftermath.'

She turned towards the bar again, laughing.

And here came Caroline. All fake smiles and teeth.

Still smiling broadly at the room, she said, 'You just can't help yourself, can you? Even at George's birthday party, you have to make a scene and embarrass me in front of my entire family.'

I pointed out that if she hadn't brought her family – who hadn't been invited, incidentally – then she wouldn't have had anyone to be embarrassed in front of, would she?

'It's true, then? You're really shagging around with that . . . ?' She stopped.

'He's got some even rougher friends if that's what floats your boat,' I said helpfully. 'I'll get him to introduce you.'

'You . . .' she hissed. 'You won't be happy until you've dragged my family down to your level. You're a tramp, Amelia Smallhope, opening your legs for anyone.' She looked across at Pennyroyal. 'And anything.'

'You should be congratulating me. We're to be married, you know. Next month. In fact, we're off to make the legal arrangements next week. You know, documents, licences . . .' I paused and assumed the expression that always gets me into such trouble. 'Wills . . .'

I was quite surprised at how calm my voice was. I'm trained

403

in all sorts of unarmed combat, but at the moment all I could think of was dragging my nails down her cheeks, watching the blood flow and then clawing her eyes out.

Perhaps something of this showed in my face because she drew back, her voice low and venomous.

'I've spent the entire evening assuring people even you wouldn't sink that low. I mean – the man looks like a child molester. I'm really not happy with him being around George.'

Pictures in my head. Pennyroyal in the kitchen at Swan Court – a whirling dervish of death. Pennyroyal stepping out of the shadows when two members of the Krantz gang appeared from nowhere and I wasn't ready. Pennyroyal lying broken on the kitchen floor. Pennyroyal standing over me, armed to the teeth and holding off all comers and buying me enough time to finish setting the charges the day we broke the Timjin cartel.

Caroline was still talking. I walked off and left her in mid-sentence. I was going to enjoy this.

'Brace yourself,' I said, appearing next to Pennyroyal who was quite happily sipping his drink in the corner and watching the room. 'I'm going to flirt with you.'

'Will it hurt?' he enquired, raising an eyebrow and fortifying himself for the coming ordeal by draining his glass.

'Only if you don't do exactly as I say.'

'Is there any particular reason for this flirting?'

'Tell you later.' I grinned at him and picked a piece of imaginary fluff off his shoulder. 'Don't just stand there like a post – you're being flirted at.'

He sighed loudly – a good man beset by continual misfortune – and then reached down and took my hand, balancing it lightly across one of his fingers. 'How's that?'

I looked down at his hand and mine. 'Is that it?'

'Well, no – I have layers.'

'Like an onion?'

'Like an ogre, actually – nothing like an onion.'

He was still balancing my hand on one finger. It felt extraordinarily intimate – barely touching me and yet . . .

I looked into his eyes, which was easy because he was only a little taller than me. They had turned very dark. The grey had almost completely disappeared. Pupils expand because of oxytocin and dopamine. Heightened excitement. I wondered what mine were doing. The size of dinner plates, probably. My heart began to thump.

I took half a step closer and whispered, 'Is anyone watching?'

'No idea,' he said. 'I only have eyes for you.'

'No, it's OK,' I said, because I had a feeling that events were beginning to get away from me. 'Purpose served.'

'Not my purpose,' he said, staring deeply into my eyes.

'You should probably stop. There are two women fanning themselves over there. I think one's about to pass out.'

'I haven't even started yet.'

He reached up and tucked a stray wisp of hair behind my ear. I noticed again how badly scarred his hands were.

'Never mind them,' I said. 'I'm going to keel over in a minute. When did you get so good at this? Is it just me or do you flirt with every woman you meet?'

'The second one.'

'How many women do you know?'

'Hundreds,' he said. 'Hundreds and hundreds and they all speak very highly of me. Except for the one who really matters. How much are you enjoying this?'

'This what? The party? Or the flirting?'

'The party.'

'Barely at all.'

'Fancy doing something more interesting?'

'What – here?'

'Would that turn you on? Not a problem if so. Name your desire.'

'Um . . .'

We were now standing very close together. 'Imagine if I ripped off all your clothes and flung you across the vol-au-vents . . .'

'Poor Mrs Tiggy might be cross. She spent all day yesterday . . .'

'Before doing something strange but imaginative with the salmon dip.'

My insides twisted. 'I really should go and talk to the vicar . . .'

'I could cover my private parts with chocolate mousse . . .'

I pulled myself together. 'Big improvement on peas.'

'What?'

'You might not remember but I once spent days covering your testicles with frozen peas. Oh, hello, vicar.'

Reverend Caldicott smiled vaguely in the manner of one determined not to believe his ears and passed on.

Pennyroyal blinked. 'Please tell me that was for medical reasons and not a new recipe you were trying out.'

'Which would you find the least disturbing?'

'I'm not actually sure.'

'I'm bored,' I said, looking him squarely in the eye.

'I'm hard.'

My insides twisted again.

'We could slip away.'

'I'd like to,' I said doubtfully. 'But someone should make sure Caroline doesn't steal the spoons.'

'Sod the spoons. I'll gift-wrap them for her if it gets you out of this room within the next ten seconds.'

'All right,' I said, wondering what on earth had got into him. And me. 'Let's slip away.'

Slipping was out of the question. We were about as far away from the door as it was possible to be. Everyone watched us go. We walked side by side. Not touching at all, which was a hundred times more arousing than . . . I don't know. For some reason my mind was full of vol-au-vents.

My sitting room was dark. I heard him lock the door behind us. I really should switch on the light – as if that would bring us both back to reality.

Slightly at a loss as to what to do next, I went to look out of the window. As I watched, a group of young people spilled out of the French windows below, shouting and laughing and heading for the bouncy castle. Enjoying the party. I suspected there might be some wild oats sown this evening. Well – good for them.

Pennyroyal came to stand very close behind me. 'What are you thinking?'

'I was just thinking – I never really got to sow my own wild oats.'

'You pulled off a major art heist at the age of seventeen. You successfully blackmailed your own sister-in-law. You've been consorting with criminals all your adult life. You've engaged in illegal time travel. You brought down an international

407

organisation hell-bent on destroying the world as we knew it. You've made us both very, very rich. Shall I go on?'

'No, I meant – you know – I've never travelled or . . .'

'You've been up and down the timeline more times than a banker collecting bonuses. Say what you mean.'

'No, I mean – I suppose – I've never . . . enjoyed myself.'

'You enjoyed yourself so much with Kester di Maggio that he says his back still doesn't work properly.'

'No, I mean – oh, I don't know.'

There was a very long silence and then, in a very different tone of voice, he said, 'I so very nearly walked off with those diamonds and left you standing there. At the mercy of Caroline Dyer. All alone.'

'I know you did.'

'I could have just turned around and walked out and left you . . .'

'Thank God you didn't. I'd probably be dead by now. Of boredom. Of marriage. Of drink. Of drugs. Of desperation.'

'I'd just be dead,' he said. 'Without you, I'd never have got up off the kitchen floor. And Uncle Albert would have died alone.'

'Max and Markham would have died at Bannockburn.'

'And an awful lot of not nearly as nice people would still be alive and threatening the world.'

'Caroline would have run Starlings into the ground. Young George would probably be quietly insane.'

'There wouldn't be a dog left alive for miles around.'

'And I'd never have . . .'

There was a long silence that, somehow, was different to the long silence that had gone before.

I found enough voice to say, 'I'm so glad you didn't walk away.'

'Same.'

I reached up behind me to unfasten the necklace.

'Leave it,' he said. 'And the bracelet. I've always wanted to see you . . .'

He was taking down my hair. My mind flew back to that night . . . all those years ago . . . when he'd put my hair up.

And then he kissed me. He kissed me in the moonlight. Something happened inside me. I don't know what. I kissed him back. He tightened his grip. I ran my fingers along the nape of his neck and he shivered.

Catching my hands in his own, he held them tight. Crushed them, nearly.

'We have a choice,' he said. 'We can stop now. This – the kiss – the moonlight – everything – it will all fade away. We carry on as before and this becomes a gentle memory but nothing more. Or – we take it further. We do what we always do and take things right to the wire. We play the game and take the consequences. You choose for both of us.'

'I want the consequences,' I said, without hesitation. 'Don't pretend you didn't know I'd say that. I want the consequences and I want them now.'

He tightened his grip again, sending my breathing all over the place.

'How do you want these consequences?'

'The way they always come for us,' I whispered. 'Hard and fast.'

He seemed to have trouble finding his voice. 'Sure?'

'Afraid you can't keep up?'

There was only one response to that.

At some point the sofa went over. And I know something smashed because I heard it go. And a picture slid down off the wall. And I've no idea how, but we somehow became entangled in the curtains and the next moment the brass curtain pole came loose from its fixing and narrowly missed braining the pair of us.

He looked down at me, enveloped in yards of curtain. 'I am never going to be able to look at green velvet again without publicly embarrassing myself.'

I laughed.

And then neither of us were wearing anything at all – well, one of us was still wearing the diamonds – and his hands, so scarred and so gentle, were everywhere.

I paused what I was doing to say, 'There's a bedroom through that door, you know.'

'You want to stop?'

I pushed him back down again. 'God, no.'

Which was the last thing I was able to say for quite some time. That's the thing with Pennyroyal. Hard and fast was what I said. Hard and fast was what I got. All night long.

I awoke the next morning. He was sitting on the end of the bed, fully clothed and putting on his shoes.

I sighed. 'Another one sneaking out without paying.'

He grinned. 'Money's on the dressing table. Don't forget my change.'

He stood up.

'Well,' I said, 'you didn't last long.'

'Telephone conference with Geoff Raikes.' Geoff Raikes trained his horses.

'Ah,' I said. 'Understandable. You'd rather talk horses than have sex. Any man would.'

He came to sit beside me and took my hand. 'I have to go. Stud procedures to discuss.'

'Yours or his? I warn you, I'm not paying for your services.'

'Come and have lunch with me later. At the cottage.'

'Will I have to sit on the floor?'

He rolled his eyes. 'There will be cushions.'

'Why?'

'For you to sit on.'

'I mean why there?'

'It's nearly finished. I want you to see it. And to talk. And eat. Some other things, perhaps.'

'I can't come before about half past twelve. I have guests to see off.'

'I'll see you then.'

Left to myself, I'd have enjoyed a long lie-in, but I had departing guests to speed on their way. Somewhat reluctantly, I came downstairs to be greeted with the excellent news that Caroline had left at dawn to catch her flight home and the two other miseries didn't breakfast. Which I should have guessed. No one in that family looked as if they'd ever had a square meal in their lives.

Confrontations averted, I joined our other party guests in the breakfast room for coffee. You can't breakfast properly if you have to jump up and down every ten minutes to say goodbye to people leaving to catch trains or make flights. George and I did our duty, waved the last car goodbye and returned – with relief – to our own breakfast at last.

I slathered some marmalade on my toast and avoided George's grinning gaze.

'Sleep well, Aunt Millie?'

'Very well, thank you, George.'

'Really? I did wonder, Aunt Millie . . .'

'What did you wonder, George?'

'I thought I heard a noise, Aunt Millie. I thought something smashed. Somewhere. In the night. Aunt Millie.'

Heroines in books are never cursed with cheeky teenage nephews.

'Did you, George?'

'I wondered if you'd heard it too, Aunt Millie.'

'No, George. I heard nothing.'

'Only it seemed to come from your room, Aunt Millie.'

'Did it, George?'

He opened his mouth again.

I grinned. 'Give it up, George. Your grandfather tried and failed. Your father never even attempted it. Learn from their example.'

He just laughed. Most teenagers don't believe anyone over twenty-five ever has sex. I don't know why George couldn't be one of those.

I could have driven chez Pennyroyal but the journey was longer by road and it would be a pleasant walk across country. I strolled through the rose garden, along the wall and out through the same door from which we'd escaped all those years ago. From there it was a gentle walk across the park, through the gate, and into the lane to follow the river downstream for just over a mile. Then over the stile, across two small fields and I'd be there. Having worked up an appetite along the way. And for lunch, too.

The day was warm, but overcast and dull. We'd have rain before long. Rather like Mrs Bennet, I was hoping for heavy rain which would mean I'd have to stay the night. I had my toothbrush and clean knickers in my pocket. Pennyroyal would be proud of my preparations.

I didn't hurry. Not only was there plenty to occupy my mind as I walked, but it was my favourite time of year. We'd had a warm, wet spring and this had resulted in a brilliant display of hawthorn blossom, daisies, buttercups and cow parsley. There was cow parsley out here nearly as tall as me. All the world was sparkling green and white. Walking was a pleasure.

I followed the river until the path picked up the right of way leading across the fields. The river flowed silently – and somewhat muddily – on its way to Rushford and a couple of birds were bouncing about and being exuberant, but other than that, it was just me and the peaceful countryside.

I set my foot on the stile and reached up for the post to steady myself, and the very second my fingers touched wood, the peace was shattered by an all too familiar eldritch ear-splitting shriek seemingly only inches from my left ear. In fact, the sound co-incided so exactly with me touching the post that for a moment I thought it was something I had done.

One microsecond later, the part of my brain that is forever Smallhope said, 'Peacock.'

Well, no, actually it said, 'Bloody peacock.'

It couldn't be the same one, surely. Papa always swore it stalked him everywhere. How old must he be by now? Although I did remember Papa once telling me they could live up to twenty-five years – even thirty to forty if well treated in captivity. True, Papa had spent years taking pot shots at him – which probably didn't come under the heading of being well treated – but let's face it, when it came to a battle of wits between them, the peacock had won hands down every time.

I twisted around to see if it was him and at the same moment something hit me hard in the chest and I flew backwards off the stile. I remember hitting the ground. I remember lying on my back, looking up at the cloudy sky. I remember the silence. I remember the first plop of rain on my face. I remember hearing a rustle in the undergrowth but being unable to turn my head. I remember hearing a shout. In the distance. Long way off. And then nothing for a while. And then vibrations. Footsteps. Running. Towards me. Closer and closer. And then a heavy weight. On my chest. And then a voice said, 'Amelia, for God's sake, don't leave me.'

And then the sky grew darker and darker and my story finishes here.

28

STARLINGS
The Present
Pennyroyal

I saw the whole thing. One of the remote alarms triggered. The one down by the stile. I knew that she would walk along the river. That she would climb the stile and come over the fields.

I was in the kitchen. The office and security screens are in a small room off to the right. I heard the alarm go off and stood in the doorway, watching the screens.

I saw her climb the stile. She stepped up on to the rickety plank. There was no sound, but I saw her stop suddenly and turn sideways as if something had caught her attention. I saw the impact. I saw her fall backwards. She didn't get up. And then I saw the shadow, moving down the hedgerow. I couldn't tell whether he was moving in or making his escape. I stood for a moment in surprise. I knew him. Then I saw his gun and that was enough for me, and I was out of the back door and running for her life and mine just as the rain started up.

I pounded across the field – realising, too late, that I was unarmed. Never mind – I would use his. I would rip his own gun from his grasp and empty it into him. Watch his body jerk and spasm and slowly disintegrate as I killed him by inches. Start with the soft fleshy bits and then move on to the joints – knees, elbows. He would be glad to die.

She wasn't dead. She couldn't be.

I vaulted the gate from one field to the next. I did have the sense to stop, look around and check the area. I hadn't thought to bring a proximity. Or even close the back door. At this, the most important moment of my life, I was no better than the most amateur of amateurs.

The rain started to come down quite heavily.

Standing in the shelter of the hedge, I shouted, 'Oi! Dave! Over here. It came from over here. Tell Chris to ring for the police. And an ambulance,' and waited to see if the shooter panicked and broke cover. Although if he had any sense, he was long gone. And if it was who I thought it was, then he would be.

No point in making myself a target. I skirted the hedge until I arrived at the stile. She was on the far side. On her back. Conscious. Both hands pressed to her chest because, out of the two of us, she was the one keeping her head.

You always approach slowly. Look before touching. I knelt beside her and pulled open her shirt. Easily as bad as I had thought it would be. I pulled off my own shirt, folded it into a pad and applied it to her wound, placing her hands on top and pressing my own over hers.

'Amelia, for God's sake, don't leave me.'

My ears heard the words, so I suppose it was me who said them.

I scrabbled for my phone.

'Which service do you require?'

'Ambulance.'

'Is the patient breathing?'

'Yes, but not for long.'

The words *gunshot wound* really shifted them. I gave them the What Three Words address. The ambulance would find us. I didn't bother with the police. They'd turn up on their own.

My shirt was nearly soaked through with blood. Ignoring the rain, I pulled off my T-shirt and pressed that over the top. Hard as I could.

'Hey,' I said. 'Stay with me.'

The rain was hammering down and there was blood every-where. She was lying in a red puddle. I was kneeling in it. She was still conscious but not for much longer. I could see her eyes closing. Her skin was transparent. Her lips paper-white. She was going.

I said, 'Open your eyes. Look at me. Look at me.' It came out more harshly than I had intended. Her eyelids fluttered.

'Look at the state of you,' I said. 'I hope you don't think you can turn up for lunch looking like this.'

Her blood continued to ooze up through my fingers. Now my T-shirt was soaked. So much blood.

I thought, in the far distance, I could hear a siren. Wishful thinking? No. I could definitely hear an ambulance. Drawing closer. They seemed to take forever to arrive. They knew exactly where to come. I could hear them bouncing along the riverside lane.

The ambulance pulled up and a paramedic jumped down.

'Let's have a look then,' he said, opening his pack while

the driver turned the vehicle round. Good thinking. Always set things up for a quick getaway.

'Amelia Smallhope,' I said. 'Early thirties. Good health. No known medical conditions. No allergies. Not currently on any medication. Keeps herself fit. Gunshot wound to the upper chest. About twenty, twenty-five minutes ago. No exit wound. No sign of the shooter. Blood group O positive. No infectious diseases or drug use.'

He nodded, saying loudly, 'Hello, Amelia. My name is Aziz. Can you hear me?'

They worked on her for a while. There was a lot of radio conversation and instructions. As soon as she was more or less stabilised, they took off.

She was unconscious by then. She would be hours in surgery and if she survived that, then she'd be unconscious for a long time afterwards. I told them I'd pack a bag for her and follow on, but in reality I had things to attend to.

The rain had eased into a cold, wet drizzle. I left my shirt and T-shirt there because it was a crime scene and walked home slowly. This was going to require some careful thinking, and the best person for that sort of thing was elsewhere, fighting for her life.

I pulled out my phone and rang Mr Treasure.

He already knew.

'News flies fast in the countryside,' was all he said.

'What about George?'

'Cleverly and I judged it best to tell him. Cleverly's doing that now. Before all the wild rumours start. I'm on my way up to Starlings at this moment.'

'Good,' I said. 'Can you get someone to pack Lady Amelia

a suitcase and bring it down to me. I'll take it in to her. I . . .'
I looked down at myself. 'I need to clean myself up a bit first.'

'Of course.'

'Thank you.'

There was a pause. 'Do we know who . . . ?'

Mr Treasure was a man of the law. I shouldn't implicate him.
I let a pause go by and then said, 'No.'

He let a pause go by and then said, 'I understand. I will have
her things sent down to you as soon as possible,' and ended
the call.

Reaching the cottage, I locked the back door behind me, ran
upstairs, showered and put my bloody jeans in a bin bag. All the
time I was thinking. Then I went into the office and replayed the
moment over again, then in slow motion, then frame by frame.
Then I downloaded it on to a couple of data sticks. Then I sat
down and made a brief timetable.

This would be all about the timing. I pulled out a burner and
rang Meilin with a list of instructions and requirements. She
was silent for a long time afterwards and then said briskly, 'Yes,
that can all be done. I will do it. And I know exactly the right
person. I shall text where and when to meet her. She will say
judgement. I will send you the Tuscany address when I have
it. Give Millie my love.'

'Thank you.'

There was a knock at the door. Milburn, the gardener. He
handed over her suitcase. I thanked him and told him no, there
was no news yet but I'd call when there was.

I ran a quick check to make sure I'd left nothing lying around
that might interest the police, left the back door unlocked because
they'd be round at some point, and went out to the pod. I stuck

419

the written timetable on the console, made a careful note of my start time, programmed in the coordinates and jumped.

I knew who was responsible for this. No – not responsible – I knew who had pulled the trigger. Him first. *Then* the person responsible.

Shifty Shifnal had been around for a very long time. He'd been semi-retired for a while now but he was still good. Careful, unspectacular, reliable, and he knew his stuff. His only problem these days was his failing eyesight. That's why he'd had to get so close and that's why he'd been picked up on the cameras. A big mistake. And his last one.

Because I knew where he lived. Less than two hours away. He'd be nearly home by now, but I would get there first. And I would be waiting for him.

Seawalls, Bristol. A quiet and respectable street. Shifty's house was two doors from the end. We'd worked together once. When I was just starting out. Before I met her. I could, of course, just gun him down as he walked to his front door but that would have been too simple. I needed confirmation.

The rain started again about twenty minutes after I got there. A big umbrella is both camouflage and weapon. As he went to pull out his door key, I said quietly, 'Shifty, me old mate.'

I was careful to keep my distance. Old he might be, and nearly half-blind, but even he couldn't miss me at that range.

He turned slowly, made me out through the rain and grinned. 'Well, I'm buggered. Thought you'd be dead long ago.'

That was reassuring. He hadn't been told of my connection with his victim. He'd probably have refused the job if he had.

'Far from it,' I said, finding a small smile. 'In fact, that's why I'm here. You still . . . um . . . in the game?'

'Yeah. Not full-time, but yeah.'

'I find myself double-booked and need to subcontract. You interested?'

'Yeah. Might be. Come on in.'

After that it was easy.

I left my umbrella outside in the porch and followed him in. We sat at the table in his little front room.

He offered tea or something stronger, which I refused. I needed to keep my gloves on.

'Thought you'd be retired by now, Shifty.'

He shook his head. 'The occasional job.'

'The ones that pay well?'

He grinned.

I glanced around. 'Nice room. Good to see you're doing well.'

'Yeah, well – planned for my retirement, didn't I? Not like some people.'

'But still doing a bit every now and then?'

'If the money's right – yeah.'

'You working now?'

'Just finished a job. Literally.'

'Ah. Does that mean you don't need the dosh?'

'A bit extra always comes in handy and the money was good for this one.'

'Yeah, well, make sure you get it, Shifty. I've been shafted more than once. *Half in advance – half on completion*, they say. You do the job and sometimes the other half never turns up.'

He shook his head. 'Paid in advance. All of it.'

421

'Well, good for you, Shifty. Bet he wasn't happy about that.'

I waited to see if he'd say *she* but he didn't.

He shook his head. 'Nasty streak of wind and piss. Didn't like him one bit and I didn't want the job, so I doubled the price and demanded it all up front. Never thought he'd agree but he wasn't bright.'

So – both of them. Caroline had provided the brains and finance. Hugo set it up.

I sat up and forced enthusiasm into my voice. 'I think I know him. If it's who I think it was, you did right to get the money first. Tall. Thin. Watery eyes. Looks you in the groin.'

He laughed. 'That's him.'

'And he paid it all up front? Good job you're honest. You could have walked off with the lot and never done the job.'

'Yeah. Well. Call it professional pride. Anyway, what can I do for you?'

I moved into business mode. 'First things first, Shifty – what are you using these days?'

As I hoped, he'd brought his little carrying case in with him. I knew he'd be wanting to clean his gun as soon as possible. He laid the case on the table. A battered and anonymous-looking briefcase, custom-made to carry his weapon. Snapping the catches, he opened it up and presented the contents for inspection.

'Nice,' I said admiringly, peering inside. 'Old-style, but you can't beat quality.'

Shifty began to fit the weapon together. 'Only seconds to assemble.'

'So I see. And to load?'

'Same. Watch.'

422

It was too easy.

'Weight? Cos that'll be important on this job.'

'See for yourself.'

He passed it over. I took it and shot him between the eyes. Quick and clean. He never knew what hit him. A professional courtesy.

I disassembled the gun, slipped it back into the carrying case, took one last look around – although I hadn't touched anything – turned out the lights and slipped out of the front door. No one was about. It wasn't that late but the sky was low and the street lights had come on in the gloom. Pulling the door to behind me, I put up my umbrella, picked up the case, walked out of the gate, and turned right. Back to the pod.

My phone rang.

'Me,' said Meilin. 'It's done.'

'All of them?'

'Every single account. Some substantial amounts of money. I suspect she has found someone else to leech off. Details texted. Get rid of this phone.'

'Thank you,' I said.

There was a pause.

'How is she?'

'Don't know.'

'How are you?'

'Tidying up loose ends.'

'Not what I asked.'

'No.'

'Take care. Call me if you need anything.'

'Thank you.'

I disconnected, pulled the phone apart and disposed of the

pieces separately as I made my way back to the pod, parked in a small allotment at the end of the road. No one was working this afternoon because of the weather. No one saw me, I made sure of it.

It might take the police a while to track things back to Shifty, but once they did, they'd find him dead. They wouldn't find the murder weapon – not then, anyway – but they would get round to investigating his bank accounts and that would give them all the evidence they needed.

Now for the next part.

I'd worked it all out very carefully. I knew that Caroline had caught a mid-morning flight. Flight time two and a half hours. Land at Pisa. An hour to clear the airport. Another hour or so to get to her villa. Thirty minutes for contingencies – plus the one-hour difference in the time zones. She should be there by now.

I had no doubt she had taken care to provide herself with some very conspicuous alibis. Taxi drivers would remember her – either for her generous tip or no tip at all. She would have made a small scene when checking in. And possibly on the plane, demanding her seat be changed. And another scene at the other end. Or she would call attention to her arrival at the villa by asking the driver the time and ostentatiously changing her watch. Or if it had updated automatically, checking its accuracy with the driver.

None of which would matter in the slightest. Caroline, unlike Shifty, was going to live long enough to regret ever having been born.

Given the beauty of the area and the surrounding houses, Caroline's villa was surprisingly ugly. Modern, architect-designed and all glass – something she must bitterly regret in the long, hot, sun-filled summers. Local people sensibly lived in stone houses with small windows.

She was very obviously home. It was growing dark by now and the villa was blazing with light. The pool was flood-lit – as were various trees and statues. Someone had thrown open most of the doors and windows. To air the place, probably, which was going to make access very easy. Keeping out of the lights, I slipped through floor-to-ceiling glass doors and into a huge room packed with fashionably uncomfortable furniture, questionable art and various bits of expensive but fragile-looking bric-a-brac.

The first thing was to carry out a quick room-to-room search. She might not be alone – alibi for the purposes of – and I half expected her useless brother to be here somewhere. But no, she was alone. Company might turn up at any moment so I moved swiftly. Kitchen, giant lounge and dining room, three bedrooms, each with their own bathroom. I nipped into her room – discarded clothes all over the bed – locked the door, pocketed the key, dimmed the lights, opened Shifty's case, dropped the gun barrel on the bed where she could see it, made myself comfortable and waited until she emerged from the shower.

God knows what she was doing in there, but she was doing it for long enough for me to start thinking that I was going to have to hurry things along a little. All this was happening in real time, and I needed to be getting back to Rushford.

She eventually emerged through the door wearing just a towel and humming a happy little tune. She didn't see me until I moved and then it was too late. In one swift movement, I'd pressed the pad of cloth over her face.

'Breathe in.'

She tried to struggle but I held her fast. We didn't even dis-lodge the towel. To give her her due, she held her breath for as long as she could manage.

'Breathe in,' I said. 'Breathe in or lose consciousness and then your body will do it for you.'

Actually, that would be the best alternative. She'd drop to the floor, inhale, and I could get her fingerprints and be gone before she even realised. That was the sensible option. But if that happened, then she'd never know . . . And I was very keen that *she should know*. Because this wasn't about justice – this was about revenge.

I felt her heave in a massive breath. And another one. I counted to fifteen, decided that was long enough and pushed her away from me.

'Good evening.'

Coughing and gasping, she backed around the bed, keeping it between us and still clutching the towel.

'*You.*'

'Yes,' I said. 'Lady Amelia's bit of rough.'

If ever I'd had any doubt she was involved in the shooting – which I didn't – it would have flown straight out of the window. Her face was a damning mixture of guilt, fear and complete bewilderment. How was I here? And so quickly? What had happened? Had something gone wrong? How much did I know? And, probably uppermost in her thoughts, was I here to kill her?

She seemed to struggle for words. 'What are you . . . ? Why are you in my bedroom? Get out. How did you . . . ?'

She stopped before she could betray the fact she knew some-thing had happened.

426

I could have told her to relax. I didn't.

I pointed to the bed. 'Sit down.'

'I will not.'

'*Do it.*'

Not taking her eyes off me, she perched on the bed, stood up again, looked down and picked up the gun barrel.

I held out my gloved hand. 'Give that to me now. Quickly.'

As I'd anticipated, she ignored me, holding the gun barrel to the light to examine it more closely. I wanted it so it must be important. She turned it over and over, trying to see what it was. Lots and lots of lovely fingerprints.

'*Now.*'

She tossed it on to the floor. I bent swiftly and put it in my pocket.

'Get out before I call the police.'

I began to head back towards the door. 'All right. Sorry to have troubled you. Goodnight.'

That took her by surprise. 'What? Wait.'

'Goodnight.'

'You're leaving?'

'I have your fingerprints on the murder weapon – that's all I needed.'

Once again her face told me everything I needed to know. She couldn't hide the sudden flash of elation. I'd said *murder*. Smallhope was dead and George and Starlings were back within her reach. And then her ears heard the bit about the fingerprints.

I watched her regain control. Quite calmly, she said, 'What murder weapon? What are you talking about?'

'You tell me, Caroline . . .'

She curled her lip. 'That's Lady Goodrich to filth like you.'

'Have you enjoyed living here?'

She just stared at me. I repeated the question, waiting for her answer. Eventually it dawned on her that I wasn't going anywhere, so she said, 'Yes.'

'Good. You'll grow to hate it but that will be your problem.'

She clutched at her towel.

'Ever heard of SmartDust?'

She shook her head.

'SmartDust is . . .'

'I'm not interested in anything you have to say. Get out.'

'As you wish. All you need to know is that you just inhaled it. Goodnight.'

I headed for the door.

'Wait. What do you mean I just inhaled it?'

'Exactly what I said. Your sinuses are now full of the stuff.'

'What does that mean?'

'It means you're dead, Caroline. You just don't know it yet.'

She clutched her towel again, her mouth slack with shock.

I gestured around. 'I'm glad you like living here. Because this is where you'll be spending the rest of your life. Any attempt to move more than a hundred yards from this place will trigger the SmartDust, which will begin to spread throughout your brain, causing you to lose control of your bladder and bowels. Unpleasant but not fatal. Yet. Struggle on a few more yards – and it will be a struggle – and you'll lose the power of speech. You might make a few animal noises but words will never come again. If you manage a few more yards, you'll lose control of your body. You won't be able to walk properly. Or at all. Areas of your brain will begin to shut down. You won't be Caroline Dyer any longer. You'll certainly never be the

Dowager Countess of Goodrich again. Only another twenty yards or so and the last part of your brain will give up and that's when things will get really messy. To the outside world it will look as if you've suffered some sort of stroke, but in reality, SmartDust will have destroyed your brain. It will be a painful and degrading death and no power on earth will be able to save you. You can't ever leave this house, Caroline. It's your prison. For the rest of your life.'

It took her a while to find her voice. 'I don't believe you. There's no such thing as this . . . dust. This is nonsense.'

'Yes, you're right – it's nonsense. I was just joking. Now I have to go.' I smiled. 'Why don't you come with me? You can give me a lift to the airport.'

I set off for the door again.

She seemed rooted to the spot.

'You're not coming? Very wise.'

'Why? Why are you doing this?'

I shrugged. 'I don't like you.'

Her jaw dropped. 'Is that it? You don't *like* me?'

'When I don't like someone, they don't tend to live for very long, so count yourself lucky you're still breathing. Oh – I knew there was something else – your bank accounts are empty.'

That hit home. She hadn't really taken the SmartDust stuff on board – but money was always close to her heart. 'You've stolen my money?'

'Well, I didn't but someone else did. You're now flat broke. So, an interesting dilemma for you: if you stay here, you'll starve to death – if you leave, then your head will explode.'

'That's rubbish. My accounts are all protected and . . .'

429

'It took a professional less than twenty minutes to get the lot. All of it. There's nothing left.'

I don't think she could take it in. 'You've left me with *nothing*?'

'Not a single penny. You'll have to do as the rest of us do. Work.' I gestured around. 'Here. In this place.'

'I'll sell it and move on.'

I sighed. 'You haven't been listening, have you?'

I think it was beginning to sink in. She looked around the room. 'I have to stay *here*?'

'You have to *work* here. If you leave, you'll die. Whoever buys this place – you work for them. You have no choice.'

She tried to laugh. 'That's ridiculous. Suppose they don't want me?'

'Understandable, but you'll just have to convince them, Caroline.'

Doubt was creeping in. And bewilderment. 'I can't ... I don't understand.'

'Whatever it takes to remain here, that's what you'll do. With a smile on your face. Because if they throw you out, you're dead. Let me tell you how the conversations will go ...

'*Work for no wages? No problem, madam, of course I will.*

'*Extracurricular activities, sir? Of course, sir. My pleasure. What would you like me to do for you? Or for your friends? Or for their friends?*'

I resumed my normal voice. 'You'll do whatever anyone wants you to do. And you'll smile, Caroline. Smile and smile and smile. You'll work from dawn to dusk. You'll cook, clean, scrub, garden – all of it. And the harder you work, the faster your looks will fade. Imagine what you'll have to do then to persuade them to keep you on here.'

She could barely speak. 'But . . . that's . . . it's . . . inhuman. It's slavery.'

'It is.'

She seemed genuinely bewildered. 'Why? What did I ever do to you?'

'You did it to Lady Amelia.'

I could see the thoughts behind her eyes. Suddenly she smiled. 'You said it yourself. She's gone. Time, perhaps, for you to consider a change of ownership. Whatever I've done – I'm sure we can come to some arrangement about that. I've got money . . . I could give you . . .'

I debated whether to tell her Smallhope was still alive. On the one hand, I'd get the pleasure of seeing Caroline's sick disappointment. On the other hand – by now she might be dead.

And I certainly wasn't going to tell her Shifty was dead because even Caroline would be able to put that two and two together. The thought of her being indicted for a murder she hadn't committed was actually quite funny.

I've heard it said I have a very specialised sense of humour.

'You weren't listening. Your money's gone, Caroline. All you have is this villa, a few clothes and the towel you're standing up in.'

She tried piteous. 'Whatever you think I've done, I don't deserve this.'

'It was inevitable, Caroline. You were doomed from the moment you hit her with that mirror. It's just taken me this long to get around to dealing with you.'

Her eyes widened as she suddenly realised who I was.

'You were there . . . that night. You were there.'

'I was. And now I'm here. As are you. For the rest of your not very long life.'

'You can't leave me here without even . . .'

'I can and I am.'

It was beginning to sink in. She began to cry. Properly. Big, ugly, gulping sobs.

Time to twist the knife. I unlocked the door.

'This . . .' I held up Shifty's case, 'will be placed in a safe deposit box somewhere not too difficult for the police to find. In your name, of course. If the police do their job properly, they'll be coming for you soon. I don't know when, of course – a few days . . . a few weeks . . . even a few months. But they'll definitely come for you one day.'

'Why? Why would they?'

'You forgot to ask what happened to all your lovely money.'

She went rigid. Her lips tried to form a word but no sound emerged, so I put her out of her misery.

'We popped it all into Shifty's bank account. Not the off-shore business account you and Hugo used, but his normal, high-street current account. And it's a very, very generous amount, Caroline. Certainly generous enough to attract attention. I should imagine that even now questions are being asked about money-laundering, the authorities have been alerted and so forth.'

'*You* did . . .'

'Not me personally. There's another someone out there who knows what you've done. Just in case you're thinking of getting Hugo to organise another shooting.'

She was now beyond speech.

'A nice thought, Caroline. Using someone I used to know.

Obviously I couldn't wait for Amelia to die before inheriting all that lovely money. If you'd succeeded, I'd have had a real job convincing the police it wasn't me. And then I remembered – your brother's done time, hasn't he? You make all sorts of useful connections in prison. And if I can work it out, you can bet the police can. Are you so confident Hugo won't grass you up at the first opportunity? No, I thought not. Really, when you think about it, it's hard to know what will get you first, isn't it?'

I turned to go. This was taking too long.

She lunged suddenly, yanking open a drawer. It was empty.

I held up her little gun and then slipped it back into my pocket.

She was beginning to pant. Even in the dim light I could see she'd gone a very funny colour.

'I have an alibi. A watertight alibi. I was on a plane the whole time and I can prove it.'

'I'm certain you can. But the point is, Caroline, once they discover the safety deposit box, the police will want to interview you at the station. Possibly the one fifteen miles away from here, but more probably back in England. And you just don't have that range any longer, do you? You could try to explain why you can't leave, of course, but they won't believe that SmartDust crap any more than you do, deep down. Imagine how surprised everyone will be when your head explodes a hundred yards down the road.'

She sat down on the bed. With a bump. Staring off into the future.

I opened the door. Time was ticking.

Suddenly, in one movement, she pulled the towel open and lay back on the bed, arranging her limbs in what she probably imagined to be an attractive invitation. 'Why don't you come here, and we can discuss this?'

I shook my head. 'When you've had silk, you don't want sacking.'

The blood flooded back into her face. She was, literally, livid with rage.

'Deep breaths,' I advised. 'Slow and steady. You don't want the SmartDust going off prematurely.'

I could almost see her mind working. She could ring her sisters for help but hers was a predatory family. What price would they force her to pay? Or Hugo? Even worse. I watched her imagine what her life would become.

I stepped out of the door.

Her voice was shrill with panic. 'Where are you going?'

'To get on with my life. Enjoy what's left of yours.'

She was hyperventilating, clutching at the silk bedcover with both hands.

'I have an alibi. I have powerful friends. I can weather this.'

'Yes, you might,' I said.

She lifted her chin. 'In which case, you think you'll kill me yourself.'

I shook my head. 'Oh, no. I'll leave that to Lady Amelia. She's a much better shot than me.'

'She's still alive? You said . . . Wait. Come back. Come back.'

Something smashed into the doorjamb next to my head. No idea what she'd thrown but it sounded expensive.

I closed the door on her hysterical screaming and walked out into the night.

29

I stopped off in London, walking the wet streets to the rendez-vous point. A blonde woman was waiting, her collar turned up against the rain. From a distance, she had a certain resemblance to Caroline.

'Judgement.'

I held out Shifty's case, the barrel now replaced.

She took it. 'There is a twenty-four-hour facility in South-wark. The safety deposit box is already set up and paid for with money from her account. I am under instructions not to tell you any more.'

She turned and walked away.

I looked at my watch. The timing was perfect. Just the right amount of time for the weapon to have been driven from Star-lings to London.

I put up my umbrella and stepped back out into the rain.

At the hospital, I parked the pod around the back, among all the working bits – the storerooms, sheds and other anonymous buildings. Engaging the camo device, I breathed deeply for a moment or so, clearing my mind of all things Caroline. Then

I took off my gloves, consulted my watch, checked I had the data sticks, picked up the suitcase, and exited.

The evening was colder and wetter than in London and much colder and wetter than Tuscany. Rain bounced off the tarmac. I weaved my way through the car park, bought myself a parking ticket, and headed towards the brightly lit front doors.

The inside seemed very warm. There was a constant stream of people making their way in and out of the hospital. I stood just inside for a few minutes, ostensibly getting my bearings so that people would remember seeing me. If I was here, then I couldn't possibly have been at Shifty's place only an hour or so ago. And certainly not in Tuscany. The hospital cameras would show me approaching from the car park. I had the ticket in my pocket. And I'd tossed the burners I'd used to contact Meilin. Caroline's little gun was at the bottom of her swimming pool. A nice detail, I thought. I ran through everything in my mind. No. Everything was accounted for. No loose ends. I like to be tidy.

I enquired at reception and was directed to Ward Nine. I bought a newspaper on the way, paying by card, carefully keeping the receipt by stuffing it seemingly carelessly into my pocket – another alibi. Which might turn out to be a complete waste of time. If she was dead, then I'd be gone in minutes. Pick up the pod and back to Home Farm. Never to return.

I made my way upstairs. Very slowly. Because these might be the last few seconds in which I could hold on to the hope she was still in this world. Ward Nine was at the end of a long corridor. I stopped at the nurses' station, took a breath and asked the question.

She was still alive. Until that moment, I hadn't realised how

436

much ... What I ... I hadn't dared even think about it. She was still alive.

I sat down heavily in the nearest seat.

There was a police officer there already. His instructions would be to stay with her, take note of visitors and anything said. That was all right. I could handle that.

About an hour later, they brought her up from recovery and installed her in a bay next to the nurses' station. I moved to a seat that gave me a view into her room. The police officer came over and made a note of my name and address.

She was surrounded by equipment. All quiet bleeping and flashing lights. There was a dim light above her bed. Her face was very white. Her hair looked dark on the pillow. She was very still.

I walked to the doorway, held up her case and indicated that I'd like to unpack. The officer nodded.

I opened it so that he could see what was inside. He nodded again. I unpacked her bag, quietly arranging her stuff as she liked it. Then I pulled up an uncomfortable plastic chair, sat down on the other side of the bed and waited.

Time passed.

I stood up and said, 'I'm off to get a tea. You want anything?'

'Tea. White. Two sugars. Thanks.'

Cordial relations established without being too obvious about it, I went off in search of refreshments. I didn't reckon I was out of the woods yet. I wouldn't be at all surprised to find myself the number one suspect. But I'd deal with that problem when it arose.

Nurses came in periodically to check patient and equipment. Obviously I asked and apparently the patient was doing as well as could be expected.

George turned up, escorted by Mr Treasure. Both of them very pale and shocked. We talked outside for a while. Conscious of the officer and his notebook, I said as little as possible. They went off to speak to the doctors, reappearing about ten minutes later. Next of kin get more info. The surgery had gone quite well. The bullet had missed her heart. The patient was strong. The longer she lived, the longer she was likely to live. They were cautiously – very cautiously – optimistic.

George had brought me something to eat. Mrs Tiggy had packed a little box for me. I thanked him. And asked him to thank her. They stayed about half an hour. Mostly we sat in silence.

As they got up to go, I let George get a little ahead and then handed over the data stick.

Mr Treasure stared at it. 'Is that . . . ?'

'Shows the attack – yes.'

'You should give this to the police.'

'I have a copy for them. This is my insurance.'

He glanced at George, nodded, and they left. More officers turned up only minutes afterwards. A man and a woman. I recognised her. The sergeant who had called at Starlings all those years ago. The night we'd stolen the diamonds. The night it all began. I ignored the thought that this might be the night it all ended.

She didn't recognise me. No reason why she should.

We stepped outside into the corridor again so as not to disturb the patient.

'Mr . . . Pennyroyal, I'm Detective Inspector Kapoor.'

She'd been promoted. Good for her.

'I believe you reported the crime. Are you able to tell me what happened?'

'I can do better.' I took the remaining data stick from my pocket. 'It's all on there. You'll even get a glimpse of the killer.'

She took it as if she couldn't believe her luck.

'You just happened to have . . . ?'

'I have excellent security.'

She was instantly suspicious. 'Why would you need excellent security?'

I had my reason all ready. 'One of my horses recently won the Derby. I have plans to put him out to stud. I leave it to you to imagine how much money that will be worth. Before I bring him here, I needed to install top-of-the-range security.'

Looking down at the stick, she nodded. 'You say it shows the killer?'

'It shows what looks like a man. You won't see him pull the trigger. You will see a face. Very briefly.'

'Did you recognise him?'

I shook my head. 'Never seen him before. Not that I can remember.'

Always qualify your answer. If I categorically denied all knowledge of Shifty and the police somehow produced proof of a past association – and you never know what's out there – then my categorical denial would be very suspicious. Hence – *not that I can remember*.

'And what is your relationship to the victim?'

'Butler.'

'You're a butler?'

'Fully qualified.'

'You have a diploma?'

Why do people have such difficulty with this? 'I have twelve diplomas, actually.'

She shifted her weight. 'And what else do you do for Lady Amelia?'

'Chauffeur, odd-job man and so forth.'

'Is that all?'

'More or less.'

'I understand you and the victim are to be married.'

'No.'

'No? No what? You're not to be married?'

'No.'

'Lady Amelia publicly stated . . .'

'Lady Amelia has a very specialised sense of humour,' I said. 'But no – there are no wedding plans.'

'Not on your side, perhaps.'

'Not on either side.'

'How would you describe her relationships with her family?'

I frowned. 'Depends on which member of her family.'

'Her nephew?'

'Excellent. They are very fond of each other.'

'Dame Indira?'

'As far as I am aware – very good.'

'Lady Goodrich?'

'Very poor.'

'As far as you are aware?'

'As far as anyone is aware.'

'Mr Hugo Dyer?'

'I think they rarely saw each other. Although she did punch his lights out after her brother's funeral.'

She blinked. 'For any particular reason?'

'He attacked her.'

'Again – why?'

I shrugged. 'Lone female. Out after dark. Easy prey.'

'Did she report the offence?'

'She dealt with it herself. No need to trouble the police.'

She stared at me. Her sergeant was staring at me as well.

Finally, she said, 'I understand that Lady Amelia has made a will in your favour.'

'No.'

'She hasn't?'

'No.'

'That's not what people are saying.'

I remained silent.

'They're saying you've persuaded her to leave everything to you.'

I smiled and shook my head.

'So you're right and everyone else is wrong?'

'Not for the first time.'

'Are you aware of the terms of Lady Amelia's will?'

'I am.'

'And they are?'

'What they've always been.'

'Which is?'

'Everything to her nephew.'

'Everything? Property? Money?'

'Well, I think she may have left me one or two small keepsakes, and the same for long-standing staff and friends – but otherwise – yes. Her solicitor will have all the details.'

She regarded me. 'And you're OK with that?'

'Why would I not be?'

'Well, we could all use a little extra cash.'

Now I regarded her. 'The investigation is in its early stages

441

so I'm sure you won't have got around to ascertaining my personal circumstances yet. Let me assist you – I don't need her money. I don't need anyone's money. Owning racehorses is not a poor man's hobby. I pay a substantial rent for my property. My outgoings – as I'm sure you will discover – are also substantial. However, all my debts are discharged. I owe no one. I'm not sure what you imagine my financial or social status to be, but it would appear you are wrong on both counts.'

She stood her ground. 'Am I?'

'In this instance – yes. I can understand your thinking. Despite the evidence, I must be the obvious suspect. The only question remaining is whether you're the sort of officer who conducts a proper investigation or the sort who simply fixes on the easiest person to fit up.'

'All my investigations are correctly conducted, Mr Pennyroyal. An innocent person has nothing to fear. I am not, however, completely convinced you are that person.'

I shrugged again. 'If you're determined to pinch me for it, there's nothing I can do about it at this stage. You should perhaps know that I've handed a duplicate data stick to Lady Amelia's solicitor. For safekeeping, you understand. I do have concerns about corruption. Of the data, I mean.'

I'd made her angry. I should stop pushing her. So I pushed a little harder.

'I am obviously your number one suspect. I have no problems with that. My only concern is that your enthusiasm for arresting me might lead you to be less diligent in pursuing other lines of investigation.'

There's a particular look. All coppers have it. I was on the receiving end now. Very softly, she said, 'Who are you?'

'Lady Amelia's butler. Would you like to see my diplomas?'

'We'll want to talk to you again.'

'I'll be here.'

'It might be a few days.'

'I'll be here.'

'They might not let you stay.'

'I'll be here.'

'Then I shall know where to find you.'

I resumed my vigil.

A nurse brought us both – me and the officer – a cup of tea. I thanked him politely.

At eleven o'clock that night, she stirred.

At eleven fifteen she opened her eyes and then closed them.

At eleven twenty-five she opened her eyes, looked around and then closed them again.

At eleven thirty she opened her eyes and they stayed open. She turned her head and looked at me.

I leaned over her and very gently took her cold hand. 'Every time I see you, I fall in love with you all over again.'

She smiled a small smile and then her eyes slid over my shoulder. I looked around. Kapoor was standing in the doorway, watching us.

I turned back to Smallhope, and in that moment there was no one else in the world. Our conversation was without words but said everything. Then she closed her eyes and went back to sleep.

I got up.

'You look as if you could do with some fresh air,' Kapoor said, and we went to stand outside.

It was still drizzling so we stood under the big porch. I waited for her to speak.

'The recording was useful.'

'Thought it would be.'

'We think we know who the figure might be.'

'Good. Can I assume I am no longer your prime suspect?'

'You were. Until I watched the data stick. And until I saw you both together just now.'

I said nothing.

'We've been to your house.'

I continued to say nothing. They wouldn't have found anything.

She gave me a lopsided smile. 'I turned the oven off.'

'I forgot,' I said, surprised. That wasn't like me.

'I suspect you're guilty of many things, but the shooting of Lady Amelia Smallhope is not one of them.'

'Will you find him? The bloke on the tape?'

'Oh yes. It might take us a while but we'll get him.'

'Thank you.'

She nodded and walked off into the rain.

Smallhope woke up properly just before eight o'clock the next morning. The police officer had gone for a slash.

I waited while she focused her eyes and took in her surroundings and her memory came back.

She blinked a few times and then croaked, 'Why are you here?'

'I'm keeping a vigil at your bedside.'

She could only manage a hoarse whisper but that wasn't going to stop her. 'Why?'

'Because.'

'I can't believe you're . . . not out avenging my death. A personal . . . quest for revenge.'

'Well, to begin with, you're not dead.'

'Give it a minute.'

'You've spent years yelling at me for taking off on personal quests for revenge. You threw a soup bowl at me for taking off on a personal quest for revenge. And then you nearly took my eye out with the spoon.'

'Why aren't you asking how I am?'

'I know how you are. I've been here ever since you were shot.'

'Yes – not avenging me.'

'You're very hard to please.' I heaved a sigh and got to my feet.

'Where are you going?'

'To avenge you. Obviously.'

'Well, it's too bloody late now.'

I sighed and sat back down again.

She regarded me. 'You've already done it, haven't you?'

I know my expression didn't change.

She smiled and closed her eyes.

She recovered. Slowly at first and then in leaps and bounds. And then we had a problem preventing her doing too much too soon. The doctors began to talk of her being discharged. Which was when the arguments started. George wanted her to come back to Starlings. As did Treasure. And Cleverly. And Mrs Tiggy. They closed ranks.

I wanted her with me. Better security. I told her it was time we had a proper home.

'We had Home Farm.'

'We still do.'

'And you have that house in London? The one you set fire to?'

'I thought it best we let that one go.'

'Good thought.'

'We still have that flat in London,' I said. 'The one where Max and Markham lived.'

'True.' She moved her arm to ease her shoulder. 'If the relevant governments knew we had all these properties, they'd be stinging us for the tax.'

I shook my head. 'I don't pay tax.'

'Well, I do.'

'Come and live with me then.'

'I've been living with you for years.'

'True, but . . .'

'Years and years.'

'Yes, but . . .'

'Ever since we ran away together.'

'We did not . . .'

She put her hand on mine, suddenly serious, and I knew then it wasn't going to happen. She wouldn't leave Starlings.

'I want to,' she said, 'and one day, I will. But not now. I can't leave George all alone. Especially not after . . . you know . . . what's happened.'

That made sense.

'But I can visit. You know . . . pop by . . .'

'For lunch.'

'If you like, but mostly I'd be there for sex. Masses and masses of noisy, vigorous sex.'

I shook my head. 'I can't hear you for the blood pounding in my ears.'

It was the sort of golden summer that comes late enough in life to be appreciated. There was good food, good wine, gentle walks, evenings in the pub. A golden, glorious summer. We gave statements to the police. Hers consisted of *I don't remember anything*. Mine consisted of *I don't know anything*. Otherwise they left us alone.

The glorious golden summer didn't last, of course. Neither of us were made for that sort of thing. It's OK for a few months but not forever.

I blame the rain.

She'd walked down to the cottage to spend the day with me, but out of nowhere, the weather turned and we were stuck inside. I talked about instituting a basic fitness regime, which she ignored – and sadly, the days of me commanding unquestioning respect and obedience were long past. If they'd ever existed at all.

I proposed a trip in the pod. A spot of convalescence in early 20th-century San Tropez, perhaps, or Christmas in 19th-century Vienna, but it seemed she had other ideas. She disappeared into the office with a jug of margaritas and a stubborn expression, saying she needed a drink and a think.

I let her be, passing the time with a weapons check and finishing off some jobs around the cottage.

She was in the office for most of the afternoon – there was obviously a great deal to think about – so I started on dinner. She finally emerged just as it began to grow dark and cocktail hour became official.

We sat at the table while dinner simmered. I'd drawn the curtains – not that it mattered because there were no sight-lines; the outside had been very carefully landscaped – but it was nice to shut out a wild night. The lights were low and the room was warm.

I sipped my whisky.

'I've had a thought,' she said.

I waited while she fiddled with her tablet.

'Our twelve months is nearly up. We have decisions to make.'

I went to speak.

'Yes,' she said, 'I know what you're going to say. I'm not match-fit. Yet. But I need to know whether I ever will be. If I'm not, then we'll need to decide whether to remain here for another twelve months or permanently retire. If I am – again we can either stay here or return to the future and Home Farm and continue with the firm. Or we can do a combination of both. Or do we split up and go our separate ways?'

'No,' I said.

'OK. Well, that's one decision made then, but I think we need more info before making anything permanent.'

She paused, looking over at me, but I said nothing.

'One job,' she said. 'Something to challenge us. Keep our hand in. Something small and discreet. Not involving anyone else. Just the two of us.'

'A sort of jobette, you mean?'

'Exactly.' She beamed at me.

'And what precisely will this jobette entail?'

'Something quite spectacular.'

'Small and discreet and yet quite spectacular?'

'Wrong word. Forget spectacular. Challenging.'

'You said that before.'

'I'm building up to my big moment.'

'If it's big moments you're after, I'm not doing anything right now and I haven't laid the table yet. Just say the word and you could be the starter.'

'Hold that thought. No, this could be history-making. Or, alternately, of course, our swansong.'

'Details of which you will no doubt get around to in your own good time.'

She grinned at me. Smallhope was back. 'Ready for this?'

'I'm growing old waiting.'

'Brace yourself.'

I slugged back more whisky. It didn't help.

'The Crown Jewels.'

You'd think I'd be used to this sort of thing by now – but no.

'*The Crown Jewels?*'

'Yes.'

'The ones in the Tower?'

'Yes.'

'Those.'

'Yes.'

'We're going to steal the Crown Jewels?'

'We are indeed.'

'Well, that will certainly make some history. Not necessarily the right sort of history, of course.' I finished my whisky and closed my eyes.

'I sense some disapproval,' she said.

'I sense too many margaritas.'

'I've done some exploratory work and I think it's perfectly doable.'

449

'Doable?'

'Very. In fact – almost too easy.'

'In that case – why bother? Where's the challenge?'

She leaned forwards, her eyes sparkling with mischief.

'The challenge, my friend, will come twenty-four hours later. When we put them back.'

THE END

AUTHOR'S NOTE

I've referenced several of Smallhope and Pennyroyal's previous adventures in this story and I wanted to do footnotes – just like a proper author. This was, however, considered to be beyond my simple capabilities.

'Beyond your simple capabilities, Taylor,' they said. 'Do an Author's Note instead.'

'But I'd be able to use asterisks and things. Grown-up punctuation.'

'If you scatter asterisks the way you scatter commas, the entire book will look like a blizzard.'

'But . . .'

'A whiteout, even,' they said, rocking with laughter at their own joke.

I sulked for ages and no one noticed so in the end I bowed to *force majeure* and went with the supposedly safer option – an Author's Note. Personally, I think it lacks the intellectuosity of asterisks, but what do I know?

Anyway, if you'd like to read more about the earlier exploits of Smallhope and Pennyroyal, how they met St Mary's at Bannockburn is told in *Why is Nothing Ever Simple?*; Site X features in *Hard Time*; and Max's adventures with those naughty people at Insight are recounted in *A Catalogue of Catastrophe* and *The Good, The Bad and The History*.

Sorry – can't resist. They'll never notice.

Asterisks – the gall!

****

ACKNOWLEDGEMENTS

Many thanks to Hazel – Agent extraordinaire, for her encouragement and support with this one.

And Stacey Beaumont – For all her excellent advice on the legalities of buying and selling land. Anything I've got wrong is all down to me, I'm afraid.

And Phillip Dawson – Consultant on everything bloody, unpleasant and slightly illegal.

And Julia Turney – Beta reader.

And everyone at Headline:

Frankie Edwards – My editor.

Jessie Goetzinger-Hall – Who somehow overcomes everything.

Hannah Sawyer – Marketing guru.

Federica Trogu – In charge of publicity.

Ellie Wheeldon – Audio production mastermind.

Everyone else involved, including the Sales, Rights, Art and Production teams.

Together with:

Sharona Selby – Copy-editor and safety net.

Jill Cole – Proofreader.

And especially to Zara Ramm – who reads my books so beautifully.